LAUGHING BILL HYDE
AND OTHER STORIES

LAUGHING BILL HYDE
AND OTHER STORIES

REX BEACH

WILDSIDE PRESS

CONTENTS

INTRODUCTION

Rex Ellingwood Beach (1877–1949) was an American novelist, playwright, and Olympic water polo player. He was born in Atwood, Michigan, but moved to Tampa, Florida, with his family where his father was growing fruit trees. He was educated at Rollins College, Florida (1891–1896), the Chicago College of Law (1896–97), and Kent College of Law, Chicago (1899–1900), but chose not to enter the legal trade. Instead, in 1900 went to Alaska during the Klondike Gold to seek his fortune. After five years of unsuccessful prospecting, he turned to writing.

His second novel *The Spoilers* (1906) was based on a true story of corrupt government officials stealing gold mines from prospectors, which he witnessed while he was prospecting in Nome, Alaska. The Spoilers became one of the best selling novels of 1906.

His adventure novels, heavily influenced by Jack London, were immensely popular throughout the early 1900s. Dubbed the "Victor Hugo of the North," by fans, critics found fault with his novels, some labelling them formulaic and predictable. However, his works struck a definite chord with readers, and his sales continued to be strong.

Due to his success in literature, many of his works were adapted into other media. *The Spoilers* became first a stage play, then was remade into movies five times between 1914 to 1955, with Gary Cooper and John Wayne each starring once as the hero, Roy Glennister. *The Silver Horde* was twice made into a movie, as a silent film in 1920 starring Myrtle Stedman, Curtis Cooksey and Betty Blythe and directed by Frank Lloyd. A talkie version in 1930 starred Jean Arthur, Joel McCrea, and Evelyn Brent.

Beach occasionally produced film adaptation of his work. "Laughing Bill Hyde" was one such project. It was filmed in 1918 and starred Will Rogers, but is now considered lost. No known copies survive.

Beach, and his most famous novel, were commemorated in 2009 by the naming of a public pedestrian/bicycle trail in Dobbs Ferry, NY, a former place of residence. The trail is called "Spoilers Run."

—Karl Wurf
Rockville, Maryland

LAUGHING BILL HYDE

Mr. William Hyde was discharged from Deer Lodge Penitentiary a changed man. That was quite in line with the accepted theory of criminal jurisprudence, the warden's discipline, and the chaplain's prayers. Yes, Mr. Hyde was changed, and the change had bitten deep; his humorous contempt for the law had turned to abiding hatred; his sunburned cheeks were pallid, his lungs were weak, and he coughed considerably. Balanced against these results, to be sure, were the benefits accruing from three years of corrective discipline at the State's expense; the knack of conversing through stone walls, which Mr. Hyde had mastered, and the plaiting of wonderful horsehair bridles, which he had learned. Otherwise he was the same "Laughing Bill" his friends had known, neither more nor less regenerate.

Since the name of Montana promised to associate itself with unpleasant memories, Mr. Hyde determined at once to bury his past and begin life anew in a climate more suited to weak lungs. To that end he stuck up a peaceful citizen of Butte who was hurrying homeward with an armful of bundles, and in the warm dusk of a pleasant evening relieved him of eighty-three dollars, a Swiss watch with an elk's-tooth fob, a pearl-handled penknife, a key-ring, and a bottle of digestive tablets.

Three wasted years of industry had not robbed Mr. Hyde of the technique of his trade, hence there was nothing amateurish or uproarious about the procedure. He merely back-heeled the pedestrian against a bill-board, held him erect and speechless by placing his left hand upon his victim's shoulder and pressing his left forearm firmly across the gentleman's apple, the while with his own dexterous right mit he placed the eighty-three dollars in circulation. During the transaction he laughed constantly. An hour later he was en route for the sunny South, there being good and sufficient reasons why he preferred that direction to any other.

Arizona helped Mr. Hyde's lungs, for the random town which he selected was high and dry, but, unfortunately, so was Laughing Bill soon after his arrival, and in consequence he was forced to engage promptly in a new business enterprise. This time he raised a pay-roll. It was an easy task, for the custodian of the pay-roll was a small man with a kindly and unsuspicious nature. As a result of this operation Bill was enabled to maintain himself, for some six weeks, in a luxury to which of late he had been unaccustomed.

At the end of this time the original bearer of the payroll tottered forth from the hospital and, chancing to overhear Mr. Hyde in altercation with a faro dealer, he was struck by some haunting note in the former's laughter, and lost no time in shuffling his painful way to the sheriff's office.

Seeing the man go, Laughing Bill realized that his health again demanded a change of climate, and since it lacked nearly an hour of train time he was forced to leave on horseback. Luckily for him he found a horse convenient. It was a wild horse, with nothing whatever to indicate that it belonged to any one, except the fact that it carried a silver-mounted saddle and bridle, the reins of which were fastened to a post in front of a saloon.

Mr. Hyde enjoyed the ride, for it kept him out in the open air. It grieved him to part with the horse, a few hours later, but being prodigal with personal property he presented the animal to a poor Mexican woman, leaving her to face any resulting embarrassments. Ten minutes later he swung himself under a west-bound freight, and in due time arrived in California, somewhat dirty and fatigued, but in excellent humor.

Laughing Bill's adventures and his aliases during his slow progress up the coast form no part of this story. It might be said, with a great deal of truth, that he was missed, if not mourned, in many towns. Finally, having found the climates of California, Oregon and Washington uniformly unsuited to one of his habits, force of circumstance in the shape of numerous hand-bills adorned with an unflattering half-tone of himself, but containing certain undeniably accurate data such as diameter of skull, length of nose, angle of ear, and the like, drove him still north and west. Bill was a modest man; he considered these statistics purely personal in character; to see them blazoned publicly on the walls of post-offices, and in the corridors of county buildings, outraged his finer feelings, so he went away from there, in haste, as usual.

Having never sailed the sea, he looked forward to such an experience with lively anticipation, only to be disappointed in the realization. It was rough off Flattery, and he suffered agonies strange and terrifying. In due time, however, he gained his sea legs and, being forever curious, even prying, he explored the ship. His explorations were interesting, for they took him into strange quarters—into the forecastle, the steerage, even into some of the first-class state-rooms, the doors of which had been left "on the hook" while their occupants were at meals. No small benefit accrued to Mr. Hyde from these investigations.

One day during the dinner-hour, as he was occupied in admiring the contents of a strange suit-case, a voice accosted him over his shoulder, and he looked up to discover a face in the cabin window. Bill realized that an explanation was due, for it was evident that the speaker had been watching him for some little time; but under the circumstances, even though the face in the window was round, youthful, good-humored, explanations promised to be embarrassing.

"How d'y?" said Mr. Hyde.

"What luck?" inquired the stranger.

Mr. Hyde sat back upon his heels and grinned engagingly. "Not much," he confessed. "Can't find it nowhere. This guy must be a missionary."

The new-comer opened the door and entered. He was a medium-sized, plump young man. "Oh, I say!" he protested. "Is it as bad as that?" Bill nodded vaguely, meanwhile carefully measuring the physical proportions of the interloper. The latter went on:

"I saw that you knew your business, and—I was hoping you'd manage to find something I had missed."

Mr. Hyde breathed deep with relief; his expression altered. "You been through ahead of me?" he inquired.

"Oh, several times; daily, in fact." The speaker tossed a bunch of keys upon the berth, saying: "Glance through the steamer-trunk while you're here and declare me in on anything-you find."

Mr. Hyde rose to his feet and retreated a step; his look of relief was replaced by one of dark suspicion. As always, in moments of extremity, he began to laugh.

"Who are you?" he demanded.

"I? Why, I live here. That's my baggage. I've been through it, as I told you, but—" The young man frowned whimsically and lit a cigarette. "It doesn't diagnose. I can't find a solitary symptom of anything worth while. Sit down, won't you?"

Mr. Hyde's manner changed for a second time. He was embarrassed, apologetic, crestfallen. "*Your* cabin? Why, then—it's my mistake!" he declared. "I must 'a' got in the wrong flat. Mac sent me up for a deck of cards, but—Say, that's funny, ain't it?"

He began to see the joke upon himself, and the youth echoed his laughter.

"It *is* funny," the latter agreed. "For Heaven's sake, don't spoil it. Sit down and have a smoke; I'm not going to eat you."

"See here! You don't mean—? D'you think for a minute—?" Mr. Hyde began with rotund dignity, but the other waved his cigarette impatiently, saying:

"Oh, drop that stuff or I'll page your friend 'Mac' and show you up."

In assuming his air of outraged innocence Laughing Bill had arched his hollow chest and inhaled deeply. As a result he began to cough, whereupon his new acquaintance eyed him keenly, saying:

"That's a bad bark. What ails you?"

"Con," said Laughing Bill.

"Pardon me. I wouldn't have smoked if I'd known." The speaker dropped his cigarette and placed a heel upon it. "What are you doing here? Alaska's no place for weak lungs."

Gingerly seating himself upon the narrow settee Mr. Hyde murmured, wonderingly: "Say! You're a regular guy, ain't you?" He began to laugh again, but now there was less of a metallic quality to his merriment. "Yes sir, dam' if you ain't." He withdrew from his pocket a silver-mounted hair-brush and comb, and placed them carefully upon the washstand. "I don't aim to quit winner on a sport like you."

"Thanks, awfully!" smiled the young man. "I'd have fought you for that comb and brush. Girl stuff, you understand? That's she." He pointed to a leather-framed photograph propped against the mirror.

Laughing Bill leaned forward and studied the picture approvingly. "Some queen, all right. Blonde, I reckon."

"Sure. You like blondes?"

"Who, me? I ain't strong for no kind of women. You hate her, don't you?"

The young man smiled more widely, his whole face lit up. "I hate her so much that I kissed her good-by and sailed away to make a quick fortune. I hope Alaska's unhealthy."

"Yeah?"

"You see, I'm a doctor. I'm a good doctor, too, but it takes a long time to prove it, out in the States, and I can't wait a long time."

Mr. Hyde pondered briefly. "I don't see's you got much on me, Doc," he said. "I frisk 'em while they're good and healthy, and you 'take' 'em when they're feeble. I don't see no difference to speak of."

"It's an interesting viewpoint," the physician agreed, seriously enough, "and I respect every man's opinion. Tell me, how did you acquire that cough?"

"Livin' in a ground-floor apartment."

"What's your business?"

"Harness-maker."

"Hm-m! You'll do well up here." The doctor was highly entertained. "I understand there's a horse at Nome."

"*A* horse!"

"Alaska isn't a stock country."

Laughing Bill was genuinely surprised. "No horses!" he murmured. "How the hell do you get away?"

"You don't. You stay and face the music."

"Now what do you know about that?" There was a brief silence. "Well, I bet I'll turn my hand to something."

"No doubt. You impress me as a man of resource." The doctor's eyes twinkled and Bill smiled. A bond of friendly understanding had already sprung up between the two men. "Now then, I'm interested in your case. I've a notion to try to cure you."

"Nothing doin' on the fees. I'm a dead card."

"Oh, I won't charge you anything! I'm merely interested in obscure ailments, and, if I'm not mistaken, you suffer from more than one—well, disease. I think you need curing about as badly as any man I ever saw."

Now Laughing Bill was not skilled in subtleties, and his relief at extricating himself from a trying predicament banished any resentment he might have felt at the doctor's double meaning. Since the latter was a good-natured, harmless individual he decided to humor him, and so, after they had visited for an hour or more, Mr. Hyde discreetly withdrew. But, oddly enough, during the days immediately following, Laughing Bill grew to like the young fellow immensely. This in itself was a novel experience, for the ex-convict had been a "loner" all his-life, and had never really liked any one. Dr. Evan Thomas, however, seemed to fill some long-felt want in Hyde's hungry make-up. He fitted in smoothly, too, and despite the latter's lifelong habit of suspicion, despite his many rough edges, he could not manage to hold the young man at a distance.

Thomas was of a type strange to the wanderer, he was educated, he had unfamiliar airs and accomplishments, but he was human and natural withal. He was totally ignorant of much that Mr. Hyde deemed fundamental, and yet he was mysteriously superior, while his indifferent good nature, his mild amusement at the antics of the world about him covered a sincere and earnest nature. He knew his business, moreover, and he revolutionized Bill's habits of hygiene in spite of the latter's protests.

But the disease which ravaged Mr. Hyde's constitution had its toes dug in, and when the steamer touched at St. Michaels he suffered a severe hemorrhage. For the first time in his life Laughing Bill stood face to face with darkness. He had fevered memories of going over side on a stretcher; he was dimly aware of an appalling weakness, which grew hourly, then an agreeable indifference enveloped him, and for a long time he lived in a land of unrealities, of dreams. The day came when he began to wonder dully how and why he found himself in a freezing cabin with Doctor Thomas, in fur cap and arctic overshoes, tending him. Bill pondered the phenomenon for a week before he put his query into words.

"I've had a hard fight for you, old man," the doctor explained. "I couldn't leave you here to die."

"I guess I must 'a' been pretty sick."

"Right! There's no hospital here, so I took this cabin—borrowed it from the Company. We don't burn much fuel, and expenses aren't high."

"You been standin' off the landlord?"

"Yes."

There was a considerable silence, then Bill said, fervently: "You're a regular guy, like I told you! But you got your pill business to attend to. I'm all right now, so you better blow."

Thomas smiled dubiously. "You're a long way from all right, and there's no place to 'blow' to. The last boat sailed two weeks ago."

"Last boat for where?"

"For anywhere. We're here for the winter, unless the mail-carrier will take us to Nome, or up the Yukon, after the trails open."

"I bet you'll do a good business right here, when folks see what you done for me," Bill ventured.

"Just wait till you look at the town—deserted warehouses, some young and healthy watchmen, and a Siwash village. You're the only possible patient in all of St. Michaels."

Bill lay silent for an hour, staring through the open cabin window at a gray curtain of falling snowflakes; then he shook his head and muttered:

"Well, I be danged!"

"Anything you want?" Thomas inquired, quickly.

"I was just thinking about that gal." Bill indicated the leather-framed photograph which was prominently featured above the other bunk. "You ain't gettin' ahead very fast, are you?"

This time the young medical man smiled with his lips only—his eyes were grave and troubled. "I've written her all the circumstances, and she'll understand. She's that sort of a girl." He turned cheerfully back to his task. "I found that I had a few dollars left, so we won't starve."

Mr. Hyde felt impelled to confess that in his war-bag there was a roll of some seven hundred dollars, title to which had vested in him on the northward trip, together with certain miscellaneous objects of virtu, but he resisted the impulse, fearing that an investigation by his nurse might lead the latter to believe that he, Bill, was not a harness-maker at all, but a jewelry salesman. He determined to spring that roll at a later date, and to present the doctor with a very thin, very choice gold watch out of State-room 27. Bill carried out this intention when he had sufficiently recovered to get about.

Later, when his lungs had healed, Bill hired the mail-man to take him and his nurse to Nome. Since he was not yet altogether strong, he rode the sled most of the way, while the doctor walked. It was a slow and tiresome trip, along the dreary shores of Behring Sea, over timberless tundras, across inlets where the new ice bent beneath their weight and where the mail-carrier cautiously tested the footing with the head of his ax. Sometimes they slept in their tent, or again in road-houses and in Indian villages.

Every hour Laughing Bill grew stronger, and with his strength of body grew his strength of affection for the youthful doctor. Bill experienced a dog-like satisfaction in merely being near him; he suffered pangs when Thomas made new friends; he monopolized him jealously. The knowledge that he had a pal was new and thrilling; it gave Bill constant food for thought and speculation. Thomas was always gentle and considerate, but his little services, his unobtrusive sacrifices never went unnoticed, and they awoke in the bandit an ever-increasing wonderment. Also, they awoke a fierce desire to square the obligation.

The two men laid over at one of the old Russian towns, and Thomas, as was his restless custom, made investigation of the native village. Of course Bill went with him. They had learned by this time to enter Indian houses without knocking, so, therefore, when they finally came to a cabin larger and cleaner than the rest they opened the door and stepped inside, quite like experienced travelers.

A squaw was bent over a tub of washing, another stood beside the tiny frosted window staring out. Neither woman answered the greeting of the white men.

"Must be the chief's house," Thomas observed.

"Must be! I s'pose the old bird is out adding up his reindeer. 'Sapolio Sue' is prob'ly his head wife." Laughing Bill ran an interested eye over the orderly interior. "Some shack, but—I miss the usual smell."

Neither woman paid them the least attention, so they continued to talk with each other.

"I wonder what she is washing," Doctor Thomas said, finally.

The figure at the window turned, exposing the face of a comely youngIndian girl. Her features were good, her skin was light. She eyed theintruders coolly, then in a well-modulated voice, and in excellentEnglish, she said:

"She is washing a pair of sealskin pants."

Both men removed their caps in sudden embarrassment. Thomas exclaimed:

"I beg your pardon! We thought this was just an ordinary native house, or we wouldn't have intruded."

"You haven't intruded. This is 'Reindeer Mary's' house." The girl had again turned her back.

"Are you Reindeer Mary?"

"No, I am Ponatah. Mary befriended me; she lets me live with her."

"Allow me to introduce Mr. Hyde. I am Doctor Thomas. We were very rude—"

"Oh, everybody comes here." The men recognized instantly in the speaker's face, as well as in her voice, that education had set its stamp. "Will you sit down and wait for her?"

"You overwhelm us." After an awkward moment the physician queried,"How in the world did you learn to speak such good English?"

"A missionary took an interest in me when I was a little girl. He sent me to Carlisle."

Laughing Bill had been an attentive listener, now he ventured to say: "I know this Carlisle. He's a swell football player, or something."

Ponatah smiled, showing a row of small, white teeth. "Carlisle is anIndian school."

"What made you come back?" Thomas inquired, curiously.

Ponatah shrugged her shoulders. "There was an end to the money. What could I do? At first I thought I'd be able to help my people, but—I couldn't. They will learn from the white people, but not from one of their own kind."

"Your parents—?"

"They died when I was a baby. Mary took me in." The girl spoke in a flat, emotionless tone.

"It must be tough to come back to this, now that you know what life really is," said Thomas, after a time.

Ponatah's eyes were dark with tragedy when she turned them to the speaker. "*God!*" she cried, unexpectedly, then abruptly she faced the window once more. It was a moment before she went on in fierce resentment:

"Why didn't they leave me as they found me? Why did they teach me their ways, and then send me back to this—this dirt and ignorance and squalor? Sometimes I think I can't stand it. But what can I do? Nobody understands. Mary can't see why I'm different from her and the others. She has grown rich, with her reindeer; she says if this is good enough for her it should be good enough for me. As for the white men who come through, they can't, or they won't, understand. They're hateful to me. Petersen, the mail-carrier, for instance! I don't know why I'm telling you this. You're strangers. You're probably just like Petersen."

"I know why you're telling us," Thomas said, slowly. "It's becauseI—because we're *not* like Petersen and the others; it's becauseI—we can help you."

"Help me?" sneered the girl. "How?"

"I don't know, yet. But you're out of place here. There's a place for you somewhere; I'll find it."

Ponatah shook her head wearily. "Mary says I belong here, with my people."

"No. You belong with white people—people who will treat you well."

This time the girl smiled bitterly. "They have treated me worse than my own people have. I know them, and—I hate them."

"Ain't you the sore-head, now?" Laughing Bill murmured. "You got a hundred-per-cent. grouch, but if the old medicine-man says he'll put you in right, you bet your string of beads he'll do it. He's got a gift for helpin' down-and-outers. You got class, Kid; you certainly rhinestone this whole bunch of red men. Why, you belong in French heels and a boodwar cap; that's how I dope you."

"There must be a chance for a girl like you in Nome," Thomas continued, thoughtfully. "You'd make a good hand with children. Suppose I try to find you a place as governess?"

"*Would* you?" Ponatah's face was suddenly eager. "Children? Oh yes! I'd work my fingers to the bone. I—I'd do *anything*—"

"Then I'll do what I can."

For some time longer the three of them talked, and gradually into the native girl's eyes there came a light, for these men were not like the others she had met, and she saw the world begin to unfold before her. When at last they left she laid a hand upon the doctor's arm and said, imploringly:

"You won't forget. You—promise?"

"I promise," he told her.

"He don't forget nothing," Bill assured her, "and if he does I'll see that he don't."

After they had gone Ponatah stood motionless for a long time, then she whispered, breathlessly:

"Children! Little white children! I'll be very good to them."

"She's a classy quilt," Laughing Bill said, on the way back to the road-house.

"She's as pretty as a picture, and little more than a child," the doctor admitted.

"You made a hit. She'd do 'most anything for you." The doctor muttered, absent-mindedly. "She's stood off Petersen and these red-necks, but she'd fall for you." Mr. Hyde was insinuating.

Thomas halted; he stared at his partner curiously, coldly. "Say! Do you think that's why I offered to help her?" he inquired.

"Come clean!" The invalid winked meaningly. "You're a long ways from home, and I've knew fellers to do a lot worse. You can grab her, easy. And if you do—"

Thomas grunted angrily. "I've put up with a lot from you," he said, then he strode on.

"And if you do," the other resumed, falling into step with him, "I'll bust you right where you're thickest."

"Eh?"

"I'll bust you wide open. Oh, me 'n' that gal in the leather frame had a long talk while I was sick in St. Mikes, and she asked me to keep you in the middle of the trail. Well, I'm the little guy that can do it."

"Bill!" Evan Thomas's eyes were twinkling. "I believe I'm going to cure you, after all," said he.

Late that afternoon Mr. Hyde disappeared; he did not show up until after dark.

"I been to see Lo, the poor squaw," he readily confessed. "She ain't the pure domestic leaf, she's a blend—part Rooshian, or something. Seems there was a gang of Rooshians or Swedes or Dagoes of some sort used to run this country. She says they horned into some of the best Injun families, and she's one of the 'overs.'"

"They were Russians."

"Rooshians is a kind of white people, ain't they? Well, that's how she come so light-complected. You remember she said our folks had treated her bad? It's a fact, Doc. She spilled the story, and it made a mouthful. It's like this: when Nome was struck a Swede feller she had knew staked her a claim, but she couldn't hold it, her bein' a squab—under age, savvy? There's something in the law that prevents Injuns gettin' in on anything good, too; I don't rightly recollect what it is, but if it's legal you can bet it's crooked. Anyhow, Uncle Sam lets up a squawk that she's only eighteen, goin' on nineteen, and a noble redskin to boot, and says his mining claims is reserved for Laps and Yaps and Japs and Wops, and such other furrin' slantheads of legal age as declare their intention to become American citizens if their claims turn out rich enough so's it pays 'em to do so.

"Well, Ponatah's Swede friend gets himself froze, somehow, so she has to pass the buck. Naturally, she turns to her pals, the missionaries. There's a he-missionary here—head mug of the whole gang. He's a godly walloper, and he tears into Satan bare-handed every Sunday. He slams the devil around something shameful, and Ponatah thinks he's a square guy if ever they come square, so she asks him to re-locate her claim, on shares, and hold it for the joint account. Old Doctor M.E. Church agrees to split fifty-fifty, half to her and half to heaven, then he vamps to Nome and chalks his monaker over the Kid's. Now get me: the claim turns out good, and Ponatah's heavenly pilot makes a Mexican divvy—he takes the money and gives her his best wishes. He grabs everything, and says he never knew nobody by the name of Ponatah—he gets so he can't even pronounce it. He allows her face is familiar, but he can't place her, and the partnership idea allus was repugnant to him. He never was partners with nobody, understand? He blows the show; he bows out and leaves the Kid flat. He forsakes the Milky Way for the Great White one, and he's out there now, smokin' Coronas and wearin' a red vest under his black coat, with a diamond horseshoe in his tie. It looks to me like the James boys could 'a' learned something from this gospel hold-up."

"Do you believe her story?" Thomas inquired.

"She don't know enough to lie, and you can't trust a guy that wears his collar backwards."

"She should go to court."

Mr. Hyde shook his head. "I been there, often, but I never picked up a bet. Somehow or other courts is usually right next to jails, and you got to watch out you don't get in the wrong place. You can't win nothing in either one. I thought I'd tell you the story, so if you ever meet up with this shave-tail preacher and he wants a headache pill you can slip him some sugar-coated arsenic."

In the days immediately following Doctor Thomas's arrival at Nome he was a busy man, but he did not forget Ponatah. He was allowed no opportunity of doing so, for Bill frequently reminded him of her, and as a result it was not long before he found a place for his charge, in the home of a leading merchant. Arrangements made, Bill went in search of the mail-carrier.

Petersen was drinking with two friends at the bar of the Last Chance, and he pressed his late passenger to join them. But alcoholism was not one of Mr. Hyde's weaknesses. The best of Bill's bad habits was much worse than drink; he had learned from experience that liquor put a traitor's tongue in his head, and in consequence he was a teetotaler.

"I got a job for you, Pete," he announced. "I got you another sled-load for your next trip. You know Ponatah?"

"Ponatah? Sure Aye know 'im." Petersen. spoke with enthusiasm.

"Well, bring her along when you come. Me 'n' the little Doc will settle."

"Dat's good yob for me, all right. Vot mak' you tank she'll come? Aye ask her plenty tams, but she ant like me."

"You slip her this billy-ducks and she'll come."

Petersen pocketed the letter which Bill handed him; his eyes brightened; the flush in his face deepened. "You bet your gum boots Aye bring her. She's svell, ant she, Bill? She's yust some svell like white voman."

"Who's this?" queried one of Petersen's companions.

"Ponatah. She's jung sqvaw. Aye got eyes on dat chicken long tam now." The burly mail-man laughed loudly and slapped his friend on the shoulder.

Mr. Hyde appeared to share in the general good nature. Carelessly, smilingly he picked up Petersen's dog-whip, which lay coiled on the bar; thoughtfully he weighed it. The lash was long, but the handle was short and thick, and its butt was loaded with shot; it had much the balance of a black-jack—a weapon not unknown to Mr. Hyde.

"Pretty soft for you mail-men." The former speaker grinned.

"Ja! Pretty soft. Aye bet Aye have good tam dis trip. Yust vait. You don't know how purty is Ponatah. She—"

Petersen's listeners waited. They are waiting yet, for the mail-man never completed his admiring recital of the Indian girl's charms, owing to the fact that the genial Mr. Hyde without warning tapped his late friend's round head with the leather butt of the dog-whip. Had it not been for the Norse-man's otter cap it is probable that a new mail-carrier would have taken the St. Michaels run.

Petersen sat down upon his heels, and rested his forehead against the cool brass foot-rail; the subsequent proceedings interested him not at all. Those proceedings were varied and sudden, for the nearest and dearest of Petersen's friends rushed upon Mr. Hyde with a roar. Him, too, Bill eliminated from consideration with the loaded whip handle. But, this done, Bill found himself hugged in the arms of the other man, as in the embrace of a bereaved she-grizzly. Now even at his best the laughing Mr. Hyde was no hand at rough-and-tumble, it being his opinion that fisticuffs was a peculiarly indecisive and exhausting way of settling a dispute. He possessed a vile temper, moreover, and once aroused half measures failed to satisfy it.

After Mr. Hyde's admirable beginning those neutrals who had seen the start of the affray were prepared to witness an ending equally quick and conclusive. They were surprised, therefore, to note that Bill put up a very weak struggle, once he had come to close quarters. He made only the feeblest resistance, before permitting himself to be borne backward to the floor, and then as he lay pinned beneath his opponent he did not even try to guard the blows that rained upon him; as a matter of fact, he continued to laugh as if the experience were highly diverting.

Seeing that the fight was one-sided, the bartender hastened from his retreat, dragged Petersen's champion to his feet, and flung him back into the arms of the onlookers, after which he stooped to aid the loser. His hands were actually upon Bill before he understood the meaning of that peculiar laughter, and saw in Mr. Hyde's shaking fingers that which caused him to drop the prostrate victim as if he were a rattlesnake.

"God'l'mighty!" exclaimed the rescuer. He retreated hurriedly whence he had come.

Bill rose and dusted himself off, then he bent over Petersen, who was stirring.

"Just give her that billy-ducks and tell her it's all right. Tell her I say you won't hurt her none." Then, still chuckling, he slipped into the crowd and out of the Last Chance. As he went he coughed and spat a mouthful of blood.

Once the mail-carrier had been apprised of the amazing incidents which had occurred during his temporary inattention, he vowed vengeance in a mighty voice, and his threats found echo in the throats of his two companions. But the bartender took them aside and spoke guardedly:

"You better lay off of that guy, or he'll fatten the graveyard with all three of you. I didn't 'make' him at first, but I got him now, all right."

"What d'you mean? Who is he?"

"His name's Hyde, 'Laughing Bill.'"

"'Laughing Bill' Hyde!" One of Petersen's friends, he who had come last into the encounter, turned yellow and leaned hard against the bar. A sudden nausea assailed him and he laid tender hands upon his abdomen. "'Laughing Bill' Hyde! That's why he went down so easy! Why, he killed a feller I knew—ribboned him up from underneath, just that way—and the jury called it self-defense." A shudder racked the speaker's frame.

"Sure! He's a cutter—a reg'lar gent's cutter and fitter. He'd 'a' had you all over the floor in another minute; if I hadn't pried you apart they'd 'a' sewed sawdust up inside of you like you was a doll. He had the old bone-handled skinner in his mit; that's why I let go of him. Laughing Bill! Take it from me, boys, you better walk around him like he was a hole in the ice."

It may have been the memory of that heavy whip handle, it may have been the moral effect of stray biographical bits garnered here and there around the gambling-table, or it may have been merely a high and natural chivalry, totally unsuspected until now, which prompted Petersen to treat Ponatah with a chill and formal courtesy when he returned from St. Michaels. At any rate, the girl arrived in Nome with nothing but praise for the mail-man. Pete Petersen, so she said, might have his faults, but he knew how to behave like a perfect gentleman.

Ponatah took up her new duties with enthusiasm, and before a month had passed she had endeared herself to her employers, who secretly assured Doctor Thomas that they had discovered a treasure and would never part with her. She was gentle, patient, sweet, industrious; the children idolized her. The Indian girl had never dreamed of a home like this; she was deliriously happy.

She took pride in discharging her obligations; she did not forget the men who had made this wonder possible. They had rented a little cabin, and, after the fashion of men, they make slipshod efforts at keeping house. Since it was Ponatah's nature to serve, she found time somehow to keep the place tidy and to see to their comfort.

Laughing Bill was a hopeless idler; he had been born to leisure and was wedded to indigence, therefore he saw a good deal of the girl on her visits. He listened to her stories of the children, he admired her new and stylish clothes, he watched her develop under the influence of her surroundings. Inasmuch as both of them were waifs, and beholden to the bounty of others, thy had ties in common—a certain mutuality—hence they came to know each other intimately.

Despite the great change in her environment, Ponatah remained in many ways quite aboriginal. For instance, she was embarrassingly direct and straightforward; she entirely lacked hypocrisy, and that which puzzled or troubled her she boldly put into words. There came a time when Bill discovered that Ponatah's eyes, when they looked at him, were more than friendly, that most of the services she performed were aimed at him.

Then one day she asked him to marry her.

There was nothing brazen or forward about the proposal; Ponatah merely gave voice to her feelings in a simple, honest way that robbed her of no dignity.

Bill laughed the proposal off. "I wouldn't marry the Queen of Sheby," said he.

"Why?"

"I ain't that kind of a bird, that's why."

"What kind of a bird are you?" Ponatah eyed him with grave curiosity. "All men marry. I'm reading a great many books, and they're all about love and marriage. I love you, and I'm pretty. Is it because I'm an Indian—?"

"Hell! That wouldn't faze me, Kiddo. You skin the white dames around this village. But you better cut out them books."

"I'd make you a good wife."

"Sure! You're aces. But I'd make a bum husband. I ain't got the breath to blow out a candle." Mr. Hyde chuckled; the idea of marriage plainly amused him. "How you know I ain't got a covey of wives?" he inquired.

"Oh, I know!" Ponatah was unsmiling. "I'm simple, but I can see through people. I can tell the good ones and the bad ones. You're a good man, Billy."

Now this praise was anything but agreeable to Mr. Hyde, for above all things he abhorred so-called "good" people. Good people were suckers, and he prided himself upon being a wise guy, with all that was meant thereby.

"You lay off of me, Kid," he warned, darkly, "and you muffle them wedding bells. You can't win nothing with that line of talk. If I was fifty inches around the chest, liked to work, and was fond of pas'ment'ries I'd prob'ly fall for you, but I ain't. I'm a good man, all right—to leave alone. I'll be a brother to you, but that's my limit." The subject was embarrassing, so he changed it. "Say! I been thinking about that claim of yours. Didn't you get no paper from that missionary?"

"No."

"Then his word's as good as yours."

"That's what the lawyer told me. I offered to give him half, but he wouldn't touch the case."

"It was a dirty deal, but you better forget it."

"I'll try," the girl promised. "But I don't forget easily."

Laughing Bill's rejection of Ponatah's offer of marriage did not in the least affect their friendly relations. She continued to visit the cabin, and not infrequently she reverted to the forbidden topic, only to meet with discouragement.

Doctor Thomas had opened an office, of course, but business was light and expenses heavy. Supplies were low in Nome and prices high; coal, for instance, was a hundred dollars a ton and, as a result, most of the idle citizens spent their evenings——but precious little else—around the saloon stoves. When April came Laughing Bill regretfully decided that it was necessary for him to go to work. The prospect was depressing, and he did not easily reconcile himself to it, for he would have infinitely preferred some less degraded and humiliating way out of the difficulty. He put up a desperate battle against the necessity, and he did not accept the inevitable until thoroughly convinced that the practice of medicine and burglary could not be carried on from the same residence without the risk of serious embarrassment to his benefactor.

However, to find employment in a community where there were two men to one job was not easy, but happily—or unhappily—Bill had a smattering of many trades, and eventually there came an opening as handy-man at a mine. It was a lowly position, and Bill had little pride in it, for he was put to helping the cook, waiting on table, washing dishes, sweeping cabins, making beds, and the like. He had been assured that the work was light, and so it was, but it was also continuous. He could summon not the slightest interest in it until he discovered that this was the very claim which rightfully belonged to Ponatah. Then, indeed, he pricked up his ears.

The Aurora Borealis, as the mine was now called, had been working all winter, and gigantic dumps of red pay-dirt stood as monuments to the industry of its workmen. Rumor had it that the "streak" was rich, and that Doctor Slayforth, the owner, would be in on the first boat to personally oversee the clean-ups. The ex-missionary, Bill discovered, had the reputation of being a tight man, and meanly suspicious in money matters. He reposed no confidence in his superintendent, a surly, saturnine fellow known as Black Jack Berg, nor in Denny Slevin, his foreman. So much Laughing Bill gathered from camp gossip.

It soon became evident that Black Jack was a hard driver, for sluicing began with the first trickle of snow water—even while the ditches were still ice-bound—and it continued with double shifts thereafter. A representative of Doctor Slayforth came out from Nome to watch the first clean-up, and Bill, in his capacity as chambermaid, set up a cot for him in the cabin shared by Black Jack and Denny. While so engaged the latter discovered him, and gruffly ordered him to remove the cot to the bunk-house.

"Put him in with the men," growled Slevin. "Serves the dam' spy right."

"Spy? Is he a gum-shoe?" Mr. Hyde paused, a pillow slip between his teeth.

"That's what! Me and Jack was honest enough to run things all winter, but we ain't honest enough to clean up. That's like old Slayforth—always lookin' to get the worst of it. I'm square, and so's Jack. Makes me sick, this spyin' on honest folks. Everybody knows we wouldn't turn a trick."

Now it was Laughing Bill's experience that honesty needs no boosting, and that he who most loudly vaunts his rectitude is he who is least certain of it.

"The boss must be a good man, him being a sort of psalm-singer," Bill ventured, guilelessly.

Denny snorted: "Oh, sure! He's good, all right. He's 'most too good—to be true. Billy, my boy, when you've seen as many crooks as I have you'll know 'em, no matter how they come dressed."

As he folded the cot Mr. Hyde opined that worldly experience must indeed be a fine thing to possess.

"You go gamble on it!" Slevin agreed. "Now then, just tell that Hawkshaw we don't want no dam' spies in our house. We're square guys, and we can't stomach 'em."

That evening Black Jack called upon the handy-man to help with the clean-up, and put him to tend the water while he and Denny, under the watchful eye of the owner's representative, lifted the riffles, worked down the concentrates, and removed them from the boxes.

Bill was an experienced placer miner, so it was not many days before he was asked to help in the actual cleaning of the sluices. He was glad of the promotion, for, as he told himself, no man can squeeze a lemon without getting juice on his fingers. It will be seen, alas! that Mr. Hyde's moral sense remained blunted in spite of the refining influence of his association with Doctor Thomas. But Aurora dust was fine, and the handy-man's profits were scarcely worth the risks involved in taking them.

One morning while Bill was cleaning up the superintendent's cabin he noticed a tiny yellow flake of gold upon the floor in front of Slevin's bed. Careful examination showed him several "colors" of the same sort, so he swept the boards carefully and took up the dust in a "blower." He breathed upon the pile, blowing the lighter particles away. A considerable residue of heavy yellow grains remained. With a grin Bill folded them in a cigarette paper and placed them in his pocket. But it puzzled him to explain how there came to be gold on the cabin floor. His surprise deepened when, a few days later, he found another "prospect" in the same place. His two sweepings had yielded perhaps a pennyweight of the precious metal—enough to set him to thinking. It seemed queer that in the neighborhood of Black Jack's bunk he could find no pay whatever.

Slevin had left his hip boots in the cabin, and as Laughing Bill turned down their tops and set them out in the wind to dry his sharp eye detected several yellow pin-points of color which proved, upon closer investigation, to be specks of gold clinging to the wet lining.

"Well, I be danged!" said Mr. Hyde. Carefully, thoughtfully, he replaced the boots where he had found them. The knowledge that he was on a hot trail electrified him.

At the next clean-up Laughing Bill took less interest in his part of the work and more in Denny Slevin's. When the riffles were washed, and the loose gravel had been worked down into yellow piles of rich concentrates, Slevin, armed with whisk broom, paddle, and scoop, climbed into the sluices. Bill watched him out of a corner of his eye, and it was not long before his vigilance was rewarded. The hold-up man turned away with a feeling of genuine admiration, for he had seen Slevin, under the very nose of the lookout, "go south" with a substantial amount of gold.

The foreman's daring and dexterity amazed Bill and deepened his respect. Slevin's work was cunning, and yet so simple as to be almost laughable. With his hip boots pulled high he had knelt upon one knee in the sluice scooping up the wet piles of gold and black iron sand, while Berg held a gold pan to receive it. During the process Black Jack had turned to address the vigilant owner's representative, and, profiting by the brief diversion, Bill had seen Denny dump a heaping scoop-load of "pay" into the gaping pocket-like top of his capacious rubber boot.

"The sons-of-a-gun!" breathed Laughing Bill. "The double-crossing sons-of-a-gun! Why, it begins to look like a big summer for me."

Bill slept well that night, for now that he knew the game which was going on he felt sure that sooner or later he would take a hand in it. Just how or when the hand would fall he could not tell, but that did not worry him in the least, inasmuch as he already held the trumps. It seemed that a kindly fortune had guided him to the Aurora; that fate had decreed he should avenge the wrongs of Ponatah. The handy-man fell asleep with a smile upon his lips.

The first ship arrived that very evening, and the next day Doctor Slayforth in person appeared at the Aurora. He was a thin, restless man with weak and shifting eyes; he said grace at dinner, giving thanks for the scanty rations of hash and brown beans over which his hungry workmen were poised like cormorants. The Aurora had won the name of a bad feeder, but its owner seemed satisfied with his meal. Later Bill overheard him talking with his superintendent.

"I'm disappointed with the clean-ups," Slayforth confessed. "The pay appears to be pinching out."

"She don't wash like she sampled, that's a fact," said Black Jack.

"I'm afraid we shall have to practise economies—"

"Look here! If you aim to cut down the grub, don't try it," counseled Berg. "It's rotten now."

"Indeed? There appeared to be plenty, and the quality was excellent. I fear you encourage gluttony, and nothing so interferes with work. We must effect a saving somehow; there is too great a variation between theoretical and actual values."

"Huh! You better try feeding hay for a while," sourly grumbled the superintendent. "If you ain't getting what you aimed to get it's because it ain't in the cards."

This conversation interested Bill, for it proved that the robbers had helped themselves with a liberal hand, but how they had managed to appropriate enough gold to noticeably affect the showing of the winter's work intensely mystified him; it led him to believe that Black Jack and Denny were out for a homestake.

That such was indeed the case and that Slevin was not the only thief Bill soon discovered, for after the next clean-up he slipped away through the twilight and took stand among the alders outside the rear window of the shack on the hill. From his point of concealment he could observe all that went on inside.

It was a familiar scene. By the light of an oil lamp Black Jack was putting the final touches to the clean-up. Two gold pans, heaped high with the mingled black sand and gold dust, as it came out of the sluices, were drying on the Yukon stove, and the superintendent was engaged in separating the precious yellow particles from the worthless material which gravity had deposited with it. This refining process was slow, painstaking work, and was effected with the help of a flat brass scoop—a "blower." By shaking this blower and breathing upon its contents the lighter grains of iron sand were propelled to the edge, as chaff is separated from wheat, and fell into a box held between the superintendent's knees. The residue, left in the heel of the blower after each blowing process, was commercial "dust," ready for the bank or the assay office. Doctor Slayforth, with his glasses on the end of his nose, presided at the gold scales, while Denny Slevin looked on. As the dust was weighed, a few ounces at a time, it was dumped into a moose-skin sack and entered upon the books.

Black Jack had the light at his back, he was facing the window, therefore Laughing Bill commanded an unobstructed view of his adept manipulations. It was not long before the latter saw him surreptitiously drop a considerable quantity of gold out of the scoop and into the box between his knees, then cover it up with the black sand. This sleight-of-hand was repeated several times, and when the last heap of gold had been weighed Bill estimated that Doctor Slayforth was poorer by at least a hundred ounces—sixteen hundred dollars. There was no question about it now; these were not common thieves; this was becoming a regular man's game, and the stakes were assuming a size to give Laughing Bill a tingling sensation along his spine. Having discovered the *modus operandi* of the pair, and having read their cards, so to speak, he next set himself to discover where they banked their swag. But this was by no means easy. His utmost vigilance went unrewarded by so much as a single clue.

Berg and Slevin had a habit of riding into town on Saturday nights, and the next time they left the claim Bill pleaded a jumping toothache and set out afoot for medical attention.

It was late when he arrived at Nome, nevertheless a diligent search of the Front Street saloons failed to locate either man. He was still looking for them when they came riding in.

With their delayed arrival Bill's apprehensions vanished, as likewise did his imaginary toothache. He had feared that they were in the habit of bringing the gold to Nome, there perhaps to bank it with some friend; but now he knew that they were too cautious for that, and preferred instead to cache it somewhere in the hills. This simplified matters immensely, so Bill looked up his little doctor for a sociable visit.

Thomas was in his office; he greeted Bill warmly.

"Say! Pill-rolling must be brisk to keep you on the job till midnight," the latter began.

"Business is rotten!" exclaimed the physician. "And it's a rotten business."

"Nobody sick? That's tough. Open a can of typhoid germs, and I'll put 'em in the well. Anything to stir up a little trade."

"I've just balanced my books and—I've just heard from Alice."

"Do the books balance?"

"Oh, perfectly—nothing equals nothing—it's a perfect equilibrium. Alice wants me to come home and start all over, and I'm tempted to do so."

"Ain't going to throw up your tail, are you?"

"I can't get along without her." Thomas was plainly in the depths; he turned away and stared moodily out into the dim-lit street. It was midnight, but already the days were shortening, already there was an hour or two of dusk between the evening and the morning light.

"Of course you can't get along without her," the ex-bandit agreed. "I seen that when I looked at her picture. Why don't you bring her in?"

"Bring her in—*here*?" Thomas faced about quickly. "Humph! Not much."

"Well, this ain't no doll's village, that's a fact. It's full of wicked men, and the women ain't wuth braggin' over. S'pose we go out and marry her?"

"We?" Thomas smiled for the first time.

"Sure. I'll stick to the bitter finish."

"I'm broke, Bill."

"Pshaw, now! Don't let that worry you. I got money."

"You?" The doctor was surprised. "Where did you get it?"

"Well, I *got* it! That's the main thing. It was—left to me."

"Honestly?"

"What d'you mean, 'honestly'?"

"How much?"

"I dunno, exactly. You see, I ain't got it actually in my mit—"

"Oh!"

"But I'll have it, all righto. It's just waiting for me to close down on it. I reckon there must be a thousand gold buzzards in the stack, mebby more. It's all yours."

"Thanks!" said the physician, unimpressed.

"Look me in the eye." Bill spoke earnestly. "Twenty thousand iron men ain't so bad. It'll buy a lot of doll's clothes. We can have a big party—I ain't kidding!" Then reading amused incredulity in his friend's face he demanded: "How you know I ain't got a rich uncle that raised me from a colt and that broke his heart at me runnin' away and turning out wild, and has had lawyers gunnin' for me ever since he knew he was gettin' old and going to croak? How you know that, eh?"

"I don't know. I don't know anything about you, Bill. That's one of the most interesting features of our friendship."

"Well, pay a little attention to me. Now then, I figger it like this:I got lungs like a grasshopper, and the money won't do me no good, soI'll stake you and Miss Alice to it."

Doctor Thomas eyed the speaker curiously. "I believe you would," said he, after a moment.

"Would I? Say! You ever seen a feather bed tied up with a rope? You sit tight and I'll slip you a roll just that size."

"Of course you know I wouldn't take it?"

"Why not? It's more'n likely it'll get me into evil company or gimme some bad habit, and I'll gargle off before I've had a chance to spend it. I ain't strong."

"I'll earn what I get, Billy."

"All right. If you feel like that I'll bet it for you on a crap game, and you can take the winnings—"

"Nothing doing. I want honest money—money that I can look in the face."

Mr. Hyde was out of patience. "All money's honest, after you get it!" he cried. "It's gettin' it that draws blood. I never knew the silver bird to fly off a dollar and scratch a guy, did you?"

"I want to make money—that's why I came up to this God-forsaken place—but—when your uncle's draft arrives you cash it."

"Ain't you the champeen bone-dome?" muttered Bill. Such an attitude seemed to him both senseless and quixotic, for he had never attached the least sentiment to money. Money was an elemental necessity, therefore he looked upon it with practical, unromantic eyes, and helped himself to it as he helped himself to such elemental necessities as air or water. Most of life's necessaries had fallen into monopolistic hands and were used to wring tribute from unfortunate mortals who had arrived too late to share in the graft, as witness, for instance, Standard Oil. So ran Bill's reasoning when he took the trouble to reason at all. Men had established arbitrary rules to govern their forays upon one another's property, to be sure, but under cover of these artificial laws they stole merrily, and got away with it. Eagles did not scruple to steal from one another, horses ate one another's fodder; why human beings should not do likewise had always puzzled Mr. Hyde. The basic principle held good in both cases, it seemed to him, and Doctor Thomas's refusal to share in the coming legacy struck him as silly; it was the result of a warped and unsound philosophy. But argue as he would he could not shake his friend's opinion of the matter.

One evening, not long after his visit to town, Bill's toothache returned again to plague him. He raised groans and hoarse profanities, and then, while the crew was still at supper, he abandoned his work and set out in search of relief. But he did not go to Nome. Once out of sight of the mine he doubled back and came out behind the superintendent's cabin. A moment later he was stretched out in the narrow, dark space beneath Black Jack's bunk. Dust irritated Bill's lungs, therefore he had carefully swept out the place that morning; likewise he had thoughtfully provided himself with a cotton comforter as protection to his bones. He had no intention of permitting himself to be taken at a disadvantage, and knowing full well the painful consequences of discovery he opened his bone-handled pocket-knife and tested its keen edge with his thumb. In the interests of peace and good-fellowship, however, he hoped he could go through the night without coughing.

Slevin was the first to return from supper. He went directly to his bunk, drew a bottle of whisky from beneath his pillow, poured himself a drink, and replaced the bottle. When Berg entered he went through a similar procedure, after which a fire was built, the men kicked off their boots, lit their pipes, and stretched out upon their beds.

"I've been thinking it over," the superintendent began, "and you can't do it."

"Why not?" queried Slevin. "I told his nibs I was sick of the grub."

"Foremen don't quit good jobs on account of the grub. You've got to stick till fall; then we'll both go. We'll strike the old man for a raise—"

"Humph! He'll let us go, quick enough, when we do that. Let's strike him now. I'm through."

"Nothing stirring," Berg firmly declared. "We'll play out the string. I'm taking no chances."

"Hell! Ain't we takin' a chance every day we stay here? I'm getting so I don't sleep. I got enough to do me; I ain't a hog. I got a bully corner all picked out, Jack—best corner in Seattle for a gin-mill."

"It'll wait. Corners don't get up and move. No, I won't hold the bag for you or for anybody," declared the former speaker. "We'll go through, arm in arm. Once we're away clean you can do what you like. Me for the Argentine and ten thousand acres of long-horns. You better forget that corner. Some night you'll get stewed and spill the beans."

"Who, me?" Slevin laughed in disdain. "Fat chance!" There was a long silence during which the only sound was the bubbling of a pipe. "I s'pose I'll have to stick, if you say so," Denny agreed finally, "but I'm fed up. I'm getting jumpy. I got a hunch the cache ain't safe; I feel like something was goin' to happen."

Mr. Slevin's premonition, under the circumstances, was almost uncanny; it gave startling proof of his susceptibility to outside influences.

"You *are* rickety," Black Jack told him. "Why, there ain't any danger; nobody goes up there." Laughing Bill held his breath, missing not a word. "If they did we'd pick 'em up with the glasses. It's open country, and we'd get 'em before they got down."

"I s'pose so. But the nights are getting dark."

"Nobody's out at night, either, you boob. I ain't losing any slumber over that. And I ain't going to lose any about your quitting ahead of me. That don't trouble me none." Berg yawned and changed the subject. Half an hour later he rose, languidly undressed and rolled into his bed. Slevin followed suit shortly after, and the rapidity with which both men fell asleep spoke volumes for the elasticity of the human conscience.

Now, Laughing Bill had come prepared to spend the night, but his throat tickled and he had a distressing habit of snoring, therefore he deemed it the part of caution to depart before he dropped off into the land of dreams. He effected the manoeuver noiselessly.

Bill lingered at the spring hole on the following morning, and lost himself in an attentive study of the surrounding scenery. It was fairly impressive scenery, and he had a keen appreciation of nature's beauty, but Black Jack's words continued to puzzle him. "Nobody goes up there." Up where? The Aurora lay in a valley, therefore most of the country round about was "up"—it was open, too. The ridges were bold and barren, garbed only with shreds and patches of short grass and reindeer moss. "We'd pick 'em up with the glasses—we'd get 'em before they got down." Manifestly the cache was in plain sight, if one only knew where to look for it, but Mr. Hyde's sharp eyes took in ten thousand likely hiding-places, and he reasoned that it would be worse than folly to go exploring blindly without more definite data than he possessed.

It was clever of the pair to hide the swag where they could oversee it every hour of the day, and they had chosen a safe location, too, for nobody wasted the effort to explore those domes and hogbacks now that they were known to contain no quartz. There was Anvil Mountain, for instance, a bold schist peak crowned with a huge rock in the likeness of a blacksmith's anvil. It guarded the entrance to the valley, rising from the very heart of the best mining section; it was the most prominent landmark hereabouts, but not a dozen men had ever climbed it, and nowadays nobody did.

As Bill pondered the enigma, out from his bed in the willows came Don Antonio de Chiquito, a meek and lowly burro, the only member of the Aurora's working force which did not outrank in social importance the man-of-all-work. Don Antonio was the pet of the Aurora Borealis, and its scavenger. He ate everything from garbage to rubber boots—he was even suspected of possessing a low appetite for German socks. It was, in fact, this very democratic taste in things edible which caused him to remain the steadiest of Doctor Slayforth's boarders. Wisdom, patience, the sagacity of Solomon, lurked in Don Antonio's eyes, and Laughing Bill consulted him as a friend and an equal.

"Tony," said he, "you've done a heap of prospecting and you know the business. There's a rich pocket on one of them hills. Which one is it?"

Don Antonio de Chiquito had ears like sunbonnets; he folded them back, lifted his muzzle toward Anvil rock, and brayed loudly.

"Mebbe you're right," said the man. He fitted the Chinese yoke to his skinny shoulders, and took up his burden. The load was heavy, the yoke bruised his bones, therefore he was moved to complain: "The idea of me totin' water for the very guys that stole my uncle's money! It's awful—the darned crooks!"

It was a rainy evening when business next took Black Jack Berg and Denny Slevin to town. Having dined amply, if not well, they donned slickers, saddled a pair of horses, and set out down the creek. Few people were abroad, therefore they felt secure from observation when they swung off the trail where it bends around the foot of Anvil Mountain and bore directly up through the scattered alders. The grass was wet, the rain erased the marks of their horses' feet almost in the passing. Tethering their mounts in the last clump of underbrush the riders labored on afoot up a shallow draw which scarred the steep slope. The murk of twilight obscured them, but even in a good light they would have run small risk of discovery, for slow-moving human figures would have been lost against the dark background.

The climb was long and arduous; both men were panting when they breasted the last rise and looked down into the valley where lay the Aurora Borealis. This was a desolate spot, great boulders, fallen from the huge rock overhead, lay all about, the earth was weathered by winter snows and summer rains. Ghostly fingers of mist writhed over the peak; darkness was not far distant.

The robbers remained on the crest perhaps twenty minutes, then they came striding down. They passed within a hundred yards of Laughing Bill Hyde, who lay flat in the wet grass midway of their descent. He watched them mount and ride out of sight, then he continued his painful progress up the hillside.

Weak lungs are not suited to heavy grades and slippery footing. Bill was sobbing with agony when he conquered the last rise and collapsed upon his face. He feared he was dying, every cough threatened a hemorrhage; but when his breath came more easily and he missed the familiar taste of blood in his mouth he rose and tottered about through the fog. He could discover no tracks; he began to fear the night would foil him, when at last luck guided his aimless footsteps to a slide of loose rock banked against a seamy ledge. The surface of the bank showed a muddy scar, already half obliterated by the rain; brief search among the near-by boulders uncovered the hiding-place of a pick and shovel.

For once in his life Mr. Hyde looked upon these tools with favor, and energetically tackled the business end of a "Number 2." He considered pick-and-shovel work the lowest form of human endeavor; nevertheless he engaged in it willingly enough, and he had not dug deeply before he uncovered the side of a packing-case, labeled "Choice California Canned Fruits." Further rapid explorations showed that the box was fitted with a loose top, and that the interior was well-nigh filled with stout canvas and moose skin bags. Bill counted them; he weighed one, then he sat down weakly and his hard, smoke-blue eyes widened with amazement.

"Suffering cats!" he whispered. He voiced other expletives, too, even more forcefully indicative of surprise. He was not an imaginative man; it did not occur to him to doubt his sanity or to wonder if he were awake, nevertheless he opened one of the pokes and incredulously examined its contents. "I'm dam' if it ain't!" he said, finally. "I should reckon they *was* ready to quit. Argentine! Why, Jack'll bust the bottom out of a boat if he takes this with him. He'll drown a lot of innocent people." Mr. Hyde shook his head and smiled pityingly. "It ain't safe to trust him with it. It ain't safe—the thievin' devil! There's five hundred pounds if there's an ounce!" He began to figure with his finger on the muddy shovel blade. "A hundred thousand bucks!" he announced, finally. "Them boys is *all right*!"

Slowly, reluctantly, he replaced the gold sacks, reburied the box, and placed the tools where he had found them; then he set out for home.

Don Antonio de Chiquito was contentedly munching an empty oat sack, doubtless impelled thereto by the lingering flavor of its former contents, when on the following morning Bill accosted him.

"Tony, I got to hand it to you," the man said, admiringly. "You're some pocket miner, and you speak up like a gent when you're spoken to. I got some nice egg-shells saved up for you." Then his voice dropped to a confidential tone. "We're in with a passel of crooks, Tony. Evil associates, I call 'em. They're bound to have a bad influence over us—I feel it a'ready, don't you? Well, s'pose you meet me to-night at the gap in the hedge and we'll take a walk?"

Don Antonio appeared in every way agreeable to the proposal, but to make certain that he would keep his appointment Bill led him down into the creek bottom and tied him securely, after which he removed a pack-saddle and a bundle of hay from the stable. The saddle he hid in the brush, the hay he spread before his accomplice, with the generous invitation: "Drink hearty; it's on the house!" In explanation he went on: "It's this way, Tony; they left the elevator out of that Anvil skyscraper, and I can't climb stairs on one lung, so you got to be my six-cylinder oat-motor. We got a busy night ahead of us."

That evening Laughing Bill ascended Anvil Mountain for a second time, but the exertion did not wind him unduly, for he made the ascent at the end of Don Antonio's tail. He was back in camp for breakfast, and despite his lack of sleep he performed his menial duties during the day with more than his usual cheerfulness.

* * * *

"Speed up, can't you?" Slevin paused midway of the steepest slope and spoke impatiently to his partner below.

"I'm coming," Black Jack panted. Being the heavier and clumsier of the two, the climb was harder for him. "You're so spry, s'pose you just pack this poke!" He unslung a heavy leather sack from his belt and gave it to Denny.

"We'd ought to 'a' got an early start," the latter complained. "The days are gettin' short and I had a rotten fall going down, last time."

Relieved of some fifteen pounds of dead, awkward weight—and nothing is more awkward to carry than a sizable gold sack—Berg made better speed, arriving at the cache in time to see Slevin spit on his hands and fall to digging.

"Every time we open her up I get a shiver," Denny confessed, with a laugh. "I'm scared to look."

"Humph! Think she's going to get up and walk out on us?" Berg seated himself, lit his pipe, and puffed in silence for a while. "We ain't never been seen," he declared, positively. "She's as safe as the Bank of England as long as you don't get drunk."

"Me drunk! Ha! Me and the demon rum is divorced forever." Slevin's shovel struck wood and he swiftly uncovered the box, then removed its top. He, stood for a full minute staring into its interior, then he cried, hoarsely, "*Jack!*"

Berg was on his feet in an instant; he strode to the excavation and bent over it. After a time he straightened himself and turned blazing eyes upon his confederate. Denny met his gaze with the glare of a man demented.

"Wha'd I tell you?" the latter chattered. "I told you they'd get it. By God! They have!"

He cast an apprehensive glance over his shoulder. Far below the lights of the valley were beginning to twinkle, in the direction of Nome the cross on the Catholic church gleamed palely against the steel-gray expanse of Behring Sea.

Berg was a man of violent temper; he choked and gasped; his face was bloated with an apoplectic rage. He began to growl curses deep in his throat. "*Who* got it?" he demanded. "Who d'you mean by '*they*'?"

"'Sh-h!" Slevin was panic-stricken; he flung out a nervous, jerky hand. "Mebbe they're here—now. Look out!"

"Who d'you mean by '*they*'?" the larger man repeated.

"I—God! I dunno! But there must 'a' been more'n one. Five hundred pounds! One man couldn't pack it!"

"You said '*they*'!" Berg persisted in an odd tone.

Slevin's madly roving gaze flew back and settled upon the discolored visage thrust toward him, then his own eyes widened. He recoiled, crying:

"Look here! You don't think I—?" His words ended in a bark.

"I ain't said what I think, but I'm thinkin' fast. Nobody knew it but us—"

"How d'you know?"

"I know."

Slowly Slevin settled himself. His muscles ceased jumping, his bullet head drew down between his shoulders. "Well, it wasn't me, so it must 'a' been—*you*!"

"Don't stall!" roared the larger man. "It won't win you anything. You can't leave here till you come through."

"That goes double, Jack. I got my gat, too, and you ain't going to run out on me."

"You wanted to quit. You weakened."

"You're a liar!"

The men stared fixedly at each other, heads forward, bodies tense; as they glared the fury of betrayal grew to madness.

"Where'd you put it?" Berg ground the words between his teeth.

"I'm askin' you that very thing," the foreman answered in a thin, menacing voice. Slowly, almost imperceptibly, he widened the distance between himself and his accuser. It was not a retreat, he merely drew himself together defensively, holding himself under control with the last supreme effort of his will.

The tension snapped suddenly.

With a harsh, wordless cry of fury Black Jack tore his six-shooter from its resting-place. But Slevin's right hand stirred in unison and it moved like light. Owing to the fact that he carried his gun beneath his left armpit he was the first to fire, by the fraction of a second. It was impossible to miss at this distance. Berg went to his knees as if hit by a sledge. But he fired from that position, and his shot caught Slevin as the latter crow-hopped nimbly. Both men were down now. Slevin, however, seemed made of rubber; he was up again almost instantly, and zigzagging toward the shelter of the nearest rocks. Berg emptied his Colt at the running target, then a shout burst from his lips as he saw Denny pitch forward out of sight.

With shaking, clumsy fingers Black Jack reloaded his hot weapon. With his left hand pressed deep into his side he rose slowly to his feet and lurched forward.

"You rat!" he yelled. "Double-cross *me*, will yeh?" He heard the sound of a body moving over loose stones and halted, weaving in his tracks and peering into the gloom.

"Come out!" he ordered. "Come out and own up and I'll let yeh off."

There was a silence. "I see yeh!" He took unsteady aim at a shadow and fired. "Never mind, I'll get yeh!" After a little while he stumbled onward between the boulders, shouting a challenge to his invisible opponent. He had gone perhaps fifty feet when the darkness was stabbed by the blaze of Slevin's gun. Three times the weapon spoke, at little more than arm's-length, and Black Jack spun on his heels, then rocked forward limply. It was a long time before the sound of his loud, slow breathing ceased. Not until then did Denny Slevin move. With a rattle in his throat the foreman crept out from hiding and went down the mountain-side upon his hands and knees.

It occasioned considerable speculation at the Aurora Borealis when neither the superintendent nor the foreman appeared for breakfast. Later, a telephone message to Doctor Slayforth having elicited the startling intelligence that neither man had been seen in town during the night, there came a flicker of excitement. This excitement blazed to white heat when Slayforth rode up on a muddy horse, accompanied by the town marshal and the chief of police. Followed more telephoning and some cross-examination. But the men were gone. They had disappeared.

It was a mystery baffling any attempt at explanation, for there were no ships in the roadstead, and hence it was impossible for the pair to have taken French leave. While a search party was being organized there came word that the missing saddle-horses had been found on the slope of Anvil Mountain, and by the time Slayforth's party had reached the ground more news awaited them. Up near the head of the draw some one had discovered the body of Denny Slevin. There was a rush thither, and thence on up the trail Slevin had left, to the scene of the twilight duel, to Black Jack Berg and the cache in the slide.

The story told itself down to the last detail; it was the story of a thieves' quarrel and a double killing. Doctor Slayforth fell upon his bag of gold as a mother falls upon her babe; he voiced loud, hysterical condemnation of the deed; he wept tears of mingled indignation and thanksgiving; he gabbled scriptural quotations about the wages of sin. Then, remembering that the wages of his men were going on, he sent them back to their work, and determined to dock half their morning's pay.

The story of the tragedy was still the sensation of Nome when, a fortnight later, Laughing Bill Hyde showed up in town with the cheerful announcement that he had been fired. Ponatah was at the cabin when he arrived, and she did not try to conceal her joy at seeing him again.

"I've been so unhappy," she told him. "You've never been out of my thoughts, Billy."

"Ain't you got nothing better to think about than me?" he asked, with a smile. "Well, the psalm-shouter let me out—jerked the piller-slip from under me, you might say—and turned me adrift. He's got a high-chested, low-browed Swede in my place. It takes a guy with hair down to his eyebrows to be a buck chamber-maid."

"The old rascal!" Ponatah's face darkened with anger. "No wonder those men robbed him. I wish they had taken all his gold, and escaped."

"You're pretty sore on his heavenly nibs, ain't you?" Ponatah clenched her hands and her eyes blazed. "Well, you got this consolation, the Aurora ain't as rich as it was."

"It would have been rich enough for us."

"Us?"

"Yes. You'd marry me if I were rich, wouldn't you?"

"No, I wouldn't," Bill declared, firmly. "What's the use to kid you?"

"Why wouldn't you? Are you ashamed of me?"

Bill protested, "Say, what is this you're giving me, the third degree?"

"If I were as rich as—well, as Reindeer Mary, wouldn't you marry me?" Ponatah gazed at the unworthy object of her affections with a yearning that was embarrassing, and Laughing Bill was forced to spar for wind.

"Ain't you the bold Mary Ann—makin' cracks like that?" he chided. "I'm ashamed of you, honest. I've passed up plenty of frills in my time, and we're all better off for it. My appetite for marriage ain't no keener than it used to be, so you forget it. Little Doc, he's the marrying kind."

"Oh yes. He tells me a great deal about his Alice. He's very much discouraged. If—if I had the Aurora I wouldn't forget him; I'd give him half."

"Would you, now? Well, he's the one stiffneck that wouldn't take it. He's funny that way—seems to think money 'll bite him, or something. I don't know how these pullanthrofists get along, with proud people always spurning their gifts. He's got my nan. You take my tip, Kid, and cling to your coin. Salt it down for winter. That's what I'm doing with mine."

"Are you?" Ponatah was not amused, she was gravely interested. "I thought you were broke, Billy."

"Where'd you get that at?" he demanded. "I've always got a pinch of change, I have. I'm lucky that way. Now then, you run along and don't never try to feint me into a clinch. It don't go."

Laughing Bill enjoyed a good rest in the days that followed. He rested hard for several weeks, and when he rested he lifted his hand to absolutely nothing. He was an expert idler, and with him indolence was but a form of suspended animation. In spite of himself, however, he was troubled by a problem; he was completely baffled by it, in fact, until, without warning and without conscious effort, the solution presented itself. Bill startled his cabin mate one day by the announcement that he intended to go prospecting.

"Nonsense!" said Thomas, when the first shock of surprise had passed."This country has been run over, and every inch is staked."

"I bet I'll horn in somewhere. All I want is one claim where I got room to sling myself."

"If that's all you want I'll give you a claim. It has twenty acres. Is that room enough?"

"Plenty. Where is it?"

"It's on Eclipse Creek, I believe. A patient gave it to me for a bill."

"He won't call for a new deal if I strike it rich?"

"No. I paid his fare out of the country. But why waste your valuable time? Your time *is* valuable, I presume?"

"Sure! I ain't got much left. You don't believe in hunches, do you? Well, I do. I've seen 'em come out. Look at Denny Slevin, for instance! I heard him say he had a hunch something unpleasant was going to happen to him, and it did. We'll go fifty-fifty on this Eclipse Creek."

The doctor shrugged his shoulders. "Suit yourself. Fresh air won't hurt you."

The first frosts of autumn had arrived before Laughing Bill returned to town with the announcement that he had struck a prospect. Doctor Thomas was at first incredulous, then amazed; finally, when the true significance of those tiny yellow grains came home to him, his enthusiasm burst all bounds. He was for at once closing his office and joining actively in his partner's work, but Bill would not hear to such a thing.

"Stick to the pills and powders, Doc," he counseled. "You know that game and I know this. It's my strike and I don't want no amachoors butting in. I got options on the whole creek—she's eclipsed for fair—'cause I don't like neighbors. You shut your trap till spring and sit tight, then we'll roll our packs, stomp on the fire, and call the dog. Old Home Week for us."

"But, Billy, we can't work out that claim in one winter," protested the physician.

"How d'you know we can't? Mebbe it's just a pocket."

"We'll find other pockets. We have the whole creek—"

"Say, how much d'you need to satisfy you?" Bill inquired, curiously.

"I—don't know. A hundred thousand dollars, perhaps."

"A hundred thousand! Whew! You got rich tastes! This ain't no bonanza."

"But if it's any good at all it will net us that much, probably more."

Bill considered briefly, then he announced: "All right, bo, I got your idea. When I hand you a hundred thousand iron men we quit—no questions, no regrets; Is that it? But you've hiked the limit on me; I dunno's I'll make good."

By the time snow flew the tent on Eclipse Creek had been replaced by a couple of warm shacks, provisions had been bought, and a crew hired. Work commenced immediately, and it continued throughout the winter with Bill in charge. The gravel was lean-looking stuff, but it seemed to satisfy the manager, and whenever Thomas came out from town he received encouraging reports from his partner. Hyde ceased playing solitaire long enough to pan samples in his tub of snow water. Now had the younger man been an experienced placer miner he might have noted with suspicion that whenever Bill panned he chewed tobacco—a new habit he had acquired—and not infrequently he spat into the tub of muddy water. But Thomas was not experienced in the wiles and artifices of mine-salters, and the residue of yellow particles left in the pan was proof positive that the claim was making good. It did strike him as strange, however, that when he selected a pan of dirt and washed it unassisted he found nothing. At such times Bill explained glibly enough that no pay dump carried steady values, and that an inexperienced sampler was apt to get "skunked" under the best of circumstances. Concentrates lay in streaks and pockets, he declared. Then to prove his assertions Bill would help his partner pan, and inasmuch as he wore long finger-nails, underneath which colors of gold could be easily concealed, it was not surprising that he succeeded in finding a prospect where the doctor had failed. For fear Thomas should still entertain some lingering doubts, Bill occasionally sent him down into the shaft alone, to sample the pay streak, but in each instance he took pains to go down beforehand with a shot-gun and some shells of his own loading and to shoot a few rounds into the face of the thawed ground.

The winter passed quickly enough, Bill's only concern arising from the fact that his strike had become common knowledge, and that men were clamoring to buy or to lease a part of the creek. It was a tiny creek, and he had it safely tied up under his options, therefore he was in a position to refuse every offer. By so doing he gained the reputation of being a cautious, cagey man and difficult to deal with.

Bill paid off his crew out of the first spring cleanup, from the dust he had managed to dump into the sluices at night. Thereafter he sent the gold to town by Doctor Thomas, who came after it regularly. When he closed down the works, in June, he and his partner held bank deposit slips for a trifle over one hundred thousand dollars. Rumor placed their profits at much more.

Bill saw little of Ponatah after his return to Nome, for the girl avoided him, and when he did see her she assumed a peculiar reserve. Her year and a half of intimate association with cultured people had in reality worked an amazing improvement in her, and people no longer regarded her as an Indian, but referred to her now as "that Russian governess," nevertheless she could retreat behind a baffling air of stolidity—almost of sullenness—when she chose, and that was precisely the mask she wore for Bill. In reality she was far from stolid and anything but sullen.

For his part he made no effort to break down the girl's guard; he continued to treat her with his customary free good nature.

Notwithstanding the liberal margin of profit on his winter's operations, Bill realized that he was still shy approximately half of the sum which Doctor Thomas had set as satisfactory, and when the latter began planning to resume work on a larger scale in the fall Mr. Hyde was stricken with panic. Fearing lest his own lack of enthusiasm in these plans and his indifference to all affairs even remotely concerning Eclipse Creek should awaken suspicion, he determined to sell out his own and his partner's interests in accordance with their original understanding. Without consulting Thomas he called upon Doctor Slayforth.

The pious mine-owner was glad to see him; his manner was not at all what it had been when Bill worked for him. His words of greeting fairly trickled prune juice and honey.

"Say, Doc, I got a load on my chest! I'm a strayed lamb and you being a sort of shepherd I turns to you," Bill began.

"I trust you have not come in vain." The ex-missionary beamed benignly. "It has been my duty and my privilege to comfort the afflicted. What troubles you, William?"

"There's a school of sharks in this village, and I don't trust 'em. They're too slick for a feller like me,"

"It *is* an ungodly place," the doctor agreed. "I have felt the call to work here, but my duties prevent. Of course I labor in the Lord's vineyard as I pass through, but—I am weak."

"Me, too, and getting weaker daily." Bill summoned a hollow cough."Listen to that hospital bark,' I gotta blow this place, Doc, orthey'll button me up in a rosewood overcoat. I gotta sell EclipseCreek and beat it."

Again he coughed.

"I am distressed. But why do you come here?"

"I aim to sell out to you."

"What is your price, William?"

"A hundred and fifty thousand, cash."

Slayforth lifted protesting palms. "My dear man—"

"That's cheaper'n good advice, and you know it. I took out 'most that much last winter with a scowegian gang of six. Here's the bank's O.K. But I ain't got use for a lot of money, Doc. I wouldn't know how to run a vineyard like you do. All I want is a nice little corner saloon or a cattle ranch."

"It is a large sum of money you ask. There is always an element of uncertainty about placer mining." Doctor Slayforth failed to conceal the gleam of avarice in his eyes.

"Doc, take it from me; there ain't a particle of uncertainty about Eclipse Creek," Bill earnestly assured his hearer. "If I told you what's there you wouldn't believe me. But Thomas, he's got a gal and I got a cough. They both need attention, and he's the only guy that can give it. We're willing to hand you Eclipse Creek if you'll take it."

There was considerable conversation, and a visit to Eclipse Creek, but the doctor, it proved, was willing to take any good bargain, and a few days later the transfer was made. When the larger part of Slayforth's winter's clean-up had changed hands the two partners adjourned to Thomas's little office.

"Well!" The physician heaved a deep sigh of relief. "It's all over, and—I feel as if I were dreaming."

"The *Oregon* sails to-morrow. It's time to stomp on the fire."

"I—I wonder if we were wise to sell out at that price," the doctor mused, doubtfully.

"You lay a bet on it, bo. Something tells me that soul-saver will go bust on Eclipse Creek. I got a hunch that way." Mr. Hyde's seamy face wrinkled into a broad grin.

"Well, I've more faith in your hunches than I used to have. You've been a good friend, Bill, and a square one." The speaker choked, then wrung his partner's hand. "I've cabled Alice to meet us. I want you to know her and—I want her to see that I cured you, after all."

"I'd admire to meet her, but my taste has allus run more to brunettes," said Mr. Hyde. Then, since he abhorred emotional display, he continued, briskly: "Now call the dog. I'm off to buy our duckets."

Laughing Bill purchased three tickets instead of two, then he went in search of Ponatah. It so chanced that he found her alone. Now neither he nor any other man had ever called upon her, therefore she was dumfounded at his coming.

"Well, Kid," he announced, "me 'n' the Doc have sold Eclipse Creek, and we bow out tomorrow on the big smoke."

Ponatah opened her lips, but no sound issued. She possessed a strong young body, but the strength, the life, seemed suddenly to go out of it, leaving her old and spiritless.

"Got a kind word for us?" the man inquired, with a twinkle.

"I'm glad you struck it rich," she murmured, dully. "You—you'll take care of yourself, Billy?"

"Who, me? I don't s'pose so. I don't know how to take care of nothing." There was a moment of silence. "Like me?" he asked.

Ponatah turned away blindly, but as she did so Laughing Bill put his hand gently upon her shoulder, saying:

"Cheer up, Kid. You're going to join the troupe. I've come to get you."

There was amazement, incredulity, in the girl's face as she lifted it to his. "What do you—mean?" she quavered. "Are you going to—marry me?"

"You guessed it!" he laughed. "I been aiming to put up that job on you for a long time, but I had a lot of deals on my hands. I was a sort of power-of-attorney for a coupla simps, and it kept me busy. If you think the two of us can do with three lungs, why, we'll grab a psalm-shouter and—"

"Billy! Billy!" Ponatah clung to him fiercely, hungrily. "Oh, Billy—I'll make you well. We'll go to Arizona, Colorado, Montana—where it is high and dry—"

"I been to them places," he told her, dubiously, "and I 'most stopped breathing altogether."

"New Mexico, then. You won't be ashamed of me there."

"Say, Kid! I wouldn't be ashamed of a harelip and warts in New Mexico. But you got me wrong; I'm plumb proud of you, and just to prove it I aim to make you carry our bank-roll in your name. That's how she stands at the bank, and that's how she's goin' to stand. From time to time you can gimme a check for what you think I'm wuth. Now then, do with me as you will; grab your lid; we'll join hands and be soldered up."

Laughing Bill stared after the girl as she hurried away; musingly he said: "The little Doc got in on no pair, for it was all her coin, of course. But she'd 'a' had to split, fifty-fifty, with a lawyer, so it ain't a bad deal all around."

THE NORTH WIND'S MALICE

It had snowed during the night, but toward morning it had grown cold; now the sled-runners complained and the load dragged heavily. Folsom, who had been heaving at the handle-bars all the way up the Dexter Creek hill, halted his dogs at the crest and dropped upon the sled, only too glad of a breathing spell. His forehead was wet with sweat; when it began to freeze in his eyebrows he removed his mittens and wiped away the drops, then watched them congeal upon his fingers. Yes, it was all of thirty below, and a bad morning to hit the trail, but—Folsom's face set itself—better thirty below in the open than the frigid atmosphere of an unhappy home.

Harkness, who had led the way up the hill, plodded onward for a time before discovering that his companion had paused; then, through the ring of hoar frost around his parka hood, he called back:

"I'll hike down to the road-house and warm up."

Folsom made no answer, he did not even turn his head. Taciturnity was becoming a habit with him, and already he was beginning to dislike his new partner. For that matter he disliked everybody this morning.

Below him lay the level tundra, merging indistinguishably with the white anchor-ice of Behring Sea; beyond that a long black streak of open water, underscoring the sky as if to emphasize the significance of that empty horizon, a horizon which for many months would remain unsmudged by smoke. To Folsom it seemed that the distant stretch of dark water was like a prison wall, barring the outside world from him and the other fools who had elected to stay "inside."

Fools? Yes; they were all fools!

Folsom was a "sour-dough." He had seen the pranks that Alaskan winters play with men and women, he had watched the alteration in minds and morals made by the Arctic isolation, and he had considered himself proof against the malice that rides the north wind—the mischief that comes with the winter nights. He had dared to put faith in his perfect happiness, thinking himself different from other men and Lois superior to other wives, wherefore he now called himself a fool!

Sprawled beside the shore, five miles away, was Nome, its ugliness of corrugated iron, rough boards, and tar paper somewhat softened by the distance. From the jumble of roofs he picked out one and centered his attention upon it. It was his roof—or had been. He wondered, with a sudden flare of wrathful indignation, if Lois would remember that fact during his absence. But he banished this evil thought. Lois had pride, there was nothing common about her; he could not believe that she would affront the proprieties. It was to spare that very pride of hers, even more than his own, that he had undertaken this adventure to the Kobuk; and now, as he looked back upon Nome, he told himself that he was acting handsomely in totally eliminating himself, thus allowing her time and freedom in which to learn her heart. He hoped that before his return she would have chosen between him and the other man.

It was too cold to remain idle long. Folsom's damp body began to chill, so he spoke to his team and once more heaved upon the handle-bars.

Leaving the crest of the ridge behind, the dogs began to run; they soon brought up in a tangle at the road-house door. When Harkness did not appear in answer to his name Folsom entered, to find his trail-mate at the bar, glass in hand.

"Put that down!" Folsom ordered, sharply.

Harkness did precisely that, then he turned, wiping his lips with the back of his hand. He was a small, fox-faced man; with a grin he invited the new-comer to "have one."

"Don't you know better than to drink on a day like this?" the latter demanded.

"Don't worry about me. I was raised on 'hootch,'" said Harkness.

"It's bad medicine."

"Bah! I'll travel further drunk than—" Harkness measured his critic with an insolent eye—"than some folks sober." He commenced to warm himself at the stove, whereupon the other cried, impatiently:

"Come along. We can't stop at every cabin."

But Harkness was in no hurry, he consumed considerable time. When he finally followed Folsom out into the air the latter, being in a peculiarly irritable mood, warned him in a voice which shook with anger:

"We're going to start with an understanding. If you take another drink during the daytime I'll leave you flat."

"Rats! How you aim to get to the Kobuk without me?" asked Harkness.

"I'll manage somehow."

The smaller man shot a startled glance at the speaker, then his insolence vanished. "All right, old top," he said, easily. "But don't cut off your nose to spite your face. Remember, I promised if you'd stick to me you'd wear gold-beaded moccasins." He set off at a trot, with the dogs following.

This fellow Harkness had come with the first snow into Nome, bearing news of a strike on the Kobuk, and despite his braggadocio he had made rather a good impression. That luck which favors fools and fakers had guided him straight to Folsom. He had appeared at a psychological moment in the latter's affairs, two disastrous seasons having almost broken Folsom and rendered him eager to grasp at anything which promised quick returns; moreover, the latter had just had a serious quarrel with his wife. Harkness had offered a half interest in his Kobuk claims for a grubstake and a working partner, and, smarting under the unaccustomed sting of domestic infelicity, the other had accepted, feeling sure in his own mind that Lois would not let him leave her when the time came to go. But the time had come, and Lois had offered no objection. She had acted strangely, to be sure, but she had made no effort to dissuade him. It seemed as if the proposal to separate for the winter had offended rather than frightened her. Well, that was the way with women; there was no pleasing them; when you tried to do the decent thing by them they pretended to misunderstand your motives. If you paid them the compliment of utter confidence they abused it on the pretext that you didn't love them; if you allowed your jealousy to show, they were offended at your lack of trust.

So ran the husband's thoughts. He hoped that six months of widowhood would teach Lois her own mind, but it hurt to hit the trail with nothing more stimulating than a listless kiss and a chill request to write when convenient. Now that he was on his way he began to think of the pranks played by malicious nature during the long, dark nights, and to wonder if he had acted wisely in teaming up with this footless adventurer. He remembered the malice that rides the winter winds, the mischief that comes to Arctic widows, and he grew apprehensive.

The travelers put up that night at the Tin Road-house, a comfortless shack sheathed with flattened kerosene cans, and Folsom's irritation at his new partner increased, for Harkness was loud, boastful, and blatantly egotistical, with the egotism that accompanies dense ignorance.

The weather held cold, the snow remained as dry as sand, so they made slow progress, and the husband had ample time to meditate upon his wrongs, but the more he considered them the less acutely they smarted him and the gentler became his thoughts of Lois. The solitudes were healing his hurt, the open air was cooling his anger.

At Kougarok City, a miserable huddle of cottonwood cabins, Harkness escaped his partner's watchful eye and got drunk. Folsom found the fellow clinging to the bar and entertaining a crowd of loafers with his absurd boastings. In a white fury he seized the wretch, dragged him from the room, and flung him into his bunk, then stood guard over him most of the night.

It was during the quieter hours when the place rumbled to snores that Folsom yielded to his desire to write his wife, a desire which had been growing steadily. He was disgusted with Harkness, disappointed with the whole Kobuk enterprise, and in a peculiarly softened mood, therefore, he wrote with no attempt to conceal his yearning, homesick tenderness.

But when he read the letter in the morning it struck him as weak and sentimental, just the sort of letter he would regret having written if it should transpire that Lois did not altogether share his feelings. So he tore it up.

Those were the days of faint trails and poor accommodations; as yet the road to the Arctic was little traveled and imperfectly known, so Harkness acted as guide. He had bragged that he knew every inch of the country, but he soon proved that his ideas of distance were vague and faulty—a serious shortcoming in a land with no food, no shelter, and no firewood except green willows in the gulch-bottoms. Folsom began to fear that the fellow's sense of direction was equally bad, and taxed him with it, but Harkness scoffed at the idea.

Leaving the last road-house behind them, they came into a hilly section of great white domes, high hog-backs, and ramifying creeks, each one exactly like its neighbor; two days' travel through this, according to Harkness, should have brought them to the Imnachuck, where there was food and shelter again. But when they pitched camp for the second night Folsom felt compelled to remind his partner that they were behind their schedule, and that this was the last of their grub.

"Are you sure you're going right?" he inquired.

"Sure? Of course I'm sure. D'you think I'm lost?"

Folsom fed some twisted willow-tops into the sheet-iron stove. "I wouldn't recommend you as a pathfinder," said he. "You said we'd sleep out one night. This is two, and to-morrow we'll walk hungry."

"Well, don't blame me!" challenged the other. "I'm going slow on your account."

Now nothing could have galled Folsom more than a reflection upon his ability to travel. His lips whitened, he was upon the point of speaking his mind, but managed to check himself in time. Harkness's personality rasped him to the raw, and he had for days struggled against an utterly absurd but insistent desire to seize the little coxcomb by the throat and squeeze the arrogance out of him as juice is squeezed out of a lemon. There is flesh for which one's fingers itch.

"I notice you're ready to camp when I am," the larger man muttered. "Understand, this is no nice place to be without grub, for it's liable to storm any hour, and storms last at this season."

"Now don't get cold feet." Harkness could be maddeningly patronizing when he chose. "Leave it to me. I'll take you a short cut, and we'll eat lunch in a cabin to-morrow noon."

But noon of the next day found Harkness still plodding up the river with the dogs close at his heels. The hills to the northward were growing higher, and Folsom's general knowledge of direction told him that they were in danger of going too far.

"I think the Imnachuck is over there," said he.

Harkness hesitated, then he nodded: "Right-o! It's just over that low saddle." He indicated a sweeping hillside ahead, and a half-mile further on he left the creek and began to climb. This was heavy work for the dogs, and mid-afternoon came before the partners had gained the summit only to discover that they were not upon a saddleback after all, but upon the edge of a vast rolling tableland from which a fanlike system of creeks radiated. In all directions was a desolate waste of barren peaks.

Folsom saw that the sky ahead was thick and dark, as if a storm impended, and realizing only too well the results of the slightest error in judgment he called to Harkness. But the latter pretended not to hear, and took advantage of the dogs' fatigue to hurry out of earshot. It was some time before the team overhauled him.

"Do you know where you are?" Folsom inquired.

"Certainly." Harkness studied the panorama spread before him. "That blue gulch yonder is the Imnachuck." He pointed to a valley perhaps four miles away.

A fine snow began to sift downward. The mountain peaks to the northward became obscured as by thin smoke, the afternoon shortened with alarming swiftness. Night, up here with a blizzard brewing, was unthinkable, so after a while the driver called another halt.

"Something informs me that you're completely lost," he said, mildly.

"Who, me? There she is." Harkness flung out a directing hand once more.

Folsom hesitated, battling with his leaping desires, and upon that momentary hesitation hinged results out of all proportions to the gravity of the situation—issues destined to change the deepest channels of his life. Folsom hesitated, then he yielded to his impulse, and the luxury of yielding made him drunk. He walked around the sled, removing his mittens with his teeth as he went. Without a word he seized his companion by the throat and throttled him until his eyes protruded and his face grew black and bloated. He relaxed his stiff fingers finally, then he shook the fellow back to consciousness.

"Just as I thought," he cried, harshly. "That's not the gulch you pointed out before. You're lost and you won't admit it."

Harkness pawed the air and fought for his breath. There was abject terror in his eyes. He reeled away, but saw there was no safety in flight.

"Own up!" Folsom commanded.

"You—said this was the way," the pathfinder whimpered. "You made me—turn off—" Folsom uttered a growl and advanced a step, whereupon his victim gurgled: "D-don't touch me! That's the Imnachuck, so help me

God! I'm—I'm almost sure it is."

"*Almost!*" The speaker stooped for his mittens and shook the snow out of them; he was still struggling to control himself. "Look here, Mr. Know-It-All, I've never been here before, and you have; somewhere in your thick skull there must be some faint remembrance of the country. You got us into this fix, and I'm going to give you one more chance to get us out of it. Don't try to think with your head, let your feet think for you, and maybe they'll carry you to the right gulch. If they don't—" Folsom scanned the brooding heavens and his lips compressed. "We're in for a storm and—we'll never weather it. Take one look while there's light to see by, then turn your feet loose and pray that they lead you right, for if they don't, by God, I'll cut you loose!"

It soon proved that memory lay neither in Harkness's head nor in his feet; when he had veered aimlessly about for half an hour, evidently fearing to commit himself to a definite course, and when the wind came whooping down, rolling a twilight smother ahead of it, Folsom turned his dogs into the nearest depression and urged them to a run. The grade increased, soon brittle willow-tops brushed against the speeding sled: this brush grew higher as the two men, blinded now by the gale, stumbled onward behind the team. They emerged from the gulch into a wider valley, after a while, and a mile further on the dogs burst through a grove of cottonwoods and fetched up before a lighted cabin window.

Harkness pulled back his parka hood and cried, boastfully: "What did I tell you? I knew where I was all the time." Then he went in, leaving his partner to unhitch the team and care for it.

Friendships ripen and enmities deepen quickly on the trail, seeds of discord sprout and flourish in the cold. Folsom's burst of temper had served to inflame a mutual dislike, and as he and Harkness journeyed northward that dislike deepened into something akin to hatred, for the men shared the same bed, drank from the same pot, endured the same exasperations. Nothing except their hope of mutual profit held them together. In our careless search for cause and effect we are accustomed to attribute important issues to important happenings, amazing consequences to amazing deeds; as a matter of fact it is the trivial action, the little thing, the thing unnoticed and forgotten which bends our pathways and makes or breaks us.

Harkness was a hare-brained, irresponsible person, incapable of steadiness in thought or action, too weak to cherish actual hatred, too changeable to nurse a lasting grudge. It is with such frail instruments that prankish fate delights to work, and, although he never suspected it, the luxury of yielding to that sudden gust of passion cost Folsom dear.

Arrived finally at the Kobuk the miner examined the properties covered by his option, and impressed by the optimism of the men who had made the gold discovery he paid Harkness the price agreed upon. The deal completed, he sent the fellow back to Candle Creek, the nearest post, for supplies. Folsom's mood had altogether changed by now, so, strangling his last doubt of Lois, he wrote her as he had written at Kougarok City, and intrusted the letter to his associate.

Harkness, promptly upon his arrival at Candle, got drunk. He stayed drunk for three days, and it was not until he was well started on his way back to the Kobuk that he discovered Folsom's letter still in his pocket.

Now, to repeat, the man was not malicious, neither was he bad, but as he debated whether he should back-track there came to him the memory of his humiliation on the Imnachuck divide.

So! His brains were in his feet, eh? Folsom had strangled him until he kicked, when, all the time, they had been on the right trail. Harkness felt a flash of rage, like the flare of loose gunpowder, and in the heat of it he tore the letter to atoms. It was a womanish, spiteful thing to do, and he regretted it, but later when he greeted the husband he lied circumstantially and declared he had given the missive into the hands of the mail-carrier on the very hour of his departure. By this time, doubtless, it was nearly to Nome. Soon thereafter Harkness forgot all about the incident.

Folsom was a fast worker. He hired men and cross-cut the most promising claim. Bed-rock was shallow, and he soon proved it to be barren, so he went on to the next property. When he had prospected this claim with no better results than before he wrote his wife confessing doubts of the district and voicing the fear that his winter's work would be wasted. Again he let his pen run as it would; the letter he gave to a neighbor who was leaving for Candle Creek in the morning.

Folsom's neighbor was a famous "musher," a seasoned, self-reliant man, thoroughly accustomed to all the hazards of winter travel, but ten miles from his destination he crossed an inch-deep overflow which rendered the soles of his muk-luks slippery, and ten yards further on, where the wind had laid the glare-ice bare, he lost his footing. He fell and wrenched his ankle and came hobbling into Candle half an hour after the monthly mail for Nome had left.

Three weeks later Folsom wrote his wife for the third time, and again a month after that. All three letters joined company in Candle Creek; for meanwhile the mail-man's lead dog had been killed in a fight with a big malamute at Lane's Landing, causing its owner to miss a trip. Now dog-fights are common; by no logic could one attribute weighty results to the loss of a sixty-pound leader, but in this instance it so happened that the mail-carrier's schedule suffered so that his contract was canceled.

Meanwhile a lonely woman waited anxiously in Nome, and as the result of a stranger's spite, a wet muk-luk, and a vicious malamute her anxiety turned to bitterness and distrust.

It is never difficult to forward mail in the north, for every "musher" is a postman. When news came to Candle Creek that the Government service had been discontinued the storekeeper, one end of whose bar served as post-office, sacked his accumulated letters and intrusted them to some friends who were traveling southward on the morrow. The trader was a canny man, but he loved to gamble, so when his friends offered to bet him that they could lower the record from Candle to Nome he went out into the night, sniffed the air and studied the stars, then laid them a hundred dollars that they could not.

Excited to recklessness by this wager the volunteer mail-men cut down their load. They left their stove and tent and grub-box behind, planning to make a road-house every night except during the long jump from the Imna-chuck to Crooked River. They argued that it was worth a hundred dollars to sleep once under the open sky.

The fruits of that sporting enterprise were bitter; the trader won his bet, but he never cashed it in. Somewhere out on the high barrens a storm swooped down upon the travelers. To one who has never faced an Arctic hurricane it seems incredible that strong men have died within call of cozy cabins or have frozen with the lashings of their sleds but half untied. Yet it is true. The sudden awful cold, the shouting wind, the boiling, blinding, suf-focating rush of snow; the sweaty clothes that harden into jointless armor; the stiff mittens and the clumsy hands inside—these tell a tale to those who know.

The two mail-carriers managed to get into their sleeping-bags, but the gale, instead of drifting them over with a protective mantle of snow, scoured the mountain-side bare to the brittle reindeer moss, and they began to freeze where they lay. Some twenty hours they stood it, then they rose and plunged ahead of the hurricane like bewildered cattle. The strongest man gave up first and lay down, babbling of things to eat. His companion buried him, still alive, and broke down the surrounding willow-tops for a landmark, then he staggered on. By some miracle of good luck, or as a result of some unsus-pected power of resistance, he finally came raving into the Crooked River Road-house. When the wind subsided they hurried him to Nome, but he was frightfully maimed and as a result of his amputations he lay gabbling until long after the spring break-up.

Folsom did not write again. In fact, when no word came from Lois, he bitterly regretted the letters he had written. He heard indirectly from her; new-comers from Nome told him that she was well, but that was all. It was enough. He did not wish to learn more.

Spring found him with barely enough money to pay his way back. He was blue, bitter, disheartened, but despite the certainty that his wife had forsaken him he still cherished a flickering hope of a reconciliation. Strangely enough he considered no scheme of vengeance upon the other man, for he was sane and healthy, and he loved Lois too well to spoil her attempt at happiness.

It so happened that the Arctic ice opened up later this spring than for many seasons; therefore the short summer was well under way before the first steam-schooner anchored off the Kobuk. Folsom turned his back upon the wreck of his high hopes, his mind solely engaged with the problem of how to meet Lois and ascertain the truth without undue embarrassment to her and humiliation to himself. The prospect of seeing her, of touching her, of hearing her voice, affected him painfully. He could neither eat nor sleep on the way to Nome, but paced the deck in restless indecision. He had come to consider himself wholly to blame for their misunderstanding, and he wished only for a chance to win back her love, with no questions asked and no favors granted.

When there were less than fifty miles to go the steamer broke her shaft. There was no particular reason why that shaft should break, but break it did, and for eighteen hours—eighteen eternities to Folsom—the ship lay crippled while its engine-room crew labored manfully.

Folsom had been so long in the solitudes that Nome looked like a big city when he finally saw it. There were several ships in the roadstead, and one of them was just leaving as the Kobuk boat came to anchor. She made a splendid sight as she gathered way.

The returning miner went ashore in the first dory and as he stepped out upon the sand a friend greeted him:

"Hello there, old settler! Where you been all winter?"

"I've been to the Kobuk," Folsom told him.

"Kobuk? I hear she's a bum."

"'Bum' is right. Maybe she'll do to dredge some day."

"Too bad you missed the *Oregon*; there she goes now." The man pointed seaward.

"Too bad?"

"Sure! Don't you know? Why, Miz Folsom went out on her!"

Folsom halted; after a momentary pause he repeated, vaguely, "Went out?"

"Exactly. Didn't you know she was going?"

"Oh yes—of course! The *Oregon*!" Folsom stared at the fading plume of black smoke; there was a curious brightness in his eyes, his face was white beneath its tan. "She sailed on the *Oregon* and I missed her, by an hour! That broken shaft—" He began to laugh, and turning his back upon the sea he plodded heavily through the sand toward the main street.

Folsom found no word from his wife, his house was empty; but he learned that "the man" had also gone to the States, and he drew his own conclusions. Since Lois had ordered her life as she saw fit there was nothing to do but wait and endure—doubtless the divorce would come in time. Nevertheless, he could not think of that broken shaft without raving.

Being penniless he looked for work, and his first job came from a small Jewish merchant, named Guth, who offered him a hundred dollars to do the assessment work on a tundra claim. For twenty days Folsom picked holes through frozen muck, wondering why a thrifty person like Guth would pay good money to hold such unpromising property as this.

The claim was in sight of Nome, and as Folsom finished his last day's labor he heard bells ringing and whistles blowing and discovered that the town was ablaze. He hurried in to find that an entire block in the business center of the city had been destroyed and with it Guth's little store, including all its contents. He found the Jew in tears.

"What a misfortune!" wailed the merchant. "Ruined, absolutely—and by a match! It started in my store—my little girl, you understand? And now, all gone!" He tore his beard and the tears rolled down his cheeks.

The little man's grief was affecting, and so Folsom inquired more gently than he intended, "I'm sorry, of course, but how about my money for the Lulu assessment?"

"Money? There's your money!" Guth pointed sadly into the smoldering ruins. "Go find it—you're welcome to anything I have left. Gott! What a country! How can a man get ahead, with no insurance?"

Folsom laughed mirthlessly. His hard luck was becoming amusing and he wondered how long it would last. He had counted on that hundred dollars to get away from Nome, hoping to shake misfortune from his heels, but a match in the hands of a child, like that broken propeller shaft, had worked havoc with his plans. Well, it was useless to cry.

To the despairing Hebrew he said: "Don't lose your grip, old man. Buck up and take another start. You have your wife and your little girl, at least, and you're the sort who makes good."

"You think so?" Guth looked up, grateful for the first word of encouragement he had heard.

"It's a cinch! Only don't lose your courage."

"I—I'll do what's right by you, Mr. Folsom," declared the other."I'll deed you a half interest in the Lulu."

But Folsom shook his head. "I don't want it. There's nothing there except moss and muck and salmon berries, and it's a mile to bed-rock. No, you're welcome to my share; maybe you can sell the claim for enough to make a new start or to buy grub for the wife and the kid. I'll look for another job."

For a month or more the lonesome husband "stevedored," wrestling freight on the lighters, then he disappeared. He left secretly, in the night, for by now he had grown fanciful and he dared to hope that he could dodge his Nemesis. He turned up in Fairbanks, a thousand miles away, and straightway lost himself in the hills.

He had not covered his tracks, however, for bad luck followed him.

Now no man starves in Alaska, for there is always work for the ablebodied; but whatever Folsom turned his hand to failed, and by and by his courage went. He had been a man of consequence in Nome; he had made money and he had handled other men, therefore his sense of failure was the bitterer.

Meanwhile, somewhere in him there remained the ghost of his faith in Lois, the faintly flickering hope that some day they would come together again. It lay dormant in him, like an irreligious man's unacknowledged faith in God and a hereafter, but it, too, vanished when he read in a Seattle newspaper, already three months old, the announcement of his wife's divorce. He flinched when he read that it had been won on the grounds of desertion, and thereafter he shunned newspapers.

Spring found him broke, as usual. He had become bad company and men avoided him. It amused him grimly to learn that a new strike had been made in Nome, the biggest discovery in the camp's history, and to realize that he had fled just in time to miss the opportunity of profiting by it. He heard talk of a prehistoric sea-beach line, a streak of golden sands which paralleled the shore and lay hidden below the tundra mud. News came of overnight fortunes, of friends grown prosperous and mighty. Embittered anew, Folsom turned again to the wilderness, and he did not reappear until the summer was over. He came to town resolved to stay only long enough to buy bacon and beans, but he had lost his pocket calendar and arrived on a Sunday, when the stores were closed.

Even so little a thing as the loss of that calendar loomed big in the light of later events, for in walking the streets he encountered a friend but just arrived from the Behring coast.

The man recognized him, despite his beard and his threadbare mackinaws and they had a drink together.

"I s'pose you heard about that Third Beach Line?" the new-comer inquired. Folsom nodded. "Well, they've opened it up for miles, and it's just a boulevard of solid gold. 'Cap' Carter's into it big, and so are the O'Brien boys and Old Man Hendricks. They're lousy with pay."

"I did the work on a tundra claim," said Folsom; "the Lulu—"

"The *Lulu*!" Folsom's friend stared at him. "Haven't you heard about the Lulu? My God! Where you been, anyhow? Why, the Lulu's a mint! Guth is a millionaire and he made it all without turning a finger."

Folsom's grip on the bar-rail tightened until his knuckles were white.

"I'm telling you right, old man; he's the luckiest Jew in the country. He let a lay to McCarthy and Olson, and they took out six hundred thousand dollars, after Christmas."

"Guth offered me a—half interest in the Lulu when his store burned and—I turned it down. He's never paid me for that assessment work."

The Nomeite was speechless with amazement. "The son-of-a-gun!" he said, finally. "Well, you can collect now. Say! That's what he meant when he told me he wanted to see you. Guth was down to the boat when I left, and he says: 'If you see Folsom up river tell him to come back. I got something for him.' Those were his very words. That little Jew aims to pay you a rotten hundred so you won't sue him for an interest. By Gorry, I wouldn't take it! I'd go back and make him do the right thing. I'd sue him. I'd bust him in the nose! A half interest—in the Lulu! My God!" The speaker gulped his drink hastily.

After consideration, Folsom said: "He'll do the right thing. Guth isn't a bad sort."

"No. But he's a Jew; trust him to get his."

"I wouldn't ask him to do more than pay his debt. You see I refused his offer."

"What of that? I'd give it a try, anyhow, and see if he wouldn't settle. There's lots of lawyers would take your case. But say, that's the toughest tough-luck story I ever heard. You've sure got a jinx on you."

"I'm going back, but I won't sue Guth. I'm sick of Alaska; it has licked me. I'm going out to God's country."

Folsom indeed acknowledged himself beaten. The narrow margin by which he had missed reward for his work and his hardships bred in him such hatred for Alaska that he abruptly changed his plans. He had no heart, perversity had killed his courage. It exasperated him beyond all measure to recall what little things his luck had hinged upon, what straws had turned his feet. A moment of pique with Lois, a broken piece of steel, a match, a momentary whim when Guth offered him payment. It was well that he did not know what part had been played by his quarrel with Harkness, that wet muk-luk, that vicious lead dog, and the storekeeper's wager.

Folsom carried cord-wood to pay for a deck passage down river. He discovered en route that Guth had really tried to get in touch with him, and in fact appeared greatly concerned over his failure to do so, for at Tanana he received another message, and again at St. Michaels. He was grimly amused at the little Jew's craftiness, yet it sorely offended him to think that any one should consider him such a welcher. He had no intention of causing trouble, for he knew he had no legal claim against the fellow, and he doubted if he possessed even a moral right to share in the Lulu's riches. To play upon the Hebrew's fears, therefore, savored of extortion. Nevertheless, he was in no agreeable frame of mind when he arrived at his destination and inquired for Guth.

The new-made millionaire was in his office; Folsom walked in unannounced. He had expected his arrival to create a scene, and he was not disappointed. But Guth's actions were strange, they left the new arrival dazed, for the little man fell upon him with what appeared to be exuberant manifestations of joy.

"Mr. Folsom!" he cried. "You have come! You got my letters, eh? Well, I wrote you everywhere, but I was in despair, for I thought you must be dead. Nobody knew what had become of you."

"I got your message in Fairbanks."

"You heard about the Lulu, eh? Gott! She's a dandy."

"Yes. I can hardly believe it. So, you're rich. Well, I congratulate you, and now I can use that hundred."

Guth chuckled. "Ha! You will have your joke, eh? But the Lulu is no joke. Come, we will go to the bank; I want them to tell you how much she has yielded. You'll blame me for leasing her, but how was I to know what she was?"

"I—Why should I blame—" Folsom stared at the speaker. "It's none of my business what the Lulu has yielded. In fact, I'll sleep better if I don't know."

Little Guth paused and his mouth opened. After a moment he inquired, curiously: "Don't you understand?" There was another pause, then he said, quietly, "I'm a man of my word."

Folsom suddenly saw black, the room began to spin, he passed his hand across his eyes. "Wait! Let's get this straight," he whispered.

"It is all very simple," Guth told him. "We are equal partners in the Lulu—we have been, ever since the day my store burned. It was a little thing you said to me then, but the way you said it, the fact that you didn't blame me, gave me new heart. Did you think I'd renig?" When Folsom found no answer the other nodded slowly. "I see. You probably said, 'That Guth is a Jew and he'll do me up if he can.' Well, I am a Jew, yes, and I am proud of it; but I am an honest man, too, like you."

Folsom turned to the wall and hid his face in the crook of his arm, but with his other hand he groped for that of the Hebrew.

The story of the Lulu is history now; in all the north that mine is famous, for it made half a dozen fortunes. In a daze, half doubting the reality of things, Folsom watched a golden stream pour into his lap. All that winter and the next summer the Lulu yielded wondrously, but one of the partners was not happy, his thoughts being ever of the woman who had left him. Prosperity gave him courage, however, and when he discovered that Lois had not remarried he determined to press his luck as a gambler should.

When the second season's sluicing was over and the ground had frozen he went outside.

The day after he sailed Lois arrived in Nome, on the last boat. She was older, graver; she had heard of the Lulu, but it was not that which had brought her back. She had returned in spite of the Lulu to solve an aching mystery and to learn the why of things. Her husband's riches—she still considered him her husband—merely made the task more trying.

Advised that Folsom had passed almost within hailing distance of her, she pressed her lips together and took up her problem of living. The prospect of another lonely Alaskan winter frightened her, and yet because of the Lulu she could not return by the ship she had come on. Now that Folsom was a Croesus she could not follow him too closely—he might misunderstand. After all, she reflected, it mattered little to her where she lived.

Guth called at her cabin, but she managed to avoid seeing him, and somehow continued to avoid a meeting.

Late in December some travelers from Candle Creek, while breaking a short cut to the head of Crooked River, came upon an abandoned sled and its impedimenta. Snow and rain and summer sun had bleached its wood, its runners were red streaks of rust, its rawhide lashings had been eaten off, but snugly rolled inside the tarpaulin was a sack of mail. This mail the travelers brought in with them, and the Nome newspapers, in commenting upon the find, reprinted the story of that tragic fight for life in the Arctic hurricane, now almost forgotten.

Folsom's three letters reached their destination on Christmas Day. They were stained and yellow and blurred in places, for they were three years old, but the woman read them with eyes wide and wondering, and with heart-beats pounding, for it seemed that dead lips spoke to her. Ten minutes later she was standing at Guth's door, and when he let her in she behaved like one demented. She had the letters hidden in her bosom, and she would not let him see them, but she managed to make known the meaning of her coming.

"You know him," she cried, hysterically. "You made him rich. You've lived alongside of him. Tell me then, has he—has he—changed? These letters are old. Does he still care, or—does he hate me, as he should?"

Guth smiled; he took her shaking hands in his, his voice was gentle. "No, no! He doesn't hate you. He has never mentioned your name to me, or to any one else, so far as I know, but his money hasn't satisfied him. He is sad, and he wants you. That is what took him to the States, I'm sure."

Lois sank into a chair, her face was white, her twisting fingers strained at each other. "I can't understand. I can't make head or tail of it," she moaned. "It seems that I wronged him, but see what ruin he has made for me! Why? Why—?"

"Who can understand the 'why' of anything?" inquired the little Hebrew. "I've heard him curse the perversity of little things, and rave at what he called the 'malice of the north wind.' I didn't dare to ask him what he meant, but I knew he was thinking of the evil which had come between you two. Who was to blame, or what separated you, he never told me. Well, his bad luck has changed, and yours, too; and I'm happy. Now then, the wireless. You can talk to him. Let us go."

An hour later a crackling message was hurled into the empty Christmas sky, a message that pulsed through the voids, was relayed over ice and brine and drifted forests to a lonely, brooding man three thousand miles away.

The answer came rushing back:

"Thank God! Am starting north tomorrow. Love and a million kisses. Wait for me."

Folsom came. Neither ice nor snow, neither winter seas nor trackless wastes, could daunt him, for youth was in his heart and fire ran through his veins. North and west he came by a rimy little steamer, as fast as coal could drive her, then overland more than fifteen hundred miles. His record stands unbroken, and in villages from Katmai to the Kuskokwim the Indians tell of the tall white man with the team of fifteen huskies who raced through as if a demon were at his heels; how he bored headlong into the blizzards and braved January's fiercest rage; how his guides dropped and his dogs died in their collars. That was how Folsom came.

He was thin and brown, the marks of the frost were bitten deep into his flesh when, one evening in early March, he drove into Nome. He had covered sixty miles on the last day's run, and his team was staggering. He left the dogs in their harnesses, where they fell, and bounded through the high-banked streets to Lois's cabin.

It was growing dark, a light gleamed from her window; Folsom glimpsed her moving about inside. He paused to rip the ice from his bearded lips, then he knocked softly, three times.

As he stood there a gentle north wind fanned him. It was deadly cold, but it was fresh and clean and vastly invigorating. There was no malice in it.

At his familiar signal he heard the clatter of a dish, dropped from nerveless fingers, he heard a startled voice cry out his name, then he pressed the latch and entered, smiling.

HIS STOCK IN TRADE

"The science of salesmanship is quite as exact as the science of astronomy," said Mr. Gross, casting his eyes down the table to see that he had the attention of the other boarders, "and much more intricate. The successful salesman is as much an artist in his line as the man who paints pictures or writes books."

"Oh, there's nothing so artistic as writing books," protested Miss Harris, the manicurist. "Nothing except acting, perhaps. Actors are artistic, too. But salesmen! I meet lots in my business, and I'm not strong for them."

Mr. Gross smiled at her indulgently; it was an expression that became him well, and he had rehearsed it often.

"The power to sell goods is a talent, my dear Miss Harris, just like the power to invent machinery or to rule a city, or—or—to keep a set of books. Don't you agree with me, Mrs. Green?"

Mrs. Green, the landlady, a brown, gray woman in black, smiled frigidly. "You're *so* original, Mr. Gross," said she, "it's a pleasure to hear you, I'm sure."

Gross was an impressive talker, due to the fact that he plagiarized office platitudes; he ran on pompously, dropping trade mottoes and shop-worn bits of philosophy until young Mitchell, unable longer to endure the light of admiration he saw in Miss Harris's eyes, rolled up his napkin to the size of a croquette and interrupted by noisily shoving back his chair and muttering under his breath:

"That stuff comes on printed cards. They give it away."

Mrs. Green called to him, "It's bread pudding, Mr. Mitchell, and very nice."

"Thanks! My gout is bad again," he said, at which some of the more frivolous-minded boarders snickered.

"Mitchell is a bright boy—in many ways," Gross remarked, a moment later, "but he's too fresh. I don't think he'll last long at the office."

Instead of climbing to his hall kennel on the fourth floor rear, Louis Mitchell went out upon the rusty little porch of the boarding-house and sat down on the topmost step, reflecting gloomily that a clerk has small chance against a head bookkeeper.

Life at Mrs. Green's pension—she called it that, rates six dollars up, terms six dollars down—had not been the same for the youthful hermit of the hall bedroom since Gross had met him and Miss Harris in the park a few Sundays before and, falling under the witchery of the manicurist's violet eyes, had changed his residence to coincide with theirs. Gross now occupied one of the front rooms, and a corresponding place in the esteem of those less fortunate boarders to whom the mere contemplation of ten dollars a week was an extravagance. Mitchell had long adored the blonde manicurist, but once the same roof sheltered her and the magnificent head bookkeeper, he saw his dream of love and two furnished rooms with kitchenette go glimmering.

Time was when Miss Harris had been content with Sundays in the park, vaudeville—first balcony—on Wednesdays, and a moving picture now and then. These lavish attentions, coupled with an occasional assault upon some delicatessen establishment, had satisfied her cravings for the higher life. Now that Gross had appeared and sown discord with his prodigality she no longer cared for animals and band concerts, she had acquired the orchestra-seat habit, had learned to dance, and, above all, she now possessed a subtle refinement in regard to victuals. She criticized Marlowe's acting, and complained that cold food gave her indigestion. No longer did she sit the summer evenings out with Mitchell, holding his hand in her lap and absent-mindedly buffing his nails, warning him in sweet familiarity that his cuticle was "growing down." In consequence of her defection, fierce resentment smoldered in the young man's breast. He was jealous; he longed to out-squander the extravagant Mr. Gross; he lusted to spend money in unstinted quantities, five dollars an evening if or when necessary.

But there seemed little hope of his ever attaining such a purse-proud position, for while he loomed fairly large in the boarding-house atmosphere of Ohio Street—or had so loomed until the advent of the reckless book-keeper—he was so small a part of the office force of Comer & Mathison, jobbers of railway supplies, as to resemble nothing multiplied by itself. He received twelve dollars a week, to be sure, for making telephone quotations and extending invoices between times; but when, as the evening shadows of pay-day descended and he drew his envelope, the procedure reminded him vaguely of blackmail, for any office-boy who did not stutter could have held his job.

When at seven forty-five Miss Harris appeared upon the porch with her hat and gloves and two-dollar-ticket air, and tripped gaily away in company with Mr. Gross, young Mitchell realized bitterly that the cost of living had increased and that it was up to him to raise his salary or lose his lady.

He recalled Gross's words at supper-time, and wondered if there really could be a science to business; if there could be anything to success except hard work. Mr. Comer, in his weekly talks to the office force, had repeatedly said so—whence the origin of the bookkeeper's warmed-over wisdom—but Mitchell's duties were so simple and so constricted as to allow no opening for science, or so, at least, it seemed to him. How could he be scientific, how could he find play for genius when he sat at the end of a telephone wire and answered routine questions from a card? Every day the General Railway Sales Manager gave him a price-list of the commodities which C. & M. handled, and when an inquiry came over the phone all he was required, all he was permitted, to do was to read the figures and to quote time of delivery. If this resulted in an order the Sales Manager took the credit. An open quotation, on the other hand, made Mitchell the subject of brusque criticism for offering a target to competitors, and when he lost an order he was the goat, not the General Railway Sales Manager.

No one around the office was too lowly to exact homage from the quotation clerk, and no one was tongue-tied in the matter of criticism, hence his position was neither one of dignity nor one that afforded scope for talent in the money-making line. And yet if salesmanship really were a science, Mitchell reasoned, there must be some way in which even a switchboard operator could profit by acquiring it. What if he were buckled to the end of a wire? Human nature is the same, face to face or voice to voice; surely then, if he set his mind to the task, he could make himself more than a mere string of words over a telephone. Heretofore he had been working wholly with his fingers, his ear-drums, and his vocal cords; he determined henceforth to exercise his intelligence, if he had any. It was indeed high time, for Miss Harris was undoubtedly slipping away, lured by luxuries no clerk could afford, and, moreover, he, Mitchell, was growing old; in a scant two years he would be able to vote. He began forthwith to analyze the situation.

There wasn't much to it. His telephone calls came almost wholly from the purchasing departments of the various railroads. Daily requisitions were filled by the stenographers in those railway offices, young ladies who through their long experience were allowed to attend to the more unimportant purchases. It was in quoting prices on these "pick-ups" that Mitchell helloed for eight hours a day. Of course no large orders ever came over his wire, but this small business carried an unusual profit for supply houses like Comer & Mathison, and in consequence it was highly prized.

After a period of intense and painful thought the young man realized, for the first time, that it was not the telephone itself which asked for price and time of delivery, but a weak, imaginative human being, like himself, at the other end of the wire. He reasoned further that if he could convince that person that the voice from Conner & Mathison likewise issued from a human throat, then it might be possible to get away, in a measure at least, from the mechanical part of the business and establish altogether new relations. If there were really a science to salesmanship, it would work at long distance as well as at collar-and-elbow holds, and Mitchell's first task, therefore, should be to project his own personality into the railroad offices. He went to bed still trying to figure the matter out.

His opportunity to test his new-born theory came on the following morning when an irritable female voice over at the Santa Fé asked the price on twenty kegs of rivets.

"Good morning, Santa Fe-male," he answered, cheerily.

There was a moment of amazed silence, then the young lady snapped: "'Good morning'? What is this, the Weather Bureau? I want Comer & Mathison."

"Gee! Can't a fellow display a little courtesy in business?" Mitchell inquired. "I'd rather be nice to you than not."

"All right, Mr. Comer," the voice replied, sarcastically. "Make a nice price on those rivets—and cut out the kidding."

"Listen; my name's not Comer; it's Mitchell. I'm not kidding, either. I want you to ask for me whenever you call up. Every little bit helps, you know."

"Oh, I see. You want the carriage man to call your number. All right, Mitch. If you're out at lunch with Mr. Carnegie the next time I want a dozen number ten sheets I'll have you paged at the Union League Club."

If the speaker liked this kind of blank verse, she had called up the right supply house, for Mitchell came back with:

"Say, if I ever get *your* number, I'll do the calling, Miss SantaFé."

"*W-what*?" came the startled reply.

"I mean what I say. I'd love to call—"

"Is that so? Well, I do all the calling for our, family, and I'm going to call you right now. What's the price of those rivets?"

"Two sixty-five."

"Too high! Good-by."

"Wait a minute." Mitchell checked the lady before she could "plug out" on him. "Now that you've got those rivets out of your system, may I get personal for an instant?"

"Just about an instant."

"I could listen to *you* all day."

"Oops, Horace; he loves me!" mocked the lady's voice.

"See here, I'm a regular person—with references. I've been talking to you every day for six months, so I feel that we're acquainted. Some pleasant evening, when your crew of hammock gladiators palls on you, let me come around and show you the difference."

"What difference?"

"I'll show you what a real porch-climber is like."

"Indeed! I'll think it over."

Ten minutes later Miss Santa Fe called up again.

"Hello! I want Mitchell, the junior partner."

"This is Mitchell."

"Did you say those rivets were two-fifty?"

"Should they be?"

"They should."

"They are."

"Ship them to Trinidad."

"That's bully of you, Miss Santa Claus. I want to—" But the wire was dead.

Mitchell grinned. Personality did count after all, and he had proved that it could be projected over a copper wire.

An hour later when Miss Northwestern called him for a price on stay-bolt iron she did not ring off for fifteen minutes, and at the end of that time she promised to take the first opportunity of having another chat. In a similar manner, once the ice had been broken at the C. & E.I., Mitchell learned that the purchasing agent was at West Baden on his vacation; that he had stomach trouble and was cranky; that the speaker loved music, particularly Chaminade and George Cohan, although Beethoven had written some good stuff; that she'd been to Grand Haven on Sunday with her cousin, who sold hats out of Cleveland and was a prince with his money, but drank; and that the price on corrugated iron might be raised ten cents without doing any damage.

On the following afternoon Murphy, the Railroad Sales Manager, stopped on his way past Mitchell's desk to inquire:

"Say, have you been sending orchids to Miss Dunlap over at the Santa Fe? I was in there this morning, and she wanted to know all about you."

"Did you boost me?" Louis inquired. "It won't hurt your sales to plug my game."

"She said you and she are 'buddies' over the wire. What did she mean?"

"Oh, wire pals, that's all. What kind of a looker is she, Mr. Murphy?"

The Sales Manager shrugged his shoulders. "She looks as if she was good to her mother." Then he sauntered away.

Mitchell, in the days that followed, proceeded to become acquainted with the Big Four, and in a short time was so close to the Lackawanna that he called her Phoebe Snow. The St. Paul asked for him three times in one afternoon, and the Rock Island, chancing to ring up while he was busy, threatened to hang crêpe on the round-house if he were not summoned immediately to enter an order for a manhole crab.

Within a week he became the most thoroughly telephoned person in the office, and had learned the tastes, the hopes, the aims, and the ambitions of his respective customers. Miss C. & E.I., for instance, whose real name was

Gratz, was a bug on music; Miss Northwestern was literary. She had read everything Marion Crawford ever wrote, and considered her the greatest writer Indiana had produced, but was sorry to learn from Mitchell that her marriage to Capt. Jack Crawford had turned out so unhappily—some men were brutes, weren't they? There was a hidden romance gnawing at the Big Four's heart, and Phoebe Snow had a picture of James K. Hackett on her desk and wanted to start a poultry farm. The Santa Fé had been married once, but had taken her maiden name, it was so much pleasanter in business.

As Mitchell's telephone orders piled up, day after day, Murphy began to treat him more like an employee than a "hand," and finally offered him a moderate expense account if he cared to entertain his railroad trade. When the young man's amazement at this offer had abated sufficiently for him to accept he sent the office-boy around to the Santa Fe on the run, instructing him to size up Miss Dunlap and report. It was the first order he had ever issued in the office, and the news spread quickly that he had been "raised."

Mr. Gross took occasion to congratulate the despised underling with pompous insincerity, whereat Louis admonished him scowlingly to beat it back to his trial balance or he'd bounce a letter-press on his dome.

When the office-boy reappeared he turned in a laconic report, "She's a peach!"

Mitchell sweated the lad for further details, then nearly strained a tendon in getting to the telephone booth.

"Hello, Miss Dunlap," he called. "Are you tied up for to-night?"

"I'm knot. The k is silent."

"Will you go to the theater with me?"

"Nickelodeon?"

"No, Montgomery and Stone."

The lady muttered something unintelligible, then she tittered nervously. "Those top balconies make me dizzy."

"How about the orchestra—sixth row? Could you keep your head there?"

"You must own a bill-board."

"No, it's a bank-book; same initials, you see. I'm an heiress."

"See here, Mitch"—Miss Dunlap became serious—"you're a good little copper-wire comedian, but I don't know you nor your people."

"Well, I come from one of the oldest families in Atwood, Michigan, and that town was settled over thirty years ago."

"But you don't know me," the lady demurred.

"I do, too. You're a tall blonde, gray eyes, blue dress; you have a dimple—"

"Well, I declare! All right, then; seven-thirty to-night, six hundred and twelve Filbert Street, fourth apartment, and many thanks."

Fifteen minutes before the appointed time Louis Mitchell was fidgeting nervously outside the Filbert Street cold-water "walk-up" known as Geraldine Manor, wondering if Miss Dunlap would notice his clothes. Twelve dollars a week had starved his wardrobe until it resembled the back-drop for a "Pity the Blind" card; but promptly on the minute he punched the button at the fourth apartment. An instant later he realized that no matter how he looked he had it on Miss Dunlap by eighty per cent.

She was a blonde, to be sure, for the time being, and by the grace of H_2O_2. One glance convinced her caller of two things—*viz.*, that his office-boy did not care much for peaches, and that the Santa Fé purchasing agent had a jealous wife. The most that possibly could be said in praise of Miss Dunlap's appearance was that she was the largest stenographer in Chicago. Then and there, however, her caller qualified as a salesman; he smiled and he chatted in a free and easy way that had the lady roped, thrown, and lashed to his chariot in three minutes by her alarm-clock.

They went to the theater, and when Montgomery sprang a joke or Stone did a fall Miss Dunlap showed her appreciation after the fashion of a laughing hyena. Between times she barked enthusiastically, giving vent to sounds like those caused when a boy runs past a picket fence with a stick in his hand. She gushed, but so does Old Faithful. Anyhow, the audience enjoyed her greatly.

At supper Mitchell secured parking space for his companion at the Union Café, and there he learned how a welsh rabbit may be humiliated by a woman. During the *débâcle* he fingered the money in his pocket, then shut his eyes and ordered a bottle of champagne, just to see if it could be done. Contrary to his expectation, the waiter did not swoon; nor was he arrested. Root-beer had been Mitchell's main intoxicant heretofore, but as he and the noisy Miss Dunlap sipped the effervescing wine over their ice-cream, they pledged themselves to enjoy Monday evenings together, and she told him, frankly:

"Mitch, you're the nickel-plated entertainer, and I'll never miss another Monday eve unless I'm in the shops or the round-house. You certainly have got class."

At breakfast Miss Harris regarded Lotus darkly, for Mr. Gross had told her just enough to excite her curiosity.

"Where were you last night?" she inquired.

"I went to a show."

"Were the pictures good?"

"They don't have pictures at the Grand."

"Oh—h!" The manicurist's violet eyes opened wide. "Louis—you *drank* something. You're awful pale. What was it?"

"Clicquot! That's my favorite brand."

Miss Harris clutched the table-cloth and pulled a dish into her lap. After a moment she said: "Maybe you'll take me somewhere to-night. We haven't been out together for the longest time."

"Oh, I see! This is Gross's night at the Maccabbees', isn't it?" Louis gloated brutally over her confusion. "Sorry, but I'll probably have to entertain some more customers. The firm is keeping me busy."

At the office things went most pleasantly for the next few weeks; sixty per cent. of the city's railroad business came to Comer & Mathison; the clerks began to treat Mitchell as if he were an equal; even Gross lost his patronizing air and became openly hateful, while Murphy—Louis no longer called him Mister—increased his assistant's expense account and confided some of his family affairs to the latter. Mr. Comer, the senior partner, began to nod familiarly as he passed the quotation clerk's desk.

Nor were Louis's customers all so eccentric as Miss Dunlap. Phoebe Snow, for instance, was very easy to entertain, and the Northwestern took to his custody like a hungry urchin to a barbecue. He gave them each one night a week, and in a short time all his evenings were taken, as a consequence of which he saw less and less of Miss Harris. But, although he and his manicurist were becoming strangers, he soon began to call the waiters at Rector's by their given names, and a number of the more prominent cab-drivers waved at him.

One morning when, for the tenth successive time, he slid into his desk-chair an hour late, Mr. Comer bowed to him, not only familiarly, but sarcastically, then invited him to step into his private office and see if he could locate the center of the carpet. It was a geometrical task that Louis had been wishing to try for some time.

The senior partner began with elaborate sarcasm. "I notice you're not getting down until nine o'clock lately, Mr. Mitchell. Is your automobile out of order?"

"I have no automobile, Mr. Comer," the youth replied, respectfully.

"No? I'm surprised. Well, if eight sharp is too early, you may set your time."

Mitchell tried his best to appear disconcerted. "You know I'm busy every evening with my trade," said he.

"Nonsense. I've seen you out with a different dressmaker every night that I've been down-town."

"Those are not dressmakers, they are stenographers from the railroad offices. I'm sorry you're not satisfied with me, but I'm glad you called me in, for I've been meaning to speak to you about this very thing. You see, I have practically all the railroad business in the city, and it takes too much of my time keeping it lined up. I have no leisure of my own. I'll quit Saturday night, if convenient."

Mr. Comer grunted like a man who has stepped off a flight of stairs one step too soon. "I didn't know it was really business. Of course, if it is, why, you needn't quit—exactly—"

"I'm afraid I'll have to." Mitchell dropped his eyes demurely. "I've had a number of offers, and in justice to myself—"

"Offers? *You*? How much?"

"One hundred a month and expenses."

Mr. Comer removed his glasses, he polished them carefully, then he readjusted them and leaned forward, looking the young man over from head to foot, as if he had never until this moment seen more than his vague outlines.

"Um-m! You're nineteen years old, I believe!"

"Yes, sir."

"Well, then, an hour's delay won't be serious. Now you go back to your desk and send Mr. Murphy here. I'll let you know shortly whether Saturday night or this noon will be convenient."

It was perhaps a half-hour before lunch-time when Mr. Comer again called for Mitchell, greeting him with the gruff inquiry:

"See here, do you think I'm going to advance you from twelve to twenty-five a week at one clip?"

"No, sir."

"Humph! I'm not. I had a talk with Murphy. I think he's a liar, but I'm going to make it fifteen hundred a year and expenses. Now get busy and work your 'trade' for all it's worth."

Young Mitchell's knees wabbled, but, having learned the value of a black mask and a gun, he went through his victim thoroughly while he had him down.

"I'd like a traveling position the first of the year, sir, if you don't mind."

"All right! If you hold your present gait I'll give you the Western roads. Anything else you'd like? Well, then, git!"

That day Louis switched from the narrow-countered bakery-lunch route to regular standard-gauge restaurants; he ordered clothes like a bookmaker's bride and he sent a cubic foot of violets to Miss Harris. At dinner-time he patronized Mr. Gross so tantalizingly that the latter threatened to pull his nose out until it resembled a yard of garden hose.

The whole boarding-house was agog at Mitchell's good fortune and Miss Harris smiled on him in a manner reminiscent of the good old ante-book-keeper—one might say "ante-vellum"—days. She hinted that Mr. Gross's company did not wholly satisfy her soul-hunger, and even confessed that she was lonely; but this was Mitchell's Rock Island evening, and although the frank surrender in Miss Harris's eyes caused him to gasp as if he were slowly settling into a barrel of ice-water, he tore himself from her side.

Louis's batting average would have reached one thousand had it not been for the Monon. Miss Day, the young lady there, had a vocabulary limited to "Hello," "Too high," and "Good-by," and it became particularly galling to learn that the fellow at James & Naughten's was pulling down the business, so Mitchell went to Murphy with a proposition which showed that his mental growth had kept pace with his financial advancement.

"You need a new stenographer," he declared.

"Oh, do I? Why do I need a new stenographer, Mr. Bones?"

"Well, it would be a good investment, and I know a corker."

"Who is she?"

"Miss Day, of the Monon."

"I didn't know you cared for Miss Day."

"I don't. That's the reason I want her to work for you."

Murphy coughed slightly, then he agreed. "You're learning the game. We'll give her a three-dollar raise, and take her on."

Shortly thereafter Mitchell began to get acquainted with the new Miss Monon along the right lines, and gave her Thursday nights. She was a great improvement over Miss Day; she was, in fact, quite different from any of the others. She was small and winsome, and she didn't care to run around. She liked her home, and so did Mitchell after he had called a few times. Before long he began to look forward eagerly to Thursday nights and Miss Monon's cozy corner with its red-plush cushions—reminiscent of chair-cars, to be sure—and its darkness illumined dimly by red and green signal lamps. Many a pleasant evening the two spent there, talking of locomotive planished iron, wire nails, and turnbuckles, and the late lunch Miss Monon served beat the system's regular buffet service a city block. Of course they lit the red fire in front of James & Naughten's and turned the green light Mitchell's way. He had the right of way on the Monon after that, and other salesmen were side-tracked.

But this was too easy to last. Human affairs never run smoothly; it is a man's ability to surmount the hummocks and the pressure ridges that enables him to penetrate to the polar regions of success. The first inkling of disaster came to Mitchell when Miss Dunlap began to tire of the gay life and chose to spend her Monday evenings at home, where they might be alone together. She spoke of the domestic habits she had acquired during her brief matrimonial experience; she boldly declared that marriage was the ideal state for any man, and that two could live as cheaply as one, although personally she saw no reason why a girl should quit work the instant she became a wife, did he? She confessed that Monday evenings had become so pleasant that if Louis could arrange to drop in on Fridays also, the week would be considerably brightened thereby and her whole disposition improved. Now Fridays were cinched tightly to the Big Four, but the young man dared not acknowledge it, so he confessed that all his evenings except Monday were taken up with night school, whereupon Miss Dunlap, in order to keep abreast of his mental development, decided to take a correspondence course in Esperanto.

It transpired also that his attentions toward the Lackawanna had been misconstrued, for one night when Phoebe bade him adieu in the vestibule she broke down and wept upon his shoulder, saying that his coldness hurt her. She confessed that a rate clerk in the freight department wanted to marry her, and she supposed she'd have to accept his dastardly proposal because a girl couldn't go on working all her life, could she? Then Miss Gratz, of the C. & E.I., following a red-letter night at Grand Opera, succeeded by a German pancake and a stein at the Edelweiss and a cab-ride home, took Louis gravely to task for his extravagance and hinted that he ought to have a permanent manager who took an interest in him, one who loved music as he did and whose tastes were simple and Teutonic.

When the literary lady of the Northwestern declined a trip to the White City and began to read Marion Crawford aloud to him Louis awoke to the gravity of the situation.

But before he had worked the matter out in his own mind that rate clerk of whom Miss Lackawanna had spoken dropped in at Comer & Mathison's, introduced himself to Mitchell and told him, with a degree of firmness which could not be ignored, that his attentions to Miss Phoebe Snow were distasteful. He did not state to whom. Louis's caller had the physical proportions of a "white hope," and he wasted few words. He had come to nail up a vacate notice, and he announced simply but firmly that Miss Snow's Wednesday evenings were to be considered open time thereafter, and if Mitchell elected to horn his way in it was a hundred-to-one shot that he'd have to give up solid foods for a month or more and take his nourishment through a glass tube.

Nor were the young man's troubles confined to the office. Miss Harris, it seemed, had seen him with a different lady each night she and Mr. Gross had been out, and had drawn her own conclusions, so, therefore, when he tried to talk to her she flared up and called him a dissipated roué, and threatened to have the head bookkeeper give him a thrashing if he dared to accost her again.

Now the various apartments where Mitchell had been calling, these past months, were opulently furnished with gifts from the representatives of the various railway supply houses of the city, each article being cunningly designed to cement in the mind of the owner a source of supply which, coupled with price and delivery, would make for good sales service. He was greatly surprised one day to receive a brass library lamp from the Santa Fé the initial destination of which had evidently been changed. Then came a mission hall-clock in the original package, redirected in the hand of Miss Gratz, of the C. & E.I., and one day the office-boy from the Lackawanna brought him a smoking-set for which Miss Phoebe Snow had no use. Gifts like these piled up rapidly, many of them bearing witness to the fact that their consignment originated from Mitchell's very rivals in the railroad trade. Judging from the quantity of stuff that ricocheted from the Santa Fé it was Miss Dunlap's evident desire to present him with a whole housekeeping equipment as quickly as possible. Louis's desk became loaded with ornaments, his room at Mrs. Green's became filled with nearly Wedgwood vases, candlesticks, and other bric-à-brac. He acquired six mission hall-clocks, a row of taborets stood outside of his door like Turkish sentinels, and his collection of ash-receivers was the best in Chicago.

Miss Harris continued to ignore him, however, and he learned with a jealous pang that she was giving Mr. Gross a gratuitous course of facial massage and scalp treatments. No longer did Mitchell entertain his trade; they entertained him. They tried to help him save his money, and every evening he was forced to battle for his freedom.

In desperation he finally went to Murphy begging quick promotion to a traveling position, but the Sales Manager told him there was no chance before the first of the year, then asked him why he had lost his grip on the Lackawanna business.

As a matter of fact, since Miss Phoebe's rate clerk had declared himself Mitchell had slipped a few Wednesday nights, trusting to hold the Lackawanna trade by virtue of his past performances, but he realized in the light of Murphy's catechism that eternal visiting is the price of safety. He sighed, therefore, and called up the lady, then apprehensively made a date.

That visit issued in disaster, as he had feared. The rate clerk, gifted with some subtle second sight, had divined his treachery and was waiting. He came to meet the caller gladly, like a paladin. Louis strove to disarm the big brute by the power of the human eye, then when that did not work he explained, politely, earnestly, that his weekly calls were but part and parcel of his business, and that there was nothing in his mind so remote as thoughts of matrimony. But the rate clerk was a stolid, a suspicious person, and he was gnawed by a low and common jealousy. Reason failing, they came together, amalgamating like two drops of quicksilver.

On the following morning Mitchell explained to Mr. Comer that in stepping out of the bathtub he had slipped and wrenched both shoulders, then while passing through the dark hall had put his face into mourning by colliding with an open door. His ankles he had sprained on the way down-town.

About nine-thirty Miss Dunlap called up, but not to leave an order. When she had finally rung off Louis looked dazedly at the wire to see if the insulation had melted. It seemed impossible that rubber and gutta-percha could withstand such heat as had come sizzling from the Santa Fé. From what the lady had said it required no great inductive powers to reason that the rate clerk had told all. Coming victorious to Miss Lackawanna's door to have his knuckles collodionized he had made known in coarse, triumphant language the base commercialism of his rival.

The result had been that Phoebe arose in her wrath. Just to verify the story she had called up the other railroad offices this morning, and the hideous truth had come out. It had come out like a herd of jack-rabbits ahead of a hound. Miss Dunlap was shouting mad, but Phoebe herself, when she called up, was indignant in a mean, sarcastic manner that hurt. The Northwestern rang Mitchell to say good-by forever and to hope his nose was broken; the Big Four promised that her brother, who was a puddler in the South Chicago steel mills, would run in and finish the rate clerk's job; Miss Gratz, of the C.&E.I., was tearfully plaintive and, being German, spoke of suicide. Of course all business relations with these offices were at an end.

During that whole day but one phone order came, and that was from Miss Monon. Mitchell had been steeling himself to hear from her, but it seemed that she took the whole thing as rather a good joke. She told him she had known all the time why he came to see her, and when he reminded her that it was Thursday she invited him to call if he thought it worth while.

When he saw Miss Harris at supper-time and undertook to explain his black eyes she assured him coldly that he and his ebony gig-lamps mattered nothing in her young life, as evidence of which she flashed a magnificent three-quarter carat diamond solitaire on her third finger. She and Mr. Gross expected to be married inside of two or three years if all went well, she told him.

At eight o'clock, disguised behind a pair of blue goggles, Louis headed for Miss Monon's door, glad that the cozy corner was so dimly lighted. When he arrived she bathed his battle-scarred features with hamamelis, which is just the same as Pond's Extract, but doesn't cost so much, and told him the other girls had acted foolishly. She was very sweet and gentle with him and young Mitchell, imperfect as was his vision, saw something in her he had never seen before.

A week went by, during which it seemed that all the railroads except the Monon had suddenly gone out of business. It was as if a strike had been declared. Another week passed and Mitchell's sales were scarcely noticeable, so Mr. Comer called him in to ask:

"Is your phone disconnected?"

"No, sir."

"Do you know the price of our goods?"

"Yes, sir."

"Don't you sleep well at home?"

"Yes, sir."

"Then what has become of those pick-ups?"

"I seem to have lost—my trade."

"Your 'trade'! Bah! Young man, you've been dissipating. That expense account turned your head. You've been blowing in our money on your friends and you've let your customers go. If you can't hold the railroad business we'll get some fellow who can. Cut out your sewing-circle wine suppers and your box parties to the North Shore débutantes and get busy. You've got a week to make good. One week."

There wasn't the slightest chance, and Mitchell told Miss Monon so when Thursday came around. He told her all about that promised position on the road and what it meant to him, and then he told her that beginning Monday he'd have to hunt a new berth at twelve dollars per. She was very quiet, very sympathetic—so sympathetic, in fact, that he told her some other things which no young man on a diminishing salary should tell. She said little at the moment, but she did considerable thinking, and she got busy on her phone early the next morning. The first number she called was the Santa Fé's. When she had finished talking with Miss Dunlap that hempen-haired sentimentalist was dabbing her eyes with her handkerchief and blowing her nose, assuring Miss Monon, at the same time, that she was a dear and that it was all right now that she knew the truth. Miss Monon blushed prettily, thanked her, and confessed that she had felt it coming on for some time. Thereupon they took turns calling the others, from the Big Four to the C.&E.I., with the result that Mitchell's wire began to heat up.

Phoebe Snow called him to say that she hadn't meant what she said, that he was a good old scout, and that the rate clerk was sorry also, and wanted to stand treat for a Dutch lunch. Then she left an order for a ton and a half of engine bolts.

Miss Gratz cried a little when she heard Mitchell's voice and told him to make his own price on forty kegs of washers and suit himself about delivery.

Miss Dunlap confessed that it was her pride which had spoken, and, anyhow, she knew altogether too much about marriage to take another chance. She'd rather have one man friend than three husbands.

One by one the flock returned, and Saturday night Mitchell sent five pounds of chocolates and a sheaf of red roses to the one who had made it all come out right. He got his share of business after that, and when the holidays came they brought him his promotion.

Murphy, who knew most of the facts, was the first to congratulate him."Jove!" he said, "that little Monon lady saved your bacon, didn't she?By. the way, you never told me what her name was."

Young Mitchell's cheeks assumed a shell-pink shade as he replied: "It doesn't matter what her name was, it's Mitchell now. We were married yesterday and—all the roads were represented at the wedding."

WITH BRIDGES BURNED

Louis Mitchell knew what the telegram meant, even though it was brief and cryptic. He had been expecting something of the sort ever since the bottom dropped out of the steel business and prices tobogganed forty dollars a ton. Nevertheless, it came as an undeniable shock, for he had hoped the firm would keep him on in spite of hard times. He wondered, as he sadly pocketed the yellow sheet, whether he had in him the makings of a good life-insurance agent, or if he had not better "join out" with a medicine show. This message led him to think his talents must lie along the latter line. Certainly they did not lie in the direction of metal supplies.

He had plenty of time to think the situation over, however, for it is a long jump from Butte to Chicago; when he arrived at the latter place he was certain of only one thing, he would not stand a cut in salary. Either Comer & Mathison would have to fire him outright or keep him on at his present wage; he would not compromise as the other salesmen had done and were doing.

Twenty-five hundred a year is a liberal piece of money where people raise their own vegetables, but to a man traveling in the West it is about equal to "no pair." Given two hundred dollars a month and a fair expense account a salesman can plow quite a respectable furrow around Plymouth Rock, but out where they roll their r's and monogram their live stock he can't make a track. Besides the loss of prestige and all that went with it, there was another reason why young Mitchell could not face a cut. He had a wife, and she was too new, too wonderful; she admired him too greatly to permit of such a thing. She might, she doubtless would, lose confidence in him if he took a step backward, and that confidence of hers was the most splendid thing in Mitchell's life. No, if Comer & Mathison wanted to make any change, they would have to promote him. Ten minutes with the "old man," however, served to jar this satisfactory determination to its foundation. Mr. Comer put the situation clearly, concisely.

"Business is rotten. We've got to lay all the younger men off or we'll go broke," he announced.

"But—I'm married," protested the young salesman.

"So am I; so is Mathison; so are the rest of the fellows. But, my boy, this is a panic. We wouldn't let you go if we could keep you."

"I can sell goods—"

"That's just it; we don't want you to. Conditions are such that we can't afford to sell anything. The less business we do the fewer losses we stand to make. Good Lord, Louis, this is the worst year the trade has ever known!"

"B-but—I'm married," blankly repeated Mitchell.

Comer shook his head. "We'd keep you in a minute if there was any way to do it. You go home and see the wife. Of course if you can show us where you're worth it, we'll let you stay; but—well, you can't. There's no chance. I'll see you to-morrow."

Ordinarily Mitchell would not have allowed himself the extravagance of a cab, but to-day the cars were too slow. He wondered how the girl would take this calamity, their very first. As a matter of fact, she divined the news even before he had voiced his exuberant greetings, and, leading him into the neat little front room, she curled up at his side, demanding all the reasons for his unexpected recall. He saw that she was wide-eyed and rather white. When he had broken the bad news she inquired, bravely:

"What is your plan, boy?"

"I haven't any."

"Nonsense!"

"I mean it. What can I do? I don't know anything except the steel business. I can lick my weight in wildcats on my own ground—but—" The wife nodded her blonde head in complete agreement. "But that lets me out," he concluded, despondently. "I can sell steel because I know it from the ground up; it's my specialty."

"Oh, we mustn't think about making a change."

"I've handled more big jobs than any man of my age and experience on the road, and yet—I'm fired." The husband sighed wearily. "I built that big pipe line in Portland; I sold those smelters in Anaconda, and the cyanide tanks for the Highland Girl. Yes, and a lot of other jobs, too. I know all about the smelter business, but that's no sign I can sell electric belts or corn salve. We're up against it, girlie."

"Have people quit building smelters?"

"They sure have—during this panic. There's nothing doing anywhere."

The wife thought for a moment before saying, "The last time you were home you told me about some Western mining men who had gone to South Africa—"

"Sure! To the Rand! They've made good, too; they're whopping big operators, now."

"You said there was a large contract of some sort coming up inLondon."

"Large! Well, rather! The Robinson-Ray job. It's the biggest ever, in my line. They're going to rebuild those plants the Boers destroyed. I heard all about it in Montana."

"Well!" Mrs. Mitchell spoke with finality. "That's the place for you. Get the firm to send you over there."

"Um-m! I thought about that, but it scared me out. It's too big. Why, it's a three-million-dollar job. You see, we've never landed a large foreign contract in this country as yet." Mitchell sat up suddenly. "But say! This panic might—" Then he relaxed. "Oh, what's the use? If there were a chance the firm wouldn't send me. Comer would go himself—he'd take the whole outfit over for a job like that. Besides, it's too big a thing for our people; they couldn't handle it."

Mrs. Mitchell's eyes were as round as buttons. "Three million dollars' worth of steel in one contract! Do you think you could land it if you went?"

"It's my line of work," the young man replied, doubtfully. "I'll bet I know more about cyanide tanks than any salesman in Europe, and if I had a decent price to work on—"

"Then it's the chance we've been waiting for."

The girl scrambled to her feet and, fetching a chair, began to talk earnestly, rapidly. She talked for a long time, until gradually the man's gray despondency gave way to her own bright optimism. Nor was it idle theory alone that she advanced; Mitchell found that she knew almost as much about the steel business as he did, and when she had finished he arose and kissed her.

"You've put new heart into me, anyhow. If you're game to do your share, why—I'll try it out. But remember it may mean all we've got in the bank, and—" He looked at her darkly.

"It's the biggest chance we'll ever have," she insisted. "It's worth trying. Don't let's wait to get rich until we are old."

When Mr. Comer returned from lunch he found his youngest salesman waiting for him, and inside of ten minutes he had learned what Mitchell had on his mind. With two words Comer blew out the gas.

"You're crazy," said he.

"Am I? It's worth going after."

"In the first place no big foreign job ever came to America—"

"I know all that. It's time we got one."

"In the second place Comer & Mathison are jobbers."

"I'll get a special price from Carnegie."

"In the third place it would cost a barrel of money to send a man toEngland."

Mitchell swallowed hard. "I'll pay my own way."

Mr. Comer regarded the speaker with genuine astonishment. "*You'll* pay your way? Why, you haven't got any money."

"I've got a thousand dollars—or the wife has. It's our nest-egg."

"It would take five thousand to make the trip."

"I'll make it on one. Yes, and I'll come back with that job. Don't you see this panic makes the thing possible? Yes, and I'm the one man to turn the trick; for it's right in my line. I'll see the Carnegie people at Pittsburgh. If they quote the right price I'll ask you for a letter, and that's all you'll have to do. Will you let me go?"

"What sort of a letter?"

"A letter stating that I am your general sales manager."

The steel merchant's mouth fell open.

"Oh, I only want it for this London trip," Mitchell explained. "I won't use it except as a credential. But I've got to go armed, you understand. Mr. Comer, if I don't land that Robinson-Ray contract, I won't come back. I—I couldn't, after this. Maybe I'll drive a bus—I hear they have a lot of them in London."

"Suppose, for instance, you should get the job on a profitable basis; the biggest job this concern ever had and one of the biggest ever let any-where—" Mr. Comer's brow was wrinkled humorously. "What would you expect out of it?"

Mitchell grinned. "Well, if I signed all those contracts as your general sales manager, I'd probably form the habit."

"There's nothing modest about you, is there?" queried the elder man.

"Not a thing. My theory of business is that a man should either be fired or promoted. If I get that job I'll leave it to you to do what's right. I won't ask any questions."

"The whole thing is utterly absurd," Mitchell's employer protested."You haven't a chance! But—Wait!" He pressed a button on his desk."We'll talk with Mathison."

Louis Mitchell took the night train for Pittsburgh. He was back in three days, and that afternoon Mr. Comer, in the privacy of his own office, dictat-ed a letter of which no carbon copy was preserved. He gave it to the young man with his own hand, and with these words: "You'd better think it over carefully, my boy. It's the most idiotic thing I ever heard of, and there isn't one chance in a million. It won't do you any good to fail, even on a forlorn hope like this."

But Mitchell smiled. "I can't fail—I'm married." Then when the other seemed unimpressed by this method of reasoning, he explained: "I guess you never saw my wife. She says I can do it."

It was only to this lady herself that Mitchell recited the details of his re-ception at Pittsburgh, and of the battle he had fought in the Carnegie office. The Carnegie men had refused to take him seriously, had laughed at him as at a mild-mannered lunatic.

"But I got my price," he concluded, triumphantly, "and it sure looks good to me. Now for the painful details and the sad good-bys."

"How long will you be gone?" his wife inquired.

"I can't stay more than a month, the bank-roll is too small."

"Oo-oo-h! A month! London is a long way off." Mrs. Mitchell's voice broke plaintively and her husband's misgivings at once took fire.

"If I fail, as they all feel sure I will, what then?" he inquired. "I'll be out of a job! I'll be a joke in the steel business; I'll be broke. What will you do?"

She gave him a ravishing, dimpled smile, and her eyes were brave once more. "Why, I haven't forgotten my shorthand, and there are always the department stores." In a high, querulous tone she cried "Ca—a—sh!" then laughed aloud at his expression. "Oh, it wouldn't hurt me any. But—you won't fail—you can't! We're going to be rich. Now, we'll divide our grand fortune." She produced a roll of currency from her purse and took four twenty-dollar bills from it.

"Only eighty dollars?" he queried.

"It's more than enough for me. You'll be back in a month." She thrust the remaining notes into his hand. "It's our one great, glorious chance, dear. Don't you understand?"

Faith, hope and enthusiasm, the three graces of salesmanship, thrive best in bright places. Had it not been for his wife's cheer during those final hours young Mitchell surely would have weakened before it came time to leave on the following day. It was a far cry to London, and he realized 'way back in his head that there wasn't one chance in a million of success. He began to doubt, to waver, but the girl seemed to feel that her lord was bound upon some flaring triumph, and even at the station her face was wreathed in smiles. Her blue eyes were brimming with excitement; she bubbled with hopeful, helpful advice; she patted her husband's arm and hugged it to her. "You're going to win, boy. You're going to win," she kept repeating. For one moment only—at the actual parting—she clung to him wildly, with all her woman's strength, then, as the warning cry sounded, she kissed him long and hungrily, and fairly thrust him aboard the Pullman. He did not dream how she wilted and drooped the instant he had gone.

As the train pulled out he ran back to the observation car to wave a last farewell, and saw her clinging to the iron fence, sobbing wretchedly; a desolate, weak little girl-wife mastered by a thousand fears. She was too blind with tears to see him. The sight raised a lump in the young husband's throat which lasted to Fort Wayne.

"Poor little thoroughbred," he mused. "I just can't lose, that's all."

The lump was not entirely gone when the luncheon call came, so Mitchell dined upon it, reasoning that this kind of a beginning augured well for an economical trip.

Now that he was away from the warmth of his wife's enthusiasm contemplation of his undertaking made the salesman rather sick. If only he were traveling at the firm's expense, if only he had something to fall back upon in case of failure, if only Comer & Mathison were behind him in any way, the complexion of things would have been altogether different. But to set out for a foreign land with no backing whatever in the hope of accomplishing that which no American salesman had ever been able to accomplish, and to finance the undertaking out of his own pocket on a sum less than he would have expected for cigarette money—well, it was an enterprise to test a fellow's courage and to dampen the most youthful optimism. His proposal to the firm to win all or lose all, he realized now, had been in the nature of a bluff, and the firm had called it. There was nothing to do, therefore, but go through and win; there could be no turning back, for he had burned his bridges.

When one enters a race-horse in a contest he puts the animal in good condition, he grooms it, he feeds it the best the stable affords, he trains and exercises it carefully. Mitchell had never owned a race-horse, but he reasoned that similar principles should apply to a human being under similar conditions. He had entered a competition, therefore he decided to condition himself physically and mentally for the race. A doped pony cannot run, neither can a worried salesman sell goods.

In line with this decision, he took one of the best state-rooms on the *Lucania*, and denied himself nothing that the ship afforded. Every morning he took his exercise, every evening a rub-down. He trained like a fighter, and when he landed he was fit; his muscles were hard, his stomach strong, his brain clear. He went first-class from Liverpool to London; he put up at the Metropole in luxurious quarters. When he stopped to think about that nine hundred and twenty, already amazingly shrunken, he argued bravely that what he had spent had gone to buy condition powders.

On the way across he had posted himself so far as possible about the proposed Robinson-Ray plant. He learned that there were to be fifteen batteries of cyanide tanks, two high—eighty-four in all—supported by steel sub- and super-structures; the work to be completed at Krugersdorpf, twenty miles out of Johannesburg, South Africa. The address of the company was No. 42-1/2 Threadneedle Street. Threadneedle Street was somewhere in London, and London was the capital of a place called England.

He knew other African contracts were under consideration, but he dismissed them from his thoughts and centered his forces upon this particular job. Once he had taken a definite scent his early trepidations vanished. He became obsessed by a joyous, purposeful, unceasing energy that would not let him rest.

The first evening in London he fattened himself for the fray with a hearty dinner, then he strove to get acquainted with his neighbors and his environment. The nervous force within him needed outlet, but he was frowned upon at every quarter. Even the waiter at his table made it patent that his social standing would not permit him to indulge in the slightest intimacy with chance guests of the hotel, while the young Earl who had permitted Mitchell to register at the desk declined utterly to go further with their acquaintance. Louis spent the evening at the Empire, and the next morning, which was Sunday, he put in on the top of a bus, laying himself open to the advances of anybody who cared to pay him the slightest attention. But he was ignored; even the driver, who spoke a foreign language, evidently considered him a suspicious character. Like a wise general, Louis reconnoitered No. 42-1/2 Threadneedle Street during the afternoon, noting the lay of the land and deciding upon modes of transportation to and from. Under the pressure of circumstance he chose a Cannon Street 'bus, fare "tuppence."

Now garrulity is a disease that must either break out or strike inward with fatal results. When Sunday night came, Mitchell was about ready to fare forth with gun and mask and take conversation away from anybody who had it to spare. He had begun to fear that his vocal cords would atrophy.

He was up early, had breakfasted, and was at 42-1/2 Threadneedle Street promptly at nine, beating the janitor by some twenty minutes. During the next hour and a half he gleaned considerable information regarding British business methods, the while he monotonously pounded the sidewalk.

At nine-thirty a scouting party of dignified office-boys made a cautious approach. At nine-thirty-five there came the main army of clerks, only they were not clerks, but "clarks"—very impressive gentlemen with gloves, spats, sticks, silk hats and sack coats. At this same time, evidently by appointment, came the charwomen—"char" being spelled s-c-r-u-b, and affording an example of how pure English has been corrupted out in the Americas.

After the arrival of the head "clarks" and stenographers at nine-forty-five, there ensued fifteen minutes of guarded conversation in front of the offices. During this time the public issues of the day were settled and the nation's policies outlined. At ten o'clock the offices were formally opened, and at ten-thirty a reception was tendered to the managers who arrived dressed as for any well-conducted afternoon function.

To Mitchell, who was accustomed to the feverish, football methods of American business life, all this was vastly edifying and instructive; it was even soothing, although he was vaguely offended to note that passers-by avoided him as if fearful of contamination.

Upon entering 42-1/2 Threadneedle Street, he was halted by an imperious office-boy. To him Louis gave his card with a request that it be handed to Mr. Peebleby, then he seated himself and for an hour witnessed a parade of unsmiling, silk-hatted gentlemen pass in and out of Mr. Peebleby's office. Growing impatient, at length, he inquired of the boy;

"Is somebody dead around here or is this where the City Council meets?"

"I beg pardon?" The lad was polite in a cool, superior way.

"I say, what's the idea of the pall-bearers?"

The youth's expression froze to one of disapproval and suspicion.

"I mean the parade. Are these fellows Congress- or minstrel-men?"

His hearer shrugged and smiled vacuously, then turned away, whereupon Mitchell took him firmly by the arm.

"Look here, my boy," he began. "There seems to be a lot of information coming to both of us. Who are these over-dressed gentlemen I see promenading back and forth?"

"Why—they're callers, customers, representatives of the firms we do business with, sir."

"Is this Guy Fawkes Day?"

"No, sir."

"Are these men here on business? Are any of them salesmen, for instance?"

"Yes, sir; some of them. Certainly, sir."

"To see Mr. Peebleby about the new construction work?"

"No doubt."

"So, you're letting them get the edge on me."

"I beg pardon?"

"Never mind, I merely wanted to assure you that I have some olive spats, a high hat, and a walking-stick, but I left them at my hotel. I'm a salesman, too. Now then let's get down to business. I've come all the way from America to hire an office-boy. I've heard so much about English office-boys that I thought I'd run over and get one. Would you entertain a proposition to go back to America and become my partner?"

The boy rolled his eyes; it was plain that he was seriously alarmed. "You are ragging me, sir," he stammered, uncertainly.

"Perish the thought!"

"I—I—Really, sir—"

"I pay twenty-five dollars a week to office-boys. That's five 'pun' in your money, I believe. But, meanwhile, now that I'm in London, I have some business with Mr. Peebleby." Mitchell produced an American silver dollar and forced it into the boy's hand, whereupon the latter blinked in a dazed manner, then hazarded the opinion that Mr. Peebleby might be at leisure if Mr. Mitchell had another card.

"Never mind the card; I can't trust you with another one. Just show me the trail and I'll take it myself. That's a way we have in America."

A moment later he was knocking at a door emblazoned, "Director General." Without awaiting an invitation, he turned the knob and walked in. Before the astonished Mr. Peebleby could expostulate he had introduced himself and was making known his mission.

Fortunately for Mitchell, Englishmen are not without a sense of humor. The announcement that this young man had come all the way from Chicago, Illinois, U.S.A., to bid on the Krugersdorpf work struck Mr. Peebleby as amusing. Not only was the idea in itself laughable, but also the fact that a mere beardless youth should venture to figure on a contract of such gigantic proportions quite convulsed the Director General, and in consequence he smiled. Then fearing that his dignity had been jeopardized, he announced politely but firmly that the proposition was absurd, and that he had no time to discuss it.

"I've come for that job, and I'm going to take it back with me," Mitchell averred, with equal firmness. "I know more about this class of work than any salesman you have over here, and I'm going to build you the finest cluster of cyanide tanks you ever saw."

"May I ask where you obtained this comprehensive knowledge of tank construction?" Mr. Peebleby inquired, with some curiosity.

"Sure!" Mitchell ran through a list of jobs with which the Director General could not have been unfamiliar. He mentioned work that caused that gentleman to regard him more respectfully. For a time questions and answers shot back and forth between them.

"I tell you, that is my line," Mitchell declared, at length. "I'll read any blueprints you can offer. I'll answer any queries you can formulate. I'm the accredited representative of a big concern, and I'm entitled to a chance to figure, at least. That courtesy is due me."

"I dare say it is," the other reluctantly agreed. "I'm very busy, but if that is the quickest way to end the discussion I'll give you the prints. I assure you, nevertheless, it is an utter waste of your time and mine." He pushed a button and five minutes later a clerk staggered back into the room with an armful of blueprints that caused Mitchell to gasp.

"The bid must be in Thursday at ten-thirty," Peebleby announced.

"Thursday? Why, good Lord! That's only three days, and there's a dray-load of drawings!"

"I told you it was a waste of time. You should have come sooner."

Mitchell ran through the pile and his heart grew sick with dismay. There were drawings of tanks, drawings of substructures and superstructures in every phase of construction—enough of them to daunt a skilled engineer. He realized that he had by no means appreciated the full magnitude of this work, in fact had never figured on a job anything like this one. He could see at least a week's hard, constant labor ahead of him—a week's work to be done in three days. There was no use trying; the time was too short; it was a physical impossibility to formulate an intelligent proposition in such a short length of time. Then to Mitchell's mind came the picture of a wretched, golden-haired girl clinging to the iron fence of the Pennsylvania depot. He gathered the rolls into his arms.

"At ten-thirty, Thursday," said he.

"Ten-thirty, sharp."

"Thank you. I'll have my bid in."

His muscles ached and his knees were trembling even before he had reached the street. When he tried to board a bus he was waved away, so he called a cab, piled his blueprints inside of it, and then clambered in on top of them. He realized that he was badly frightened.

To this day the sight of a blueprint gives Louis Mitchell a peculiar nausea and a fluttering sensation about the heart. At three o'clock the next morning he felt his way blindly to his bed and toppled upon it, falling straightway into a slumber during which he passed through monotonous, maddening wastes of blue and white, over which ran serpentine rows of figures.

He was up with the dawn and at his desk again, but by four that afternoon he was too dazed, too exhausted to continue. His eyes were playing him tricks, the room was whirling, his hand was shaking until his fingers staggered drunkenly across the sheets of paper. Ground plans, substructures, superstructures, were jumbled into a frightful tangle. He wanted to yell. Instead he flung the drawings about the room, stamped savagely upon them, then rushed down-stairs and devoured a table d'hôte dinner. He washed the meal down with a bottle of red wine, smoked a long cigar, then undressed and went to bed amid the scattered blueprints. He slept like a dead man.

He arose at sun-up, clear-headed, calm. All day he worked like a machine, increasing his speed as the hours flew. He took good care to eat and drink, and, above all, to smoke at regular intervals, but he did not leave his room. By dark he had much of the task behind him; by midnight he began to have hope; toward dawn he saw the end; and when daylight came he collapsed.

He had deciphered the tank and superstructure plans on forty-five sets of blueprints, had formulated a proposition, exclusive of substructure work, basing a price per pound on the American market then ruling, f.o.b. tide-water, New York. He had the proposition in his pocket when he tapped on the ground-glass door of Mr. Peebleby's office at ten-twenty-nine Thursday morning.

The Director General of the great Robinson-Ray Syndicate was genuinely surprised to learn that the young American had completed a bid in so short a time, then requested him, somewhat absent-mindedly, to leave it on his desk where he could look it over at his leisure.

"Just a moment," said his caller. "I'm going to sit down and talk to you again. How long have you been using cyanide tanks, Mr. Peebleby?"

"Ever since they were adopted." Mr. Peebleby was visibly annoyed at this interruption to his morning's work.

"Well, I can give you a lot of information about them."

The Director General raised his brows haughtily. "Ah! Suggestions, amendments, improvements, no doubt."

"Exactly."

"In all my experience I never sent out a blueprint which some youthful salesman could not improve upon. Generally the younger the salesman the greater the improvement."

In Mitchell's own parlance he "beat Mr. Peebleby to the punch." "If that's the case, you've got a rotten line of engineers," he frankly announced.

"Indeed! I went over those drawings myself. I flattered myself that they were comprehensive and up-to-date." Mr. Peebleby was annoyed, nevertheless he was visibly interested and curious.

"Well, they're not," the younger man declared, eying him boldly. "For instance, you call for cast-iron columns in your sub-and super-structures, whereas they're obsolete. We've discarded them. What you save in first cost you eat up, twice over, in freight. Not only that, but their strength is a matter of theory, not of fact. Then, too, in your structural-steel sections your factor of safety is wrongly figured. To get the best results your lower tanks are twenty inches too short and your upper ones nine inches too short. For another thing, you're using a section of beam which is five per cent. heavier than your other dimensions call for."

The Director General sat back in his chair, a look of extreme alertness replacing his former expression.

"My word! Is there anything else?" He undertook to speak mockingly, but without complete success.

"There is. The layout of your platework is all wrong—out of line with modern practice. You should have interchangeable parts in every tank. The floor of your lower section should be convex, instead of flat, to get the run-off. You see, sir, this is my line of business."

"Who is your engineer?" inquired the elder man. "I should like to talk to him."

"You're talking to him now. I'm him—it—them. I'm the party! I told you I knew the game."

There was a brief silence, then Mr. Peebleby inquired, "By the way, who helped you figure those prints?"

"Nobody."

"You did that *alone*, since Monday morning?" The speaker was incredulous.

"I did. I haven't slept much. I'm pretty tired."

There was a new note in Mr. Peebleby's voice when he said: "Jove! I've treated you badly, Mr. Mitchell, but—I wonder if you're too tired to tell my engineers what you told me just now? I should like them to hear you."

"Trot them in." For the first time since leaving this office three days before, Mitchell smiled. He was getting into his stride at last. After all, there seemed to be a chance.

There followed a convention of the draftsmen and engineers of theRobinson-Ray Syndicate before which an unknown American youthdelivered an address on "Cyanide Tanks. How to Build Them; Where toBuy Them."

It was the old story of a man who had learned his work thoroughly and who loved it. Mitchell typified the theory of specialization; what he knew, he knew completely, and before he had more than begun his talk these men recognized that fact. When he had finished, Mr. Peebleby announced that the bids would not be opened that day.

The American had made his first point. He had gained time in which to handle himself, and the Robinson-Ray people had recognized a new factor in the field. When he was again in the Director General's room, the latter said:

"I think I will have you formulate a new bid along the lines you have laid down."

"Very well."

"You understand, our time is up. Can you have it ready by Saturday, three days from now?"

Mitchell laughed. "It's a ten days' job for two men."

"I know, but we can't wait."

"Then give me until Tuesday; I'm used to a twenty-four-hour shift now. Meanwhile I'd like to leave these figures here for your chief draftsman to examine. Of course they are not to be considered binding."

"Isn't that a bit—er—foolish?" inquired Peebleby? "Aren't you leaving a weapon behind you?"

"Yes, but not the sort of a weapon you suspect," thought Mitchell. "This is a boomerang." Aloud, he answered, lightly: "Oh, that's all right. I know I'm among friends."

When his request was granted he made a mental note, "Step number two!"

Again he filled a cab with drawings, again he went back to the Metropole and to maddening columns of new figures—back to the monotony of tasteless meals served at his elbow.

But there were other things besides his own bid to think of now. Mitchell knew he must find what other firms were bidding on the job, and what prices they had bid. The first promised to require some ingenuity, the second was a Titan's task.

Salesmanship, in its highest development, is an exact science. Given the data he desired, Louis Mitchell felt sure he could read the figures sealed up in those other bids to a nicety, but to get that data required much concentrated effort and much time. Time was what he needed above all things; time to refigure these myriad drawings, time to determine when the other bids had gone in, time to learn trade conditions at the competitive plants, time to sleep. There were not sufficient hours in the day for all these things, so he rigidly economized on the least important, sleep. He laid out a program for himself; by night he worked in his room, by day he cruised for information, at odd moments around the dawn he slept. He began to feel the strain before long. Never physically robust, he began to grow blue and drawn about the nostrils. Frequently his food would not stay down. He was forced to drive his lagging spirits with a lash. To accomplish this he had to think often of his girl-wife. Her letters, written daily, were a great help; they were like some God-given cordial that infused fresh blood into his brain, new strength into his flagging limbs. Without them he could not have held up.

With certain definite objects in view he made daily trips to Threadneedle Street. Invariably he walked into the general offices unannounced; invariably he made a new friend before he came out. Peebleby seemed to like him; in fact asked his opinion on certain forms of structure and voluntarily granted the young man two days of grace. Two days! They were like oxygen to a dying man.

Mitchell asked permission to talk to the head draftsman and received it, and following their interview he requested the privilege of dictating some notes regarding the interview. In this way he met the stenographer. When he had finished with her he flipped the girl a gold sovereign, stolen from the sadly melted nine hundred and twenty.

As Mitchell was leaving the office the Director General yielded to a kindly impulse and advised his new acquaintance to run over to Paris and view the Exposition.

"You can do your figuring there just as well as here," said he."I don't want your trip from Chicago to be altogether wasted, Mr. Mitchell."

Louis smiled and shook his head. "I can't take that Exposition back with me, and I can take this contract. I think I'll camp with my bid."

In the small hours of that night he made a discovery that electrified him. He found that the most commonly used section in his specifications, a twelve-inch I-beam, was listed under the English custom as weighing fifty-four pounds per foot, whereas the standardized American section, which possessed the same carrying strength, weighed four pounds less. Here was an advantage of eight per cent. in cost and freight! This put another round of the ladder beneath him; he was progressing well, but as yet he had learned nothing about his competitors.

The next morning he had some more dictation for Peebleby's stenographer, and niched another sovereign from his sad little bank-roll. When the girl gave him his copy he fell into conversation with her and painted a picture of Yankeeland well calculated to keep her awake nights. They gossiped idly, she of her social obligations, he of the cyanide-tank business—he could think of nothing else to talk about. Adroitly he led her out. They grew confidential. She admitted her admiration for Mr. Jenkins from Edinburgh. Yes, Mr. Jenkins's company was bidding on the Krugersdorpf job. He was much nicer than Mr. Kruse from the Brussels concern, and, anyhow, those Belgian firms had no chance at this contract, for Belgium was pro-Boer, and—well, she had heard a few things around the office.

Mitchell was getting "feed-box" information. When he left he knew the names of his dangerous competitors as well as those whom, in all likelihood, he had no cause to fear. Another step! He was gaining ground.

In order to make himself absolutely certain that his figures would be low, there still remained three things to learn, and they were matters upon which he could afford to take no slightest chance of mistake. He must know, first, the dates of those other bids; second, the market-price of English steel at such times; and, third, the cost of fabrication at the various mills. The first two he believed could be easily learned, but the third promised to afford appalling difficulties to a man unfamiliar with foreign methods and utterly lacking in trade acquaintances. He went at them systematically, however, only to run against a snag within the hour. Not only did he fail to find the answer to question number one, but he could find no market quotations whatever on structural steel shapes such as entered into the Krugersdorpf job.

He searched through every possible trade journal, through reading rooms and libraries, for the price of I-beams, channels, Z-bars, and the like; but nowhere could he even find mention of them. His failure left him puzzled and panic-stricken; he could not understand it. If only he had more time, he reflected, time in which to learn the usages and the customs of this country. But time was what he had not. He was tired, very tired from his sleepless nights and hours of daylight strain—and meanwhile the days were rushing past.

While engaged in these side labors, he had, of course, been working on his draftsmen friends, and more assiduously even than upon his blue-prints. On Tuesday night, with but one more day of grace ahead of him, he gave a dinner to all of them, disregarding the fact that his bank-roll had become frightfully emaciated.

For several days after that little party blue-printing in the Robinson-Ray office was a lost art. When his guests had dined and had settled back into their chairs, Mitchell decided to risk all upon one throw. He rose, at the head of the table, and told them who he was. He utterly destroyed their illusions regarding him and his position with Comer & Mathison, he bared his heart to those stoop-shouldered, shabby young men from Threadneedle Street and came right down to the nine hundred and twenty dollars and the girl. He told them what this Krugersdorpf job meant to him and to her, and to the four twenty-dollar bills in Chicago, Illinois, U.S.A.

Those Englishmen listened silently. Nobody laughed. Perhaps it was the sort of thing they had dreamed of doing some day, perhaps there were other girls in other tiny furnished flats, other hearts wrapped up in similar struggles for advancement. They were good mathematicians, it seemed, for they did not have to ask Mitchell how the nine hundred and twenty was doing, or to inquire regarding the health of the other eighty. One of them, a near-sighted fellow with thick lenses, arose with the grave assertion that he had taken the floor for the purpose of correcting a popular fallacy; Englishmen and Yankees, he declared, were not cousins, they were brothers, and their interests ever had been and ever would be identical. He said, too, that England wanted to do business with America, and as for this particular contract, not only did the British nation as a whole desire America to secure it, but the chaps who bent over the boards at No. 42-1/2 Threadneedle Street were plugging for her tooth and nail. His hollow-chested companions yelled their approval of this statement, whereupon Mitchell again arose, alternately flushing and paling, and apologized for what had happened in 1776. He acknowledged himself ashamed of the 1812 affair, moreover, and sympathized with his guests over their present trouble with the Boers. When he had finished they voted him the best host and the best little cyanide tank-builder known to them—and then everybody tried to tell him something at once.

They told him among other things that every bid except his had been in for two weeks, and that they were in the vault under the care of Mr. Pitts, the head draftsman. They promised to advise him if any new bids came in or if any changes occurred, and, most important of all, they told him that in England all structural steel shapes, instead of being classified as in America, are known as "angles," and they told him just how and where to find the official reports giving the price of the same for every day in the year.

The word "angles" was the missing key, and those official market reports formed the lock in which to fit it. Mitchell had taken several mighty strides, and there remained but one more step to take.

When his guests had finally gone home, swearing fealty, and declaring this to be the best dinner they had ever drunk, he hastened back to his room, back to the desert of blueprints and to the interminable columns of figures, and over them he worked like a madman.

He slept two hours before daylight, then he was up and toiling again, for this was his last day. Using the data he had gathered the night before, he soon had the price of English and Scottish steel at the time the last bids were closed. Given one thing more—namely, the cost of fabrication in these foreign shops, and he would have reduced this hazard to a certainty, he would be able to read the prices contained in those sealed bids as plainly as if they lay open before him. But his time had narrowed now to hours.

He lunched with John Pitts, the head draughtsman, going back to pick up the boomerang he had left the week before.

"Have you gone over my first bid?" he asked, carelessly.

"I have—lucky for you," said Pitts. "You made a mistake."

"Indeed! How so?"

"Why, it's thirty per cent. too low. It would be a crime to give you the business at those figures."

"But, you see, I didn't include the sub-structure. I didn't have time to figure that." Mitchell prayed that his face might not show his eagerness. Evidently it did not, for Pitts walked into the trap.

"Even so," said he; "it's thirty per cent. out of the way. I made allowance for that."

The boomerang had finished its flight!

Once they had separated, Mitchell broke for his hotel like a hunted man. He had made no mistake in his first figures. The great Krugersdorpf job was his; but, nevertheless, he wished to make himself absolutely sure and to secure as much profit as possible for Comer & Mathison. Without a handsome profit this three-million-dollar job might ruin a firm of their standing.

In order to verify Pitts's statement, in order to swell his proposed profits to the utmost, Mitchell knew he ought to learn the "overhead" in English mills; that is, the fixed charges which, added to shop costs and prices of material, are set aside to cover office expenses, cost of operation, and contingencies. Without this information he would have to go it blind, after a fashion, and thereby risk penalizing himself; with it he could estimate very closely the amounts of the other bids and insure a safe margin for Comer & Mathison. In addition to this precaution he wished to have his own figures checked up, for even under normal conditions, if one makes a numerical error in work of this sort, he is more than apt to repeat it time and again, and Mitchell knew himself to be deadly tired—almost on the verge of collapse. He was inclined to doze off whenever he sat down; the raucous noises of the city no longer jarred or startled him, and his surroundings were becoming unreal, grotesque, as if seen through the spell of absinthe. Yes, it was necessary to check off his figures.

But who could he get to do the work? He could not go to Threadneedle Street. He thought of the Carnegie representative and telephoned him, explaining the situation and his crying need, only to be told that no one in that office was capable of assisting him. He was referred, however, to an English engineer who, it was barely possible, could handle the job. In closing, the Carnegie man voiced a vague warning:

"His name is Dell, and he used to be with one of the Edinburgh concerns, so don't let him know your inside figures. He might spring a leak."

A half-hour later Mitchell, his arms full of blue-prints, was in Mr. Dell's office. But the English engineer hesitated; he was very busy; he had numerous obligations. Mitchell gazed over the threadbare rooms and hastily estimated how much of the nine hundred and twenty dollars would be left after he had paid his hotel bill. What there was to do must be done before the next morning's sun arose.

"This job is worth ten sovereigns to me if it is finished tonight," he declared, briskly.

Mr. Dell hesitated, stumbled, and fell. "Very well. We'll begin at once," said he.

He unrolled the blue-prints, from a drawer he produced a sliding-rule. He slid this rule up; he slid it down; he gazed through his glasses at space; he made microscopic Spencerian figures in neat rows and columns. He seemed to pluck his results from the air with necromantic cunning, and what had taken the young man at his elbow days and nights of cruel effort to accomplish—what had put haggard lines about his mouth and eyes—the engineer accomplished in a few hours by means of that sliding-rule. Meanwhile, with one weary effort of will, his visitor summoned his powers and cross-examined him adroitly. Here was the very man to supply the one missing link in the perfect chain; but Mr. Dell would not talk. He did not like Americans nor American methods, and he made his dislike apparent by sealing his lips. Mitchell played upon his vanity at first, only to find the man wholly lacking in conceit. Changing his method of attack, Mitchell built a fire under Mr. Dell. He grilled everything British, the people, their social customs, their business methods, even English engineers, and he did it in a most annoying manner. Mr. Dell began to perspire. He worked doggedly on for a while, then he arose in defense of his country, whereupon Mitchell artfully shifted his attack to English steel-mills. The other refuted his statements flatly. At length the engineer was goaded to anger, he became disputative, indignant, loquacious.

When Louis Mitchell flung himself into the dark body of his cab, late that evening, and sank his legs knee-deep into those hateful blue-prints, he blessed that engineer, for Dell had told him all he wished to know, all he had tried so vainly to discover through other sources. The average "overhead" in British mills was one hundred and thirty per cent., and Dell *knew*.

The young man laughed hysterically, triumphantly, but the sound was more like a tearful hiccough. To-morrow at ten-thirty! It was nearly over. He would be ready. As he lolled back inertly upon the cushions he mused dreamily that he had done well. In less than two weeks, in a foreign country, and under strange conditions, without acquaintance or pull or help of any sort, he had learned the names of his competitive firms, the dates of their bids, and the market prices ruling on every piece of steel in the Krugersdorpf job when those bids were figured. He had learned the rules governing English labor unions; he knew all about piece-work and time-work, fixed charges and shop costs, together with the ability of every plant figuring on the Robinson-Ray contract to turn out the work in the necessary time. All this, and more, he had learned legitimately and without cost to his commercial honor. Henceforth that South-African contract depended merely upon his own ability to add, subtract, and multiply correctly. It was his just as surely as two and two make four—for salesmanship is an exact science.

The girl would be very happy, he told himself. He was glad that she could never know the strain it had been.

Again, through the slow, silent hours of that Wednesday night, Mitchell fought the fatigue of death, going over his figures carefully. There were no errors in them.

Dawn was creeping in on him when he added a clean thirty-per-cent. profit for his firm, signed his bid, and prepared for bed. But he found that he could not leave the thing. After he had turned in he became assailed by sudden doubts and fears. What if he had made a mistake after all? What if some link in his chain were faulty? What if some other bidder had made a mistake and underfigured? Such thoughts made him tremble. Now that it was all done, he feared that he had been overconfident, for could it really be possible that the greatest steel contract in years would come to him? He grew dizzy at the picture of what it meant to him and to the girl.

He calmed himself finally and looked straight at the matter, sitting up in bed, his knees drawn up under his chin. While so engaged he caught sight of his drawn face in the mirror opposite and started when he realized how old and heavy with fatigue it was. He determined suddenly to shave that profit to twenty-nine per cent. and make assurance doubly sure, but managed to conquer his momentary panic. Cold reasoning told him that his figures were safe.

Louis Mitchell was the only salesman in Mr. Peebleby's office that morning who did not wear a silk hat, pearl gloves, and spats. In consequence the others ignored him for a time—but only for a time. Once the proposals had been read, an air of impenetrable gloom spread over the room. The seven Scotch, English, and Belgian mourners stared cheerlessly at one another and then with growing curiosity at the young man from overseas who had underbid the lowest of them by six thousand pounds sterling, less than one per cent. After a while they bowed among themselves, mumbled something to Mr. Peebleby, and went softly out in their high hats, their pearl gloves, and their spats—more like pall-bearers now than ever.

"Six hundred and thirty-seven thousand five hundred pounds sterling!" said the Director General. "By Jove, Mitchell, I'm glad!" They shook hands. "I'm really glad."

"That's over three million dollars in real money," said the youth."It's quite a tidy little job."

Peebleby laughed. "You've been very decent about it, too. I hope to see something of you in the future. What?"

"You'll see my smoke, that's all."

"You're not going back right away?"

"To-morrow; I've booked my passage and cabled the girl to meet me inNew York."

"My word! A girl! She'll be glad to hear of your success."

"Oh, I've told her already. You see, I knew I'd won."

The Director General of the Robinson-Ray Syndicate stared in open amazement, but Mitchell hitched his chair closer, saying:

"Now let's get at those signatures. I've got to pack."

* * * *

That night Louis Mitchell slept with fifteen separate contracts under his pillow. He double-locked the door, pulled the dresser in front of it, and left the light burning. At times he awoke with a start and felt for the documents. Toward morning he was seized with a sudden fright, so he got up and read them all over for fear somebody had tampered with them. They were correct, however, whereupon he read them a second time just for pleasure. They were strangely interesting.

On the *Deutschland* he slept much of the way across, and by the time Liberty Statue loomed up he could dream of other things than blue-prints—of the girl, for instance.

She had enough left from the eighty dollars to bring her to New York and to pay for a week's lodging in West Thirty-fourth Street, though how she managed it Mitchell never knew. She was at the dock, of course. He knew she would be. He expected to see her with her arms outstretched and with the old joyous smile upon her dimpled face, and, therefore, he was sorely disappointed when he came down the gang-plank and she did not appear. He searched high and low until finally he discovered her seated over by the letter "M," where his trunk was waiting inspection. There she was, huddled up on a coil of rope, crying as if her heart would break; her nerve was gone, along with the four twenty-dollar bills; she was afraid to face him, afraid there had been an error in his cablegram.

Not until she lay in his arms at last, sobbing and laughing, her slender body all aquiver, did she believe. Then he allowed her to feel the fifteen contracts inside his coat. Later, when they were in a cab bound for her smelly little boarding-house, he showed them to her. In return she gave him a telegram from his firm—a telegram addressed as follows:

Mr. LOUIS MITCHELL,

General Sales Manager, Comer & Mathison, New York City.

The message read:

That goes. COMER.

Mitchell opened the trap above his head and called up to the driver: "Hey, Cabbie! We've changed our minds. Drive us to the Waldorf—at a gallop."

WITH INTEREST TO DATE

This is the tale of a wrong that rankled and a great revenge. It is not a moral story, nor yet, measured by the modern money code, is it what could be called immoral. It is merely a tale of sharp wits which clashed in pursuit of business, therefore let it be considered unmoral, a word with a wholly different commercial significance.

Time was when wrongs were righted by mace and battle-ax, amid fanfares and shoutings, but we live in a quieter age, an age of repression, wherein the keenest thrust is not delivered with a yell of triumph nor the oldest score settled to the blare of trumpets. No longer do the men of great muscle lord it over the weak and the puny; as a rule they toil and they lift, doing unpleasant, menial duties for hollow-chested, big-domed men with eye-glasses. But among those very spindle-shanked, terra-cotta dwellers who cower at draughts and eat soda mints, the ancient struggle for supremacy wages fiercer than ever. Single combats are fought now as then, and the flavor of victory is quite as sweet to the pallid man back of a roll-top desk as to the swart, bristling baron behind his vizored helmet.

The beginning of this story runs back to the time Henry Hanford went with the General Equipment Company as a young salesman full of hope and enthusiasm and a somewhat exaggerated idea of his own importance. He was selling shears, punches, and other machinery used in the fabrication of structural steel. In the territory assigned to him, the works of the Atlantic Bridge Company stuck up like a sore thumb, for although it employed many men, although its contracts were large and its requirements numerous, the General Equipment Company had never sold it a dollar's worth of anything.

In the course of time Hanford convinced himself that the Atlantic Bridge Company needed more modern machinery, so he laid siege to Jackson Wylie, Sr., its president and practical owner. He spent all of six months in gaining the old man's ear, but when he succeeded he laid himself out to sell his goods. He analyzed the Atlantic Bridge Company's needs in the light of modern milling practice, and demonstrated the saving his equipment would effect. A big order and much prestige were at stake, both of which young Hanford needed badly at the time. He was vastly encouraged, therefore, when the bridge-builder listened attentively to him.

"I dare say we shall have to make a change," Mr. Wylie reluctantly agreed. "I've been bothered to death by machinery salesmen, but you're the first one to really interest me."

Hanford acknowledged the compliment and proceeded further to elaborate upon the superiority of the General Equipment Company's goods over those sold by rival concerns. When he left he felt that he had Mr. Wylie, Sr., "going."

At the office they warned him that he had a hard nut to crack; that Wylie was given to "stringing" salesmen and was a hard man to close with, but Hanford smiled confidently. Granting those facts, they rendered him all the more eager to make this sale; and the bridge company really did need up-to-date machinery.

He instituted an even more vigorous selling campaign, he sent much printed matter to Mr. Wylie, Sr., he wrote him many letters. Being a thoroughgoing young saleman, he studied the plant from the ground up, learning the bridge business in such detail as enabled him to talk with authority on efficiency methods. In the course of his studies he discovered many things that were wrong with the Atlantic, and spent days in outlining improvements on paper. He made the acquaintance of the foremen; he cultivated the General Superintendent; he even met Mr. Jackson Wylie, Jr., the Sales Manager, a very polished, metallic young man, who seemed quite as deeply impressed with Hanford's statements as did his father.

Under our highly developed competitive system, modern business is done very largely upon personality. From the attitude of both father and son, Hanford began to count his chickens. Instead of letting up, however, he redoubled his efforts, which was his way. He spent so much time on the matter that his other work suffered, and in consequence his firm called him down. He outlined his progress with the Atlantic Bridge Company, declared he was going to succeed, and continued to camp with the job, notwithstanding the firm's open doubts.

Sixty days after his first interview he had another visit with Wylie, senior, during which the latter drained him of information and made an appointment for a month later. Said Mr. Wylie:

"You impress me strongly, Hanford, and I want my associates to hear you. Get your proposition into shape and make the same talk to them that you have made to me."

Hanford went away elated; he even bragged a bit at the office, and the report got around among the other salesmen that he really had done the impossible and had pulled off something big with the Atlantic. It was a busy month for that young gentleman, and when the red-letter day at last arrived he went on to Newark to find both Wylies awaiting him.

"Well, sir, are you prepared to make a good argument?" the father inquired.

"I am." Hanford decided that three months was not too long a time to devote to work of this magnitude, after all.

"I want you to do your best," the bridge-builder continued, encouragingly, then he led Hanford into the directors' room, where, to his visitor's astonishment, some fifty men were seated.

"These are our salesmen," announced Mr. Wylie. He introduced Hanford to them with the request that they listen attentively to what the young man had to say.

It was rather nervous work for Hanford, but he soon warmed up and forgot his embarrassment. He stood on his feet for two long hours pleading as if for his life. He went over the Atlantic plant from end to end; he showed the economic necessity for new machinery; then he explained the efficiency of his own appliances. He took rival types and picked them to pieces, pointing out their inferiority. He showed his familiarity with bridge work by going into figures which bore out his contention that the Atlantic's output could be increased and at an actual monthly saving. He wound up by proving that the General Equipment Company was the one concern best fitted to effect the improvement.

It had taken months of unremitting toil to prepare himself for this exposition, but the young fellow felt he had made his case. When he took up the cost of the proposed instalment, however, Mr. Jackson Wylie, Sr., interrupted him.

"That is all I care to have you cover," the latter explained. "Thank you very kindly, Mr. Hanford."

Hanford sat down and wiped his forehead, whereupon the other stepped forward and addressed his employees.

"Gentlemen," said he, "you have just listened to the best argument I ever heard. I purposely called you in from the road so that you might have a practical lesson in salesmanship and learn something from an outsider about your own business. I want you to profit by this talk. Take it to heart and apply it to your own customers. Our selling efficiency has deteriorated lately; you are getting lazy. I want you to wake up and show better results. That is all. You might thank this young gentleman for his kindness."

When the audience had dispersed, Hanford inquired, blankly, "Don't you intend to act on my suggestions?"

"Oh no!" said Mr. Wylie, in apparent surprise. "We are doing nicely, as it is. I merely wanted you to address the boys."

"But—I've spent three months of hard labor on this! You led me to believe that you would put in new equipment."

The younger Wylie laughed, languidly exhaling a lungful of cigarette smoke. "When Dad gets ready to purchase, he'll let you know," said he.

Six months later the Atlantic Bridge Company placed a mammoth order with Hanford's rival concern, and he was not even asked to figure on it.

That is how the seeds of this story were sown. Of course the facts got out, for those Atlantic salesmen were not wanting in a sense of humor, and Hanford was joshed in every quarter. To make matters worse, his firm called him to account for his wasted time, implying that something was evidently wrong with his selling methods. Thus began a lack of confidence which quickly developed into strained relations. The result was inevitable; Hanford saw what was coming and was wise enough to resign his position.

But it was the ridicule that hurt him most. He was unable to get away from that. Had he been at all emotional, he would have sworn a vendetta, so deep and lasting was the hurt, but he did not; he merely failed to forget, which, after all, is not so different.

It seemed queer that Henry Hanford should wind up in the bridge business himself, after attempting to fill several unsatisfactory positions, and yet there was nothing remarkable about it, for that three months of intense application at the Atlantic plant had given him a groundwork which came in handy when the Patterson Bridge Company offered him a desk. He was a good salesman; he worked hard and in time he was promoted. By and by the story was forgotten—by every one except Henry Hanford. But he had lost a considerable number of precious years.

* * * * *

When it became known that the English and Continental structural shops were so full of work that they could not figure on the mammoth five-million-dollar steel structure designed to span the Barrata River in Africa, and when the Royal Commission in London finally advertised broadcast that time was the essence of this contract, Mr. Jackson Wylie, Sr., realized that his plant was equipped to handle the job in magnificent shape, with large profit to himself and with great renown to the Wylie name. He therefore sent his son, Jackson Wylie, the Second, now a full-fledged partner, to London armed with letters to almost everybody in England from almost everybody in America.

Two weeks later—the Patterson Bridge Company was not so aggressive as its more pretentious rival—Henry Hanford went abroad on the same mission, but he carried no letters of introduction for the very good reason that he possessed neither commercial influence nor social prestige. Bradstreets had never rated him, and *Who's Who* contained no names with which he was familiar.

Jackson Wylie, the Second had been to London frequently, and he was accustomed to English life. He had friends with headquarters at Prince's and at Romano's, friends who were delighted to entertain so prominent an American; his letters gave him the entree to many of the best clubs and paved his way socially wherever he chose to go.

It was Hanford's first trip across, and he arrived on British soil without so much as a knowledge of English coins, with nothing in the way of baggage except a grip full of blue-prints, and with no destination except the Parliament buildings, where he had been led to believe the Royal Barrata Bridge Commission was eagerly and impatiently awaiting his coming. But when he called at the Parliament buildings he failed not only to find the Commission, but even to encounter anybody who knew anything about it. He did manage to locate the office, after some patient effort, but learned that it was nothing more than a forwarding address, and that no member of the Commission had been there for several weeks. He was informed that the Commission had convened once, and therefore was not entirely an imaginary body; beyond that he could discover nothing. On his second visit to the office he was told that Sir Thomas Drummond, the chairman, was inside, having run down from his shooting-lodge in Scotland for the day. But Sir Thomas's clerk, with whom Hanford had become acquainted at the time of his first call, informed him that Mr. Jackson Wylie, the Second, from America, was closeted with his lordship, and in consequence his lordship could not be disturbed. Later, when Hanford got more thoroughly in touch with the general situation, he began to realize that introductions, influence, social prestige would in all probability go farther toward landing the Barrata Bridge than mere engineering, ability or close figuring—facts with which the younger Wylie was already familiar, and against which he had provided. It also became plain to Hanford as time went on that the contract would of necessity go to America, for none of the European shops were in position to complete it on time.

Owing to government needs, this huge, eleven-span structure had to be on the ground within ninety days from the date of the signing of the contract, and erected within eight months thereafter. The Commission's clerk, a big, red-faced, jovial fellow, informed Hanford that price was not nearly so essential as time of delivery; that although the contract glittered with alluring bonuses and was heavily weighted with forfeits, neither bonuses nor forfeitures could in the slightest manner compensate for a delay in time. It was due to this very fact, to the peculiar urgency of the occasion, that the Commissioners were inclined to look askance at prospective bidders who might in any way fail to complete the task as specified.

"If all that is true, tell me why Wylie gets the call?" Hanford inquired.

"I understand he has the very highest references," said theEnglishman.

"No doubt. But you can't build bridges with letters of introduction, even in Africa."

"Probably not. But Sir Thomas is a big man; Mr. Wylie is one of his sort. They meet on common ground, don't you see?"

"Well, if I can't arrange an interview with any member of theCommission, I can at least take you to lunch. Will you go?"

The clerk declared that he would, indeed, and in the days that followed the two saw much of each other. This fellow, Lowe by name, interested Hanford. He was a cosmopolite; he was polished to the hardness of agate by a life spent in many lands. He possessed a cold eye and a firm chin; he was a complex mixture of daredeviltry and meekness. He had fought in a war or two, and he had led hopes quite as forlorn as the one Hanford was now engaged upon. It was this bond, perhaps, which drew the two together.

In spite of Lowe's assistance Hanford found it extremely difficult, nay, almost impossible, to obtain any real inside information concerning the Barrata Bridge; wherever he turned he brought up against a blank wall of English impassiveness: he even experienced difficulty in securing the blue-prints he wanted.

"It looks pretty tough for you," Lowe told him one day. "I'm afraid you're going to come a cropper, old man. This chap Wylie has the rail and he's running well. He has opened an office, I believe."

"So I understand. Well, the race isn't over yet, and I'm a good stayer. This is the biggest thing I ever tackled and it means a lot to me—more than you imagine."

"How so?"

Hanford recited the story of his old wrong, to Lowe's frank amazement.

"What a rotten trick!" the latter remarked.

"Yes! And—I don't forget."

"You'd better forget this job. It takes pull to get consideration from people like Sir Thomas, and Wylie has more than he needs. A fellow without it hasn't a chance. Look at me, for instance, working at a desk! Bah!"

"Want to try something else?"

"I do! And you'd better follow suit."

Hanford shook his head. "I never quit—I can't. When my chance at this bridge comes along—"

Lowe laughed.

"Oh, the chance will come. Chances always come; sometimes we don't see them, that's all. When this one comes I want to be ready. Meanwhile, I think I'll reconnoiter Wylie's new office and find out what's doing."

Day after day Henry Hanford pursued his work doggedly, seeing much of Lowe, something of Wylie's clerk, and nothing whatever of Sir Thomas Drummond or the other members of the Royal Barrata Bridge Commission. He heard occasional rumors of the social triumphs of his rival, and met him once, to be treated with half-veiled amusement by that patronizing young man. Meanwhile, the time was growing short and Hanford's firm was not well pleased with his progress.

Then the chance came, unexpectedly, as Hanford had declared chances always come. The remarkable thing in this instance was not that the veiled goddess showed her face, but that Hanford was quick enough to recognize her and bold enough to act. He had taken Lowe to the Trocadero for dinner, and, finding no seats where they could watch the crowd, he had selected a stall in a quiet corner. They had been there but a short time when Hanford recognized a voice from the stall adjacent as belonging to the representative of the Atlantic Bridge Company. From the sounds he could tell that Wylie was giving a dinner-party, and with Lowe's aid he soon identified the guests as members of the Royal Barrata Bridge Commission. Hanford began to strain his ears.

As the meal progressed this became less of an effort, for young Wylie's voice was strident. The Wylie conversation had ever been limited largely to the Wylies, their accomplishments, their purposes, and their prospects; and now having the floor as host, he talked mainly about himself, his father, and their forthcoming Barrata Bridge contract. It was his evident endeavor this evening to impress his distinguished guests with the tremendous importance of the Atlantic Bridge Company and its unsurpassed facilities for handling big jobs. A large part of young Wylie's experience had been acquired by manipulating municipal contracts and the aldermen connected therewith; he now worked along similar lines. Hanford soon learned that he was trying in every way possible to induce Drummond and his associates to accompany him back to America for the purpose of proving beyond peradventure that the Atlantic could take care of a five-million-dollar contract with ease.

"As if they'd go!" Lowe said, softly. "And yet—by Jove! he talks as if he had the job buttoned up."

The Englishman was alert, his dramatic instinct was at play; recognizing the significance of Wylie's offer and its possible bearing upon Hanford's fortunes, he waved the waiter away, knowing better than to permit the rattle of dishes to distract his host's attention.

Meanwhile, with clenched teeth and smoldering eyes Henry Hanford heard his rival in the next compartment identify the State of New Jersey by the fact that the works of the Atlantic Bridge Company were located therein, and dignify it by the fact that the Jackson Wylies lived there.

"You know, gentlemen," Wylie was saying, "I can arrange the trip without the least difficulty, and I assure you there will be no discomfort. I am in constant cipher communication with my father, and he will be delighted to afford you every courtesy. I can fix it up by cable in a day."

Hanford arose with a silent gesture to his guest, then, although the meal was but half over, he paid the bill. He had closed his campaign. Right then and there he landed the great Barrata Bridge contract.

Lowe, mystified beyond measure by his friend's action, made no comment until they were outside. Then he exclaimed:

"I say, old top, what blew off?"

Hanford smiled at him queerly. "The whole top of young Wylie's head blew off, if he only knew it. It's my day to settle that score, and the interest will be compounded."

"I must be extremely stupid."

"Not at all. You're damned intelligent, and that's why I'm going to need your help." Hanford turned upon the adventurer suddenly. "Have you ever been an actor?"

Lowe made a comical grimace. "I say, old man, that's pretty rough. My people raised me for a gentleman."

"Exactly. Come with me to my hotel. We're going to do each other a great favor. With your help and the help of Mr. Jackson Wylie the Second's London clerk, I'm going to land the Barrata Bridge."

Hanford had not read his friend Lowe awrong, and when, behind locked doors, he outlined his plan, the big fellow gazed at him with amazement, his blue eyes sparkling with admiration.

"Gad! That appeals to me. I—think I can do it." There was no timidity in Lowe's words, merely a careful consideration of the risks involved.

Hanford gripped his hand. "I'll attend to Wylie's clerk," he declared."Now we'd better begin to rehearse."

"But what makes you so positive you can handle his clerk?" queried-Lowe.

"Oh, I've studied him the same way I've studied you! I've been doing nothing else for the last month."

"Bli' me, you're a corker!" said Mr. Lowe.

* * * * *

Back in Newark, New Jersey, Jackson Wylie, Sr., was growing impatient. In spite of his son's weekly reports he had begun to fret at the indefinite nature of results up to date. This dissatisfaction it was that had induced him to cable his invitation to the Royal Commission to visit the Atlantic plant. Mr. Jackson Wylie, Sr., had a mysterious way of closing contracts once he came in personal contact with the proper people. In the words of his envious competitors, he had "good terminal facilities," and he felt sure in his own mind that he could get this job if only he could meet some member of that Commission who possessed the power to act. Business was bad, and in view of his son's preliminary reports he had relied upon the certainty of securing this tremendous contract; he had even turned work away so that his plant might be ready for the rush, with the result that many of his men now were idle and that he was running far below capacity. But he likewise had his eye upon those English bonuses, and when his associates rather timidly called his attention to the present state of affairs he assured them bitingly that he knew his business. Nevertheless, he could not help chafing at delay nor longing for the time to come to submit the bid that had lain for a month upon his desk. The magnitude of the figures contained therein was getting on Mr. Wylie's nerves.

On the tenth of May he received a cablegram in his own official cipher which, translated, read:

Meet Sir Thomas Drummond, Chairman Royal Barrata Bridge Commission, arriving Cunard Liner *Campania*, thirteenth, stopping Waldorf. Arrange personally Barrata contract. Caution.

The cablegram was unsigned, but its address, "Atwylie," betrayed not only its destination, but also the identity of its sender. Mr. Jackson Wylie, Sr., became tremendously excited. The last word conjured up bewildering possibilities. He was about to consult his associates when it struck him that the greatest caution he could possibly observe would consist of holding his own tongue now and henceforth. They had seen fit to criticize his handling of the matter thus far; he decided he would play safe and say nothing until he had first seen Sir Thomas Drummond and learned the lay of the land. He imagined he might then have something electrifying to tell them. He had "dealt from the bottom" too often, he had closed too many bridge contracts in his time, to mistake the meaning of this visit, or of that last word "caution."

During the next few days Mr. Jackson Wylie, Sr., had hard work to hold himself in, and he was at a high state of nervous tension when, on the morning of the fourteenth day of May, he strolled into the Waldorf-Astoria and inquired at the desk for Sir Thomas Drummond.

There was no Sir Thomas stopping at the hotel, although a Mr. T. Drummond from London had arrived on the *Campania* the day before. Mr. Jackson Wylie placed the heel of his right shoe upon the favorite corn of his left foot and bore down upon it heavily. He must be getting into his dotage, he reflected, or else the idea of a five-million-dollar job had him rattled. Of course Sir Thomas would not use his title.

At the rear desk he had his card blown up through the tube to "Mr. T. Drummond," and a few moments later was invited to take the elevator.

Arriving at the sixth floor, he needed no page to guide him; boots pointed his way to the apartment of the distinguished visitor as plainly as a lettered sign-board; boots of all descriptions—hunting-boots, riding-boots, street shoes, lowshoes, pumps, sandals—black ones and tan ones—all in a row outside the door. It was a typically English display. Evidently Sir Thomas Drummond was a personage of the most extreme importance and traveled in befitting style, Mr. Wylie told himself. Nothing was missing from the collection, unless perhaps a pair of rubber hip-boots.

A stoop-shouldered old man with a marked accent and a port-wine nose showed Mr. Wylie into a parlor where the first object upon which his active eyes alighted was a mass of blue-prints. He knew these drawings; he had figured on them himself. He likewise noted a hat-box and a great, shapeless English bag, both plastered crazily with hotel and steamship labels hailing from every quarter of the world. It was plain to be seen that Sir Thomas was a globe-trotter.

"Mr. Drummond begs you to be seated," the valet announced, with what seemed an unnecessary accent on the "mister," then moved silently out.

Mr. Wylie remarked to himself upon the value of discreet servants. They were very valuable; very hard to get in America. This must be some lifelong servitor in his lordship's family.

There was no occasion to inquire the identity of the tall, floridEnglishman in tweeds who entered a moment later, a bundle of estimatesin his hand. "Sir Thomas Drummond, Chairman of the Royal BarrataBridge Commission," was written all over him in large type.

His lordship did not go to the trouble of welcoming his visitor, but scanned him frigidly through his glasses.

"You are Mr. Jackson Wylie, Senior?" he demanded, abruptly.

"That is my name."

"President of the Atlantic Bridge Company, of Newark, New Jersey?"

"The same."

"You received a cablegram from your son in London?"

"Yes, your lordship."

Sir Thomas made a gesture as if to forego the title. "Let me see it, please."

Mr. Wylie produced the cablegram, and Drummond scanned it sharply .Evidently the identification was complete.

"Does any one besides your son and yourself know the contents of this message?"

"Not a soul."

"You have not told any one of my coming?"

"No, sir!"

"Very well." Sir Thomas appeared to breathe easier; he deliberately tore the cablegram into small bits, then tossed the fragments into a wastepaper basket before waving his caller to a chair. He still remained very cold, very forceful, although his stiff formality had vanished.

"Do you understand all about this bridge?" he inquired.

Wylie senior took the cue of brusqueness and nodded shortly.

"Can you build it in the time specified?"

"With ease."

"Have you submitted your bid?"

"Not yet. I—"

"What is the amount of your proposal?"

The president of the Atlantic Bridge Company gasped. This was the boldest, the coldest work he had ever experienced. Many times he had witnessed public officials like Sir Thomas Drummond approach this delicate point, but never with such composure, such matter-of-fact certainty and lack of moral scruple. Evidently, however, this Englishman had come to trade and wanted a direct answer. There was no false pose, no romance here. But Jackson Wylie, Sr., was too shrewd a business man to name a rock-bottom price to begin with. The training of a lifetime would not permit him to deny himself a liberal leeway for hedging, therefore he replied, cautiously:

"My figures will be approximately £1,400,000 sterling." It was his longest speech thus far.

For what seemed an hour to the bridge-builder Sir Thomas Drummond gazed at him with a cold, hard eye, then he folded his papers, rolled up his blue-prints, placed them in the big traveling-bag, and carefully locked it. When he had finished he flung out this question suddenly:

"Does that include the Commissioners?"

Up to this point Mr. Jackson Wylie had spoken mainly in monosyllables; now he quit talking altogether; it was no longer necessary. He merely shook his head in negation. He was smiling slightly.

"Then I shall ask you to add £200,000 sterling to your price," his lordship calmly announced. "Make your bid £1,600,000 sterling, and mail it in time for Wednesday's boat. I sail on the same ship. Proposals will be opened on the twenty-fifth. Arrange for an English indemnity bond for ten per cent. of your proposition. Do not communicate in any manner whatsoever with your son, except to forward the sealed bid to him. He is not to know of our arrangement. You will meet me in London later; we will take care of that £200,000 out of the last forty per cent. of the contract price, which is payable thirty days after completion, inspection, and acceptance of the bridge. You will not consult your associates upon leaving here. Do I make myself clear? Very well, sir. The figures are easy to remember: £1,600,000; £1,400,000 to you. I am pleased with the facilities your plant offers for doing the work. I am confident you can complete the bridge on time, and I beg leave to wish you a very pleasant good day."

Jackson Wylie, Sr., did not really come to until he had reached the street; even then he did not know whether he had come down the elevator or through the mail-chute. Of one thing only was he certain: he was due to retire in favor of his son. He told himself that he needed a trip through the Holy Land with a guardian and a nursing-bottle; then he paused on the curb and stamped on his corn for a second time.

"Oh, what an idiot I am!" he cried, savagely. "I could have gotten £1,600,000 to start with, but—by gad, Sir Thomas is the coldest-blooded thing I ever went against! I—I can't help but admire him."

Having shown a deplorable lack of foresight, Mr. Wylie determined to make up for it by an ample display of hindsight. If the profits on the job were not to be so large as they might have been, he would at least make certain of them by obeying instructions to the letter. In accordance with this determination, he made out the bid himself, and he mailed it with his own hand that very afternoon. He put three blue stamps on the envelope, although it required but two. Then he called up an automobile agency and ordered a foreign town-car his wife had admired. He decided that she and the girls might go to Paris for the fall shopping—he might even go with them, in view of that morning's episode.

For ten days he stood the pressure, then on the morning of the twenty-fourth he called his *confrères* into the directors' room, that same room in which young Hanford had made his talk a number of years before. Inasmuch as it was too late now for a disclosure to affect the opening of the bids in London, he felt absolved from his promise to Sir Thomas.

"Gentlemen, I have the honor to inform you," he began, pompously, "that the Barrata Bridge is ours! We have the greatest structural steel job of the decade." His chest swelled with justifiable pride.

"How? When? What do you mean?" they cried.

He told them of his mysterious but fruitful interview at the Waldorf ten days previously, enjoying their expressions of amazement to the full; then he explained in considerable detail the difficulties he had surmounted in securing such liberal figures from Sir Thomas.

"We were ready to take the contract for £1,300,000, as you will remember, but by the exercise of some diplomacy"—he coughed modestly—"I may say, by the display of some firmness and independence, I succeeded in securing a clean profit of $500,000 over what we had expected." He accepted, with becoming diffidence, the congratulations which were showered upon him. Of course, the news created a sensation, but it was as nothing to the sensation that followed upon the receipt of a cablegram the next day which read:

ATWYLIE,
Newark, New Jersey.
　　Terrible mistake somewhere. We lost. Am coming home to-day.

Mr. Jackson Wylie, Sr., also went home that day—by carriage, for, after raving wildly of treachery, after cursing the name of some English nobleman, unknown to most of the office force, he collapsed, throwing his employees into much confusion. There were rumors of an apoplectic stroke; some one telephoned for a physician; but the president of the Atlantic Bridge Company only howled at the latter when he arrived.

What hit the old man hardest was the fact that he could not explain to his associates—that he could not even explain to himself, for that matter. He could make neither head nor tail of the affair; his son was on the high seas and could not be reached; the mystery of the whole transaction threatened to unseat his reason. Even when his sorrowing heir arrived, a week after the shock, the father could gather nothing at first except the bare details.

All he could learn was that the Royal Barrata Bridge Commission had met on the twenty-fifth day of May, for the second time in its history, with Sir Thomas Drummond in the chair. In the midst of an ultra-British solemnity the bids had been opened and read—nine of them—two Belgian, one German, two French, one English, one Scottish, and two American.

The only proposals that conformed to the specifications in every respect were the last named. They were perfect. The Atlantic Bridge Company, of Newark, New Jersey, offered to do the work as specified for £1,600,000 sterling. The Patterson Bridge Company, through its authorized agent, Mr. Henry Hanford, named a price of £1,550,000. The rest was but a matter of detail.

Having concluded this bald recital, Jackson Wylie, the Second, spread his hands in a gesture of despair. "I can't understand it," he said, dolefully. "I thought I had it cinched all the time."

"*You* had it cinched!" bellowed his father. "*You*! Why, you ruined it all! Why in hell did you send him over here?"

"I? Send who? What are you talking about?"

"That man with the boots! That lying, thieving scoundrel, Sir Thomas-Drummond, of course."

The younger Wylie's face showed blank, uncomprehending amazement. "Sir Thomas Drummond was in London all the time I was there. I saw him daily," said he.

Not until this very moment did the president of the Atlantic Bridge Company comprehend the trap he had walked into, but now the whole hideous business became apparent. He had been fooled, swindled, and in a way to render recourse impossible; nay, in a manner to blacken his reputation if the story became public. He fell actually ill from the passion of his rage and not even a long rest from the worries of business completely cured him. The bitter taste of defeat would not down. He might never have understood the matter thoroughly had it not been for a missive he received one day through the mail. It was a bill from a London shoe-store for twelve pairs of boots, of varying styles, made out to Henry Hanford, and marked "paid."

Mr. Jackson Wylie, Sr., noted with unspeakable chagrin that the last word was heavily under-scored in ink, as if by another hand. Hanford's bill was indeed paid, and with interest to date.

THE CUB REPORTER

Why he chose Buffalo Paul Anderson never knew, unless perhaps it had more newspapers than Bay City, Michigan, and because his ticket expired in the vicinity of Buffalo. For that matter, why he should have given up an easy job as the mate of a tugboat to enter the tortuous paths of journalism the young man did not know, and, lacking the introspective faculty, he did not stop to analyze his motives. So far as he could discover he had felt the call to higher endeavor, and just naturally had heeded it. Such things as practical experience and educational equipment were but empty words to him, for he was young and hopeful, and the world is kind at twenty-one.

He had hoped to enter his chosen field with some financial backing, and to that end, when the desire to try his hand at literature had struck him, he had bought an interest in a smoke-consumer which a fireman on another tugboat had patented. In partnership with the inventor he had installed one of the devices beneath a sawmill boiler as an experiment. Although the thing consumed smoke surprisingly well, it likewise unharnessed such an amazing army of heat-units that it melted the crown-sheet of the boiler; whereupon the sawmill men, being singularly coarse and unimaginative fellows, set upon the patentee and his partner with ash-rakes, draw-bars, and other ordinary, unpatented implements; a lumberjack beat hollowly upon their ribs with a peavy, and that night young Anderson sickened of smoke-consumers, harked anew to the call of journalism, and hiked, arriving in Buffalo with seven dollars and fifty cents to the good.

For seven dollars, counted out in advance, he chartered a furnished room for a week, the same carrying with it a meal at each end of the day, which left in Anderson's possession a superfluity of fifty cents to be spent in any extravagance he might choose.

Next day he bought a copy of each newspaper and, carefully scanning them, selected the one upon which to bestow his reportorial gifts. This done, he weighed anchor and steamed through the town in search of the office. Walking in upon the city editor of *The Intelligencer*, he gazed with benevolent approval upon that busy gentleman's broad back. He liked the place, the office suited him, and he decided to have his desk placed over by the window.

After a time the editor wheeled, displaying a young, smooth, fat face, out of which peered gray-blue eyes with pin-point pupils.

"Well?" he queried.

"Here I am," said Anderson.

"So it appears. What do you want?"

"Work."

"What kind?"

"Newspapering."

"What can you do?"

"Anything."

"Well, well!" cried the editor. "You don't look much like a newspaper man."

"I'm not one—yet. But I'm going to be."

"Where have you worked?"

"Nowhere! You see, I'm really a playwright."

The editor's face showed a bit of interest. "Playwright, eh? Anderson! Anderson!" he mused. "Don't recall the name."

"No," said Paul; "I've never written any plays yet, but I'm going to. That's why I want to sort of begin here and get the hang of this writing game."

A boy entered with some proofs at that moment and tossed them upon the table, distracting the attention of the newspaper man. The latter wheeled back to his work and spoke curtly over his shoulder.

"I'm not running a school of journalism. Good-by."

"Maybe you'd like me to do a little space work—?"

"I'd never like you. Get out. I'm busy."

Anderson retired gracefully, jingling his scanty handful of nickels and dimes, and a half-hour later thrust himself boldly in upon another editor, but with no better result. He made the rounds of all the offices; although invariably rebuffed he became more firmly convinced than ever that journalism was his designated sphere.

That night after dinner he retired to his room with the evening papers, wedged a chair against his bed, and, hoisting his feet upon the wash-stand, absorbed the news of the day. It was ineffably sweet and satisfying to be thus identified with the profession of letters, and it was immeasurably more dignified than "tugging" on the Saginaw River. Once he had schooled himself in the tricks of writing, he decided he would step to higher things than newspaper work, but for the present it was well to ground himself firmly in the rudiments of the craft.

In going through the papers he noted one topic which interested him, a "similar mystery" story on the second page. From what he could gather, he judged that much space had already been given to it; for now, inasmuch as no solution offered, the item was dying slowly, the major portion of each article being devoted to a rehash of similar unsolved mysteries.

Anderson read that the body of the golden-haired girl still lay at the Morgue, unidentified. Bit by bit he pieced together the lean story that she was a suicide and that both the police and the press had failed in their efforts to unearth the least particle of information regarding her. In spite of her remarkable beauty and certain unusual circumstances connected with her death investigation had led nowhere.

On the following day Anderson again walked into the editorial-rooms of *The Intelligencer* and greeted the smooth, fat-faced occupant thereof.

"Anything doing yet?" he inquired.

"Not yet," said the newspaper man, with a trace of annoyance in his voice. As the applicant moved out he halted him at the door with the words: "Oh! Wait!"

Anderson's heart leaped. After all, he thought, perseverance would—

"Not yet, nor soon." The editor smiled broadly, and Paul realized that the humor in those pin-point eyes was rather cruel.

Five other calls he made that day, to be greeted gruffly in every instance except one. One man encouraged him slightly by saying:

"Come back next week; I may have an opening then."

In view of the "pay-as-you-enter" policy in vogue at Anderson's boarding-house he knew there could be no next week for him, therefore he inquired:

"How about a little space work in the meantime? I'm pretty good at that stuff."

"You are?"

"Surest thing you know."

"Did you ever do any?"

"No. But I'm good, just the same."

"Huh!" the editor grunted. "There's no room now, and, come to think of it, you needn't bother to get around next week. I can't break in new men."

That evening young Anderson again repaired to his room with his harvest of daily papers, and again he read them thoroughly. He was by no means discouraged as yet, for his week had just begun—there were still five days of grace, and prime ministers have been made overnight, nations have fallen in five days. Six calls a day for five days, that meant thirty chances for a job. It was a cinch!

Hidden away among the back pages once more he encountered the golden-haired-girl story, and although one paper featured it a bit because of some imaginary clue, the others treated it casually, making public the information that the body still lay at the Morgue, a silent, irritating thing of mystery.

On the third day Paul made his usual round of calls. He made them more quickly now because he was recognized, and was practically thrown out of each editorial sanctum. His serenity remained unruffled, and his confidence undisturbed. Of all the six editors, Burns, of *The Intelligencer*, treated him worst, adding ridicule to his gruffness, a refinement of cruelty which annoyed the young steamboat man. Anderson clenched his hard-knuckled hand and estimated the distance from editorial ear to point of literary chin, but realized in time that steamboat methods were out of place here in the politer realms of journalism.

Four times more he followed his daily routine, and on Monday morning arose early to avoid his landlady. His week was up, his nickels and dimes were gone, nevertheless he spent the day on his customary rounds. He crept in late at night, blue with the cold and rather dazed at his bad luck; he had eaten nothing since the morning before, and he knew that he dared not show up at the breakfast-table the next morning. For the time being discouragement settled upon him; it settled suddenly like some heavy smothering thing; it robbed him of hope and redoubled his hunger. He awoke at daylight, roused by the sense of his defeat, then tiptoed out while yet the landlady was abed, and spent the day looking for work along the water-front. But winter had tied up the shipping, and he failed, as he likewise failed at sundry employment agencies where he offered himself in any capacity.

At noon he wandered into the park, and, finding a sheltered spot, sunned himself as best he could. He picked up the sheets of a wind-scattered paper and read until the chill December afternoon got into his bones and forced him to his feet. The tale of the unidentified girl at the Morgue recurred to him when he read the announcement that she would be buried two days later in the Potter's Field. Perhaps the girl had starved for lack of work, he reflected. Perhaps hunger and cold had driven her to her death. Certainly those two were to blame for many a tragedy calculated to mystify warmly clad policemen and well-fed reporters.

When he stole, shivering, into his bleak bedroom, late that night, he found a note pinned upon his pillow. Of course the landlady needed her rent—all landladies were in need of money—and of course he would get out in the morning. He was glad she had not turned him out during the day, for this afforded him sanctuary for another night at least. After to-morrow it would be a park bench for his.

He left his valise behind in the morning, rather lamenting the fact that the old lady could not wear the shirts it contained, and hoping that she would realize a sufficient sum from their sale to pay his bill.

It was late afternoon when he commenced his listless tramp toward the newspaper offices. Since Burns had become his pet aversion, he saved him for the last, framing a few farewell remarks befitting the death of hopes like his, and rehearsing an exit speech suitable to mark his departure from the field of letters.

When he finally reached *The Intelligencer* editorial-rooms, Burns rounded on him angrily.

"For the love of Mike! Are you here again?" he demanded.

"I thought you might like to have some space work—"

"By heavens! You're persistent."

"Yes."

"We editors are an unfeeling lot, aren't we?" the fat young man inquired. "No temperament, no appreciation." He laughed noiselessly.

"Give me a job," Anderson cried, his voice breaking huskily. "I'll make good. I'll do anything."

"How long do you intend to keep bothering me?" questioned Burns.

Anderson's cheeks were blue and the backs of his legs were trembling from weakness, but he repeated, stolidly: "Give me a job. I—I won't bother you after that. I'll make good, see if I don't."

"You think well of yourself, don't you?"

"If you thought half as well of me as I do," Paul assured him, "I'd be your star reporter."

"Star hell!" testily cried the editor. "We haven't got such a thing. They don't know they're alive, except on pay-day. Look at this blond girl at the Morgue—they've wasted two weeks on that case." He paused suddenly, then his soft lips spread, showing his sharp, white teeth. Modifying his tone, he continued: "Say, I rather like you, Anderson, you're such a blamed nuisance. You've half convinced me that you're a genius."

The younger man's hunger, which had given up in despair, raised its head and bit into his vitals sharply.

"Maybe I—"

"I've a notion to give you a chance."

"That's all I want," the caller quavered, in a panic. "Just give me a toe-hold, that's all," His voice broke in spite of his effort to hold it steady. Burns wasn't a bad sort, after all; just grouchy and irritable. Perhaps this was merely his way.

Burns continued: "Well, I will give you an assignment, a good assignment, too, and if you cover it I'll put you on permanently. I'll do more than that, I'll pay you what we pay our best man, if you make good. That's fair, isn't it?"

He smiled benignly, and the soon-to-be reporter's wits went capering off in a hysterical stampede. Anderson felt the desire to wring the fellow's hand.

"All that counts in this office is efficiency," the latter went on. "We play no favorites. When a man delivers the goods we boost him; when he fails we fire him. There's no sentiment here, and I hold my job merely because I'm the best man in the shop. Can you go to work to-night?"

"Why—why—yes, sir!"

"Very well. That's the spirit I like. You can take your time on the story, and you needn't come back till you bring it."

"Yes, sir."

"Now pay attention, here it is. About two weeks ago a blond girl committed suicide in a Main Street boarding-house. The body's down at the Morgue now. Find out who she is." He turned back to his desk and began to work.

The hungry youth behind him experienced a sudden sinking at the stomach. All at once he became hopelessly empty and friendless, and he felt his knees urging him to sit down. He next became conscious that the shoulders of Mr. Burns were shaking a bit, as if he had encountered a piece of rare humor. After an instant, when Anderson made no move to go, the man at the desk wheeled about, exposing a bloated countenance purple with suppressed enjoyment.

"What's the matter?" he giggled. "Don't you want the job? I can't tell you any more about the girl; that's all we know. The rest is up to you. You'll find out everything, won't you? Please do, for your own sake and the sake of *The Intelligencer*. Yes, yes, I'm sure you will, because you're a good newspaper man—you told me so yourself." His appreciation of the jest threatened to strangle him.

"Mr. Burns," began the other, "I—I'm up against it. I guess you don't know it, but I'm hungry. I haven't eaten for three days."

At this the editor became positively apoplectic.

"Oh yes—yes, I do!" He nodded vigorously. "You show it in your face. That's why I went out of my way to help you. He! He! He! Now you run along and get me the girl's name and address while I finish this proof. Then come back and have supper with me at the Press Club." Again he chortled and snickered, whereupon something sullen and fierce awoke in young Anderson. He knew of a way to get food and a bed and a place to work even if it would only last thirty days, for he judged Burns was the kind of man who would yell for the police in case of an assault. Paul would have welcomed the prospect of prison fare, but he reasoned that it would be an incomplete satisfaction merely to mash the pudgy face of Mr. Burns and hear him clamor. What he wanted at this moment was a job; Burns's beating could hold over. This suicide case had baffled the pick of Buffalo's trained reporters; it had foiled the best efforts of her police; nevertheless, this fat-paunched fellow had baited a starving man by offering him the assignment. It was impossible; it was a cruel joke, and yet—there might be a chance of success. Even while he was debating the point he heard himself say:

"Very well, Mr. Burns. If you want her name I'll get it for you."

He crammed his hat down over his ears and walked out, leaving the astonished editor gazing after him with open mouth.

Anderson's first impulse had been merely to get out of Burns's office, out of sight of that grinning satyr, and never to come back, but before he had reached the street he had decided that it was as well to starve striving as with folded hands. After all, the dead girl had a name.

Instead of leaving the building, he went to the files of the paper and, turning back, uncovered the original story, which he cut out with his pen-knife, folded up, and placed in his pocket. This done, he sought the lobby of a near-by hotel, found a seat near a radiator, and proceeded to read the clipping carefully.

It was a meager story, but it contained facts and was free from the confusion and distortions of the later accounts, which was precisely what he wished to guard against. Late one afternoon, so the story went, the girl had rented a room in a Main Street boarding-house, had eaten supper and retired. At eleven o'clock the next day, when she did not respond to a knock on her door, the room had been broken into and she had been found dead, with an empty morphine-bottle on the bureau. That was all. There were absolutely no clues to the girl's identity, for the closest scrutiny failed to discover a mark on her clothing or any personal articles which could be traced. She had possessed no luggage, save a little hand-satchel or shopping-bag containing a few coins. One fact alone stood out in the whole affair. She had paid for her room with a two-dollar Canadian bill, but this faint clue had been followed with no result. No one knew the girl; she had walked out of nowhere and had disappeared into impenetrable mystery. Those were the facts in the case, and they were sufficiently limited to baffle the best efforts of Buffalo's trained detective force.

It would seem that there can be no human creature so obscure as to have neither relatives, friends, nor acquaintances, and yet this appeared to be the case, for a full description of this girl had been blazoned in the papers of every large city, had been exposed in countless country post-offices, and conveyed to the police of every city of the States and Canada. It was as if the mysterious occupant of the Morgue had been born of the winter wind on that fateful evening two weeks before. The country had been dragged by a net of publicity, that marvelous, fine-meshed fabric from which no living man is small or shrewd enough to escape, and still the sad, white face at the Morgue continued to smile out from its halo of gold as if in gentle mockery.

For a long time Paul Anderson sat staring into the realms of speculation, his lips white with hunger, his cheeks hollow and feverish from the battle he had waged. His power of exclusion was strong, therefore he lost himself to his surroundings. Finally, however, he roused himself from his abstraction and realized the irony of this situation. He, the weakest, the most inexperienced of all the men who had tried, had been set to solve this mystery, and starvation was to be the fruit of his failure.

He saw that it had begun to snow outside. In the lobby it was warm and bright and vivid with jostling life; the music of a stringed orchestra somewhere back of him was calling well-dressed men and women in to dinner. All of them seemed happy, hopeful, purposeful. He noted, furthermore, that three days without food makes a man cold, even in a warm place, and light-headed, too. The north wind had bitten him cruelly as he crossed the street, and now as he peered out of the plate-glass windows the night seemed to hold other lurking horrors besides. His want was like a burden, and he shuddered weakly, hesitating to venture out where the wind could harry him. It was a great temptation to remain here where there was warmth and laughter and life; nevertheless, he rose and slunk shivering out into the darkness, then laid a course toward the Morgue.

While Anderson trod the snowy streets a slack-jowled editor sat at supper with some friends at the Press Club, eating and drinking heartily, as is the custom of newspaper men let down for a moment from the strain of their work. He had told a story, and his caustic way of telling it had amused his hearers, for each and every one of them remembered the shabby applicant for work, and all of them had wasted baffling hours on the mystery of this girl with the golden hair.

"I guess I put a crimp in him," giggled Mr. Burns. "I gave him a chance to show those talents he recommends so highly."

"The Morgue, on a night like this, is a pretty dismal place for a hungry man," said one of the others. "It's none too cheerful in the daytime."

The others agreed, and Burns wabbled anew in his chair in appreciation of his humor.

Young Anderson had never seen a morgue, and to-night, owing to his condition, his dread of it was child-like. It seemed as if this particular charnel-house harbored some grisly thing which stood between him and food and warmth and hope; the nearer he drew to it the greater grew his dread. A discourteous man, shrunken as if from the chill of the place, was hunched up in front of a glowing stove. He greeted Anderson sourly:

"Out into that courtyard; turn to the left—second door," he directed."She's in the third compartment."

Anderson lacked courage to ask the fellow to come along, but stumbled out into a snow-filled areaway lighted by a swinging incandescent which danced to the swirling eddies.

Compartment! He supposed bodies were kept upon slabs or tables, or something like that. He had steeled himself to see rows of unspeakable sights, played upon by dripping water, but he found nothing of the sort.

The second door opened into a room which he discovered was colder than the night outside, evidently the result of artificial refrigeration. He was relieved to find the place utterly bare except for a sort of car or truck which ran around the room on a track beneath a row of square doors. These doors evidently opened into the compartments alluded to by the keeper.

Which compartment had the fellow said? Paul abruptly discovered that he was rattled, terribly rattled, and he turned back out of the place. He paused shortly, however, and took hold of himself.

"Now, now!" he said, aloud. "You're a bum reporter, my boy." An instant later he forced himself to jerk open the first door at his hand.

For what seemed a full minute he stared into the cavern, as if petrified, then he closed the door softly. Sweat had started from his every pore. Alone once more in the great room, he stood shivering. "God!" he muttered. This was newspaper training indeed.

He remembered now having read, several days before, about an Italian laborer who had been crushed by a falling column. To one unaccustomed to death in any form that object, head-on in the obscurity of the compartment, had been a trying sight. He began to wonder if it were really cold or stiflingly hot.

The boy ground his teeth and flung open the next door, slamming it hurriedly again to blot out what it exposed. Why didn't they keep them covered? Why didn't they show a card outside? Must he examine every grisly corpse upon the premises?

He stepped to the third door and wrenched it open. He knew the girl at once by her wealth of yellow hair and the beauty of her still, white face. There was no horror here, no ghastly sight to weaken a man's muscles and sicken his stomach; only a tired girl asleep. Anderson felt a great pity as he wheeled the truck opposite the door and reverently drew out the slab on which the body lay. He gazed upon her intently for some time. She was not at all as he had pictured her, and yet there could be no mistake. He took the printed description from his pocket and reread it carefully, comparing it point by point. When he had finished he found that it was a composite word photograph, vaguely like and yet totally unlike the person it was intended to portray, and so lacking in character that no one knowing the original intimately would have been likely to recognize her from it.

So that was why no word had come in answer to all this newspaper publicity. After all, this case might not be so difficult as it had seemed; for the first time the dispirited youth felt a faint glow of encouragement. He began to formulate a plan.

Hurriedly he fumbled for his note-book, and there, in that house of death, with his paper propped against the wall, he wrote a two-hundred-word description; a description so photographically exact that to this day it is preserved in the Buffalo police archives as a perfect model.

He replaced the body in its resting-place and went out. There was no chill in him now, no stumbling nor weakness of any sort. He had found a starting-point, had uncovered what all those trained newspaper men had missed, and he felt that he had a chance to win.

Twenty minutes later Burns, who had just come in from supper, turned back from his desk with annoyance and challenge in his little, narrow eyes.

"Well?"

"I think I've got her, Mr. Burns."

"Nonsense!"

"Anyhow, I've got a description that her father or her mother or her friends can recognize. The one you and the other papers printed disguised her so that nobody could tell who she was—it might have covered a hundred girls."

Rapidly, and without noting the editor's growing impatience, Paul read the two descriptions, then ran on, breathlessly:

"All we have to do is print ten or twenty thousand of these and mail them out with the morning edition—separate sheets, posters, you under-stand?—so they can be nailed up in every post-office within two hundred miles. Send some to the police of all the cities, and we'll have a flash in twenty-four hours."

Burns made no comment for a moment. Instead, he looked the young man over angrily from his eager face to his unblacked shoes. His silence, his stare, were eloquent.

"Why? Why not?" Anderson demanded, querulously. "I tell you this description isn't right. It—it's nothing like her, nothing at all."

"Say! I thought I'd seen the last of you," growled the corpulent man."Aren't you on to yourself yet?"

"Do you—mean that your talk this evening don't go?" Paul demanded, quietly. "Do you mean to say you won't even give me the chance you prom-ised?"

"No! I don't mean that. What I said goes, all right, but I told *you* to iden-tify this girl. I didn't agree to do it. What d'you think this paper is, anyhow? We want stories in this office. We don't care who or what this girl is unless there's a story in her. We're not running a job-print shop nor a mail-order business to identify strayed females. Twenty thousand posters! Bah! And say—don't you know that no two men can write similar descriptions of any-body or anything? What's the difference whether her hair is burnished gold or 'raw gold' or her eyes bluish gray instead of grayish blue? Rats! Beat it!"

"But I tell you—"

"What's her name? Where does she live? What killed her? That's what I want to know. I'd look fine, wouldn't I, circularizing a dead story? Wouldn't that be a laugh on me? No, Mr. Anderson, author, artist, and playwright, I'm getting damned tired of being pestered by you, and you needn't come back here until you bring the goods. Do I make myself plain?"

It was anger which cut short the younger man's reply. On account of petty economy, for fear of ridicule, this editor refused to relieve some withered old woman, some bent and worried old man, who might be, who probably were, waiting, waiting, waiting in some out-of-the-way village. So Anderson reflected. Because there might not be a story in it this girl would go to the Potter's Field and her people would never know. And yet, by Heaven, they *would* know! Something told him there *was* a story back of this girl's death, and he swore to get it. With a mighty effort he swallowed his chagrin and, disregarding the insult to himself, replied:

"Very well. I've got you this time."

"Humph!" Burns grunted, viciously.

"I don't know how I'll turn the trick, but I'll turn it." For the second time that evening he left the office with his jaws set stubbornly.

Paul Anderson walked straight to his boarding-house and bearded his landlady. "I've got a job," said he.

"I'm very glad," the lady told him, honestly enough. "I feared you were going to move out."

"Yes!" he repeated. "I've got a job that carries the highest salary on the paper. You remember the yellow-haired girl who killed herself awhile ago?" he asked.

"Indeed I do. Everybody knows about that case."

"Well, it got too tough for the police and the other reporters, so they turned it over to me. It's a bully assignment, and my pay starts when I solve the mystery. Now I'm starved; I wish you'd rustle me some grub."

"But, Mr. Anderson, you're bill for this week? You know I get paid in—"

"Tut, tut! You know how newspapers are. They don't pay in advance, andI can't pay you until they pay me. You'll probably have to wait untilSaturday, for I'm a little out of practice on detective stuff. ButI'll have this thing cleared up by then. You don't appreciate—you*can't* appreciate—what a corking assignment it is."

Anderson had a peculiarly engaging smile, and five minutes later he was wrecking the pantry of all the edibles his fellow-boarders had overlooked, the while his landlady told him her life's history, wept over the memory of her departed husband, and confessed that she hoped to get out of the boarding-house business some time.

A good night's sleep and a hearty breakfast put the young man in fine fettle, and about ten o'clock he repaired to a certain rooming-house on Main Street, the number of which he obtained from the clipping in his pocket.

A girl answered his ring, but at sight of him she shut the door hurriedly, explaining through the crack:

"Mrs. MacDougal is out and you can't come in."

"But I want to talk to you."

"I'm not allowed to talk to reporters," she declared. "Mrs. MacDougal won't let me."

A slight Scotch accent gave Anderson his cue. "MacDougal is a good-Scotch name. I'm Scotch myself, and so are you." He smiled hisboarding-house smile, and the girl's eyes twinkled back at him."Didn't she tell you I was coming?"

"Why, no, sir. Aren't you a reporter?"

"I've been told that I'm not. I came to look at a room."

"What room?" the girl asked, quickly. "We haven't any vacant rooms."

"That's queer," Anderson frowned. "I can't be mistaken. I'm sure Mrs. MacDougal said there was one."

The door opened slowly. "Maybe she meant the one on the second floor."

"Precisely." An instant later he was following his guide up-stairs.

Anderson recognized the room at a glance, from its description, but the girl did not mention the tragedy which had occurred therein, so he proceeded to talk terms with her, prolonging his stay as long as possible, meanwhile using his eyes to the best advantage. He invented an elaborate ancestry which he traced backward through the pages of *Scottish Chiefs*, the only book of the sort he had ever read, and by the time he was ready to leave the girl had thawed out considerably.

"I'll take the room," he told her, "and I'm well pleased to get it. I don't see how such a good one stands vacant in this location."

There was an instant's pause, then his companion confessed: "There's a reason. You'll find it out sooner or later, so I may as well tell you. That's where the yellow-haired girl you hear so much about killed herself. I hope it won't make any difference to you, Mr.—"

"Gregor. Certainly not. I read about the case. Canadian, wasn't she?"

"Oh yes! There's no doubt of it. She paid her rent with a Canadian bill, and, besides, I noticed her accent. I didn't tell the reporters, however, they're such a fresh lot."

Paul's visit, it appeared, had served to establish one thing, at least, a thing which the trained investigators had not discovered. Canadian money in Buffalo was too common to excite comment, therefore none of them had seen fit to follow out that clue of the two-dollar bill.

"The papers had it that she was some wealthy girl," the former speaker ran on, "but I know better."

"Indeed? How do you know?"

"Her hands! They were good hands, and she used them as if she knew what they were made for."

"Anything else?"

"No. She seemed very sad and didn't say much. Of course I only saw her once."

Anderson questioned the girl at some further length, but discovered nothing of moment, so he left, declaring that he would probably move into the room on the following day.

Prom the rooming-house he went directly to the Morgue, and for a second time examined the body, confining his attention particularly to the hands. The right one showed nothing upon which to found a theory, save that it was, indeed, a capable hand with smooth skin and well-tended nails; but on examining the left Paul noted a marked peculiarity. Near the ends of the thumb and the first finger the skin was roughened, abrased; there were numerous tiny black spots beneath the skin, which, upon careful scrutiny, he discovered to be microscopic blood-blisters.

For a long time he puzzled over this phenomenon which had escaped all previous observers, but to save him he could invent no explanation for it. He repaired finally to the office of the attendant and asked for the girl's clothes, receiving permission to examine a small bundle.

"Where's the rest?" he demanded.

"That's all she had," said the man.

"No baggage at all?"

"Not a thing but what she stood up in. The coroner has her jewelry and things of that sort."

Anderson searched the contents of the bundle with the utmost care, but found no mark of any sort. The garments, although inexpensive, were beautifully neat and clean, and they displayed the most marvelous examples of needlework he had ever seen. Among the effects was a plush muff, out of which, as he picked it up, fell a pair of little knitted mittens—or was there a pair? Finding but the one, he shook the muff again, then looked through the other things.

"Where's the other mitten?" he inquired.

"There ain't been but the one," the attendant told him.

"Are you sure?"

"See here, do you think I'm trying to hold out a yarn mitten on you? I say there ain't been but the one. I was here when she came, and I know."

Discouraged by the paucity of clues which this place offered, Anderson went next to the coroner's office.

The City Hall newspaper squad had desks in this place, but Paul paid no attention to them or to their occupants. He went straight to the wicket and asked for the effects of the dead girl.

It appeared that Burns had told his practical joke broadcast, for the young man heard his name mentioned, and then some one behind him snickered. He paid no attention, however, for the clerk had handed him a small leather bag or purse, together with a morphine-bottle, about the size and shape of an ordinary vaseline-bottle. The bag was cheap and bore no maker's name or mark. Inside of it was a brooch, a ring, a silver chain, and a slip of paper. Stuck to the bottom of the reticule was a small key. Paul came near overlooking the last-named article, for it was well hidden in a fold near the corner. Now a key to an unknown lock is not much to go on at best, therefore he gave his attention to the paper. It was evidently a scrap torn from a sheet of wrapping-paper, and bore these figures in pencil:

9.25 6.25 —— 3.00

While he was reading these figures Paul heard a reporter say, loudly, "Now that I have written the paper, who will take it?"

Another answered, "I will."

"Who are you?" inquired the first voice.

"Hawkshaw, the detective."

Anderson's cheeks flushed, but he returned the bag and its contents without comment and walked out, heedless of the laughter of the six reporters. The injustice of their ridicule burnt him like a branding-iron, for his only offense lay in trying the impossible. These fellows had done their best and had failed, yet they jeered at him because he had tackled a forlorn hope. They had taken the trail when it was hot and had lost it; now they railed at him when he took it cold.

All that afternoon he tramped the streets, thinking, thinking, until his brain went stale. The only fresh clues he had discovered thus far were the marks on finger and thumb, the fact that the girl was a Canadian, and that she had possessed but one mitten instead of two. This last, for obvious reasons, was too trivial to mean anything, and yet in so obscure a case it could not be ignored. The fact that she was a Canadian helped but little, therefore the best point upon which to hang a line of reasoning seemed to be those black spots on the left hand. But they stumped Anderson absolutely.

He altered his mental approach to the subject and reflected upon the girl's belongings. Taken in their entirety they showed nothing save that the girl was poor, therefore he began mentally to assort them, one by one. First, clothes. They were ordinary clothes; they betrayed nothing. Second, the purse. It was like a million other purses and showed no distinguishing mark, no peculiarity. Third, the jewelry. It was cheap and common, of a sort to be found in any store. Fourth, the morphine-bottle. Paul was forced likewise to dismiss consideration of that. There remained nothing but the scrap of paper, torn from the corner of a large sheet and containing these penciled figures:

9.25 6.25 —— 3.00

It was a simple sum in subtraction, a very simple sum indeed; too simple, Anderson reflected, for any one to reduce to figures unless those figures had been intended for a purpose. He recalled the face at the morgue and vowed that such a girl could have done the sum mentally. Then why the paper? Why had she taken pains to tear off a piece of wrapping-paper, jot down figures so easy to remember, and preserve them in her purse? Why, she did so because she was methodical, something answered. But, his alter ego reasoned, if she had been sufficiently methodical to note a trivial transaction so carefully, she would have been sufficiently methodical to use some better, some more methodical method. She would not have torn off a corner of thick wrapping-paper upon which to keep her books. There was but one answer, memorandum!

All right, memorandum it was, for the time being. Now then, in what business could she have been engaged where she found it necessary to keep memoranda of such inconsiderable sums? Oh, Lord! There were a million! Paul had been walking on thin ice from the start; now it gave way beneath him, so he abandoned this train of thought and went back once more to the bundle of clothes. Surely there was a clue concealed somewhere among them, if only he could find it. They were poor clothes, and yet, judging by their cut, he fancied the girl had looked exceedingly well in them—nay, even modish. She had evidently spent much time on them, as the beautiful needlework attested. At this point Anderson's mind ran out on to thin ice again, so he reverted to the girl herself for the _n_th time. She was Canadian, her hands were useful, there were tiny blood-blisters on the left thumb and index finger, and the skin was roughened and torn minutely, evidently by some sharp instrument. What instrument? He answered the question almost before he had voiced it. A needle, of course!

Paul stopped in his walk so abruptly that a man poked him in the back with a ladder; but he paid no heed, for his mind was leaping. That thickening of the skin, those tiny scratches, those blood-blisters, those garments without mark of maker, yet so stylish in cut and so carefully made, and furthermore that memorandum:

9.25 6.25 —— 3.00

"Why, she was a dressmaker!" said Anderson, out loud. He went back over his reasoning, but it held good—so good that he would have wagered his own clothes that he was right. Yes, and those figures represented some trifling purchases or commission—for a customer, no doubt.

It followed naturally that she was not a Buffalo dressmaker, else she would have been identified long since; nor was it likely that she came from any city, for her clothes had not given him the impression of being city-made, and, moreover, the publicity given to the case through the press, even allowing for the fact that the printed description had been vague, would have been sure to uncover her identity. No, she was a Canadian country seamstress.

The young man's mind went back a few years to his boyhood on a Michigan farm, where visiting dressmakers used to come and stay by the week to make his mother's clothes. They usually carried a little flat trunk filled with patterns, yard sticks, forms, and other paraphernalia of the trade. Paul remembered that the owners used to buy the cloths and materials at the country stores, and render a strict accounting thereof to his mother. Well, where was the trunk that went with this country dressmaker?

The question of baggage had puzzled him from the start. Had the girl been possessed of a grip or bundle of any kind at the time of her death that question would have been answered. But there was absolutely nothing of the sort in her room. Her complete lack of luggage had made him doubt, at first, that she was an out-of-town visitor; but, following his recent conclusions, he decided now that directly the opposite was true. She had come to Buffalo with nothing but a trunk, otherwise she would have taken her hand-luggage with her to the Main Street rooming-house. It remained to find that trunk.

This problem threatened even greater difficulties than any hitherto, and Paul shivered as the raw Lake wind searched through his clothes. He wondered if it had been as cold as this when the girl arrived in Buffalo. Yes, assuredly. Then why did she go out with only one mitten? His reason told him that the other one had been lost by the police. But the police are careful, as a rule. They had saved every other article found in the girl's possession, even to a brooch and pin and scrap of paper. Probably the girl herself had lost it. But country dressmakers are careful, too; they are not given to losing mittens, especially in cold weather. It was more reasonable to believe that she had mislaid it among her belongings; inasmuch as those belongings, according to Paul's logic, were doubtless contained in her trunk, that was probably where the missing mitten would be found. But, after all, had she really brought a trunk with her?

Like a flash came the recollection of that key stuck to the bottom of the girl's leather purse at the coroner's office. Ten minutes later Paul was back at the City Hall.

For a second time he was greeted with laughter by the reportorial squad; again he paid no heed.

"Why, you saw those things not two hours ago," protested the coroner's clerk, in answer to his inquiry.

"I want to see them again."

"Well, I'm busy. You've had them once, that's enough."

"Friend," said Anderson, quietly, "I want those things and I want them quick. You give them to me or I'll go to the man higher up and get them— and your job along with them."

The fellow obeyed reluctantly. Paul picked the key loose and examined it closely. While he was thus engaged, one of the reporters behind him said:

"Aha! At last he has the key to the mystery."

The general laughter ceased abruptly when the object of this banter thrust the key into his pocket and advanced threateningly toward the speaker, his face white with rage. The latter rose to his feet; he undertook to execute a dignified retreat, but Anderson seized him viciously, flung him back, and pinned him against the wall, crying, furiously:

"You dirty rat! If you open your face to me again, I'll brain you, and that goes for all of this death-watch." He took in the other five men with his reddened eyes. "When you fellows see me coming, hole up. Understand?"

His grip was so fierce, his mouth had such a wicked twist to it, that his victim understood him perfectly and began to grin in a sickly, apologetic fashion. Paul reseated the reporter at his desk with such violence that a chair leg gave way; then he strode out of the building.

For the next few hours Anderson tramped the streets in impotent anger, striving to master himself, for that trifling episode had so upset him that he could not concentrate his mind upon the subject in hand. When he tried to do so his conclusions seemed grotesquely fanciful and farfetched. This delay was all the more annoying because on the morrow the girl was to be buried, and, therefore, the precious hours were slipping away. He tried repeatedly to attain that abstract, subconscious mood in which alone shines the pure light of inductive reasoning.

"Where is that trunk? Where is that trunk? Where is that trunk?" he repeated, tirelessly. Could it be in some other rooming-house? No. If the girl had disappeared from such a place, leaving her trunk behind, the publicity would have uncovered the fact. It might be lying in the baggage-room of some hotel, to be sure; but Paul doubted that, for the same reason. The girl had been poor, too; it was unlikely that she would have gone to a high-priced hotel. Well, he couldn't examine all the baggage in all the cheap hotels of the city—that was evident. Somehow he could not picture that girl in a cheap hotel; she was too fine, too patrician. No, it was more likely that she had left her trunk in some railroad station. This was a long chance, but Paul took it.

The girl had come from Canada, therefore Anderson went to the Grand Trunk Railway depot and asked for the baggage-master. There were other roads, but this seemed the most likely.

A raw-boned Irish baggage-man emerged from the confusion, and of a sudden Paul realized the necessity of even greater tact here than he had used with the Scotch girl, for he had no authority of any sort behind him by virtue of which he could demand so much as a favor.

"Are you a married man?" he inquired, abruptly.

"G'wan! I thought ye wanted a baggage-man," the big fellow replied.

"Don't kid me; this is important."

"Shure, I am, but I don't want any accident insurance. I took a chance and I'm game."

"Have you any daughters?"

"Two of them. But what's it to ye?"

"Suppose one of them disappeared?"

The baggage-man seized Anderson by the shoulder; his eyes dilated; with a catch in his voice he cried:

"Love o' God, speak out! What are ye drivin' at?"

"Nothing has happened to your girls, but—"

"Then what in hell—?"

"Wait! I had to throw a little scare into you so you'd understand whatI'm getting at. Suppose one of your girls lay dead and unidentifiedin the morgue of a strange city and was about to be buried in thePotter's Field. You'd want to know about it, wouldn't you?"

"Are ye daft? Or has something really happened? If not, it's a damn fool question. What d'ye want?"

"Listen! You'd want her to have a decent burial, and you'd want her mother to know how she came to such a pass, wouldn't you?"

The Irishman mopped his brow uncertainly. "I would that."

"Then listen some more." Paul told the man his story, freely, earnestly, but rapidly; he painted the picture of a shy, lonely girl, homeless, hopeless and despondent in a great city, then the picture of two old people waiting in some distant farmhouse, sick at heart and uncertain, seeing their daughter's face in the firelight, hearing her sigh in the night wind. He talked in homely words that left the baggage-man's face grave, then he told how Burns, in a cruel jest, had sent a starving boy out to solve the mystery that had baffled the best detectives. When he had finished his listener cried:

"Shure it was a rotten trick, but why d'ye come here?"

"I want you to go through your baggage-room with me till we find a trunk which this key will fit."

"Come on with ye. I'm blamed if I don't admire yer nerve. Of course ye understand I've no right to let ye in—that's up to the station-master, but he's a grouchy divil." The speaker led Paul into a room piled high with trunks, then summoned two helpers. "We'll move every dam' wan of them till we fit your little key," he declared; then the four men fell to.

A blind search promised to be a job of hours, so Paul walked down the runway between the piles of trunks, using his eyes as he went. At least he could eliminate certain classes of baggage, and thus he might shorten the search; but half-way down the row he called sharply to the smashers:

"Come here, quick!" At his tone they came running. "Look! that one in the bottom row!" he cried. "That's it. Something tells me it is."

On the floor underneath the pile was a little, flat, battered tin trunk, pathetically old-fashioned and out of place among its more stylish neighbors; it was the kind of trunk Paul had seen in his mother's front room on the farm. It was bound about with a bit of rope.

His excitement infected the others, and the three smashers went at the pile, regardless of damage. Anderson's suspense bid fair to choke him; what if this were not the one? he asked himself. But what if it were the right one? What if this key he clutched in his cold palm should fit the lock? Paul pictured what he would see when he lifted the lid: a collection of forms, hangers, patterns, yard-sticks, a tape measure, and somewhere in it a little black yarn mitten. He prayed blindly for courage to withstand disappointment.

"There she is," panted his Irish friend, dragging the object out into the clear. The other men crowded closer. "Come on, lad. What are ye waitin' for?"

Anderson knelt before the little battered trunk and inserted the key. It was the keenest moment he had ever lived. He turned the key; then he was on his feet, cold, calm, his blue eyes glittering.

"Cut those ropes. Quick!" he ordered. "We're right."

The man at his side whipped out a knife and slashed twice.

"Come close, all of you," Paul directed, "and remember everything we find. You may have to testify."

He lifted the lid. On the top of the shallow tray lay a little black yarn mitten, the mate to that one in the city Morgue.

Anderson smiled into the faces of the men at his side. "That's it," he said, simply.

The tall Irishman laid a hand on his shoulder, saying: "Yer all right, boy. Don't get rattled,"

Paul opened the till and found precisely the paraphernalia he had expected: there were forms, hangers, patterns, yard-sticks, and a tape measure. In the compartment beneath were some neatly folded clothes, the needlework of which was fine, and in one corner a bundle of letters which Anderson examined with trembling fingers. They were addressed to "Miss Mabel Wilkes, Highland, Ontario, Canada, Care of Captain Wilkes."

The amateur detective replaced the letters carefully; he closed and locked the trunk; then he thanked his companions.

"If I had a dollar in the world," said he, "I'd ask you boys to have a drink, but I'm broke." Then he began to laugh foolishly, hysterically, until the raw-boned man clapped him on the back again.

"Straighten up, lad. Ye've been strained a bit too hard. I'll telephone for the cops."

In an instant Paul was himself. "You'll do nothing of the sort," he cried. "Why, man, you'll spoil the whole thing. I've worked this out alone, and if the police hear of it they'll notify all the papers and I'll have no story. Burns won't give me that job, and I'll be hungry again."

"True! I forgot that fat-headed divil of an editor. Well, you say the word and nobody won't know nothin' from us. Hey, boys?"

"Sure not," the other men agreed. This lad was one of their kind; he was up against it and fighting for his own, therefore they knew how to sympathize. But Paul had been seized with terror lest his story might get away from him, therefore he bade them a hasty good-by and sped up-town. His feet could not carry him swiftly enough.

Burns greeted him sourly when he burst into the editorial sanctum. It was not yet twenty-four hours since he had sent this fellow away with instructions not to return.

"Are you back again?" he snarled. "I heard about your assaulting Wells down at the City Hall. Don't try it on me or I'll have you pinched."

Paul laughed lightly. "I don't have to fight for my rights any more."

"Indeed! What are you grinning about? Have you found who that girl is?"

"I have."

"*What?*" Burns's jaw dropped limply; he leaned forward in his chair.

"Yes, sir! I've identified her."

The fat man was at first incredulous, then suspicious. "Don't try any tricks on me," he cried, warningly. "Don't try to put anything over—"

"Her name is Mabel Wilkes. She is the daughter of Captain Wilkes, of Highland, Ontario. She was a country dressmaker and lived with her people at that place. Her trunk is down at the Grand Trunk depot with the rest of her clothes in it, together with the mate to the mitten she had when she killed herself. I went through the trunk with the baggage-master, name Corrigan. Here's the key which I got from her purse at the coroner's office."

Burns fixed his round eyes upon the key, then he shifted them slowly to Anderson's face. "Why—why—this is amazing! I—I—" He cleared his throat nervously. "How did you discover all this? Who told you?"

"Nobody told me. I reasoned it out."

"But how—Good Lord! Am I dreaming?"

"I'm a good newspaper man. I've been telling you that every day. Maybe you'll believe me now."

Burns made no reply. Instead, he pushed a button and Wells, of the City Hall squad, entered, pausing abruptly at sight of Anderson. Giving the latter no time for words, Mr. Burns issued his instructions. On the instant he was the trained newspaper man again, cheating the clock dial and trimming minutes: his words were sharp and decisive.

"That suicide story has broken big and we've got a scoop. Anderson has identified her. Take the first G.T. train for Highland, Ontario, and find her father, Captain Wilkes. Wire me a full story about the girl Mabel, private life, history, everything. Take plenty of space. Have it in by midnight."

Wells's eyes were round, too; they were glued upon Paul with a hypnotic stare, but he managed to answer, "Yes, sir!" He was no longer grinning.

"Now, Anderson," the editor snapped, "get down-stairs and see if you can write the story. Pile it on thick—it's a corker."

"Very good, sir, but I'd like a little money," that elated youth demanded, boldly. "Just advance me fifty, will you? Remember I'm on top salary."

Burns made a wry face. "I'll send a check down to you," he promised, "but get at that story and make it a good one or I'll fire you tonight."

Anderson got. He found a desk and began to write feverishly. A half-hour later he read what he had written and tore it up. Another half-hour and he repeated the performance. Three times he wrote the tale and destroyed it, then paused, realizing blankly that as a newspaper story it was impossible. Every atom of interest surrounding the suicide of the girl grew out of his own efforts to solve the mystery. Nothing had happened, no new clues had been uncovered, no one had been implicated in the girl's death, there was no crime. It was a tale of Paul Anderson's deductions, nothing more, and it had no newspaper value. He found he had written about himself instead of about the girl.

He began again, this time laboriously eliminating himself, and when he had finished his story it was perhaps the poorest journalistic effort ever written.

Upon lagging feet he bore the copy to Burns's office. But the editor gave him no time for explanation, demanding, fiercely:

"Where's that check I sent you?"

"Here it is." The youth handed it to him. "Make a mistake?"

"I certainly did." Burns tore up the check before saying, "Now you get out, you bum, and stay out, or take the consequences."

"Get out? What for?"

"You know what for." Burns was quivering with rage. "You ran a good bluff and you nearly put it over; but I don't want to advertise myself as a jackass, so I shan't have you pinched unless you come back."

"Come back? I intend to stay. What's the matter?"

"I had an idea you were fourflushing," stormed the editor, "so I went down to the G.T. depot myself. There's no trunk of the sort there; Corrigan never saw you or anybody like you. Say, why didn't you walk out when you got that check? What made you come back?"

Anderson began to laugh softly. "Good old Corrigan! He's all right, isn't he? Well, he gets half of that check when you rewrite it, if I don't laugh myself to death before I get to the bank."

"What d'you mean?" Burns was impressed by the other's confidence.

"Nothing, except that I've found one square man in this village. One square guy is a pretty big percentage in a town the size of Buffalo. Corrigan wouldn't let you see the depot if I wasn't along. Put on your coat and come with me—yes, and bring a couple of hired men if it will make you feel any better."

At the depot he called the baggage-master to him, and said:

"Mr. Corrigan, this is Mr. Burns, the city editor of *TheIntelligencer*."

"That's what he told me," grinned the Irishman, utterly ignoring the young editor; "but you didn't give him no references, and I wouldn't take a chance."

Burns maintained a dignified silence; he said little even when the contents of the trunk were displayed to him. Nor did he open his mouth on the way back to the office. But when he was seated at his desk and had read Anderson's copy he spoke.

"This is the rottenest story ever turned in at this office," said he.

"I know it is," Paul agreed, frankly, then explained his difficulty in writing it.

"I'll do it myself," Burns told him. "Now, you go home and report tomorrow."

A very tired but a very happy young man routed out the landlady of a cheap boarding-house that night and hugged her like a bear, explaining joyously that he had done a great big thing. He waltzed her down the hall and back, while she clutched wildly at her flapping flannel wrapper and besought him to think of her other boarders. He waltzed her out of her bedroom slippers, gave her a smacking big kiss on her wrinkled cheek, then left her, breathless and scandalized, but all aflutter.

The city had read the story when Anderson awoke the next morning, for *The Intelligencer* had made a clean "beat," and Burns had played up the story tremendously, hence it was with jumping pulses that Paul scanned the front page of that journal. The further he read, however, the greater grew his indignation.

The history of Mabel Wilkes, under the magic touch of Burns, had, to be sure, become a wonderful, tragic story; but nowhere in it was mention made of Paul Anderson. In the patient and ingenious solution of the mystery of the girl's identity no credit was given to him. The cleverness and the perseverance of *The Buffalo Intelligencer* was exploited, its able reportorial staff was praised, its editorial shrewdness extolled, but that was all. When he had concluded reading the article Anderson realized that it was no more than a boost for the city editor, who it was plain to be seen, had uncovered the story bit by bit, greatly to the confusion of the police and the detective bureau.

It astounded as well as angered Paul to realize how cleverly Burns had covered him up, therefore the sense of injustice was strong in him when he entered the office. His enemy recognized his mood, and seemed to gloat over it.

"That was good work you did," he purred, "and I'll keep you on as long as you show ability. Of course you can't write yet, so I'll let you cover real-estate transactions and the market. I'll send for you when you're needed."

Anderson went back to his desk in silent rage. Real estate! Burns evidently intended to hold him down. His gloomy meditations were somewhat lightened by the congratulations of his fellow-reporters, who rather timidly ventured to introduce themselves. They understood the facts and they voiced a similar indignation to his. Burns had played him a rotten trick, they agreed. Not content with robbing his new reporter of the recognition which was justly his, the fellow was evidently determined to vent his spite in other ways. Well, that was like Burns. They voiced the opinion that Anderson would have a tough job getting through interference of the kind that their editor would throw in his way.

Hour after hour Paul sat around the office nursing his disappointment, waiting for Burns to send him out. About two o'clock Wells hurried into the office, bringing with him the afternoon papers still wet from the press. In his eyes was an unwonted sparkle. He crossed directly to Anderson and thrust out his palm.

"Old man, I want to shake with you," said he. "And I want to apologize for being a rotter."

Paul met him half-way, and the fellow went on:

"Burns gave us the wrong tip on you—said you were a joke—that's why we joshed you. But you showed us up, and I'm glad you did."

"Why—thank you!" stammered the new reporter, upon whom this manly apology had a strong effect. "It—it was more luck than anything."

"Luck nothing! You're a genius, and it's a dirty shame the way the boss tried to steal your credit. However, it seems he overreached himself." Wells began to laugh.

"*Tried* to steal it! Good Lord! he did steal it! How do you mean he overreached himself?"

"Haven't you seen the afternoon papers?"

"No."

"Well! Read 'em!" Mr. Wells spread his papers out before Paul, whose astonished eyes took in for a second time the story of the Wilkes suicide. But what a story!

He read his own name in big, black type; he read head-lines that told of a starving boy sent out on a hopeless assignment as a cruel joke; he read the story as it had really occurred, only told in the third person by an author who was neither ashamed nor afraid to give credit where it was due. The egotistical pretense of *The Buffalo Intelligencer* was torn to shreds, and ridicule was heaped upon its editor. Paul read nervously, breathlessly, until Wells interrupted him.

"I'm to blame for this," said he. "I couldn't stand for such a crooked deal. When I got in this morning and saw what that fat imbecile had done to you I tipped the true facts off to the others—all of the facts I knew. They got the rest from Corrigan, down at the Grand Trunk depot. Of course this means my job, if the old man finds it out; but I don't give a damn."

As yet Anderson was too dazed to grasp what had happened to him, but the other continued:

"The boys have had it in for Burns, on the quiet, for months, and nowI guess they're even."

"I—I don't know how to thank you," stammered Anderson.

"Don't try. You're a born reporter, and the other papers will give you a job even if the baby hippo in yonder fires you."

A boy touched Paul on the arm with the announcement, "Mr. Burns wants to see you."

"Oho!" cried Wells. "He's got the bad news. Gee! I'd like to hear what he says. I'll bet he's biting splinters out of his desk. Let me know what comes off, will you?"

When Anderson entered the office of his editor he was met by a white-faced man whose rage had him so by the throat that speech for a moment was impossible. Beneath Mr. Burns's feet, and strewn broadcast about the room, were the crumpled sheets of the afternoon papers. Burns glared at the newcomer for a moment, then he extended a shaking finger, crying, furiously:

"You did this!"

"Did what?"

"You put up this job. You made a fool of me!"

"No, sir! I did not. Your parents saw to that."

"Don't tell me you didn't, you—you damned ungrateful—" Burns seemed about to assault his reporter, but restrained himself. "You're fired! Do you understand? Fired—discharged."

"Say, Burns—"

"Not a word. I'm done with you. I—"

"Just a minute," young Anderson cried, in a tone that stilled the other. "I'm fired, am I, for something I didn't do? Very well! I'm glad of it, for now you can't stand in my way. You tried to double-cross me and failed. You robbed me of what was mine and got caught at it. You're a big man, in your way, Burns, but some day people will tell you that the biggest thing you ever did was to fire Paul Anderson. That's how small you'll be, and that's how big I'm going to grow. You've 'welched' on your own word; but there's one thing you gave me that you can't take away, and that's the knowledge that

I'm a newspaper man and a good one. Now just one thing more: I'm broke today, but I'm going to lick you as soon as I save up enough for the fine."

With studied insolence the speaker put on his hat, slammed the door behind him, and walked out of *The Intelligencer* office, leaving the apoplectic editor thereof secure in the breathless knowledge that for once in his life he had heard the truth spoken. Mr. Burns wondered how long it would take that young bully to save up ten dollars and costs.

OUT OF THE NIGHT

"There is but one remedy for your complaint." Doctor Suydam settled deeper into his chair. "Marry the girl."

"That is the only piece of your professional advice I ever cared to follow. But how?"

"Any way you can—use force if necessary—only marry her. Otherwise I predict all sorts of complications for you—melancholia, brain-fag, bankruptcy—"

Austin laughed. "Could you write me a prescription?"

"Oh, she'll have you, Bob. You don't seem to realize that you are a good catch."

Austin finished buckling his puttee before rising to his full height. "That doesn't mean anything to her. She doesn't need to make a catch."

"Nonsense! She's just like all the others, only richer and nicer. Go at her as if she were the corn-market; she won't be half so hard to corner. You have made a name for yourself, and a blamed sight more money than you deserve; you are young—comparatively, I mean."

The elder man stroked his shock of iron-gray hair for answer.

"Well, at any rate you are a picturesque personage, even if you can't wear riding-clothes."

"Doesn't a man look like the devil in these togs?" Austin posed awkwardly in front of a mirror.

"There's only one person who can look worse in riding-clothes than a man—that's a woman."

"What heresy, particularly in a society doctor! But I agree with you. I learned to ride on her account, you know. As a matter of fact, I hate it. The sight of a horse fills me with terror."

Doctor Suydam laughed outright at this. "She tells me that you have a very good seat."

"Really!" Austin's eyes gleamed suddenly. "You know I never had a chance to ride when I was a youngster—in fact, I never had an opportunity to do anything except work. That's what makes me so crude and awkward. What I know I have picked up during the last few years."

"You make me tired!" declared the former. "You aren't—"

"Oh, I don't skate on waxed floors nor spill tea, nor clutch at my chauffeur in a tight place, but you know what I mean. I feel lonesome in a dress-suit, a butler fills me with gloom, and—Well, I'm not one of you, that's all."

"Perhaps that's what makes a hit with Marmion. She's used to the other kind."

"It seems to me that I have always worked," ruminated the former speaker. "I don't remember that I ever had time to play, even after I came to the city. It's a mighty sad thing to rob a boy of his childhood; it makes him a dull, unattractive sort when he grows up. I used to read about people like Miss Moore, but I never expected to know them until I met you. Of course, that corn deal rather changed things."

"Well, I should rather say it did!" Suydam agreed, with emphasis.

"The result is that when I am with her I forget the few things I have done that are worth while, and I become the farm-hand again. I'm naturally rough and angular, and she sees it."

"Oh, you're too sensitive! You have a heart like a girl underneath that saturnine front of yours, and while you look like the Sphinx, you are really as much of a kid at heart as I am. Where do you ride to-day?"

"Riverside Drive."

"What horse is she riding?"

"Pointer."

The doctor shook his head. "Too many automobiles on the Drive. He's a rotten nag for a woman, anyhow. His mouth is as tough as a stirrup, and he has the disposition of a tarantula. Why doesn't she stick to the Park?"

"You know Marmion."

"Say, wouldn't it be great if Pointer bolted and you saved her life? She couldn't refuse you then."

Austin laughed. "That's not exactly the way I'd care to win her. However, if Pointer bolted I'd probably get rattled and fall off my own horse. I don't like the brutes. Come on, I'm late."

"That's right," grumbled the other, "leave me here while you make love to the nicest girl in New York. I'm going down to the office and amputate somebody."

They descended the single flight to the street, where Austin's groom was struggling with a huge black.

"It's coming pretty soft for you brokers," the doctor growled, as his companion swung himself into the saddle. "The next time I get a friend I'll keep him to myself."

Austin leaned forward with a look of grave anxiety upon his rugged features and said: "Wish me luck, Doc. I'm going to ask her to-day."

"Good for you, old fellow." There was great fondness in the younger man's eyes as he wrung the rider's hand and waved him adieu, then watched him disappear around the corner.

"She'll take him," he mused, half aloud. "She's a sensible girl even if all New York has done its best to spoil her." He hailed a taxicab and was hurried to his office.

It was perhaps two hours later that he was called on the telephone.

"Hello! Yes, yes! What is it?" he cried, irritably. "Mercy Hospital! *What?*" The young physician started. "Hurt, you say? Run-away? Go on, quick!" He listened with whitening face, then broke in abruptly: "Of course he sent for me. I'll be right up."

He slammed the receiver upon its hook and, seizing his hat, bolted out through a waiting-room full of patients. His car was in readiness, and he called to his chauffeur in such tones that the fellow vaulted to his seat.

"Go up Madison Avenue; there's less traffic there. And for God's sake *hurry!*"

During two years' service with New York's most fashionable physician the driver had never received a command like this, and he opened up his machine. A policeman warned him at Thirty-third Street and the car slowed down, at which Suydam leaned forward, crying, roughly:

"To hell with regulations! There's a man dying!"

The last word was jerked from him as he was snapped back into his seat. Regardless of admonitory shouts from patrolmen, the French car sang its growing song, while truck-drivers bellowed curses and pedestrians fled from crossings at the scream of its siren. A cross-town car blocked them, and the brakes screeched in agony, while Doctor Suydam was well-nigh catapulted into the street; then they were under way again, with the car leaping from speed to speed. It was the first time the driver had ever dared to disregard those upraised, white-gloved hands, and it filled his joy-riding soul with exultation. A street repair loomed ahead, whereupon, with a sickening skid, they swung into a side street; the gears clashed again, and an instant later they shot out upon Fifth Avenue. At the next corner they lay motionless in a blockade, while the motor shuddered; then they dodged through an opening where the mud-guards missed by an inch and were whirling west toward Broadway. At 109th Street a bicycle officer stared in amazement at the dwindling number beneath the rear axle, then ducked his head and began to pedal. He overhauled the speeding machine as it throbbed before the doors of Mercy Hospital, to be greeted by a grinning chauffeur who waved him toward the building and told of a doctor's urgency.

Inside, Doctor Suydam, pallid of face and shaking in a most unprofessional manner, was bending over a figure in riding-clothes, the figure of a tall, muscular man who lay silent, deaf to his words of greeting.

They told him all there was to tell in the deadly, impersonal way of hospitals, while he nodded swift comprehension. There had been a runaway—a woman on a big, white-eyed bay, that had taken fright at an automobile; a swift rush up the Driveway, a lunge over the neck of the pursuing horse, then a man wrenched from his saddle and dragged beneath cruel, murderous hoofs. The bay had gone down, and the woman was senseless when the ambulance arrived, but she had revived and had been hurried to her home. In the man's hand they had found the fragment of a bridle rein gripped with such desperation that they could not remove it until he regained consciousness. He had asked regarding the girl's safety, then sighed himself into oblivion again. They told Suydam that he would die.

With sick heart the listener cursed all high-spirited women and high-strung horses, declaring them to be works of the devil, like automobiles; then he went back to the side of his friend, where other hands less unsteady were at work.

"Poor lonely old Bob!" he murmured. "Not a soul to care except Marmion and me, and God knows whether she cares or not."

* * * * *

But Robert Austin did not die, although the attending surgeons said he would, said he should, in fact, unless all the teachings of their science were at fault. He even offended the traditions of the hospital by being removed to his own apartments in a week. There Suydam, who had watched him night and day, told him that Miss Moore had a broken shoulder and hence could not come to see him.

"Poor girl!" said Austin, faintly. "If I'd known more about horses I might have saved her."

"If you'd known more about horses you'd have let Pointer run," declared his friend. "Nobody but an idiot or a Bob Austin would have taken the chance you did. How is your head?"

The sick man closed his eyes wearily. "It hurts all the time. What's the matter with it?"

"We've none of us been able to discover what isn't the matter with it! Why in thunder did you hold on so long?"

"Because I—I love her, I suppose."

"Did you ask her to marry you?" Suydam had been itching to ask the question for days.

"No, I was just getting to it when Pointer bolted. I—I'm slow at such things." There was a moment's pause. "Doc, what's the matter with my eyes? I can't see very well."

"Don't talk so much," ordered the physician. "You're lucky to be here at all. Thanks to that copper-riveted constitution of yours, you'll get well."

But it seemed that the patient was fated to disappoint the predictions of his friend as well as those of the surgeons at Mercy Hospital. He did not recover in a manner satisfactory to his medical adviser, and although he regained the most of his bodily vigor, the injury to his eyes baffled even the most skilled specialists.

He was very brave about it, however, and wrung the heart of Doctor Suydam by the uncomplaining fortitude with which he bore examination after examination. Learned oculists theorized vaporously about optic atrophies, fractures, and brain pressures of one sort and another; and meanwhile Robert Austin, in the highest perfection of bodily vigor, in the fullest possession of those faculties that had raised him from an unschooled farm-boy to a position of eminence in the business world, went slowly blind. The shadows crept in upon him with a deadly, merciless certainty that would have filled the stoutest heart with gloom, and yet he maintained a smiling stoicism that deceived all but his closest associates. To Doctor Suydam, however, the incontestable progress of the malady was frightfully tragic. He alone knew the man's abundant spirits, his lofty ambitions, and his active habits. He alone knew of the overmastering love that had come so late and was destined to go unvoiced, and he raved at the maddening limits of his profession. In Austin's presence he strove to be cheerful and to lighten the burden he knew was crushing the sick man; but at other times he bent every energy toward a discovery of some means to check the affliction, some hand more skilled than those he knew of. In time, however, he recognized the futility of his efforts, and resigned himself to the worst. He had a furious desire to acquaint Marmion Moore with the truth, and to tell her, with all the brutal frankness he could muster, of her part in this calamity. But Austin would not hear of it.

"She doesn't dream of the truth," the invalid told him. "And I don't want her to learn. She thinks I'm merely weak, and it grieves her terribly to know that I haven't recovered. If she really knew—it might ruin her life, for she is a girl who feels deeply. I want to spare her that; it's the least I can do."

"But she'll find it out some time."

"I think not. She comes to see me every day—"

"Every day?"

"Yes. I'm expecting her soon."

"And she doesn't know?"

Austin shook his head. "I never let her see there's anything the matter with my sight. She drives up with her mother, and I wait for her there in the bay-window. It's getting hard for me to distinguish her now, but I recognize the hoofbeats—I can tell them every time."

"But—I don't understand."

"I pretend to be very weak," explained the elder man, with a guilty flush. "I sit in the big chair yonder and my Jap boy waits on her. She is very kind." Austin's voice grew husky. "I'm sorry to lose sight of the Park out yonder, and the trees and the children—they're growing indistinct. I—I like children. I've always wanted some for myself. I've dreamed about—that." His thin, haggard face broke into a wistful smile. "I guess that is all over with now."

"Why?" questioned Suydam, savagely. "Why don't you ask her to marry you, Bob? She couldn't refuse—and God knows you need her."

"That's just it; she couldn't refuse. This is the sort of thing a fellow must bear alone. She's too young, and beautiful, and fine to be harnessed up to a worn-out old—cripple."

"Cripple!" The other choked. "Don't talk like that. Don't be so blamed resigned. It tears my heart out. I—I—why, I believe I feel this more than you do."

Austin turned his face to the speaker with a look of such tragic suffering that the younger man fell silent.

"I'm glad I can hide my feelings," Austin told him, slowly, "for that is what I have to do every instant she is with me. I don't wish to inflict unnecessary pain upon my friends, but don't you suppose I know what this means? It means the destruction of all my fine hopes, the death of all I hold dear in the world. I love my work, for I am—or I was—a success; this means I must give it up. I'm strong in body and brain; this robs me of my usefulness. All my life I have prayed that I might some time love a woman; that time has come, but this means I must give her up and be lonely all my days. I must grope my way through the dark with never a ray of light to guide me. Do you know how awful the darkness is?" He clasped his hands tightly. "I must go hungering through the night, with a voiceless love to torture me. Just at the crowning point of my life I've been snuffed out. I must fall behind and see my friends desert me."

"Bob!" cried the other, in shocked denial.

"Oh, you know it will come to that. People don't like to feel pity forever tugging at them. I've been a lonely fellow and my friends are numbered. For a time they will come to see me, and try to cheer me up; they will even try to include me in their pleasures; then when it is no longer a new story and their commiseration has worn itself out they will gradually fall away. It always happens so. I'll be 'poor Bob Austin,' and I'll go feeling my way through life an object of pity, a stumbling, incomplete thing that has no place to fill, no object to work for, no one to care. God! I'm not the sort to go blind! Where's the justice of it? I've lived clean. Why did this happen to me? Why? Why? I know what the world is; I've been a part of it. I've seen the spring and the autumn colors and I've watched the sunsets. I've looked into men's faces and read their souls, and when you've done that you can't live in darkness. I can't and—I won't!"

"What do you mean?"

"I'm going away."

"When? Where?"

"When I can no longer see Marmion Moore and before my affliction becomes known to her. Where—you can guess."

"Oh, that's cowardly, Bob! You're not that sort. You mustn't! It's unbelievable," his friend cried, in a panic.

Austin smiled bitterly. "We have discussed that too often, and—I'm not sure that what I intend doing is cowardly. I can't go now, for the thing is too fresh in her memory, she might learn the truth and hold herself to blame; but when she has lost the first shock of it I shall walk out quietly and she won't even suspect. Other interests will come into her life; I'll be only a memory. Then—" After a pause he went on, "I couldn't bear to see her drop away with the rest."

"Don't give up yet," urged the physician. "She is leaving for the summer, and while she is gone we'll try that Berlin chap. He'll be here in August."

"And he will fail, as the others did. He will lecture some clinic about me, that's all. Marmion will hear that my eyes have given out from overwork, or something like that. Then I'll go abroad, and—I won't come back." Austin, divining the rebellion in his friend's heart, said, quickly: "You're the only one who could enlighten her, Doc, but you won't do it. You owe me too much."

"I—I suppose I do," acknowledged Suydam, slowly. "I owe you more thanI can ever repay—"

"Wait—" The sick man raised his hand, while a sudden light blazed up in his face. "She's coming!"

To the doctor's trained ear the noises of the street rose in a confused murmur, but Austin spoke in an awed, breathless tone, almost as if he were clairvoyant.

"I can hear the horses. She's coming to—see me."

"I'll go," exclaimed the visitor, quickly, but the other shook his head.

"I'd rather have you stay."

Austin was poised in an attitude of the intensest alertness, his angular, awkward body was drawn to its full height, his lean face was lighted by some hidden fire that lent it almost beauty.

"She's getting out of the carriage," he cried, in a nervous voice; then he felt his way to his accustomed arm-chair. Suydam was about to go to the bay-window when he paused, regarding his friend curiously.

"What are you doing?"

The blind man had begun to beat time with his hand, counting under his breath: "One! Two! Three!—"

"She'll knock when I reach twenty-five. 'Sh! 'sh!" He continued his pantomime, and Suydam realized that from repeated practice Austin had gauged to a nicety the seconds Marmion Moore required to mount the stairs. This was his means of holding himself in check. True to prediction, at

"Twenty-five" a gentle knock sounded, and Suydam opened the door.

"Come in, Marmion."

The girl paused for the briefest instant on the threshold, and the doctor noted her fleeting disappointment at seeing him; then she took his hand.

"This *is* a surprise," she exclaimed. "I haven't seen you for ever so long."

Her anxious glance swept past him to the big, awkward figure against the window's light. Austin was rising with apparent difficulty, and she glided to him.

"Please! Don't rise! How many times have I told you not to exert yourself?"

Suydam noted the gentle, proprietary tone of her voice, and it amazed him.

"I—am very glad that you came to see me." The afflicted man's voice was jerky and unmusical. "How are you to-day, Miss?"

"He shouldn't rise, should he?" Miss Moore appealed to the physician."He is very weak and shouldn't exert himself."

The doctor wished that his friend might see the girl's face as he saw it; he suddenly began to doubt his own judgment of women.

"Oh, I'm doing finely," Austin announced. "Won't you be seated?" He waved a comprehensive gesture, and Suydam, marveling at the manner in which the fellow concealed his infirmity, brought a chair for the caller.

"I came alone to-day. Mother is shopping," Miss Moore was saying. "See! I brought these flowers to cheer up your room." She held up a great bunch of sweet peas. "I love the pink ones, don't you?"

Austin addressed the doctor. "Miss Moore has been very kind to me; I'm afraid she feels it her duty—"

"No! No!" cried the girl.

"She rarely misses a day, and she always brings flowers. I'm very fond of bright colors."

Suydam cursed at the stiff formality in the man's tone. How could any woman see past that glacial front and glimpse the big, aching heart beyond? Austin was harsh and repellent when the least bit self-conscious, and now he was striving deliberately to heighten the effect.

The physician wondered why Marmion Moore had gone even thus far in showing her gratitude, for she was not the self-sacrificing kind. As for a love match between two such opposite types, Suydam could not conceive of it. Even if the girl understood the sweet, simple nature of this man, even if she felt her own affections answer to his, Suydam believed he knew the women of her set too well to imagine that she could bring herself to marry a blind man, particularly one of no address.

"We leave for the mountains to-morrow," Marmion said, "so I came to say good-by, for a time."

"I—shall miss your visits," Austin could not disguise his genuine regret, "but when you return I shall be thoroughly recovered. Perhaps we can ride again."

"Never!" declared Miss Moore. "I shall never ride again. Think of the suffering I've caused you. I—I—am dreadfully sorry."

To Suydam's amazement, he saw the speaker's eyes fill with tears. A doubt concerning the correctness of his surmises came over him and he rose quickly. After all, he reflected, she might see and love the real Bob as he did, and if so she might wish to be alone with him in this last hour. But Austin laughed at his friend's muttered excuse.

"You know there's nobody waiting for you. That's only a pretense to find livelier company. You promised to dine with me." To Miss Moore he explained: "He isn't really busy; why, he has been complaining for an hour that the heat has driven all his patients to the country, and that he is dying of idleness."

The girl's expression altered curiously. She shrank as if wounded; she scanned the speaker's face with startled eyes before turning with a strained smile to say:

"So, Doctor, we caught you that time. That comes from being a high-priced society physician. Why don't you practise among the masses? I believe the poor are always in need of help."

"I really have an engagement," Suydam muttered.

"Then break it for Mr. Austin's sake. He is lonely and—I must be going in a moment."

The three talked for a time in the manner all people adopt for a sick-room, then the girl rose and said, with her palm in Austin's hand:

"I owe you so much that I can never hope to repay you, but you—you will come to see me frequently this season. Promise! You won't hide yourself, will you?"

The blind man smiled his thanks and spoke his farewell with meaningless politeness; then, as the physician prepared to see her to her carriage, Miss Moore said:

"No! Please stay and gossip with our invalid. It's only a step."

She walked quickly to the door, flashed them a smile, and was gone.

Suydam heard his patient counting as before.

"One! Two! Three—!"

At "Twenty-five" the elder man groped his way to the open bay-window and bowed at the carriage below. There came the sound of hoofs and rolling wheels, and the doctor, who had taken stand beside his friend, saw Marmion Moore turn in her seat and wave a last adieu. Austin continued to nod and smile in her direction, even after the carriage was lost to view; then he felt his way back to the arm-chair and sank limply into it.

"Gone! I—I'll never be able to see her again."

Suydam's throat tightened miserably. "Could you see her at all?"

"Only her outlines; but when she comes back in the fall I'll be as blind as a bat." He raised an unsteady hand to his head and closed his eyes. "I can stand anything except that! To lose sight of her dear face—" The force of his emotion wrenched a groan from him.

"I don't know what to make of her," said the other. "Why didn't you let me go, Bob? It was her last good-by; she wanted to be alone with you. She might have—"

"That's it!" exclaimed Austin. "I was afraid of myself; afraid I'd speak if I had the chance." His voice was husky as he went on. "It's hard—hard, for sometimes I think she loves me, she's so sweet and so tender. At such times I'm a god. But I know it can't be; that it is only pity and gratitude that prompts her. Heaven knows I'm uncouth enough at best, but now I have to exaggerate my rudeness. I play a part—the part of a lumbering, stupid lout, while my heart is breaking." He bowed his head in his hands, closing his dry, feverish eyes once more. "It's cruelly hard. I can't keep it up."

The other man laid a hand on his shoulder, saying: "I don't know whether you're doing right or not. I half suspect you are doing Marmion a bitter wrong."

"Oh, but she can't—she *can't* love me!" Austin rose as if frightened. "She might yield to her impulse and—well, marry me, for she has a heart of gold, but it wouldn't last. She would learn some time that it wasn't real love that prompted the sacrifice. Then I should die."

The specialist from Berlin came, but he refused to operate, declaring bluntly that there was no use, and all during the long, hot summer days Robert Austin sat beside his open window watching the light die out of the world, waiting, waiting, for the time to make his sacrifice.

Suydam read Marmion's cheery letters aloud, wondering the while at the wistful note they sounded now and then. He answered them in his own handwriting, which she had never seen.

One day came the announcement that she was returning the first week in October. Already September was partly gone, so Austin decided to sail in a week. At his dictation Suydam wrote to her, saying that the strain of overwork had rendered a long vacation necessary. The doctor writhed internally as he penned the careful sentences, wondering if the hurt of the deliberately chosen words would prevent her sensing the truth back of them. As days passed and no answer came he judged it had.

The apartment was stripped and bare, the trunks were packed on the afternoon before Austin's departure. All through the dreary mockery of the process the blind man had withstood his friend's appeal, his stern face set, his heavy heart full of a despairing stubbornness. Now, being alone at last, he groped his way about the premises to fix them in his memory; then he sank into his chair beside the window.

He heard a knock at the door and summoned the stranger to enter, then he rose with a gasp of dismay. Marmion Moore was greeting him with sweet, yet hesitating effusiveness.

"I—I thought you were not coming back until next week," he stammered.

"We changed our plans." She searched his face as best she could in the shaded light, a strange, anxious expression upon her own. "Your letter surprised me."

"The doctor's orders," he said, carelessly. "They say I have broken down."

"I know! I know what caused it!" she panted. "You never recovered from that accident. You did not tell me the truth. I've always felt that you were hiding something from me. Why? Oh, why?"

"Nonsense!" He undertook to laugh, but failed in a ghastly manner."I've been working too hard. Now I'm paying the penalty."

"How long will you be gone?" she queried.

"Oh, I haven't decided. A long time, however." His tone bewildered her. "It is the first vacation I ever had; I want to make the most of it."

"You—you were going away without saying good-by to—your old friends?" Her lips were white, and her brave attempt to smile would have told him the truth had he seen it, but he only had her tone to go by, so he answered, indifferently:

"All my arrangements were made; I couldn't wait."

"You are offended with me," Miss Moore said, after a pause. "How haveI hurt you? What is it; please? I—I have been too forward, perhaps?"

Austin dared not trust himself to answer, and when he made no sign the girl went on, painfully:

"I'm sorry. I didn't want to seem bold. I owe you so much; we were such good friends—" In spite of her efforts her voice showed her suffering.

The man felt his lonely heart swell with the wild impulse to tell her all, to voice his love in one breathless torrent of words that would undeceive her. The strain of repression lent him added brusqueness when he strove to explain, and his coldness left her sorely hurt. His indifference filled her with a sense of betrayal; it chilled the impulsive yearning in her breast. She had battled long with herself before coming and now she repented of her rashness, for it was plain he did not need her. This certainty left her sick and listless, therefore she bade him adieu a few moments later, and with aching throat went blindly out and down the stairs.

The instant she was gone Austin leaped to his feet; the agony of death was upon his features. Breathlessly he began to count:

"One! Two! Three—!"

He felt himself smothering, and with one sweep of his hand ripped the collar from his throat.

"Five! Six! Seven—!"

He was battling like a drowning man, for, in truth, the very breath of his life was leaving him. A drumming came into his ears. He felt that he must call out to her before it was too late. He was counting aloud now, his voice like the moan of a man on the rack.

"Nine! Ten—!"

A frenzy to voice his sufferings swept over him, but he held himself. Only a moment more and she would be gone; her life would be spared this dark shadow, and she would never know, but he—he would indeed be face to face with darkness.

Toward the last he was reeling, but he continued to tell off the seconds with the monotonous regularity of a timepiece, his every power centered on that process. The idea came to him that he was counting his own flickering pulse-throbs for the last time. With a tremendous effort of will he smoothed his face and felt his way to the open window, for by now she must be entering the landau. A moment later and she would turn to waft him her last adieu. Her last! God! How the seconds lagged! That infernal thumping in his ears had drowned the noises from the street below. He felt that for all time the torture of this moment would live with him.

Then he smiled! He smiled blindly out into the glaring sunlight, and bowed. And bowed and smiled again, clinging to the window-casing to support himself. By now she must have reached the corner. He freed one hand and waved it gaily, then with outflung arms he stumbled back into the room, the hot tears coursing down his cheeks.

Marmion Moore halted upon the stairs and felt mechanically for her gold chatelaine. She recalled dropping it upon the center-table as she went forward with hands outstretched to Austin; so she turned back, then hesitated. But he was leaving to-morrow; surely he would not misinterpret the meaning of her reappearance. Summoning her self-control, she remounted the stairs quickly.

The door was half ajar as she had left it in her confusion. Mustering a careless smile, she was about to knock, then paused. Austin was facing her in the middle of the room, beating time. He was counting aloud—but was that his voice? In the brief instant she had been gone he had changed astoundingly. Moreover, notwithstanding the fact that she stood plainly revealed, he made no sign of recognition, but merely counted on and on, with the voice of a dying man. She divined that something was sadly amiss; she wondered for an instant if the man had lost his senses.

She stood transfixed, half-minded to flee, yet held by some pitying desire to help; then she saw him reach forward and grope his way uncertainly to the window. In his progress he stumbled against a chair; he had to feel for the casing. Then she knew.

Marmion Moore found herself inside the room, staring with wide, affrighted eyes at the man whose life she had spoiled. She pressed her hands to her bosom to still its heavings. She saw Austin nodding down at the street below; she saw his ghastly attempt to smile; she heard the breath sighing from his lungs and heard him muttering her name. Then he turned and lurched past her, groping, groping for his chair. She cried out, sharply, in a stricken voice:

"Mr. Austin!"

The man froze in his tracks; he swung his head slowly from side to side, as if listening.

"What!" The word came like the crack of a gun. Then, after a moment, "Marmion!" He spoke her name as if to test his own hearing. It was the first time she had ever heard him use it.

She slipped forward until within an arm's-length of him, then stretched forth a wildly shaking hand and passed it before his unwinking eyes, as if she still disbelieved. Then he heard her moan.

"Marmion!" he cried again. "My God! little girl, I—thought I heard you go!"

"Then this, *this* is the reason," she said. "Oh-h-h!"

"What are you doing here? Why did you come back?" he demanded, brutally.

"I forgot my—No! God sent me back!"

There was a pause, during which the man strove to master himself; then he asked, in the same harsh accents:

"How long have you been here?"

"Long enough to see—and to understand."

"Well, you know the truth at last. I—have gone—blind." The last word caused his lips to twitch. He knew from the sound that she was weeping bitterly. "Please don't. I've used my eyes too much, that is all. It is—nothing."

"No! No! No!" she said, brokenly. "Don't you think I understand? Don't you think I see it all now? But why—why didn't you tell me? Why?" When he did not answer she repeated: "God sent me back. I—I was not meant to be so unhappy."

Austin felt himself shaken as if by a panic. He cried, hurriedly: "You see, we've been such good friends. I knew it would distress you. I—wanted to spare you that! You were a good comrade to me; we were like chums. Yes, we were chums. No friend could have been dearer to me than you, Miss Moore. I never had a sister, you know. I—I thought of you that way, and I—" He was struggling desperately to save the girl, but his incoherent words died on his lips when he felt her come close and lay her cheek against his arm.

"You mustn't try to deceive me any more," she said, gently. "I was here. I know the truth, and—I want to be happy."

Even then he stood dazed and disbelieving until she continued:

"I know that you love me, and that I love you."

"It is pity!" he exclaimed, hoarsely. "You don't mean it."

But she drew herself closer to him and turned her tear-stained face up to his, saying, wistfully, "If your dear eyes could have seen, they would have told you long ago."

"Oh, my love!" He was too weak to resist longer. His arms were trembling as they enfolded her, but in his heart was a gladness that comes to but few men.

"And you won't go away without me, will you?" she questioned, fearfully.

"No, no!" he breathed. "Oh, Marmion, I have lost a little, but I have gained much! God has been good to me."

THE REAL AND THE MAKE-BELIEVE

On his way down-town Phillips stopped at a Subway news-stand and bought all the morning papers. He acknowledged that he was vastly excited. As he turned in at the stage door he thrilled at sight of the big electric sign over the theater, pallid now in the morning sunshine, but symbolizing in frosted letters the thing for which he had toiled and fought, had hoped and despaired these many years. There it hung, a dream come true, and it read, "A Woman's Thrall, By Henry Phillips."

The stage-door man greeted him with a toothless smile and handed him a bundle of telegrams, mumbling: "I knew it would go over, Mr. Phillips. The notices are swell, ain't they?"

"They seem to be."

"I ain't seen their equal since 'The Music Master' opened. We'll run a year."

This differed from the feverish, half-hysterical praise of the evening before. Phillips had made allowances then for the spell of a first-night enthusiasm and had prepared himself for a rude awakening this morning—he had seen too many plays fail, to put much faith in the fulsomeness of first-nighters—but the words of the doorman carried conviction. He had felt confident up to the last moment, to be sure, for he knew he had put his life's best work into this drama, and he believed he had written with a master's cunning; nevertheless, when his message had gone forth a sudden panic had seized him. He had begun to fear that his judgment was distorted by his nearness to the play, or that his absorption in it had blinded him to its defects. It was evident now, however, that these fears had been ill-founded, for no play could receive such laudatory reviews as these and fail to set New-Yorkers aflame.

Certain printed sentences kept dancing through his memory: "Unknown dramatist of tremendous power," "A love story so pitiless, so true, that it electrifies," "The deep cry of a suffering heart," "Norma Berwynd enters the galaxy of stars."

That last sentence was the most significant, the most wonderful of all. Norma Berwynd a star! Phillips could scarcely credit it; he wondered if she had the faintest notion of how or why her triumph had been effected.

The property man met him, and he too was smiling.

"I just came from the office," he began. "Say! they're raving. It's the biggest hit in ten years."

"Oh, come now! It's too early for the afternoon papers—"

"The papers be blowed! It's the public that makes a play; the whole town knows about this one already. It's in and over, I tell you; we'll sell out tonight. Believe me, this is a knock-out—a regular bull's-eye. It won't take no government bonds to bridge us over the next two weeks."

"Did you get the new props?"

"Sure! The electrician is working on the drop light for the first act; we'll have a better glass crash tonight, and I've got a brand-new dagger. That other knife was all right, but Mr. Francis forgot how to handle it."

"Nevertheless, it's dangerous. We came near having a real tragedy last evening. Don't let's take any more chances."

"It wasn't my fault, on the level," the property man insisted."Francis always 'goes up' at an opening."

"Thank Heaven the papers didn't notice it."

"Huh! We could *afford* to kill an actor for notices like them. It would make great advertising and please the critics. Say! I knew this show was a hit."

Under the dim-lit vault of the stage Phillips found the third-act scenery set for the rehearsal he had called, then, having given his instructions to the wardrobe woman, he drew a chair up before a bunch light and prepared to read for a second time the morning reviews.

He had attempted to read them at breakfast, but his wife—The playwright sighed heavily at the memory of that scene. Léontine had been very unjust, as usual. Her temper had run away with her again and had forced him to leave the house with his splendid triumph spoiled, his first taste of victory like ashes in his mouth. He was, in a way, accustomed to these endless, senseless rows, but their increasing frequency was becoming more and more trying, and he was beginning to doubt his ability to stand them much longer. It seemed particularly nasty of Léontine to seize upon this occasion to vent her open dislike of him—their relations were already sufficiently strained. Marriage, all at once, assumed a very lopsided aspect to the playwright; he had given so much and received so little.

With an effort he dismissed the subject from his mind and set himself to the more pleasant task of looking at his play through the eyes of the reviewers.

They had been very fair, he decided at last. Their only criticism was one which he had known to be inevitable, therefore he felt no resentment.

"Norma Berwynd was superb," he read; "she combined with rare beauty a personality at once bewitching and natural. She gave life to her lines; she was deep, intense, true; she rose to her emotional heights in a burst of power which electrified the audience. We cannot but wonder why such an artist has remained so long undiscovered."

The dramatist smiled; surely that was sufficient praise to compensate him for the miserable experience he had just undergone. He read further:

"Alas, that the same kind things cannot be said of Irving Francis, whose name is blazoned forth in letters of fire above the theater. He has established himself as one of America's brightest stars; but the rôle of John Danton does not enhance his reputation. In his lighter scenes he was delightful, but his emotional moments did not ring true. In the white-hot climax of the third act, for instance, which is the big scene of the play, he was stiff, unnatural, unconvincing. Either he saw Miss Berwynd taking the honors of stardom away from him and generously submerged his own talent in order to enhance her triumph, or it is but another proof of the statement that husband and wife do not make convincing lovers in the realm of the make-believe. It was surely due to no lack of opportunity on his part—"

So the writer thought Irving Francis had voluntarily allowed his wife to rival him. Phillips smiled at this. Some actors might be capable of such generosity, but hardly Irving Francis. He recalled the man's insistent demands during rehearsals that the script be changed to build up his own part and undermine that of his wife; the many heated arguments which had even threatened to prevent the final performance of the piece. Irving's egotism had blinded him to the true result of these quarrels, for although he had been given more lines, more scenes, Phillips had seen to it that Norma was the one to really profit by the changes. Author and star had been upon the verge of rupture more than once during that heartbreaking period of preparation, but Phillips was supremely glad now that he had held himself in control. Léontine's constant nagging had borne fruit, after all, in that it had at least taught him to bite down on his words, and to smile at provocation.

Yes! Norma Berwynd was a star in spite of herself, in spite of her husband. She was no longer merely the wife of Irving Francis, the popular idol. Phillips was glad that she did not know how long it had taken him to effect her independence, nor the price he had paid for it, since, under the circumstances, the truth could help neither of them.

He was aroused from his abstraction by the rustle of a woman's garments, and leaped to his feet with a glad light in his eyes, only to find Léontine, his wife, confronting him.

"Oh!" he said; then with an effort, "What is the matter?"

"Nothing."

"I didn't know you were coming down-town."

"Whom were you expecting?" Léontine mocked, with that slight accent which betrayed her Gallic origin.

"No one."

She regarded him with fixed hostility. "I came down to see your rehearsal. You don't object, I hope?"

"Why should I object?" Phillips turned away with a shrug. "I'm surprised, that's all—after what you said this morning. Isn't your interest in the play a trifle—tardy?"

"No! I've been greatly interested in it all the time. I read it several times in manuscript."

"Indeed! I didn't know that. It won't be much of a rehearsal this morning; I'm merely going to run over the third act with Mr. and Mrs. Francis."

"You can rehearse her forty years and she'll never play the part."

"The critics don't agree with you; they rave over her. If Francis himself—"

Mrs. Phillips uttered an exclamation of anger. "Oh, of course, *she* is perfect! You wouldn't give me the part, would you? No. You gave it to her. But it's mine by rights; I have the personality."

"I wrote it for her," said the husband, after a pause. "I can't see you in it."

"Naturally," she sneered. "Well, *I* can, and it's not too late to make the change. I'll replace her. My name will help the piece."

"Léontine!" he exclaimed, in amazement. "What are you talking about? The play is a tremendous success as it is, and Miss Berwynd is a big hit. I'd be crazy to make a change."

"You won't give me the part?"

"Certainly not. You shouldn't ask it."

"Doesn't Léontine Murat mean more to the public than Norma Berwynd?" she demanded.

"Until last night, yes. To-day—well, no. She has created this rôle. Besides—you—couldn't play the part."

"And why not, if you please?"

"I don't want to hurt your feelings, Léontine."

"Go on!" she commanded, in a voice roughened by passion.

"In the first place you're not—young enough." The woman quivered. "In the second place, you've grown heavy. Then, too, your accent—"

She broke out at him furiously. "So! I'm old and fat and foreign. I've lost my beauty. You think so, eh? Well, other men don't. I'll show you what men think of me—"

"This is no time for threats," he interrupted, coldly.

"Bah! I don't threaten." Seizing him by the arm, she swung him about, for she was a large woman and still in the fullest vigor of her womanhood. "Listen! You can't fool me. I know why you wrote this play. I know why you took that girl and made a star of her. I've known the truth all along."

"You have no cause to—"

"Don't lie!" she stormed at him. "I can read you like a book. But I won't stand for it." She flung his arm violently from her and turned away.

"I think you'd better go home," he told her. "You'll have the stage hands talking in a minute."

She laughed disagreeably, ignoring his words. "I watched you write this play! I have eyes, even if Irving Francis is blind. It's time he knew what is going on."

"There is nothing going on," Phillips cried, heatedly; but his wife merely shrugged her splendid shoulders and, opening her gold vanity case, gave her face a deft going over with a tiny powder puff. After a time the man continued: "I could understand your attitude if you—cared for me, but some years ago you took pains to undeceive me on that point."

Léontine's lip curled, and she made no answer.

"This play is a fine piece of property; it will bring us a great deal of money; it is the thing for which I have worked years."

"I am going to tell Francis the truth about you and his wife!" she said.

"But there's nothing to tell," the man insisted, with an effort to restrain himself. "Besides, you must know the result if you start a thing like that. He'll walk out and take his wife with him. That would ruin—"

"Give me her part."

"I won't be coerced," he flared up, angrily. "You are willing to ruin me, out of pique, I suppose, but I won't permit it. This is the biggest thing I ever did, or ever will do, perhaps; it means honor and recognition, and—you're selfish enough to spoil it all. I've never spoken to Norma Berwynd in any way to which her husband or you could object. Therefore I resent your attitude."

"My attitude! I'm your wife."

He took a turn across the stage, followed by her eyes. Pausing before her at length, he said, quietly: "I've asked you to go home and now I insist upon it. If you are here when I return I shall dismiss the rehearsal. I refuse to allow our domestic relations to interfere with my business." He strode out to the front of the house and then paced the dark foyer, striving to master his emotions. A moment later he saw his wife leave the stage and assumed that she had obeyed his admonitions and gone home.

The property-man appeared with an armful of draperies and mechanical appliances, interrupting his whistling long enough to call out.

"Here's the new hangings, Mr. Phillips, and the Oriental rugs. I've got the dagger, too." He held a gleaming object on high. "Believe me, it's some Davy Crockett. There's a newspaper guy out back and he wants your ideas on the American drama. I told him they were great. Will you see him?"

"Not now. Tell him to come back later."

"Say! That John Danton is some character. Why don't you let him have the gal?"

"Because—well, because it doesn't happen in real life, and I've tried to make this play real, more than anything else."

When Norma Berwynd and her husband arrived Phillips had completely regained his composure, and he greeted them cordially. The woman seemed awed, half-frightened, by her sudden rise to fame. She seemed to be walking in a dream, and a great wonder dwelt in her eyes. As for Francis, he returned the author's greeting curtly, making it plain that he was in no agreeable temper.

"I congratulate you, Phillips," he said. "You and Norma have become famous overnight."

The open resentment in his tone angered the playwright and caused him to wonder if their long-deferred clash was destined to occur this morning. He knew himself to be overwrought, and he imagined Francis to be in no better frame of mind; nevertheless, he answered, pacifically:

"If that is so we owe it to your art."

"Not at all. I see now what I failed to detect in reading and rehearsing the piece, and what you neglected to tell me, namely, that this is a woman's play. There's nothing in it for me. There's nothing in my part."

"Oh, come now! The part is tremendous; you merely haven't got the most out of it as yet."

Francis drew himself up and eyed the speaker coldly. "You're quoting the newspapers. Pray be more original. You know, of course, how I stand with these penny-a-liners; they never have liked me, but as for the part—" He shrugged. "I can't get any more out of it than there is in it."

"Doubtless that was my fault at rehearsals. I've called this one so we can fix up the weak spot in the third act."

"Well! We're on time. Where are the others?" Francis cast an inquiring glance about.

"I'll only rehearse you and Mrs. Francis."

"Indeed!" The former speaker opened his mouth for a cutting rejoinder, but changed his mind and stalked away into the shadowy depths of the wings.

"Please make allowances for him," Norma begged, approaching Phillips in order that her words might not be overheard. "I've never seen him so broken up over anything. He is always unstrung after an opening, but he is—terrible, this morning."

There was trouble, timidity, and another indefinable expression in the woman's eyes as they followed the vanishing figure of her husband; faint lines appeared at the corners of her mouth, lines which had no place in the face of a happily married woman. She was trembling, moreover, as if she had but recently played some big, emotional rôle, and Phillips felt the old aching pity for her tugging at his heart. He wondered if those stories about Francis could be true.

"It has been a great strain on all of us," he told her. "But you? How do you feel after all this?" He indicated the pile of morning papers, and at sight of them her eyes suddenly filled with that same wonder and gladness he had noticed when she first arrived.

"Oh-h! I—I'm breathless. Something clutches me—here." She laid her hand upon her bosom. "It's so new I can't express it yet, except—well, all of my dreams came true in a night. Some fairy waved her wand and, lo! poor ugly little me—" She laughed, although it was more like a sob. "I had no idea my part was so immense. Had you?"

"I had. I wrote it that way. My dreams, also, came true."

"But why?" A faint flush stole into her cheeks. "There are so many women who could have played the part better than I. You had courage to risk your piece in my hands, Mr. Phillips."

"Perhaps I knew you better than you knew yourself." She searched his face with startled curiosity. "Or better at least than the world knew you. Tell me, there is something wrong? I'm afraid he—resents your—"

"Oh no, no!" she denied, hastily, letting her eyes fall, but not before he had seen them fill again with that same expression of pain and bewilderment. "He's—not himself, that's all. I—You—won't irritate him? Please! He has such a temper."

Francis came out of the shadows scowling. "Well, let's get at it," said he.

Phillips agreed. "If you don't mind we'll start with your entrance. I wish you would try to express more depth of feeling, more tenderness, if you please, Mr. Francis. Remember, John Danton has fought this love of his for many years, undertaking to remain loyal to his wife. He doesn't dream that Diane returns his love, for he has never spoken, never even hinted of his feelings until this instant. Now, however, they are forced into expression. He begins reluctantly, frightened at the thing which makes him speak, then when she responds the dam breaks and his love over-rides his will power, his loyalty, his lifelong principles; it sweeps him onward and it takes her with him. The truth appals them both. They recognize its certain consequences and yet they respond freely, fiercely. You can't overplay the scene, Mr. Francis."

"Certainly I can overplay it," the star declared. "That's the danger. My effects should come from repression."

"I must differ with you. Repressive methods are out of place here. You see, John Danton loses control of himself—"

"Nonsense!" Francis declared, angrily.

"The effectiveness of the scene depends altogether upon its—well, its savagery. It must sweep the audience off its feet in order that the climax shall appear logical."

"Nonsense again! I'm not an old-school actor, and I can't chew scenery. I've gained my reputation by repressive acting, by intensity."

"This is not acting; this is real life."

Francis's voice rose a tone in pitch, and his eyes flashed at this stubborn resistance to his own set ideas.

"Great heavens, Phillips! Don't try to tell me my own business. People don't behave that way in real life; they don't explode underpassion—not even jealousy or revenge; they are reserved. Reserve! That's the real thing; the other is all make-believe."

Seeing that it was useless to argue with the man, Phillips said nothing more, so Francis and his wife assumed their positions and began their lines.

It was a long scene and one demanding great force to sustain. It was this, in fact, which had led to the choice of Irving Francis for the principal rôle, for he was a man of tremendous physical power. He had great ability, moreover, and yet never, even at rehearsals, had he been able to invest this particular scene with conviction. Phillips had rehearsed him in it time and again, but he seemed strangely incapable of rising to the necessary heights. He was hollow, artificial; his tricks and mannerisms showed through like familiar trade marks. Strangely enough, the girl also had failed to get the most out of the scene, and this morning, both star and leading woman seemed particularly cold and unresponsive. They lacked the spark, the uplifting intensity, which was essential, therefore, in desperation, Phillips finally tried the expedient of altering their "business," of changing positions, postures, and crosses; but they went through the scene for a second time as mechanically as before.

Knowing every line as he did, feeling every heart throb, living and suffering as John Danton was supposed to be living and suffering, Phillips was nearly distracted. To him this was a wanton butchery of his finest work. He interrupted, at last, in a heart-sick, hopeless tone which sorely offended the already irritated Francis.

"I'm—afraid it's no use. You don't seem to get it."

"What is it I don't get?" roughly demanded the actor.

"You're not genuine—either of you. You don't seem to feel it."

"Humph! We're married!" said the star, so brutally that his wife flushed painfully. "I tell you I get all it's possible to get out of the scene. You wrote it and you see a lot of imaginary values; but they're not there. I'm no superman—no god! I can't give you more than the part contains."

"Look at it in this light," Phillips argued, after a pause. "Diane is a married woman; she, too, is fighting a battle; she is restrained by every convention, every sense of right, every instinct of wifehood and womanhood. Now, then, you must sweep all that aside; your own fire must set her ablaze despite—"

"I? *I* must do all this?" mocked the other, furiously. "Why must *I* do it all? Make Norma play up to me. She underplays me all the time; she's not in my key. That's what's the matter—and I'm damned tired of this everlasting criticism."

There was a strained silence, during which the two men faced each other threateningly, and a panic seized the woman.

She managed to say, uncertainly: "Perhaps I—should play up to you,Irving."

"On the contrary, I don't think the fault is yours," Phillips said, stiffly.

Again there was a dramatic silence, in which there was no element of the make-believe. It was the clash of two strong men who disliked each other intensely and whose masks were slipping. Neither they nor the leading woman detected a figure stealing out from the gloom, as if drawn by the magnetism of their anger.

"My fault, as usual," Francis sneered. "Understand this, Phillips, my reputation means something to me, and I won't be forced out of a good engagement by a—well, by you or by any other stage manager."

Phillips saw that same fearful look leap into the woman's eyes, and it checked his heated retort. "I don't mean to find fault with you," he declared, evenly. "I have the greatest respect for your ability as an actor, but—"

The star tossed his massive head in a peculiarly aggravating manner. "Perhaps you think you can play the part better than I?"

"Irving! *Please!*" breathed his wife.

"Show me how it should be done, if you feel it so strongly."

"Thank you, I will," Phillips answered, impulsively. "I'm not an actor, but I wrote this piece. What's more, I lived it before I wrote it. It's my own story, and I think I know how it should be played."

Francis smiled mockingly. "Good!" said he; "I shall learn something."

"Do you mind?" The author turned to the real Diane, and she shook her head, saying, uncertainly:

"It's—very good of you."

"Very well. If you will hold the manuscript, Mr. Francis, I'll try to show what I feel the scene lacks. However, I don't think I'll need any prompting. Now, then, we'll begin at John Danton's entrance."

With the mocking smile still upon his lips, Francis took the manuscript and seated himself upon the prompter's table.

It was by no means remarkable that Henry Phillips should know something about acting, for he had long been a stage manager, and in emergencies he has assumed a good many divergent rôles. He felt no self-consciousness, therefore, as he exchanged places with Francis; only an intense desire to prove his contentions. He nerved himself to an unusual effort, but before he had played more than a few moments he forgot the hostile husband and began to live the part of John Danton as he had lived it in the writing, as he invariably lived it every time he read the play or saw it acted.

Nor, as he had said, did he need prompting, for the lines were not the written speeches of another which had been impressed upon his brain by the mechanical process of repetition; they were his own thoughts expressed in the simplest terms he knew, and they came forth unbidden, hot, eager. Once he began to voice them he was seized by that same mighty current which had drawn them from him in the first place and left them strewn upon paper like driftwood after a flood. He had acted every part of his play; he had spoken every line many times in solitude; but this was the first time he had faced the real Diane. He found himself mastered by a fierce exultation; he forgot that he was acting or that the woman opposite him was playing a rôle of his creation; he began to live his true life for the first time since he had met the wife of Irving Francis. Clothed in the make-believe, the real Henry Phillips spoke freely, feelingly. His very voice changed in timbre, in quality; it became rich, alive; his eyes caressed the woman and stirred her to a new response.

As for Irving Francis, he watched the transformation with astonishment. Grudgingly, resentfully, he acknowledged that this was indeed fine acting. He realized, too, that his blind egotism had served merely to prove the truth of the author's criticism and to emphasize his own shortcomings. The idea enraged him, but the spectacle held him enthralled.

Norma Berwynd was not slow to appreciate the truth. Accustomed thoroughly to every phase of the make-believe world in which she dwelt, she recognized unerringly in the new John Danton's words and actions something entirely unreal and apart from the theatrical. The conviction that Henry Phillips was not acting came to her with a blinding suddenness, and it threw her into momentary confusion, hence her responses were mechanical. But soon, without effort on her part, this embarrassment fell away and she in turn began to blaze. The flame grew as Phillips breathed upon it. She realized wildly that her heart had always hungered for words like these, and that, coming from his lips, they carried an altogether new and wondrous meaning; that they filled some long-felt, aching want of which she had been ignorant until this moment. The certainty that it was Phillips himself who spoke, and not a mere character of his creation, filled her with an exultant recklessness. She forgot her surroundings, her husband's presence, even the fact that the lines she spoke were not of her own making.

Never had the scene been played like this. It grew vital, it took on a tremendous significance. No one could have observed it and remained unresponsive. Francis let fall the manuscript and stared at the actors wondering-ly. Since he was an actor, nothing was so real to him, nothing so thrilling, as the make-believe. He realized that this was indeed a magnificent exhibition of the artificial. With parted lips and pulse athrob he followed the wooing of that imaginary John Danton, in whom he could see no one but himself.

After a time he became conscious of a presence at his side, and heard some one breathing heavily. Turning with a start, he found Léontine Phillips at his shoulder. She, too, was aroused, but in her sneering visage was that which brought the actor abruptly out of his spell. She had emerged from the shadows noiselessly, and was leaning forward, her strong hands gripping the edge of the table littered with its many properties.

Mrs. Phillips had played emotional scenes herself, but never with such melodramatic intensity as she now unconsciously displayed. Her whole body shook as with an ague, her dark face was alive with a jealous fury which told Irving Francis the story he had been too dull to suspect. The truth, when it came home, smote him like a blow; his hatred for the author, which had been momentarily forgotten—momentarily lost in his admiration of the artist—rose up anew, and he recognized this occult spell which had held him breathless as the thrall of a vital reality, not, after all, the result of inspired acting. Instantly he saw past the make-believe, into the real, and what he saw caused him to utter a smothered cry.

Léontine turned her face to him. "You fool!" she whispered through livid lips.

Francis was a huge, leonine man; he rose now to his full height, as a cat rises. But the drama drew his gaze in spite of himself; he could not keep his eyes from his wife's face. Léontine plucked at his sleeve and whispered again:

"You *fool*!"

Something contorted the actor's frame bitterly, and he gasped like a man throttled. Léontine could feel his muscles stiffen.

But the two players were in Elysium. They had reached the climax of the scene; Danton had told his love as only a great, starved love can tell itself, and with swimming eyes and fluttering lids, with heart pounding beneath her folded hands, Diane swayed toward him and his arms enfolded her. Her body met his, yielded; her face was upturned; her fragrant, half-opened lips were crushed to his in a fierce, impassioned kiss of genuine ecstasy.

* * * *

Up to this moment the intensity of Francis's rage had held him para-lyzed, despite the voice which was whispering so constantly at his ear; but now, when he saw his wife swooning upon the breast of the man who had played his part, he awoke.

"She knows he loves her," Léontine was saying. "You let him tell her in front of your face. He has taken her away from you!"

Mrs. Phillips's eyes fell upon the working fingers of the man as they rested beside her own. They were opening and closing hungrily. She also saw the naked knife which lay upon the table, and she moved it forward cautiously until the eager fingers twined about it. Then she breathed, "Go!" and shoved him forward fiercely.

It was Irving Francis's cry of rage as he rushed upon them which aroused Norma Berwynd from her dream, from her intoxication. She saw him towering at Phillips's back, and with a scream she tried to save the latter.

The husband's blow fell, however; it was delivered with all the savage fury that lay in Irving Francis's body, and his victim was fairly driven to his knees beneath it. The latter rose, then staggered, and, half sliding through the woman's sheltering embrace, crumpled limply into a massive upholstered chair. He, too, was dazed by the sudden transition from his real world to his make-believe.

When his eyes cleared he saw Norma Berwynd struggling with her husband, interposing her own slender body in his path. Francis was cursing her foully for her unfaithfulness; his voice was thick and brutal.

"Yes! It's true!" she cried, with hysterical defiance. "I never knew till now; but it's true! It's *true!*"

"You've killed him!" Léontine chattered, shrilly, and emerged from the shadows, her dark features ashen, her eyes ringed with white. Mrs. Francis turned from her husband and flung her arms about the recumbent man, calling wildly to him.

The dénouement had come with such swiftness that it left all four of them appalled at their actions. Seeing what his brief insanity had led him into, Francis felt his strength evaporate; his face went white, his legs buckled beneath him. He scanned the place wildly in search of means of escape.

"My God! My God!" Léontine was repeating. "Why doesn't somebody come?"

Now that his brain had cleared, and he knew what hand had smitten him, and why, Phillips was by far the calmest of the four. He saw the knife at his feet and smiled, for no steel could rob him of that gladness which was pulsing through his veins. He was still smiling when he stooped and picked up the weapon. He arose, lifting Norma to her feet; then his hand slid down and sought hers.

"You needn't worry," he said to Francis. "You see—this is the new dagger I got for the end of the act."

He held it out in his open palm for all of them to see, and they noted that it was strangely shortened—that the point of the sliding blade was barely exposed beneath the hilt.

Francis wiped his wet face, then shuddered and cursed weakly with relief, meanwhile groping at the prompter's table for support. "Sold! A prop knife!" he cried.

"You—you're not really—" Norma swayed forward with eyes closed.

Léontine laughed.

"By God! I meant it," the star exclaimed, uncertainly. "You can't deny—" He gasped and tugged at his collar.

"I believe there is nothing to deny," the author said, quietly. He looked first at his wife, then at his enemy, and then down at the quivering, white face upturned to his. "There is nothing to deny, is there?" he inquired of Norma.

"Nothing!" she said. "I—I'm glad to know the truth, that's all."

Francis glared first at one, then at the other, and as he did so he began to realize the full cost of his action. When it came home to him in terms of dollars and cents, he showed his true character by stammering:

"I—I made a frightful mistake. I'm—not myself; really, I'm not. It was your wife's fault." In a panic he ran on, unmindful of Léontine's scorn. "She did it, Mr. Phillips. She gave me the knife. She whispered things—she made me—I—I'm very sorry—Mr. Phillips, and I'll play the part the way you want it. I will, indeed."

Léontine met her husband's look defiantly; hence it was as much to her as to the cringing actor that the playwright said:

"Your salary will go on as usual, under your contract, Mr. Francis—that is, until the management supplies you with a new play; but I'm the real John Danton, and I shall play him tonight and henceforth."

"Then, I'm—discharged? Norma—d'you hear that? We're canceled. Fired!"

"No, Miss Berwynd's name will go up in lights as the star, if she cares to stay," said Phillips. "Do you wish to remain?" He looked down at the woman, and she nodded.

"Yes, oh yes!" she said. "I *must* stay. I daren't go back." That hunted look leaped into her eyes again, and Phillips recognized it now as fear, the abject physical terror of the weaker animal. "I want to go—forward—not backward, if there is any way."

"I'll show you the way," he told her, gently. "We'll find it together."

He smiled reassuringly, and with a little gasping sigh she placed her hand in his.

RUNNING ELK

Up from the valley below came the throb of war drums, the faint rattle of shots, and the distant cries of painted horsemen charging. From my vantage-point on the ridge I had an unobstructed view of the encampment, a great circle of tepees and tents three miles in circumference, cradled in a sag of the timberless hills. The sounds came softly through the still Dakota air, and my eye took in every sharp-drawn detail of the scene—ponies grazing along the creek bottom, children playing beneath the blue smoke of camp-fires, the dense crowd ringed about a medicine pole in their center, intent on a war-dance.

Five thousand Sioux were here in all their martial splendor. They were painted and decked and trapped for war, living again their days of plenty, telling anew their tales of might, and repeating on a mimic scale their greatest battles. Five days the feasting had continued; five mornings had I been awakened at dawn to see a thousand ochered, feathered horsemen come thundering down upon the camp, their horses running flat, their rifles popping, while the valley rocked to their battle-cries and to the answering clamor of the army which rode forth to meet them. Five sultry days had I spent wandering unnoticed, ungreeted, and disdained, an alien in a hostile land, tolerated but unwelcome. Five evenings had I witnessed the tents begin to glow and the campfires kindle until the valley became hooped about as if by a million giant fireflies. Five nights had I strayed, like a lost soul, through an unreal wilderness, harkening to the drone of stories told in an unfamiliar tongue, to the minor-keyed dirges of an unknown race, to the thumping of countless moccasined feet in the measures of queer dances. The odors of a savage people had begun to pall on me, and the sound of a strange language to annoy; I longed for another white man, for a word in my own tongue.

It was the annual "Give-away" celebration, when all the tribe assembles to make presents, to race, to tell stories, and to recount the legends of their prowess. They had come from all quarters of the reservation, bringing their trunks, their children, and their dogs. Of the last named more had come, by far, than would go back, for this was a week of feasting, and every day the air was heavy with the smell of singeing hair, and the curs that had been spared gnawed at an ever-increasing pile of bones.

I had seen old hags strangle dogs by pulling on opposite ends of a slipnoose, or choke them by laying a tent-pole on their throats and standing on the ends; I had seen others knock them down with billets of wood, drag them kicking to the fires, and then knock them down again when they crawled out of the flames. All in all, I had acquired much information regarding the carnival appetites of the noble red man, learning that he is poetic only in the abstract.

It was drawing on toward sunset, so I slipped into my camera strap and descended the slope. I paused, however, while still some distance away from my tent, for next to it another had been erected during my absence. It was a tiny affair with a rug in front of it, and upon the rug stood a steamer-chair.

"Hello, inside!" I shouted, then ran forward, straddling papooses and shouldering squaws out of my way.

"Hello!" came an answer, and out through the flap was thrust the head of my friend, the Government doctor.

"Gee! I'm glad to see you!" I said as I shook his hand. "I'm as lonesome as a deaf mute at a song recital."

"I figured you would be," said the doctor, "so I came out to see the finish of the feast and to visit with you. I brought some bread from the Agency."

"Hoorah! White bread and white conversation! I'm hungry for both."

"What's the matter? Won't the Indians talk to you?"

"I guess they would if they could, but they can't. I haven't found one among the whole five thousand who can understand a word I say. Your Government schools have gone back in the betting with me, Doc. You must keep your graduates under lock and key."

"They can all speak English if they want to—that is, the younger ones. Some few of the old people are too proud to try, but the others can talk as well as we can, until they forget."

"Do you mean to say these people have been fooling me? I don't believe it," said I. "There's one that can't talk English, and I'll make a bet on it." I indicated a passing brave with an eagle-feather head-dress which reached far down his naked legs. He was a magnificent animal; he was young and lithe, and as tall and straight as a sapling. "I've tried him twice, and he simply doesn't understand."

My friend called to the warrior: "Hey, Tom! Come here a minute." The Indian came, and the doctor continued, "When do you hold the horse-races, Thomas?"

"To-morrow, at four o'clock, unless it rains," said the fellow. He spoke in an odd, halting dialect, but his words were perfectly understandable.

"Are you going to ride?"

"No; my race-horse is sick."

As the ocher-daubed figure vanished into the dusk the old man turned to me, saying, "College man."

"What?"

"Yes. B.A. He's a graduate."

"Impossible!" I declared. "Why, he talks like a foreigner, or as if he were just learning our language."

"Exactly. In another three years he'll be an Indian again, through and through. Oh, the reservation is full of fellows like Tom." The doctor heaved a sigh of genuine discouragement. "It's a melancholy acknowledgment to make, but our work seems to count for almost nothing. It's their blood."

"Perhaps they forget the higher education," said I; "but how about the Agency school, where you teach them to farm and to sew and to cook, as well as to read and to write? Surely they don't forget that?"

"I've heard a graduating class read theses, sing cantatas, and deliver sounding orations; then I've seen those same young fellows, three months later, squatting in tepees and eating with their fingers. It's a common thing for our 'sweet girl graduates' to lay off their white commencement-day dress, their high-heeled shoes and their pretty hats, for the shawl and the moccasin. We teach them to make sponge-cake and to eat with a fork, but they prefer dog-soup and a horn spoon. Of course there are exceptions, but most of them forget much faster than they learn."

"Our Eastern ideas of Mr. Lo are somewhat out of line with the facts," I acknowledged. "He's sort of a hero with us. I remember several successful plays with romantic Indians in the lead."

"I know!" My friend laughed shortly. "I saw some of them. If you like, however, I'll tell you how it really happens. I know a story."

When we had finished supper the doctor told me the story of Running Elk. The night was heavy with unusual odors and burdened by weird music; the whisper of a lively multitude came to us, punctuated at intervals by distant shouts or shots or laughter. On either hand the campfires stretched away like twinkling stars, converging steadily until the horns joined each other away out yonder in the darkness. It was a suitable setting for an epic tale of the Sioux.

"I've grown gray in this service," the old man began, "and the longer I live the less time I waste in trying to understand the difference between the Indian race and ours. I've about reached the conclusion that it's due to some subtle chemical ingredient in the blood. One race is lively and progressive, the other is sluggish and atavistic. The white man is ever developing, he's always advancing, always expanding; the red man is marking time or walking backward. It is only a matter of time until he will vanish utterly. He's different from the negro. The negro enlarges, up to a certain limit, then he stops. Some people claim, I believe, that his skull is sutured in such a manner as to check his brain development when his bones finally harden and set. The idea sounds reasonable; if true, there will never be a serious conflict between the blacks and the whites. But the red man differs from both. To begin with, his is not a subject race by birth. Physically he is as perfect as either; Nature has endowed him with an intellect quite as keen as the white man's, and with an open articulation of the skull which permits the growth of his brain. Somewhere, nevertheless, she has cunningly concealed a flaw, a flaw which I have labored thirty years to find.

"I have a theory—you know all old men have theories—that it is a physical thing, as tangible as that osseous constriction of the cranium which holds the negro in subjection, and that if I could lay my finger on it I could raise the Indian to his ancient mastery and to a dignified place among the nations; I could change them from a vanishing people into a race of rulers, of lawgivers, of creators. At least that used to be my dream.

"Some years ago I felt that I was well on my way to success, for I found a youth who offered every promise of great manhood. I studied him until I knew his every trait and his every strength—he didn't seem to have any weaknesses. I raised him according to my own ideas; he became a tall, straight fellow, handsome as a bronze statue of a god. Physically he was perfect, and he had a mind as fine as his body. He had the best blood of his nation in him, being the son of a war chief, and he was called Thomas Running Elk. I educated him at the Agency school under my own personal supervision, and on every occasion I studied him. I spent hours in shaping his mind and in bending him away from the manners and the habits of his tribe. I taught him to think like a white man. He responded like a growing vine; he became the pride of the reservation—a reserved but an eager youth, with an understanding and a wit beyond that of most white boys of his age. Search him as rigorously as I might, I couldn't find a single flaw. I believed I was about to prove my theory.

"Running Elk romped through our school, and he couldn't learn fast enough; when he had finished I sent him East to college, and, in order to wean him utterly away from the past, instead of sending him to an Indian school I arranged for him to enter one of the big Eastern universities, where no Indian had ever been, where constant association with the flower of our race would by its own force raise him to a higher level. Well, it worked. He led his classes as a stag leads a herd. He was a silent, dignified, shadowy figure; his fellow-students considered him unapproachable, nevertheless they admired and they liked him. In all things he excelled; but he was best, perhaps, in athletics, and for this I took the credit—a Jovian satisfaction in my work.

"News of his victories on track and field and gridiron came to me regularly, for his professors were interested in my experiment. As for the boy himself, he never wrote; it was not his nature. Nor did he communicate with his people. He had cut himself off from them, and I think he looked down upon them. At intervals his father came to the Agency to inquire about Running Elk, for I did not allow my protégé to return even during vacations. That was a part of my plan. At my stories of his son's victories the father made no comment; he merely listened quietly, then folded his blanket about him and slipped away. The old fellow was a good deal of a philosopher; he showed neither resentment nor pleasure, but once or twice I caught him smiling oddly at my enthusiasm. I know now what was in his mind.

"It was in Running Elk's senior year that a great thing came to him, a thing I had counted upon from the start. He fell in love. A girl entered his life. But this girl didn't enter as I had expected, and when the news reached me I was completely taken aback. She was a girl I had dandled on my knees as a child, the only daughter of an old friend. Moreover, instead of Running Elk being drawn to her, as I had planned, she fell desperately in love with him.

"I guess the gods were offended at my presumption and determined by one hair's-breadth shift to destroy the balance of my whole structure. They're a jealous lot, the gods. I didn't understand, at that time, how great must have been the amusement which I offered them.

"You've heard of old Henry Harman? Yes, the railroad king. It was his daughter Alicia. No wonder you look incredulous.

"In order to understand the story you'll have to know something about old Henry. You'll have to believe in heredity. Henry is a self-made man. He came into the Middle West as a poor boy, and by force of indomitable pluck, ability, and doggedness he became a captain of industry. We were born on neighboring farms, and while I, after a lifetime of work, have won nothing except an underpaid Government job, Henry has become rich and mighty. He had that indefinable, unacquirable faculty for making money, and he became a commanding figure in the financial world. He's dominant, he's self-centered, he's one-purposed; he's a rough-hewn block of a man, and his unbounded wealth, his power, and his contact with the world have never smoothed nor rounded him. He's just about the same now as when he was a section boss on his own railroad. His daughter Alicia is another Henry Harman, feminized. Her mother was a pampered child, born to ease and enslaved to her own whims. No desire of hers, however extravagant, ever went ungratified, and right up to the hour of her death old Henry never said no to her—partly out of a spirit of amusement, I dare say, and partly because she was the only unbridled extravagance he had ever yielded to in all his life. Well, having sowed the wind, he reaped the whirlwind in Alicia. She combined the distinguishing traits of both parents, and she grew up more effectively spoiled than her mother.

"When I got a panicky letter from one of Running Elk's professors coupling her name vaguely with that of my Indian, I wavered in my determination to see this experiment out; but the analyst is unsentimental, and a fellow who sets out to untangle the skein of nature must pay the price, so I waited.

"That fall I was called to Washington on department business—we were fighting for a new appropriation—and while there I went to the theater one night. I was extremely harassed, and my mind was filled with Indian matters, so I went out alone to seek an evening's relief, not caring whither my feet took me.

"The play was one of those you spoke of; it told the story of a young Indian college man in love with a white girl. Whether or not it was well written I don't know; but it seemed as if the hand of destiny had led me to it, for the hero's plight was so similar to the situation of Running Elk that it seemed almost uncanny, and I wondered if this play might afford me some solution of his difficulty.

"You will remember that the Indian in the play is a great football hero, and a sort of demi-god to his fellows. He begins to consider himself one of them—their equal—and he falls in love with the sister of his chum. But when this fact is made known his friends turn against him and try to show him the barrier of blood. At the finish a messenger comes bearing word that his father is dead and that he has been made chief in the old man's place. He is told that his people need him, and although the girl offers to go with him and make her life his, he renounces her for his duty to the tribe.

"Well, it was all right up to that point, but the end didn't help me in shaping the future of Running Elk, for his father was hale, hearty, and contented, and promised to hang on in that condition as long as we gave him his allowance of beef on Issue Day.

"That night when I got back to the hotel I found a long-distance call from old Henry Harman. He had wired me here at the Agency, and, finding I was in Washington, he had called me from New York. He didn't tell me much over the phone, except that he wanted to see me at once on a matter of importance. My work was about finished, so I took the train in the morning and went straight to his office. When I arrived I found the old fellow badly rattled. There is a certain kind of worry which comes from handling affairs of importance. Men like Henry Harman thrive upon it; but there's another kind which searches out the joints in their coats of mail and makes women of them. That's what Henry was suffering from.

"'Oh, Doc, I'm in an awful hole!' he exclaimed. 'You're the only man who can pull me out. It's about Alicia and that damned savage of yours.'

"'I knew that was it,' said I.

"'If you've heard about it clear out there,' Harman declared, with a catch in his voice, 'it's even worse than I thought.' He strode up and down his office for a few moments; then he sank heavily into his chair and commenced to pound his mahogany desk, declaring, angrily:

"'I won't be defied by my own flesh and blood! I won't! That's all there is to it. I'm master of my own family. Why, the thing's fantastic, absurd, and yet it's terrible! Heavens! I can't believe it!'

"'Have you talked with Alicia?'

"'Not with her, *to* her. She's like a mule. I never saw such a will in a woman. I—I've fought her until I'm weak. Where she got her temper I don't know.' He collapsed feebly and I was forced to smile, for there's only one thing stubborn enough to overcome a Harman's resistance, and that is a Harman's desire.

"'Then it isn't a girlish whim?' I ventured.

"'*Whim!* Look at me!' He held out his trembling hands. 'She's licked me, Doc. She's going to marry that—that—' He choked and muttered, unintelligibly: 'I've reasoned, I've pleaded, I've commanded. She merely smiles and shrugs and says I'm probably right, in the abstract. Then she informs me that abstract problems go to pieces once in a while. She says this—this—Galloping Moose, this yelping ghost-dancer of yours, is the only real man she ever met.'

"'What does he have to say?'

"'Humph!' grunted Harman. 'I offered to buy him off, but he threatened to serve me up with dumplings and wear my scalp in his belt. Such insolence! Alicia wouldn't speak to me for a week.'

"'You made a mistake there,' said I. 'Running Elk is a Sioux. As for Alicia, she's thoroughly spoiled. She's never been denied any single thing in all her life, and she has your disposition. It's a difficult situation.'

"'Difficult! It's scandalous—hideous!'

"'How old is Alicia?'

"'Nineteen. Oh, I've worn out that argument! She says she'll wait. You know she has her own money, from her mother.'

"'Does Running Elk come to your house?'

"At this my old friend roared so fiercely that I hastened to say: 'I'll see the boy at once. I have more influence with him than anybody else.'

"'I hope you can show him how impossible, how criminal, it is to ruin my girl's life.' Harman said this seriously. 'Yes, and mine, too, for that matter. Suppose the yellow newspapers got hold of this!' He shuddered. 'Doc, I love that girl so well that I'd kill her with my own hands rather than see her disgraced, ridiculed—'

"'Tut, tut!' said I. 'That's pride—just plain, selfish pride.'

"'I don't care a damn what it is, I'd do it. I earned my way in the world, but she's got blue blood in her and she was born to a position; she goes everywhere. When she comes out she'll be able to marry into the best circles in America. She could marry a duke, if she wanted to. I'd buy her one if she said the word. Naturally, I can't stand for this dirty, low-browed Injun.'

"'He's not dirty,' I declared, 'and he's not as low-browed as some foreigner you'd be glad to pick out for her.'

"'Well, he's an Injun,' retorted Harman, 'and that's enough. We've both seen 'em tried; they all drop back where they started from. You know that as well as I do.'

"'I don't know it,' said I, thinking of my theories. 'I've been using him to make an experiment, but—the experiment has gotten away from me. I dare say you're right. I wanted him to meet and to know white girls, but I didn't want him to marry one—certainly not a girl like Alicia. No, we must put a stop to this affair. I'll see him right away.'

"'To-morrow is Thanksgiving,' said Henry. 'Wait over and go up with us and see the football game.'

"'Are you going?'

"Harman grimaced. 'Alicia made me promise. I'd rather take her than let her go with friends—there's no telling what she might do.'

"'Why let her go at all?' I objected.

"The old fellow laughed mirthlessly. 'Why *let* her? Running Elk plays full-back! How *stop* her? We'll pick you up at your hotel in the morning and drive you up in the car. It's the big game of the year. You'll probably enjoy it. I won't!'

"Miss Harman seemed glad to see me on the following day. She must have known that I was in her father's confidence, but she was too well schooled to show it. As we rode out in the big limousine I undertook to study her, but the reading of women isn't my game. All I could see was a beautiful, spirited, imperious girl with the Harman eyes and chin. She surprised me by mentioning Running Elk of her own free will; she wasn't the least bit embarrassed, and, although her father's face whitened, she preserved her quiet dignity, and I realized that she was in no wise ashamed of her infatuation. I didn't wonder that the old gentleman chose to accompany her to this game, although he must have known that the sight of Running Elk would pain him like a branding-iron.

"It was the first great gridiron battle I had ever seen, and so I was unprepared for the spectacle. The enthusiasm of that immense crowd astonished me, and in spite of the fact that I had come as a tired old man, it got into my veins until my heart pounded and my pulses leaped. The songs, the shouts, the bellows of that multitude were intensely thrilling, for youth was in them. I grew young again, and I was half ashamed of myself until I saw other people of my own age who had also become boys and girls for the day. And the seriousness of it! Why, it was painful! Not one of those countless thousands was a disinterested spectator; they were all intensely partisan, and you'd have thought life or death hung on the victory.

"Not one, did I say? There was one who held himself aloof from all the enthusiasm. Old Henry sat like a lump of granite, and out of regard for him I tried to restrain myself.

"We had a box, close to the side lines, with the élite of the East on either hand—people whose names I had read. They bowed and smiled and waved to our little party, and I felt quite important.

"You've probably seen similar games, so there's no need of my describing this one, even if I could. It was my first experience, however, and it impressed me greatly. When the teams appeared I recognized Running Elk at a distance. So did the hordes of madmen behind us, and I began to understand for the first time what it was that the old man in the seat next to mine was combating.

"A dancing dervish in front of the grandstand said something through a megaphone, then he waved a cane, whereupon a tremendous barking, 'Rah! Rah! Rah!' broke out. It ended with my Sioux boy's name, and I wished the old chief back in Dakota were there to see his son and to witness the honor done him by the whites.

"Quite as impressive to me as this demonstration was the death-like silence which settled over that tremendous throng when the teams scattered out in readiness. The other side kicked off, and the ball sailed high and far. As it settled in its downward flight, I saw a lithe, tall shadow of a man racing toward it, and I recognized my boy. I'd lost his position for the moment, but I knew that hungry, predatory stride which devoured the yards as if he were a thing of the wind. He was off with the ball in the hollow of his arm, right back into the heart of his enemies, dodging, darting, leaping, twisting, always advancing. They tore his interference away from him, but, nevertheless, he penetrated their ranks and none of them could lay hands upon him. He was running free when tackled; his assailant launched himself with such savage violence that the sound of their impact came to us distinctly. As he fell I heard Alicia Harman gasp. Then the crowd gave tongue.

"From that time on to the finish of the game my eyes seldom left Running Elk, and then only long enough to shoot covert glances at my companions.

"Although the skill of my young Sioux overtopped that of all the other contestants, the opposing team played as one man; they were like a wonderful, well-oiled piece of machinery, and—they scored. All through the first half our side struggled to retaliate, but at the intermission they had not succeeded.

"So far Running Elk hadn't noticed our presence, but when the teams returned for the second half he saw us. He didn't even know that I was in the East; in fact, he hadn't laid eyes on me for more than three years. The sight of me there in the box with Alicia and her father must have been an unpleasant shock to him; my face must have seemed an evil omen; nevertheless, he waved his hand at me and smiled—one of his rare, reserved smiles. I couldn't help marveling at the fellow's physical beauty.

"I had been secretly hoping that his side would be defeated, so that Miss Harman might see him for once as a loser; but the knowledge of our presence seemed to electrify him, and by the spark of his own magnetism he fired his fellows until they commenced to play like madmen; I have no doubt they were precisely that. His spirit was like some galvanic current, and he directed them with a master mind. He was a natural-born strategist, of course, for through him ran the blood of the craftiest race of all the earth, the blood of a people who have always fought against odds, to whom a forlorn hope is an assurance of victory. On this day the son of a Sioux chief led the men of that great university with the same skill that Hannibal led his Carthaginian cohorts up to the gates of Rome. He led them with the cunning of Chief Joseph, the greatest warrior of his people. He was indefatigable, irresistible, magnificent—and he himself tied the score.

"In spite of myself I joined madly in the cheering; but the boy didn't let down. Now that his enemies recognized the source of their peril, they focused upon him all their fury. They tried to destroy him. They fell upon him like animals; they worried and they harried and they battered him until I felt sick for him and for the girl beside me, who had grown so faint and pale. But his body was of my making; I had spent careful years on it, and although they wore themselves out, they could not break Running Elk. He remained a fleeting, an elusive thing, with the vigor of a wild horse. He tackled their runners with the ferocity of a wolf.

"It was a grand exhibition of coolness and courage, for he was every-where, always alert and always ready—and it was he who won the game.

"There came some sort of a fumble, too fast for the eye to follow, and then the ball rolled out of the scrimmage. Before we knew what had happened, Running Elk was away with it, a scattered field ahead of him.

"I dare say you have heard about that run, for it occurred in the last three minutes of play, and is famous in football annals to this day, so I'm told. It was a spectacular performance, apparently devised by fate to make more difficult the labors of old Henry and me. Every living soul on those high-banked bleachers was on his feet at the finish, a senseless, screaming demon. I saw Alicia straining forward, her face like chalk, her very lips blanched, her whole high-strung body aquiver. Her eyes were distended, and in them I saw a look which told me that this was no mere girlish whim, that this was more than the animal call of youth and sex. Running Elk had become a fetish to her.

"The father must likewise have recognized this, for as we passed out he stammered into my ear:

"'You see, Doc, the girl's mad. It's awful—awful. I don't know what to do.'

"We had become momentarily separated from her, and therefore I urged him: 'Get her away, quick, no matter how or where. Use force if you have to, but get her out of this crowd, this atmosphere, and keep her away. I'll see *him* to-night.'

"The old fellow nodded. 'I—I'll kidnap her and take her to Europe,' he mumbled. 'God! It's awful!'

"I didn't go back to the city with the Harmans; but I told Alicia good-by at the running-board of the machine. I don't think she heard me.

"Running Elk was glad to see me, and I spent that evening with him. He asked all about his people; he told me of his progress, and he spoke lightly of his victory that day. But sound him as I would, I could elicit no mention of Alicia Harman's name. He wasn't much of a talker, anyhow, so at last I was forced to bring up the subject myself. At my first word the silence of his forefathers fell upon him, and all he did was listen. I told him forcibly that any thoughts of her were ridiculous and impossible.

"'Why?' said he, after I had finished.

"I told him a thousand reasons why; I recounted them cruelly, unfeelingly, but he made no sign. As a matter of fact, I don't think he understood them any more than he understood the affair itself. He appeared to be blinded, confused by the splendor of what had come to him. Alicia was so glorious, so different, so mysterious to him, that he had lost all sense of perspective and of proportion. Recognizing this, I descended to material things which I knew he could grasp.

"'I paid for your education,' said I, 'and it is almost over with. In a few months you'll be turned out to make your own living, and then you'll encounter this race prejudice I speak of in a way to effect your stomach and your body. You're a poor man, Running Elk, and you've got to earn your way. Your blood will bar you from a good many means of doing it, and when your color begins to affect your earning capacity you'll have all you can do to take care of yourself. Life isn't played on a gridiron, and the first thing you've got to do is to make a man of yourself. You've got no right to fill your head with dreams, with insane fancies of this sort.'

"'Yes, sir!' said he, and that was about all I could get out of him. His reticence was very annoying.

"I didn't see him again, for I came West the next day, and the weeks stretched into months without word of him or of the others.

"Shortly before he was due to return I was taken sick—the one big illness of my life, which came near ending me, which made me into the creaking old ruin that I am. They sent me away to another climate, where I got worse, then they shifted me about like a bale of goods, airing me here and there. For a year and a half I hung over the edge, one ailment running into another, but finally I straightened out a bit and tottered back into Washington to resume operations.

"For six months I hung around headquarters, busied on department matters. I had lost all track of things out here, meanwhile, for the agent had been changed shortly after I left, and no one had taken the trouble to keep me posted; but eventually I showed up on the reservation again, reaching here on the first of July, three days before the annual celebration of the people.

"Many changes had occurred in my two years' absence, and there was no one to bring me gossip, hence I heard little during the first day or two while I was picking up the loose ends of my work. One thing I did find out, however—namely, that Running Elk had come straight home from college, and was still on the reserve. I determined to look him up during the festival.

"But on the morning of the Fourth I got the surprise of my life. The stage from the railroad brought two women, two strange women, who came straight to my office—Alicia Harman and her French maid.

"Well, I was fairly knocked endwise; but Alicia was as well-poised and as self-contained as on that Thanksgiving morning in New York when she and old Henry had picked me up in their automobile—a trifle more stunning and a bit more determined, perhaps. Oh, she was a splendid creature in the first glory of her womanhood, a perfectly groomed and an utterly spoiled young goddess. She greeted me graciously, with that queenly air of all great ladies.

"'Where is your father?' I asked, as she laid off her dust-coat.

"'He's in New York,' said she. 'I'm traveling alone.'

"'And where have you been all this time?'

"'In Europe, mainly; Rome, Naples, Cairo, India, St. Petersburg, London— all about, in fact. Father took me abroad the day after Thanksgiving—you remember? And he has kept me there. But I came of age two weeks ago.'

"'Two weeks!' I ejaculated.

"'Yes, I took the first ship after my birthday. I've been traveling pretty constantly ever since. This is a long way from the world out here, isn't it?' She looked around curiously.

"'From your world, yes,' said I, and when she offered nothing further I grew embarrassed. I started to speak; then, noting the maid, I hesitated; but Alicia shook her head faintly.

"'Lisette doesn't understand a word of English,' said she.

"'Why have you come out here, Alicia?' I inquired. I was far more ill at ease than she.

"'Do you need to ask?' She eyed me defiantly. 'I respected father's wishes when I was in my minority. I traveled and studied and did all the tiresome things he commanded me to do—as long as he had the right to command. But when I became my own mistress I—took my full freedom.

He made his life to suit himself; I intend to make mine to suit myself. I'm sorry I can't please him, but we don't seem to see things the same way, and I dare say he has accepted the inevitable.'

"'Then you consider this—this move you evidently contemplate as inevitable?'

"She lifted her dainty brows. 'Inevitable isn't a good word. I wish a certain thing; I have wished it from the first; I have never ceased for an instant to wish it; I feel that I must have it; therefore, to all intents and purposes, it is inevtable. Anyhow, I'm going to have it.'

"'You have—er—been in communication with—'

"'Never! Father forbade it.'

"'Then how did you know he is here?'

"'He wrote me when he left college. He said he was coming home. I've heard nothing since. He is here, isn't he?'

"'So I believe. I haven't seen him yet; you know I've been away myself.'

"'Will you take me to him?'

"'Have you really weighed this thing?' I remonstrated. 'Do you realize what it means?'

"'Please don't.' She smiled wearily. 'So many people have tried to argue me out of my desires. I shall not spoil my life, believe me; it is too good a thing to ruin. That is precisely why I'm here.'

"'If you insist.' I gave in reluctantly. 'Of course I'll put myself at your service. We'll look for him to-morrow.' All sorts of wild expedients to thwart a meeting were scurrying through my mind.

"'We'll go to-day,' said she.

"'But—'

"'At once! If you're too busy I'll ask somebody else—'

"'Very well!' said I. 'We'll drive out to the encampment.' And I sent for my buckboard.

"I was delayed in spite of myself until nearly sundown, and meanwhile Alicia Harman waited in my office, pacing the floor with ill-concealed impatience. Before starting I ventured one more remonstrance, for I was filled with misgivings, and the more I saw of this girl the more fantastic and unnatural this affair seemed. But the unbridled impulses of her parents were bearing fruit, and no one could say her nay. She afforded the most illuminating study in heredity that I have ever witnessed.

"We didn't say much during our fifteen-mile drive, for I was worried and Alicia was oddly torn between apprehension and exultation. We had left the French maid behind. I don't know that any woman ever went to her lover under stranger circumstances or in greater perturbation of spirit than did this girl, behind whom lay a generation of selfishness and unrestraint.

"It was well along in the evening when we came over the ridge and saw the encampment below us. You can imagine the fairy picture it made with its myriad of winking fires, with the soft effulgence of a thousand glowing tents, and with the wonderful magic of the night over it all. As we drew nearer, the unusual sounds of a strange merrymaking came to us—the soft thudding of drums, the weird melody of the dances, the stir and the confusion of crowded animal life. In the daylight it would have been sufficiently picturesque, but under the wizard hand of the darkness it became ten times more so.

"When I finally tied my horses and led the girl into the heart of it I think she became a bit frightened, for these Indians were the Sioux of a bygone day. They were barbaric in dress and in demeanor.

"I guided her through the tangle of tepees, through glaring fire-lit circles and through black voids where we stumbled and had to feel our way. We were jostled and elbowed by fierce warriors and by sullen squaws. At every group I asked for Running Elk, but he was merely one of five thousand and nobody knew his whereabouts.

"The people have ever been jealous of their customs, and as a result we were frequently greeted by cold looks and sudden silences. Recognizing this open resentment, my companion let down a thick automobile veil which effectually hid her face. Her dust-coat was long and loose and served further to conceal her identity.

"At one time we came upon a sight I would gladly have spared her—the spectacle of some wrinkled hags strangling a dog by the light of a fire. The girl at my side stifled a cry at the apparition.

"'What are they doing?' she gasped.

"'Preparing the feast,' I told her.

"'Do they—really—'

"'They do,' said I. 'Come!' I tried to force her onward, but she would not stir until the sacrifice had been dragged to the flames, where other carcasses were singeing among the pots and kettles. From every side came the smell of cooking meat, mingled with the odor of burning hair and flesh. I could hear Miss Harman panting as we went on.

"We circled half the great hoop before we came upon the trail of our man, and were directed to a near-by tepee, upon the glowing walls of which many heads were outlined in silhouette, and from which came the monotonous voice of a story-teller.

"I don't know what hopes the girl had been nursing; she must have looked upon these people not as kindred of Running Elk, but rather as his servants, his slaves. Realizing that her quest was nearly ended, her strength forsook her and she dropped behind me. The entrance to the tepee was congested by those who could not find space inside, but they rose silently, upon recognizing me, and made room. I lifted the flap and peered within, clearing a view for Miss Harman.

"We beheld a circle of half-naked braves in full war regalia, squatting haunch to haunch, listening to a story-teller. In front of them was a confusion of blackened pails and steaming vessels, into which they dipped with their naked fingers. Their faces were streaked with paint, their lips were greasy with traces of the dish, the air of the place was reeking from their breaths. My eyes were slower than Alicia's, and so I did not distinguish our quarry at first, although a slow sigh at my ear and a convulsive clutch at my arm told me that he was there.

"And then I, too, saw Running Elk. It was he who was talking, to whom the others listened. What a change two years had wrought! His voice was harsh and guttural, his face, through the painted daubs and streaks, was coarser and duller than when I had seen him. His very body was more thin and shrunken.

"He finished his tale while we stared at him; the circle broke into commendatory grunts, and he smiled in childlike satisfaction at the impression he had made. He leaned forward and, scrutinizing the litter of sooty pots, plunged his hand into the nearest one.

"Miss Harman stumbled back into the crowd and her place was taken by a squaw.

"'Running Elk,' I called, over the heads of those next the entrance, and, seeing my face against the night, he arose and came out, stepping over the others.

"'How do you do?' I said. 'You haven't forgotten me, have you?'

"He towered head and shoulders above me, his feather head-dress adding to his stature. The beaded patterns of his war-harness stood out dimly in the half-light.

"'No, no! I will never forget you, doctor. You—you have been sick.' The change in his speech was even more noticeable when he turned his tongue to English. He halted over his words and he mouthed them hesitatingly.

"'Yes, pretty sick. And you, what are you doing?'

"'I do what the rest do,' said he. 'Nothing! I have some horses and a few head of cattle, that is all.'

"'Are you satisfied?' I demanded, sharply. He eyed me darkly for an instant, then he answered, slowly:

"'I am an Indian. I am satisfied.'

"'Then education didn't do you any good, after all?' I was offended, disappointed; I must have spoken gruffly.

"This time he paused a long while before he replied.

"'I had dreams,' said he, 'many dreams, and they were splendid; but you told me that dreams were out of place in a Sioux, so I forgot them, along with all the things I had learned. It is better so.'

"Alicia Harman called me in a voice which I did not recognize, so I shook hands with Running Elk and turned away. He bowed his head and slunk back through the tepee door, back into the heart of his people, back into the past, and with him went my experiment. Since then I have never meddled with the gods nor given them cause to laugh at me."

The doctor arose and stretched himself, then he entered his tent for a match. The melancholy pulse of the drums and the minor-keyed chant which issued out of the night sounded like a dirge sung by a dying people.

"What became of Running Elk?" I inquired.

The old man answered from within. "That was he I asked about the horse-races. He's the man you couldn't understand, who wouldn't talk to you. He's nearly an Indian again. Alicia Harman married a duke."

THE MOON, THE MAID, AND THE WINGED SHOES

The last place I locked wheels with Mike Butters was in Idaho. I'd just sold a silver-lead prospect and was proclaimin' my prosperity with soundin' brass and ticklin' symbols. I was tuned up to G and singin' quartettes with the bartender—opery buffet, so to speak—when in Mike walked. It was a bright morning out-side and I didn't reco'nize him at first against the sunlight.

"Where's that cholera-morbus case?" said he.

"Stranger, them ain't sounds of cramps," I told him. "It's me singin' 'Hell Amongst the Yearlin's.'" Then I seen who he was and I fell among him.

When we'd abated ourselves I looked him over.

"What you doin' in all them good clothes?" I inquired.

"I'm a D.D.S."

"Do tell! All I ever took was the first three degrees. Gimme the grip and the password and I'll believe you."

"That ain't a Masonic symbol," said he. "I'm a dentist—a bony fido dentist, with forceps and a little furnace and a gas-bag and a waitin'-rooms". He swelled up and bit a hang-nail off of his cigar.

"Yep! A regular toothwright."

Naturally I was surprised, not to say awed. "Have you got much of a practice?" I made bold to ask.

"Um-m—It ain't what it ought to be, still I can't complain. It takes time to work into a fashionable clienteel. All I get a whack at now is Injuns, but I'm gradually beginnin' to close in on the white teeth."

Now this was certainly news to me, for Mike was a foot-racer, and a good one, too, and the last time I'd seen him he didn't know nothing about teeth, except that if you ain't careful they'll bite your tongue. I figured he was lyin', so I said:

"Where did you get your degree—off of a thermometer?"

"Nothing of the tall. I run it down. I did, for a God's fact. It's like this: three months ago I crep' into this burg lookin' for a match, but the professions was overcrowded, there bein' fourteen lawyers, a half-dozen doctors, a chiropodist, and forty-three bartenders here ahead of me, not to speak of a tooth-tinker. That there dentist thought he could sprint. He come from some Eastern college and his pa had grub-staked him to a kit of tools and sent him out here to work his way into the confidences and cavities of the Idahobos.

"Well, sir, the minute I seen him I realized he was my custard. He wore sofy cushions on his shoulders, and his coat was cut in at the back. He rolled up his pants, too, and sometimes he sweetened the view in a vi'lent, striped sweater. I watered at the mouth and picked my teeth over him—he was that succ'lent.

"He'd been lookin' down on these natives and kiddin' 'em ever since he arrived, and once a week, reg'lar, he tried to frame a race so's he could wear his runnin'-pants and be a hero. I had no trouble fixin' things. He was a good little runner, and he done his best; but when I breasted the tape I won a quick-claim deed to his loose change, to a brand-new office over a drug-store, and to enough nickel-plated pliers for a wire-tapper. I staked him to a sleeper ticket, then I moved into his quarters. The tools didn't have no directions on 'em, but I've figgered out how to use most of 'em."

"I gather that this here practice that you're buildin' up ain't exactly remunerative," I said to Mike.

"Not yet it ain't, but I'm widenin' out. There ain't a day passes that I don't learn something. I was out drummin' up a little trade when your groans convinced me that somebody in here had a jumpin' toothache. If you ain't busy, mebbe you can help me get a patient."

This particular saloon had about wore out its welcome with me, so I was game for any enterprise, and I allowed a little patient-huntin' would prob'ly do me good. I drawed my six gun and looked her over.

"It's a new sport, but I bet I'll take to it," said I. "What d'you do, crease 'em or cripple 'em?"

"Pshaw! Put up that hearse ticket," Mike told me. "Us doctors don't take human life, we save it."

"I thought you said you was practisin' on Injuns."

"Injuns is human. For a fact! I've learned a heap in this business. Not that I wouldn't bust one if I needed him, but it ain't necessary. Come, I'll show you."

This here town had more heathens than whites in it, and before we'd gone a block I seen a buck Injun and his squaw idlin' along, lookin' into the store winders. The buck was a hungry, long-legged feller, and when we neared him Mike said to me:

"Hist! There's one. I'll slip up and get him from behind. You grab him if he runs."

This method of buildin' up a dental practice struck me as some strange, but Butters was a queer guy and this was sort of a rough town. When he got abreast of Mr. Lo, Mike reached out and garnered him by the neck. The

Injun pitched some, but Mike eared him down finally, and when I come up I seen that one side of the lad's face was swelled up something fearful.

"Well, well," said I. "You've sure got the dentist's eye. You must have spied that swellin' a block away."

Mike nodded, then he said: "Poor feller! I'll bet it aches horrible. My office is right handy; let's get him in before the marshal sees us."

We drug the savage up-stairs and into Mike's dental stable, then we bedded him down in a chair. He protested considerable, but we got him there in a tollable state of preservation, barring the fact that he was skinned up on the corners and we had pulled a hinge off from the office door.

"It's a shame for a person to suffer thataway," Mike told me; "but these ignorant aborigines ain't educated up to the mercies of science. Just put your knee in his stummick, will you? What could be finer than to alleviate pain? The very thought in itself is elevatin'. I'm in this humanity business for life—Grab his feet quick or he'll kick out the winder."

"Whoa!" I told the Injun. "Plenty fix-um!" I poked the swellin' on his face and he let out a yelp.

"It's lucky we got him before multiplication set in," Mike assured me. "I lay for 'em that-away at the foot of the stairs every day; but this is the best patient I've had. I've a notion to charge this one."

"Don't you charge all of 'em?" I wanted to know.

"Nope. I got a tin watch off of one patient when he was under gas, but the most of 'em ain't worth goin' through. You got to do a certain amount of charity work."

"Don't look like much of a business to me," I said.

"There's something about it I like," Mike told me. "It sort of grows on a feller. Now that you're here to help catch 'em, I calc'late to acquire a lot of skill with these instruments. I've been playin' a lone hand and I've had to take little ones that I could handle."

When Mike produced a pair of nickel-plated nail-pullers, Mr. Injun snorted like a sea-lion, and it took both of us to hold him down; but finally I tied his hair around the head-rest and we had him. His mane was long and I put a hard knot in it, then I set on his moccasins while Doctor Butters pried into his innermost secrets.

"There she is—that big one." Mike pointed out a tooth that looked like the corner monument to a quartz claim.

"You're on the wrong side," I told him.

"Mebbe I am. Here's one that looks like it would come loose easier." Mike got a half-Nelson over in the east-half-east quarter-section of the buck's mouth and threw his weight on the pliers.

The Injun had pretty well wore himself out by this time, and when he felt those ice-tongs he just stiffened out—an Injun's dead game that-away;

he won't make a holler when you hurt him. His squaw was hangin' around with her eyes poppin' out, but we didn't pay no attention to her.

Somehow Mike's pinchers kept jumpin' the track and at every slip a new wrinkle showed in the patient's face—patient is the right word, all right—and we didn't make no more show at loosenin' that tusk than as if we'd tried to pull up Mount Bill Williams with a silk thread. At last two big tears come into the buck's eyes and rolled down his cheeks. First time I ever seen one cry.

Now that weakness was plumb fatal to him, for right there and then he cracked his plate with his missus. Yes, sir, he tore his shirt-waist proper. The squaw straightened up and give him a look—oh, what a look!

"Waugh!" she sniffed. "Injun heap big squaw!" And with that she swished out of the office and left him flat. Yes, sir, she just blew him on the spot.

I s'pose Mike would have got that tooth somehow—he's a perseverin' party—only that I happened to notice something queer and called him off.

"Here, wait a minute," said I, and I loosened him from the man's chest. Mike was so engorsed in the pursuit of his profession that he was astraddle of his patient's wishbone, gougin' away like a quartz miner. "Take your elbow out of his mouth and lemme talk to him a minute." When the savage had got his features together, I said to him, "How you catch um bump, hey?" And I pointed to his jaw.

"Bzz-zz-zz!" said he.

I turned to Doctor Butters. "Hornet!" I declared.

When Mike had sized up the bee-sting he admitted that my diagnosis was prob'ly correct. "That's the trouble with these patients," he complained. "They don't take you into their confidence. Just the same, I'm goin' to attend to his teeth, for there's no tellin' when I'll catch another one."

"What's wrong with his teeth?" I questioned. "They look good to me, except they're wore down from eatin' camus. If he was a horse I'd judge him to be about a ten-year-old."

"You never can tell by lookin' at teeth what's inside of 'em. Anyhow, a nice fillin' would set 'em off. I ain't tried no fillin's yet. Gimme that Burley drill."

I wheeled out a kind of sewing-machine; then I pedaled it while Mike dug into that Injun's hangin' wall like he had a round of holes to shoot before quittin'-time. This here was more in my line, bein' a hard-rock miner myself, and we certainly loaded a fine prospect of gold into that native's bi-cuspidor. We took his front teeth because they was the easiest to get at.

It was just like I said, this Injun's white keys was wore off short and looked like they needed something, so we laid ourselves out to supply the want. We didn't exactly fill them teeth; we merely riveted on a sort of a plowshare—a gold sod-cutter about the size of your finger-nail. How Mike got it to stick I don't know, but he must have picked up quite a number of dentist's tricks before I came. Anyhow, there she hung like a brass name-plate, and she didn't wabble hardly at all. You'd of been surprised to see what a difference it made in that redskin's looks.

We let our patient up finally and put a lookin'-glass in his hand. At first he didn't know just what to make of that fillin'; but when he seen it was real gold a grin broke over his face, his chest swelled up, and he walked out of the office and across the street to a novelty store. In a minute out he came with a little round lookin'-glass and a piece of buckskin, and the last we seen of him he was hikin' down the street, grinnin' into that mirror as happy as a child and polishin' that tusk like it had started to rust.

"Which I sure entitle a gratifyin' operation," said Mike.

"I'm in no ways proud of the job," I told him. "I feel like I'd salted a mine."

Well, me and Mike lived in them dental parlors for a couple of weeks, decoyin' occasional natives into it, pullin', spilin', fillin', and filin' more teeth than a few, but bimeby the sport got tame.

One day Mike was fakin' variations on his guitar, and I was washin' dishes, when I said: "This line is about as excitin' as a game of jack-straws. D'you know it's foot-racin' time with the Injuns?"

"What?"

"Sure. They're gettin' together at old Port Lewis to run races this week. One tribe or the other goes broke and walks home every year. If we could meet up with the winnin' crowd, down on the La Plata—"

I didn't have to say no more, for I had a hackamore on Mike's attention right there, and he quit climbin' the "G" string and put up his box.

The next day we traded out of the tooth business and rode south down the old Navajo trail. We picked a good campin' spot—a little "flat" in a bend of the river where the grazin' was good—and we turned the ponies out.

We didn't have to wait long. A few evenings later, as we et supper we heard a big noise around the bend and knew our visitors was comin'. They must of had three hundred head of horses, besides a big outfit of blankets, buckskin, baskets, and all the plunder that an Injun outfit travels with. At sight of us in their campin'-place they halted, and the squaws and the children rode up to get a look at us.

I stepped out in front of our tent and throwed my hand to my forehead, shading my eyes—that's the Injun sign of friendship. An old chief and a couple of warriors rode forrad, Winchester to pommel, but, seein' we was alone, they sheathed their guns, and we invited 'em to eat.

It didn't take much urgin'. While we fed hot biscuits to the head men the squaws pitched camp.

They was plumb elated at their winnin' up at Fort Lewis, and the gamblin' fever was on 'em strong, so right after supper they invited us to join 'em in a game of Mexican monte. I let Mike do the card-playin' for our side, because he's got a pass which is the despair of many a "tin-horn." He can take a clean Methodist-Episcopal deck, deal three hands, and have every face card so it'll answer to its Christian name. No, he didn't need no lookout, so I got myself into a game of "bounce the stick," which same, as you prob'ly know, is purely a redskin recreation. You take a handful of twigs in your hand, then throw 'em on to a flat rock endways, bettin' whether an odd or an even number will fall outside of a ring drawed in the dirt. After a couple of hours Mike strolled up and tipped me the wink that he'd dusted his victims.

"Say," he began, "there's the niftiest chicken down here that I ever see."

"Don't start any didos with the domestic relations of this tribe," I told him, "or they'll spread us out, and spread us thin. Remember, you're here on business bent, and if you bend back and forrads, from business to pleasure, and versy visa, you'll bust. These people has scrooplous ideas regardin' their wives and I respect 'em."

"She ain't married," Mike told me. "She's the chief's daughter, and she looks better to me than a silver mine."

Durin' that evening we give the impression that we was well heeled, so the tribe wasn't in no hurry to break camp on the following morning.

Along about noon I missed Mike, and I took a stroll to look for him. I found him—and the chief's daughter—alongside of a shady trout pool. She was weavin' a horsehair bracelet onto his wrist, and I seen the flash of his ring on her finger. Mike could travel some.

He was a bit flustered, it seemed to me, and he tried to laugh the matter off, but the girl didn't. There was something about the look of her that I didn't like. I've seen a whole lot of trouble come from less than a horsehair bracelet. This here quail was mebbe seventeen; she was slim and shy, and she had big black eyes and a skin like velvet. I spoke to Mike in words of one syllable, and I drug him away with me to our tent.

That afternoon some half-grown boys got to runnin' foot-races and Mike entered. He let 'em beat him, then he offered to bet a pony that they couldn't do it again. The kids was game, and they took him quick. Mike faked the race, of course, and lost his horse, that bein' part of our progam.

When it was all over I seen the chief's daughter had been watchin' us, but she didn't say nuthin'. The next mornin', however, when we got up we found a bully pinto pony tied to one of our tent stakes.

"Look who's here," said I. "Young Minnie Ha-ha has made good your losin's."

"That pony is worth forty dollars," said Mike.

"Sure. And you're as good as a squaw-man this minute. You're betrothed."

"Am I?" The idy didn't seem to faze Mike. "If that's the case," said he, "I reckon I'll play the string out. I sort of like it as far as I've gone."

"I wish she'd gave us that cream-colored mare or hers," I said. "It's worth two of this one."

"I'll get it to-day," Mike declared. And sure enough, he lost another foot-race, and the next morning the cream-colored mare was picketed in front of our tent.

Well, this didn't look good to me, and I told Mike so. I never was much of a hand to take money from women, so I served a warnin' on him that if we didn't get down to business pretty quick and make our clean-up I proposed to leave him flat on his back.

That day the young men of the tribe did a little foot-runnin', and Mike begged 'em to let him in. It was comical to see how pleased they was. They felt so sure of him that they began pro-ratin' our belongin's among one another. They laid out a half-mile course, and everybody in camp went out to the finish-line to see the contest and to bet on it. The old chief acted as judge, bookmaker, clerk of the course, referee, and stakeholder. I s'pose by the time the race was ready to start there must of been fifty ponies up, besides a lot of money, but the old bird kept every wager in his head. He rolled up a couple of blankets and placed 'em on opposite sides of the track, and showed us by motions that the first man between 'em would be declared the winner. All the money that had been bet he put in little piles on a blanket; then he give the word to get ready.

I had no trouble layin' our money at one to five, and our ponies at the same odds; then, when everything was geared up, I called Mike from his tent. Say, when he opened the fly and stepped out there was a commotion, for all he had on was his runnin'-trunks and his spiked shoes. The Injuns was in breech-cloths and moccasins, and, of course, they created no comment; but the sight of a half-nekked white man was something new to these people, and the first flash they got at Mike's fancy togs told 'em they'd once more fell a victim to the white man's wiles.

They was wise in a minute, and some of the young hot-bloods was for smokin' us up, but the chief was a sport—I got to give the old bird credit. He rared back on his hind legs and made a stormy palaver; as near as I could judge he told his ghost-dancers they'd been cold-decked, but he expected 'em to take their medicine and grin, and, anyhow, it was a lesson to 'em. Next time they'd know better'n to monkey with strangers. Whatever it was he said, he made his point, and after a right smart lot of powwowin' the entertainment proceeded. But Mike and me was as popular with them people as a couple of polecats at a picnic.

Mike certainly made a picture when he lined up at the start; he stood out like a marble statue in a slate quarry. I caught a glimpse of the chief's daughter, and her eyes was bigger than ever, and she had her hands clinched at her side. He must have looked like a god to her; but, for that matter, he was a sight to turn any untamed female heart, whether the owner et Belgian hare off of silver service or boiled jack-rabbit out of a coal-oil can. Women are funny thataway.

It's a pot-hunter's maxim never to win by a big margin, but to nose out his man at the finish. This Mike did, winnin' by a yard; then he acted as if he was all in—faked a faint, and I doused him with a sombrero of water from the creek. It was a spectacular race, at that, for at the finish the runners was bunched till a blanket would of covered 'em. When they tore into the finish I seen the chief's girl do a trick. Mike was runnin' on the outside, and when nobody was watchin' her the little squaw kicked one of them blanket bundles about two feet down the course, givin' Mike that much the "edge." She done it clever and it would have throwed a close race.

Them savages swallered their physic and grinned, like the chief had told 'em, and they took it standin' up. They turned over the flower of their pony herd to us, not to mention about six quarts of silver money and enough blankets to fill our tent. The old chief patted Mike on the back, then put both hands to his temples with his fingers spread out, as much as to say, "He runs like a deer."

Bimeby a buck stepped up and begun makin' signs. He pointed to the sun four times, and we gathered that he wanted us to wait four days until he could go and get another man.

Mike tipped me the wink, sayin': "They're goin' after the champeen of the tribe. That phony faint of mine done it. Will we wait? Why, say, we'd wait four years, wouldn't we? Sweet pickin's, I call it. Champeen, huh?"

"For me, I'd wait here till I was old folks," I said. "I don't aim to leave these simple savages nothin'. Nothin' at all, but a lot of idle regrets."

Well, sir, there was a heap of excitement in that camp for the next three days. All them Injuns done, was to come and look at Mike and feel of his legs and argue with one another. The first night after the race Mike tuned up his guitar, and later on I heard snatches of the "Spanish Fandango" stealin' up from the river bank. I knew what was on; I knew without lookin' that the old chief's girl was right there beside him, huggin' her knees and listenin' with both ears. I didn't like to think about it, for she was a nice little yearlin', and it looked to me like Mike was up to his usual devilment. Seemed like a low-down trick to play on an injunoo like her, and the more I studied it the warmer I got. It was a wonderful night; the moonlight drenched the valley, and there was the smell of camp-fires and horses over everything—just the sort of a night for a guitar, just the sort of a night to make your blood run hot and to draw you out into the glitter and make you race with your shadow.

When Mike moseyed in, along about ten o'clock, he was plumb loco; the moon-madness was on him strong. His eyes was as bright as silver coins, and his voice had a queer ring to it.

"What a night!" said he. "And what a life this is Lord! I'm tired of pot-huntin'. I've trimmed suckers till I'm weary; I've toted a gold brick in my pocket till my clothes bag. I'm sick of it. I'm goin' to beat this Injun champeen, take my half of our winnin's, sell off the runty ones, and settle down."

"Where do you aim to settle?" I inquired.

"Oh, anywhere hereabouts. These are good people, and I like 'em."

"You mean you're goin' to turn out with the Injuns?" I inquired, with my mouth open. Mike had led so sudden that he had me over the ropes.

"I'm goin' to do that very little thing," he declared. "I dunno how to talk much Navajo, but I'm learnin' fast, and she got my meanin'. We understand each other, and we'll do better as time goes on. She calls me 'Emmike'! Sweet, ain't it?" He heaved a sigh, then he gargled a laugh that sounded like boilin' mush. "It ain't often a feller like me gets a swell little dame that worships him. Horses, guns, camp-fires! Can you beat it?"

"If that squaw had a soft palate or a nose like a eeclair, you wouldn't be so keen for this simple life," I told him. "She has stirred up your wickedness, Mike, and you've gone nutty. You're moon-crazy, that's all. You cut it out."

I argued half the night; but the more I talked the more I seen that Mike was stuck to be a renegade. It's a fact. If he hadn't of been a nice kid I'd of cut his hobbles and let him go; but—pshaw! Mike Butters could run too fast to be wasted among savages, and, besides, it's a terrible thing for a white man to marry an Injun. The red never dies out in the woman, but the white in the man always changes into a dirty, muddy red. I laid awake a long while tryin' to figger out a way to block his game, but the only thing I could think of was to tie him up and wear out a cinch on him. Just as I was dozin' off I had an idy. I didn't like it much at first; I had to swaller hard to down it, but the more I studied it the better it looked, so for fear I'd weaken I rolled over and went to sleep.

Mike was in earnest, and so was the girl; that much I found out the next day. And she must of learned him enough Navajo to propose marriage with, and he must of learned her enough English to say "yes," for she took possession of our camp and begun to order me around. First thing she lugged our Navajo blankets to the creek, washed 'em, then spread 'em over some bushes and beat 'em with a stick until they were as clean and soft as thistledown. I'll admit she made a pleasant picture against the bright colors of them blankets, and I couldn't altogether blame Mike for losin' his head. He'd lost it, all right. Every time she looked at him out of them big black eyes he got as wabbly as clabber. It was plumb disgustin'.

That evenin' he give her a guitar lesson. Now Mike himself was a sad musician, and the sound of him fandangoin' uncertainly up and down the fretful spine of that instrument was a tribulation I'd put up with on account of friendship, pure and simple, but when that discord-lovin' lady cliff-dweller set all evenin' in our tent and scraped snake-dances out of them catguts with a fish-bone, I pulled my freight and laid out in the moonlight with the dogs.

Mike's infatuation served one purpose, though; he spent so much time with the squab that it give me an opportunity to work out my scheme. That guitar lesson showed me that vig'rous measures was necessary, so I dug up a file, a shoemaker's needle and some waxed thread, all of which we had in our kit.

On the fourth morning there was a stir in the camp, and we knew that the courier had got back with his runner. Pretty soon the whole village stormed up to our tent in a body.

"Let's go out and look him over," I said.

"What's the use of lookin' at him?" Mike inquired. "All Injuns look alike—except one."

I pulled back the tent fly and stepped out; then I called to Mike, for the first thing I seen was that gold fillin' of ours. Yes, sir, right there, starin' me in the eye, was the sole and shinin' monument to me and Mike's brief whirl at the science of dentistry. The face surroundin' it was stretched wide and welcome, and the minute this here new-comer reco'nized me, he drawed back his upper lip and pointed proudly to his ornament, then he dug up his lookin'-glass and his polishin'-rag and begun to dust it off. It was plain to be seen that he thought more of it than his right eye. And it impressed the other Injuns, too; they crowded up and studied it. They took turns feelin' of it, especially the squaws, and I bet if we'd had our dentist outfit with us we could of got rich right there. The chief's daughter, in particular, was took with the beauties of that gew-gaw, and she made signs to us that she wanted one just like it.

"I never noticed he was so rangy," Mike told me, when he'd sized up the new arrival. "Say, this guy looks good. He's split plumb to the larynx and I bet he can run, for all of that wind-shield."

I noticed that Mike was pretty grave when he come back in the tent, and more than once that day I caught him lookin' at the champeen, sort of studyin' him out. But for that matter this new party was gettin' his full share of attention; everywhere he went there was a trail of kids at his heels, and every time he opened his mouth he made a hit with the grown folks. The women just couldn't keep their eyes offen him, and I seen that Mike was gettin' pretty sore.

In the evenin' he made a confession that tipped off the way his mind was workin'. "This is the first time I ever felt nervous before a race," said he. "Mebbe it's because it's goin' to be my last race; mebbe it's because that Injun knows me and ain't scared of me. Anyhow, I'm scared of *him*. That open-faced, Elgin-movement buck has got me tickin' fast."

"That ain't what's got your goat," I told him.

"Your cooin' dove is dazzled by that show of wealth, and you know it."

"Hell! She's just curious, that's all. She's just a kid. I—I wish I'd of known who he was when I treated him. I'd of drove a horse-shoe nail in his knee."

But all the same Mike looked worried.

It rained hard that night, and the next morning the grass was pretty wet. Mike tried it, first thing, and come back grinnin' till the top of his head was an island.

"That sod is so slippery old Flyin' Cloud can't get a good stride in his moccasins. Me, I can straddle out and take holt with my spikes. Them spikes is goin' to put us on easy street. You see! I don't care how good he is, they're goin' to give me four hundred head of broncs and a cute little pigeon to look out for 'em. Me, I'm goin' to lay back and learn to play the guitar. I'm goin' to learn it by note."

"You sure got the makin's of a squaw-man," I told him. "Seems like I've over-read your hand. I used to think you had somethin' in you besides a appetite, but I was wrong. You're plumb cultus, Mike."

"Don't get sore," he grinned. "I got my chance to beat the game and I'm goin' to take it. I can't run foot-races, and win 'em, all my life. Some day I'll step in my beard and sprain my ankle. Ambition's a funny thing. I got the ambition to quit work. Besides, she—you know—she's got a dimple you could lay your finger in. You'd ought to hear her say 'Emmike'; it's certainly cute."

We bet everything we had—everything except that pinto pony and the cream-colored mare. I held them two out, for I figgered we was goin' to need 'em and need 'em bad, if my scheme worked out.

The course—it was a quarter-mile, straight-away—was laid out along the bottom-land where the grass was thick and short. Me and the chief and his girl set on a blanket among the little piles of silver, and the rest of the merry villagers lined up close to the finish-line. We white men had been the prime attraction up till now, but it didn't take me long to see that we wasn't any more. Them people was all wrapped up in the lad with the gold name-plate, and they was rootin' for him frantic. Last thing he done was to give his eighteen-carat squaw-catcher the once-over with his buckskin buffer, then he shined it at the chief's girl and trotted down to the startin'-line. I noticed that she glued her big-and-liquids on him and kept 'em there.

It was beautiful to watch those two men jockey for a start; the Injun was lean and hungry and mighty smart—but Mike was smarter still. Of course he got the jump.

It was a pretty start, and Mike held his lead for fifty yards or more. I'll admit I was worked up. I've had my heart in my mouth so often over his races that it's wore smooth from swallerin', but this time it just wouldn't go down. Our dental patient was runnin' an awful race, but it looked like Mike had him; then, just as the boy settled down and reached out into that long, strong stride of his'n, something happened. He slipped. He would have fell, except that he caught himself. The next second he slipped again, and Mr. "Man in Love with a Gold Fillin'" passed him.

With that them Injuns begun to speak. Some of their yells brought hunks of throat with 'em, and that whole region begun to echo as far south as the Rio Bravo.

My scheme had worked, all right. You see, when Mike was doin' his heavy courtin' I'd planted my ace in the hole; I'd took off the outer soles of his runnin'-shoes and filed the spikes almost in two, close up to the plate. When I sewed the leather back on, it never showed, but the minute he struck his gait they broke with him and he begin to miss his pull. He might have won at that, for he's got the heart of a lion, but I s'pose the surprise did as much as anything else to beat him. It made my heart bleed to see the fight he put up, but he finished six feet to the bad and fell across the mark on his face, sobbin' like a child. It's the game ones that cry when they're licked; analyze a smilin' loser and you'll find the yellow streak. I lifted him to his feet, but he was shakin' like a bush in the wind.

"Them shoes!" he wailed. "Them damned shoes!" Then he busted out again and blubbered like a kid.

Right then I done some actin'; but, pshaw! anybody can act when he has to. If I'd of overplayed my hand a nickel's worth he'd of clumb up me like a rat up a rafter and there would of been human reminders all over that neighborhood. Not but what I would have got him eventually, bein' as I had my side-arms, but I liked Mike and I wouldn't kill nobody if I was sober.

It happened that he fell right at the feet of the chief's girl, and when I lifted him up he seen her. But, say, it must have been a shock to him. Her eyes was half shut, her head was throwed back, and she was hissin' like a rattlesnake. Mike stiffened and sort of pawed at her, but she drawed away just like that other squaw in our dentist office had drawed away from her liege lord and master.

"Waugh! White man heap squaw!" said she, and with that she flirted her braids and turned to the winner of the race. She went up to him and lifted his lip with her thumb like she just had to have another look at his gold tooth, then she smiled up into his face and they walked away together without a glance in our direction.

Mike follered a step or two, then he stopped and stared around at the crowd. It was a big minute for him, and for me, too, and I'll prob'ly never forget the picture of that pantin' boy at bay among them grinnin' barbarians. The curs was yappin' at his heels, the squaws was gigglin' and makin' faces, the bucks was showin' their teeth and pointin' at his tears.

Mike never said a word. He just stooped down and peeled off his runnin'-shoes, then he throwed 'em as far as he could, right out into the river. "Who the hell would marry a dame like that?" he sobbed. "She's stuck on his jewelry."

"Come on, lad," said I; and I led him to our tent. Then, while he put on his clothes, I saddled the pinto pony and the cream-colored mare, for it was six days to the railroad.

FLESH

I

Should you chance, in crossing a certain mountain pass in southern Catalonia, to find yourself poised above a little valley against the opposite side of which lies a monastery, look to the heights above it. Should you piece out from among the rocks the jagged ruins of a castle, ask its name. Your guide will perhaps inform you that those blackened stones are called "The Teeth of the Moor," and if he knows the story he will doubtless tell it to you, crossing himself many times during the recital. In all probability, however, he will merely shrug his shoulders and say it is a place of bad repute, nothing more.

Even the monks of the monastery, who are considered well versed in local history, have forgotten the reason for the name, although they recall the legend that once upon a time the castle harbored a haughty Moslem lord. Few of them ever heard the story of Joseph the Anchorite, and how he sought flesh within its portals; those who have will not repeat it. Time was, however, when the tale was fresh, and it runs this wise:

Away back in the reign of Abderamus the Just, First Caliph of the West, Hafiz, a certain warlike Moor, amazed at the fertility of this region, established on the edge of the plateau a stronghold of surprising security. His house he perched upon the crest of the cliff overlooking the valley below. It was backed by verdant, sun-kissed slopes which quickly yielded tribute in such quantity as to render him rich and powerful. Hafiz lived and fought and died beneath the Crescent banner, leaving in his place a son, who likewise waged war to the northward on behalf of the Prophet and all True Believers, at the same time farming his rich Catalonian acres.

Generations came and went, and, although the descendants of Hafiz waxed strong, so also did the power of the hated Christians. Living as they did upon the very fringe of the Mussulman empire, the Moors beheld with consternation the slow encroachment of the Unbelievers—more noticeable here than farther to the southward. At intervals these enemies were driven back, but invariably they reappeared, until at length, upon the plain beneath the castle, monks came and built a monastery which they called San Sebastian. Beneath the very eyes of Abul Malek, fourth descendant of Hafiz, they raised their impious walls; although he chafed to wreak a bloody vengeance for this outrage, his hands were tied by force of circumstance. Wearied with interminable wars, the Moorish nation had sought respite; peace dozed upon the land. Men rested and took from the earth new strength with which to resume the never-ending struggle between the Crescent and the Cross, wherefore Abul Malek's rage availed him nothing. From his embrasured windows he beheld the cassocked enemies of his creed passing to and fro about their business; he heard his sacred hour of prayer desecrated by their Christian bells, and could do no more than revile them for dogs, the while he awaited the will of Allah. It was scant comfort for a man of his violent temper.

But the truce threatened never to be broken. Years passed and still peace continued to reign. Meanwhile the Moor fed upon his wrongs and, from incessant brooding over them, became possessed of a fury more fanatical, more poisonous even than had been engendered by his many battles.

Finally, when the wrong had bit too deep for him to endure, he summoned all his followers, and selecting from their number one hundred of the finest horsemen, he bade them make ready for a journey to Cordova; then in their presence he kissed the blue blade of his scimitar and vowed that the shackles which had hampered him and them would be struck off.

For many days there ensued the bustle and the confusion of a great preparation in the house of the Moor; men came and went, women sewed and cleaned and burnished; horses were groomed, their manes were combed and their hoofs were polished; and then one morning, ere the golden sun was an hour high, down the winding trail past the monastery of San Sebastian, came a brilliant cavalcade. Abul Malek led, seated upon an Arabian steed whiter than the clouds which lay piled above the westward mountains. His two sons, Hassam and Elzemah, followed astride horses as black as night— horses the distinguished pedigrees of which were cited in the books of Ibn Zaid. Back of them came one hundred swarthy warriors on other coal-black mounts, whose flashing sides flung back the morning rays. Their flowing linen robes were like the snow, and from their turbans gleamed gems of value. Each horseman bore at his girdle a purse, a kerchief, and a poinard; and in their purses lay two thousand dinars of gold. Slaves brought up the rear of the procession, riding asses laden with bales, and they led fifty blood-red bays caparisoned as for a tournament.

With scowling glances at the monastery the band rode on across the valley, climbed to the pass, and disappeared. After many days they arrived at Cordova, then when they had rested and cleansed themselves, Abul Malek craved audience of the Caliph, Aboul-Abbas El Hakkam. Being of distinguished reputation, his wish was quickly granted; and on the following day in the presence of the Hadjeb, the viziers, the white and black eunuchs, the archers, and the cuirassiers of the guard, he made a gift to his sovereign of those hundred northern horsemen and their mounts, those fifty blooded bays and their housings, those bales of aloe-wood and camphor, those silken pieces and those two thousand dinars of yellow Catalonian gold. This done, he humbly craved a favor in return, and when bade to speak, he began by telling of the indignities rendered him by the monks of San Sebastian.

"Five generations my people have dwelt upon our lands, serving the true God and His Prophet," he declared, with quivering indignation; "but now those idolaters have come. They gibe and they mock at me beneath my very window. My prayers are broken by their yammerings; they defile my casement, and the stench of their presence assails my nostrils."

"What do you ask of me?" inquired the Caliph.

"I ask for leave to cleanse my doorstep."

The illustrious Moslem shook his head, whereat Abul Malek cried:

"Does not the Koran direct us to destroy the unbelieving and the impious? Must I then suffer these infidels to befoul my garden?"

"God is merciful; it is His will that for a time the Unbelievers shall appear to flourish," said the Caliph. "We are bound by solemn compact with the kings of Leon and Castile to observe an armistice. That armistice we shall observe, for our land is weary of wars, our men are tired, and their scars must heal. It is not for you or for me to say: 'This is good, or this is evil.' Allah's will be done!"

Abul Malek and his sons returned alone to their mountains, but when they reined in at the door of their castle the father spat venomously at the belfried roof of the monastery beneath and vowed that he would yet work his will upon it.

Now that the Law forbade him to make way with his enemies by force, he canvassed his brain for other means of effecting their downfall; but every day the monks went on with their peaceful tasks, unmindful of his hatred, and their impious religion spread about the countryside. Abul Malek's venom passed them by; they gazed upon him with gentle eyes in which there was no spleen, although in him they recognized a bitter foe.

As time wore on his hatred of their religion became centered upon the monks themselves, and he undertook by crafty means to annoy them. Men said these Christian priests were good; that their lives were spent in prayer, in meditation, and in works of charity among the poor; tales came to the Moor of their spiritual existence, of their fleshly renunciation; but at these he scoffed. He refused to credit them.

"Pah!" he would cry, tugging at his midnight beard; "how can these men be aught but liars, when they live and preach a falsehood? Their creed is impious, and they are hypocrites. They are not superior beings, they are flesh like you or me. They have our passions and our faults, but a thousand times multiplied, for they walk in darkness and dwell in hypocrisy. Beneath their cassocks is black infamy; their hearts are full of evil—aye, of lust and of every unclean thing. Being false to the true God, they are false to themselves and to the religion they profess; and I will prove it." Thus ran his reasoning.

In order to make good his boast Abul Malek began to study the monks carefully, one after another. He tried temptation. A certain gross-bellied fellow he plied with wine. He flattered and fawned upon the simple friar; he led him into his cellars, striving to poison the good man's body as well as his mind; but the visitor partook in moderation, and preached the gospel of Christ so earnestly that the Saracen fled from his presence, bathing himself in clean water to be rid of the pollution.

Next he laid a trap for the Abbot himself. He selected the fairest of his slaves, a well-rounded woman of great physical charm, and bribed her with a girdle of sequins. She sought out the Abbot and professed a hunger for his creed. Bound thus by secrecy to the pious man, she lured him by every means at her command. But the Abbot had room for no passion save the love of Christ, and her wiles were powerless against this armor.

Abul Malek was patient; he renewed his vow to hold the false religion up to ridicule and laughter, thinking, by encompassing the downfall of a single advocate, thus to prove his contention and checkmate its ever-widening influence. He became obsessed by this idea; he schemed and he contrived; he used to the utmost the powers of his Oriental mind. From his vantage-point above the cloister he heard the monks droning at their Latin; his somber glances followed them at their daily tasks. Like a spider he spun his web, and when one victim broke through it he craftily repaired its fabric, luring another into its meshes.

At times he shared his vigil with his daughter Zahra, a girl of twelve, fast growing into womanhood; and since she had inherited his wit and temperament, he taught her to share his hatred of the black-robed men.

This Moorish maiden possessed the beauty of her mother, who had died in childbirth; and in honor of that celebrated favorite of Abderamus III. she had been christened "Flower of the World." Nor was the title too immoderate, as all men who saw her vowed. Already the hot sun of Catalonia had ripened her charms, and neighboring lords were beginning to make extravagant overtures of marriage. But seeing in her a possible weapon more powerful than any he had yet launched against the monks of San Sebastian, the father refused to consider even the best of them. He continued to keep her at his side, pouring his hatred into her ears until she, too, was ablaze with it.

Zahra was in her fourteenth year when Abul Malek beheld, one day, a new figure among those in the courtyard of the monastery below. Even from his eminence the Saracen could see that this late-comer was a giant man, for the fellow towered head and shoulders above his brethren. Inquiry taught him that the monk's name was Joseph. Nor was their meeting long delayed, for a sickness fell among the people of the valley, and Abul Malek, being skilled in medicine, went out to minister among the poor, according to his religion. At the sick-bed of a shepherd the two men came face to face.

Joseph was not young, nor was he old, but rather he had arrived at the perfect flower of his manhood, and his placid soul shone out through features of unusual strength and sweetness. In him the crafty Moor beheld a difference which for a time was puzzling. But eventually he analyzed it. The other monks had once been worldly men—they showed it in their faces; the countenance of Fray Joseph, on the contrary, was that of a boy, and it was without track of temptation or trace of evil. He had lived a sheltered life from his earliest youth, so it transpired, and Abul Malek rejoiced in the discovery, it being his belief that all men are flesh and that within them smolder flames which some day must have mastery. If this monk had never let his youth run free, if he had never met temptation and conquered it, those pent-up forces which inhabit all of us must be gathering power, year by year, and once the joint of this armor had been found, once it could be pierced, he would become earthly like other men, and his false religion would drop away, leaving him naked under the irksome garb of priesthood.

Accordingly, the Moor tested Fray Joseph, as he had tested the Abbot and the others, but to no avail, and he was in despair, until one day the secret of his failure was unexpectedly revealed.

Being busied with his accounts, he had repaired to the shade of a pomegranate grove near the cliff, the better to escape the heat; while so engaged up the path from the monastery came the good brother. Just abreast of Abul Malek's point of vantage Joseph paused to listen. A songbird was trilling wondrously and the monk's face, raised toward the pomegranate trees, became transfigured. He changed as if by magic; his lips parted in a tender smile, his figure grew tense with listening; not until the last note had died away did he move. Then a great breath stirred his lungs, and with shining eyes and rapt countenance he went on into the fields.

Abul Malek rose, his white teeth gleaming through his beard.

"Allah be praised!" he exclaimed. "It is music!" And rolling up his papers, he went into the house.

Early on the following morning another cavalcade filed down past the monastery of San Sebastian; but this procession was in great contrast to the one that had gone by five years before. Instead of gaily caparisoned warriors, it was composed mainly of women and slaves, with a mere handful of guards to lead the way. There were bondmaidens and seamstresses, an ancient nurse and a tutor of languages; while astride of a palfrey at her father's side rode the youthful lady of the castle. Her veil was wet upon her cheeks, her eyes were filled with shadows; yet she rode proudly, like a princess.

Once more the train moved past the sun-baked walls of the monastery, across the plain to the mountain road that led to the land of bounty and of culture. Late that afternoon Brother Joseph learned from the lips of a herdsman that the beauteous Zahra, flower of all the Moorish race, had gone to Cordova to study music.

II

Abul Malek once more rode home alone to his castle; but this time as he dismounted at his door he smiled at the monastery below.

Four years crept by, during which the Saracen lord brooded over the valley and the monk Joseph went his simple way, rendering service where he could, preaching, by the example of his daily life and his unselfish devotion, a sermon more powerful than his lips could utter. Through it all the Moor watched him carefully, safeguarding him as a provident farmer fattens a sheep for the slaughter. Once a year the father rode southward to Cordova, bringing news with his return that delighted the countryside, news that penetrated even the walls of San Sebastian and filled the good men therein with gladness. It seemed that the maiden Zahra was becoming a great musician. She pursued her studies in the famous school of Ali-Zeriab, and not even Moussali himself, that most gifted of Arabian singers, could bring more tender notes from the lute than could this fair daughter of Catalonia. Her skill transcended that of Al Farabi, for the harp, the tabor, and the mandolin were wedded to her dancing fingers; and, most marvelous of all, her soul was so filled with poetry that her verses were sung from Valencia to Cadiz. It was said that she could move men to laughter, to tears, to deeds of heroism—that she could even lull them to sleep by the potency of her magic. She had once played before the Caliph under amazing circumstances.

The Prince of True Believers, so ran the story, had quarreled with his favorite wife, and in consequence had fallen into a state of melancholy so deep as to threaten his health and to alarm his ministers. Do what they would, he still declined, until in despair the Hadjeb sent for Zahra, daughter of Abul Malek. She came, surrounded by her servants, and sang before El Hakkam. So cunningly did she contrive her verses, so tender were her airs, so potent were her fluttering fingers, that those within hearing were moved to tears, and the unhappy lover himself became so softened that he sped to the arms of his offended beauty and a reconciliation occurred. In token of his gratitude he had despatched a present of forty thousand drachmas of gold to the singer, and her renown went broadcast like a flame.

When Abul Malek heard of this he praised his God, and, gathering his horsemen, he set out to bring his daughter home, for the time was ripe.

One evening in early spring, that magic season when nature is most charming, Fray Joseph, returning to his cell, heard from behind a screen of verdure alongside his path a woman singing. But was this singing? he asked himself. Could mortal lips give birth to melody like this? It was the sighing of summer winds through rustling leaves, the music of crystal brooks on stony courses, the full-throated worship of birds. Joseph listened, enthralled, like a famished pilgrim in the desert. His simple soul, attuned to harmonies of the woodland, leaped in answer; his fancy, starved by years of churchly rigor, quickened like a prisoner at the light of day. Not until the singer had ceased did he resume his way, and through his dreams that night ran the song of birds, the play of zephyrs, the laughter of bubbling springs.

A few evenings later he heard the voice again, and paused with lips apart, with heart consumed by eagerness. It was some slave girl busied among the vines of Abul Malek, he decided, for she translated all the fragmentary airs that float through summer evenings—the songs of sweethearts, the tender airs of motherhood, the croon of distant waterfalls, the voice of sleepy locusts—and yet she wove them into an air that carried words. It was most wonderful.

Joseph felt a strong desire to mingle his voice with the singer's, but he knew his throat to be harsh and stiff from chanting Latin phrases. He knew not whither the tune would lead, and yet, when she sang, he followed, realizing gladly that she voiced the familiar music of his soul. He was moved to seek her out and to talk with her, until he remembered with a start that she was a woman and he a priest.

Each night he shaped his course so as to bring him past the spot where the mysterious singer labored, and in time he began to feel the stirring of a very earthly curiosity, the which he manfully fought down. Through the long, heated hours of the day he hummed her airs and repeated her verses, longing for the twilight hour which would bring the angel voice from out the vineyard. Eventually the girl began to sing of love, and Joseph echoed the songs in solitude, his voice as rasping and untrue as that of a frog.

Then, one evening, he heard that which froze him in his tracks. The singer accompanied herself upon some instrument the like of which he had never imagined. The music filled the air with heavenly harmony, and it set him to vibrating like a tautened string; it rippled forth, softer than the breeze, more haunting than the perfume of the frangipani. Joseph stood like a man in a trance, forgetful of all things save these honeyed sounds, half minded to believe himself favored by the music of the seraphim.

Never had he dreamed of such an intoxication. And then, as if to intensify his wild exultation, the maiden sang a yearning strain of passion and desire.

The priest began to tremble. His heart-beats quickened, his senses became unbridled; something new and mighty awoke within him, and he was filled with fever. His huge thews tightened, his muscles swelled as if for battle, yet miracle of miracles, he was melting like a child in tears! With his breath tugging at his throat, he turned off the path and parted the verdure, going as soundlessly as an animal; and all the while his head was whirling, his eyes took note of nothing. He was drawn as by a thousand invisible strings, which wound him toward the hidden singer.

But suddenly the music ended in a peal of rippling laughter and there came the rustle of silken garments. Fray Joseph found himself in a little open glade, so recently vacated that a faint perfume still lingered to aggravate his nostrils. Beyond stretched the vineyard of the Moor, a tangle of purpling vines into the baffling mazes of which the singer had evidently fled.

So she had known of his presence all along, the monk reflected, dizzily. It followed, therefore, that she must have waited every evening for his coming, and that her songs had been sung for him. An ecstasy swept over him. Regaining the path, he went downward to the monastery, his brain afire, his body tingling.

Joseph was far too simple for self-analysis, and he was too enchanted by those liquid strains to know what all this soul confusion foretold; he merely realized that he had made the most amazing of discoveries, that the music of the spheres had been translated for his privileged ears, that a door had opened allowing him to glimpse a glory hidden from other mortals. It was not the existence of the singer, but of the music, that excited him to adoration. He longed to possess it, to take it with him, and to cherish it like a thing of substance, to worship it in his solitude.

The song had been of love; but, after all, love was the burden of his religion. Love filled the universe, it kept the worlds a-swinging, it was the thing that dominated all nature and made sweet even the rigid life of an anchorite. It was doubtless love which awoke this fierce yet tender yearning in him now, this ecstasy that threatened to smother him. Love was a holy and an impersonal thing, nevertheless it blazed and melted in his every vein, and it made him very human.

Through all that night Fray Joseph lay upon his couch, rapt, thankful, wondering. But in the morning he had changed. His thoughts became unruly, and he recalled again that tantalizing perfume, the shy tones of that mischief laughter. He began to long intensely to behold the author of this music-magic, to behold her just once, for imagination graced her with a thousand witching forms. He wished ardently, also, to speak with her about this miracle, this hidden thing called melody, for the which he had starved his life, unknowingly.

As the afternoon aged he began to fear that he had frightened her, and therefore when he came to tread his homeward path it was with a strange commingling of eagerness and of dread. But while still at a distance, he heard her singing as usual, and, nearing the spot, he stopped to drink in her message. Again the maiden sang of love; again the monk felt his spirit leaping as she fed his starving soul even more adroitly than she fingered the vibrant strings. At last her wild, romantic verses became more unrestrained; the music quickened until, regardless of all things, Fray Joseph burst the thicket asunder and stood before her, huge, exalted, palpitant.

"I, too, have sung those songs," he panted, hoarsely. "That melody has lived in me since time began; but I am mute. And you? Who are you? What miracle bestowed this gift—?"

He paused, for with the ending of the song his frenzy was dying and his eyes were clearing. There, casting back his curious gaze, was a bewitching Moorish maid whose physical perfection seemed to cause the very place to glow. The slanting sunbeams shimmered upon her silken garments; from her careless hand drooped an instrument of gold and of tortoise-shell, an instrument strange to the eyes of the monk. Her feet were cased in tiny slippers of soft Moroccan leather; her limbs, rounded and supple and smooth as ivory, were outlined beneath wide flowing trousers which were gathered at the ankles. A tunic of finest fabric was flung back, displaying a figure of delicate proportions, half recumbent now upon the sward.

The loveliness of Moorish women has been heralded to the world; it is not strange that this maid, renowned even among her own people, should have struck the rustic priest to dumbness. He stood transfixed; and yet he wondered not, for it was seemly that such heavenly music should have sprung from the rarest of mortals. He saw that her hair, blacker than the night, rippled in a glorious cascade below her waist, and that her teeth embellished with the whiteness of alabaster the vermilion lips which smiled at him.

That same intoxicating scent, sweeter than the musk of Hadramaut, enveloped her; her fingers were jeweled with nails which flashed in rivalry with their burden of precious stones as she toyed with the whispering strings.

For a time she regarded the monk silently.

"I am Zahra," she said at length, and Joseph thrilled at the tones of her voice. "To me, all things are music."

"Zahra! 'Flower of the World,'" he repeated, wonderingly. After an instant he continued, harshly, "Then you are the daughter of the Moor?"

"Yes. Abul Malek. You have heard of me?"

"Who has not? Aye, you were rightly called 'Flower of the World.' But—this music! It brought me here against my will; it pulls at me like straining horses. Why is that? What wizardry do you possess? What strange chemistry?"

She laughed lightly. "I possess no magic art. We are akin, you and I. That is all. You, of all men, are attuned to me."

"No," he said, heavily. "You are an Infidel, I am a Christian. There is no bond between us."

"So?" she mocked. "And yet, when I sing, you can hear the nightingales of Aden; I can take you with me to the fields of battle, or to the innermost halls of the Alhambra. I have watched you many times, Brother Joseph, and I have never failed to play upon your soul as I play upon my own. Are we not, then, attuned?"

"Your veil!" he cried, accusingly. "I have never beheld a Moorish woman's face until now."

Her lids drooped, as if to hide the fire behind them, and she replied, without heeding his words: "Sit here, beside me. I will play for you."

"Yes, yes!" he cried, eagerly. "Play! Play on for me! But—I will stand."

Accordingly she resumed her instrument; and o'er its strings her rosy fingers twinkled, while with witchery of voice and beauty she enthralled him. Again she sang of love, reclinging there like an *houri* fit to grace the paradise of her Prophet; and the giant monk became a puppet in her hands. Now, although she sang of love, it was a different love from that which Joseph knew and worshiped; and as she toyed with him his hot blood warred with his priestly devotion until he was racked with the tortures of the pit. But she would not let him go. She lured him with her eyes, her lips, her luscious beauty, until he heard no song whatever, until he no longer saw visions of spiritual beatitude, but flesh, ripe flesh, aquiver and awake to him.

A cry burst from him. Turning, he tore himself away and went crashing blindly through the thicket like a bull pursued. On, on he fled, down to the monastery and into the coolness of his cell, where, upon the smooth, worn flags, he knelt and struggled with this evil thing which accursed his soul.

For many days Joseph avoided the spot which had witnessed his temptation; but of nights, when he lay spent and weary with his battle, through the grating of his window came the song of the Saracen maid and the whisper of her golden lute. He knew she was calling to him, therefore he beat his breast and scourged himself to cure his longing. But night after night she sang from the heights above, and the burden of her song was ever the same, of one who waited and of one who came.

Bit by bit she wore down the man's resistance, then drew him up through the groves of citron and pomegrante, into the grape fields; time and again he fled. Closer and closer she lured him, until one day he touched her flesh— woman's flesh—and forgot all else. But now it was her turn to flee.

She poised like a sunbeam just beyond his reach, her bosom heaving, her lips as ripe and full as the grapes above, her eyes afire with invitation. In answer to his cry she made a glowing promise, subtle, yet warm and soft, as of the flesh.

"To-night, when the moon hangs over yonder pass, I shall play on the balcony outside my window. Beneath is a door, unbarred. Come, for I shall be alone in all the castle, and there you will find music made flesh, and flesh made music." Then she was gone.

The soul of the priest had been in torment heretofore, but chaos engulfed it during the hours that followed. He was like a man bereft of reason; he burned with fever, yet his whole frame shook as from a wintry wind. He prayed, or tried to, but his eyes beheld no vision save a waiting Moorish maid with hair like night, his stammering tongue gave forth no Latin, but repeated o'er and o'er her parting promise:

"There you will find music made flesh and flesh made music."

He realized that the foul fiend had him by the throat, and undertook to cast him off; but all the time he knew that when the moon came, bringing with it the cadence of a song, he would go, even though his going led to perdition. And go he did, groveling in his misery. His sandals spurned the rocky path when he heard the voice of Zahra sighing through the branches; then, when he had reached the castle wall, he saw her bending toward him from the balcony above.

"I come to you," she whispered; and an instant later her form showed white against the blackness of the low stone door in front of him. There, in the gloom, for one brief instant, her yielding body met his, her hands reached upward and drew his face down to her own; then out from his hungry arms she glided, and with rippling laughter fled into the blackness.

"Zahra!" he cried.

"Come!" she whispered, and when he hesitated, "Do you fear to follow?"

"Zahra!" he repeated; but his voice was strange, and he tore at the cloth that bound his throat, stumbling after her, guided only by her voice.

Always she was just beyond his reach; always she eluded him; yet never did he lose the perfume of her presence nor the rustle of her silken garments. Over and over he cried her name, until at last he realized from the echo of his calling that he had come into a room of great dimensions and that the girl was gone.

For an instant he was in despair, until her voice reached him from above:

"I do but test you, Christian priest. I am waiting."

"'Flower of the World,'" he stammered, hoarsely. "Whence lead the stairs?"

"And do you love me, then?" she queried, in a tone that set him all ablaze.

"Zahra," he repeated, "I shall perish for want of you."

"How do you measure this devotion?" she insisted, softly. "Will it cool with the dawn, or are you mine in truth forever and all time?"

"I have no thought save that of you. Come, Light of my Soul, or I shall die."

"Do you then adore me above all things, earthly and heavenly, that you forsake your vows? Answer, that my arms may enfold you."

He groaned like a man upon a rack, and the agony of that cry was proof conclusive of his abject surrender.

Then, through the dead, black silence of the place there came a startling sound. It was a peal of laughter, loud, evil, triumphant; and, as if it had been a signal, other mocking voices took it up, until the great vault rang to a fiendish din.

"Ho! Hassam! Elzemah! Close the doors!" cried the voice of Abul Malek."Bring the lights."

There followed a ponderous clanging and the rattle of chains, the while Fray Joseph stood reeling in his tracks. Then suddenly from every side burst forth the radiance of many lamps. Torches sprang into flame, braziers of resin wood began to smoke, flambeaux were lit, and, half blinded by the glare, the Christian monk stood revealed in the hall of Abul Malek.

He cast his eyes about, but on every side he beheld grinning men of swarthy countenance, and at sight of his terror the hellish merriment broke forth anew, until the whole place thundered with it. Facing him, upon an ornamental balcony, stood the Moor, and beside him, with elbows on the balustrade and face alight with sinister enjoyment, stood his daughter.

Stunned by his betrayal, Joseph imploringly pronounced her name, at which a fresh guffaw resounded. Then above the clamor she inquired, with biting malice:

"Dost thou any longer doubt, oh, Christian, that I adore thee?" At this her father and her brothers rocked back and forth, as if suffocated by the humor of this jest.

The lone man turned, in mind to flee, but every entrance to the hall was closed, and at each portal stood a grinning Saracen. He bowed his shaven head, and his shame fell slowly upon him.

"You have me trapped," he said. "What shall my punishment be?"

"This," answered the Moorish lord; "to acknowledge once again, before us all, the falseness of your faith."

"That I have never done; that I can never do," said Joseph.

"Nay! But a moment ago you confessed that you adored my daughter above all things, earthly or heavenly. You forswore your vows for her. Repeat it, then."

"I have sinned before God; but I still acknowledge Him and crave His mercy," said the wretched priest.

"Hark you, Joseph. You are the best of monks. Have you ever done evil before this night?"

"My life has been clean, but the flesh is weak. It was the witchcraft of Satan in that woman's music. I prayed for strength, but I was powerless. My soul shall pay the penalty."

"What sort of God is this who snares His holiest disciple, with the lusts of the flesh?" mocked Abul Malek. "Did not your prayers mount up so high? Or is His power insufficient to forestall the devil? Bah! There is but one true God, and Mohammed is His Prophet. These many years have I labored to rend your veil of holiness asunder and to expose your faith to ridicule and laughter. This have I done to-night."

"Stop!" cried the tortured monk. "Bring forth a lance."

"Nay! Nay! You shall hear me through," gloated Abul Malek; and again-Joseph bowed his tonsured head, murmuring:

"It is my punishment."

Ringed about thus by his enemies, the priest stood meekly, while the sweat came out upon his face; as the Saracen mocked and jeered at him he made no answer, except to move his lips in whispered grayer. Had it not been for this sign they might have thought him changed to stone, so motionless and so patient did he stand. How long the baiting lasted no one knew; it may have been an hour, then Joseph's passive silence roused the anger of the overlord, who became demoniac in his rage. His followers joined in harrying the victim, until the place became a babel. Finally Elzemah stepped forward, torch in hand, and spat upon the giant black-robed figure.

The monk's face whitened, it grew ghastly; but he made no movement. Then in a body the infidels rushed forth to follow the example of Abul Malek's son. They swarmed about the Christian, jeering, cursing, spitting, snatching at his garments, until their master cried:

"Enough! The knave has water in his veins. His blood has soured. Deserted by his God, his frame has withered and his vigor fled."

"Yes," echoed his daughter. "He is great only in bulk. Had he been a Man I might have loved him; but the evil has fled out of him, leaving nothing but his cassock. Off with his robe, Elzemah. Let us see if aught remains."

With swift movement her brother tore at the monk's habit, baring his great bosom. At this insult to his cloth a frightful change swept over the victim. He upheaved his massive shoulders, his gleaming head rose high, and in the glaring light they saw that his face had lost all sweetness and humility; it was now the visage of a madman. All fleshly passion stored through thirty years of cloister life blazed forth, consuming reason and intelligence; with a sweep of his mighty arms he cleared a space about him, hurling his enemies aside as if they were made of straw. He raised his voice above the din, cursing God and men and Moors. As they closed in upon him he snatched from the hands of a lusty slave a massive wrought-iron brazier, and whirling it high above his head, he sent its glowing coals flying into the farthest corners of the room. Then with this weapon he laid about him right and left, while men fell like grain before the reaper.

"At him!" shouted Abul Malek, from his balcony. "Pull down the weapons from the walls! The fool is mad!"

Zahra clutched at her father's sleeve and pointed to a distant corner, where a tongue of flame was licking the dry woodwork and hangings. Her eyes were flashing and her lips were parted; she bent forward, following the priest with eagerness.

"Allah be praised!" she breathed. "He is a Man!"

Elzemah strove to sheathe his poinard in the monk's bare breast, but the brazier crushed him down. Across the wide floor raged the contest, but the mighty priest was irresistible. Hassam, seeing that the priest was fighting toward the balcony, flung himself upon the stairs, crying to his father and his sister to be gone. By now the castle echoed with a frightful din through which arose a sinister crackling. The light increased moment by moment, and there came the acrid smell of smoke.

Men left the maniac to give battle to the other fury. Some fled to the doors and fought with their clumsy fastenings, but as they flung them back a draught sucked through, changing the place into a raging furnace.

With his back against the stairs, Hassam hewed at the monk with his scimitar; he had done as well had he essayed to fell an oak with a single blow. Up over him rushed the giant, to the balcony above, where Abul Malek and his daughter stood at bay in the trap of their own manufacture. There, in the glare of the mounting flames, Fray Joseph sank his mighty fingers through the Moor's black beard.

The place by now was suffocating, and the roar of the conflagration had drowned all other sounds. Men wrapped their robes about their heads and hurled themselves blindly at the doors, fighting with one another, with the licking flames, with the dead that clogged the slippery flags. But the maid remained. She tore at the tattered cassock of the priest, crying into his ear:

"Come, Joseph! We may yet escape."

He let the writhing Abul Malek slip from out his grasp and peered at her through the smother.

"Thou knowest me not?" she queried. "I am Zahra." Her arms entwined his neck for a second time that night, but with a furious cry he raised his hands and smote her down at his feet, then he fled back to the stairs and plunged down into the billows that raged ahead of the fresh night wind.

The bells of San Sebastian were clanging the alarm, the good monks were toiling up the path toward the inferno which lit the heavens, when, black against the glare, they saw a giant figure approaching. It came reeling toward them, vast, mighty, misshapen. Not until it was in their very midst did they recognize their brother, Joseph. He was bent and broken, he was singed of body and of raiment, he gibbered foolishly; he passed them by and went staggering to his cell. Long ere they reached the castle it was but a seething mountain of flame; and in the morning naught remained of Abul Malek's house but heated ruins.

Strange tales were rife concerning the end of the Moor and of his immediate kin, but the monks could make little out of them, for they were garbled and too ridiculous for belief. No Mussulman who survived the fire could speak coherently of what had happened in the great hall, nor could Fray Joseph tell his story, for he lay stricken with a malady which did not leave him for many weeks. Even when he recovered he did not talk; for although his mind was clear on most matters, nay, although he was as simple and as devout as ever, a kind Providence had blotted out all memory of Zahra, of his sin, and of the temptation that had beset his flesh.

So it is that even to this day "The Teeth of the Moor" remains a term of mystery to most of the monks of San Sebastian.